I0727909

Moon Dragon Falling

Dragon Shadows, Book 2

By G.S. Carline

This is a work of fiction. All characters, organizations, places, and events portrayed in this novel are either products of the author's imagination or are used fictitiously.

Cover art by Joe Felipe of Market Me
(http://www.marketme.us)

MOON DRAGON FALLING
Copyright © 2022 G.S. Carline
All rights reserved

ISBN-13 978-1-943654-23-9

 Published in the USA by Dancing Corgi
Press

This book is dedicated to badass
mothers.

A Brief Note

I love writing fiction because I believe that in fiction is where we find eternal truths. That being said, the Caribbean islands I am about to transport you to, do not exist. I wanted to tell a pirate story and I wanted it to have a Caribbean feel. What I did not want was Caribbean reality. I don't want everyone getting fussy about what year it is and who was ruling Europe and attempting to establish themselves in Jamaica or Tortuga or whatever island that really exists. It means a lot of research on my end just for insignificant details that detract from the story of a young noblewoman who is transformed into a pirate—and more.

So, my story takes place in a small group of make-believe islands, an archipelago if you will, somewhere to the east of Tobago and Trinidad, called Los Peces Pequeña (The Little Fishes). Back in Europe, there are always kings who send nobles to conquer islands because everybody wants to rule the world. And there is magic wherever you look.

Moon Dragon Falling

One river
Many streams
Paths are chosen
Feeding dreams

Dragon Shadows, Book 2

Lisette de Lille strode down the jungle path, trying to catch her breath as she followed Lamya de Sang. According to Lamya, they were on their way to a place on Île des Anciens where Lisette could have her baby under the Ancient One's magical guidance.

"Why…do we…" Lisette puffed as she hastened to keep up. "Have…to…hurry?"

She blanched at Lamya's annoyed glance and kept going, her shorter legs taking two strides to make up for Lamya's one. At last, the Ancient One stopped at a grove of trees and pointed. "That is our destination."

The trees grew close together. Lamya grabbed Lisette's hand and pulled her between the first two trunks of rough bark. There was barely room for her body to squeeze sideways. Lisette was yanked left as Lamya pulled her through another tiny space.

"You must move faster." The Ancient One quickened her pace as she zigged between the trunks, dragging Lisette along.

Lisette hurried to keep up, attempting to anticipate Lamya's moves. The spaces between the trees seemed to be shrinking to the point that her clothes were catching on the bark, and her knuckles were skinned. The two rushed left and right, past the trees that leaned in their way.

At one point, Lamya darted right, then left, then right again. Lisette tripped, trying to keep up with her. That's when she saw the trees actually move together to prevent her travel. She hesitated, her eyes wide.

"Jump!" Lamya shouted as she leapt through the small passage.

Lisette sprang and felt a tug on her skirt. Landing in soft brush outside the grove, she rolled over, gasping. A piece of her clothing had been torn away. She glanced up at the tree, where the scrap hung on a small branch. Knotholes in the trunk made a mocking smile.

"I'm glad I'm not large with child." Lisette ran her hands across the small bulge at her stomach. "What just happened?"

Lamya stood and smoothed her clothes. "They don't want us here, of course."

"They? You mean the trees? That's amazing."

"No. It is this island's magic."

"I thought the magic on this island was yours."

"I have explained this before. We are merely the…mmm…gardeners of magic." Lamya shook her head. "The magic on this island is its own, needed for survival. Some places are more fragile than others. The island must protect itself."

"What's so fragile here that magic must protect it?"

"Look around you." She gestured and Lisette studied

her environment for the first time.

All of the islands in the Caribbean were beautiful, from their sparkling sand beaches to brilliant displays of flowers. And yet none could compare with the vision before her. The underbrush was a soft glow of dark green, layered with flowering vines that wound gently up palm trees, weaving a canopy that framed an azure lagoon. Colors popped everywhere, deep reds and sunny yellows and even royal purple.

"This is the Cradle of the Caribbean," Lamya said. "You will have your baby here."

Lisette let her vision wander, taking in the beauty, and inhaling the fragrant air, until Lamya's hand pulled her along again.

"Come. It is time to speak of important things."

At last, they arrived at a hidden swath of white sand by the lagoon, tucked in a glade of palms. Lamya sat her pack down. Soon she was pulling out bowls, cooking implements, and silks for their beds. Lisette watched the woman work, wondering at her shape-shifting abilities.

When she was turning into a blood dragon, Lamya had appeared to her as a warrior, strong and tall.

Now she was a crone, bent and wrinkled. Lisette understood that each of these versions of Lamya were designed to suit human expectations, but she was still surprised by the familiar purring voice coming from this new, yet old, body.

"I will gather our food," Lamya said. "You will start the fire."

Lisette gathered dry sticks and piled them together as Lamya picked ripe mangos. "I forgot—I don't have my knife."

Lamya turned and smiled. "You do not need your knife. Focus on the sticks and place a fire firmly in your mind."

Lisette looked at the sticks, listening to the sound of

Lamya digging roots. *It is distinctly silly, staring at a pile of wood, and wishing for it to spark.*

"Do not wish and stop paying attention to me." Lamya's words were clipped. "Look at the sticks and tell them to light."

Her scolding lit Lisette's cheeks in embarrassed anger. She glared at the pile and pushed an image of fire onto it. It exploded into a roaring blaze, and she fell back in shock.

Lamya pulled a yam from the soil. "You don't have to yell. Next time, just ask it to light."

Lisette sat up. "Is this the kind of magic a moon dragon does?"

"This is the kind of magic this island does."

Soon they were eating roasted yams, fresh flowers, and mangos. Lisette did not know how hungry she was until she tasted the first sweet piece of fruit. Lamya ate slowly, gazing at the ground, seemingly lost in thought. Each time Lisette put her bowl down, Lamya urged her to pick it up again and have more.

"You must finish the coconut milk," she said. "You will need it for your journey."

"What journey? Are we climbing the Dragon's Breath again?"

Lamya laughed. "No, you have already been on the journey of being a dragon. I speak of your journey to motherhood."

"Oh, that." Lisette shrugged. "Women have been having babies for a long time. It happens whether you are ready or not."

"It is true, the physical act is the same as of old, but your path to motherhood is, hmm, different. One is your transformation to moon dragon. Unlike your blood dragon curse, being a moon dragon is a gift, one that you can call upon. I must teach you how to ask."

Lisette frowned. "If I only change when I ask, why

did I change on Begum's ship?"

"Hmm…" Lamya drew circles in the sand. "Let us say, I required your presence on the island, and Alara helped me in this manner."

"I don't know that I like having my child in control of my body."

Lamya gazed at her drawings. "It was necessary."

"I'm still not happy about it," Lisette said. "So, what do you want of me now?"

"You must be prepared for your child. She has already shown herself to be a force."

"What kind of child—or dragon—will she be?"

Lamya was silent for some time. At last, she muttered, "I do not know. We have never encountered a child born of two blood dragons. Alara will be a surprise to all."

"But I thought…" Lisette searched for the words. "You are an Ancient One. I assumed that means all knowing."

"We know much, but we are not gods." Lamya brushed at the sand on her toes. "Do no worrying. Even not knowing what she is, I have the wisdom to help you."

Lisette's shoulders slumped. "I should have been more careful. I was such an arrogant child, so full of myself. This is the price I pay, to tread this unwanted road."

"It may not be the path you planned, but it is the path you chose."

"If I hadn't been kidnapped, none of this would have happened." Lisette hurled her empty bowl at the sand. "Before that, I wanted—what? Nothing, except to live the life I was born to."

Lamya's face remained calm, her eyes soft. "Every day of your life, you have chosen what you wanted. That you do not admit your own desires does not make them go away."

"How did I desire this?" She pointed to her stomach.

The Ancient One stood, her lips pursed and her eyes boring icily into Lisette's. Straightening, she stretched to a height her unbent crone-body should never reach. As she continued to grow taller, Lisette's eyes widened. Lamya kept rising, expanding until she assumed her true form as an Ancient One. Gnarled as a tree, gray as granite, with hair of wild grasses and large eyes of sea foam, she was wondrous but terrifying. All of earth and sky were revealed in her being.

Lisette trembled, bowing her head in reverence.

"Lift your head and look," Lamya commanded.

Lisette obeyed. The Ancient One splayed her fingers, shooting sparks that formed an image. It was a kind of a map, with a large river that turned this way and that, leaving rills at the turns that fed tributaries, which in turn fed other bodies of water.

"This is your life, Lisette de Lille. It is a river, and each choice you make turns you toward another. You chose your nature from childhood." She pointed to an early winding. "Whether to find happiness in obedience or turn away in rebellion. You chose obedience because it was easy and cost you nothing. The feigning of a good girl, presenting a calm surface, so that underneath the water could rush and whirl, and you could be free to think as you wish."

She went through the map, highlighting Lisette's choices, until she got to Rocco. "Here are several places where you could have stayed on an island and perhaps gotten help to return to your family. Instead, you found your way back to Rocco. And here—did people tell you to get rid of the feather?"

"Just Poussin."

"How many people did you show it to?"

Lisette's eyes lowered. "Only him."

"Yes, because you knew everyone would tell you the same thing. Why did you keep it?"

She had no answer.

Lamya continued. "You chose to lie with Rocco. You chose to believe that you were invincible. Impregnable. The path was there all along. You chose it."

With a sigh of surrender, Lisette walked to the edge of the lagoon and picked up the bowl. "What do I do now?"

Lamya brought her arms down, ending the river of light and returning to her form as the wrinkled woman in the cotton dress. "Now you learn to be a moon dragon and you have a baby."

"What about Rocco?"

"Rocco is your love," Lamya said. "He is not my concern."

A tall ship stood outside a shallow cove, backlit in the morning sun. On the beach, a young girl stood in the doorway of a small hovel, squinting against the sunlight, and pushing beads of sweat from her temples.

"Satasnae alualihat tryqan," she said to the warm air. "The gods will make a way."

A dinghy approached carrying two dark figures, one of them in steady motion as his shoulders swept forward and back. She found herself breathing in and out to the rhythm of his rowing. The other figure was smaller and spent his time looking up at the beach, then down at something in the boat.

The *something* was why she was here and why she fingered her braid nervously, dabbed at the moisture on her temples, and whispered words of faith and courage under her breath. Her captain, Begum Derya, had dropped her here with orders to receive a wounded sailor and use her skills to heal him. Captain Derya had not bothered with particulars, but Ruhee heard the ship's gossip.

This was Tristan de Rocco, captain of *L'Implacable*.

The dinghy hit sand, and both men jumped out to pull it onto the beach. A third figure rose from the boat and fell back, causing both men to rush to his aid. They gathered a tarp and made a sort of gurney to carry him.

Ruhee picked up one leaden foot and set it forward, hoping it would goad her legs into action. This was no time for shyness. She breathed deeply and staggered forward to meet them.

"You the healer?" The large man nodded at her. He was broad-shouldered and ruddy-faced, with an unruly head of rust-colored curls. "Name's Chunk."

She gave a slight bow. "I am Ruhee Vaishya of the *Dişi Aslan*. Captain Derya sends her regards. She wishes me to heal your captain and return him to you."

"Sure you can do the job?" Worry pierced his voice. "Cap'n's awful sick with fever from a knife wound, like nuthin' I ever seen."

Ruhee led them inside the one-room shack and gestured to the bed. "How long has he had the sickness?"

"Stabbed two weeks ago."

Chunk worked with the younger man to carefully lift Rocco and place him on the straw mattress. They moved away to fold their makeshift gurney, while she approached her patient, lifting his shirt to see the damage. Rocco flinched and moaned as she touched him.

"We thought we got it all cleaned up," Chunk said, "but he ain't stopped moanin' or heatin' up."

She slipped the shirt from his body and removed the bandage. After poking around the edges of the wound, she put the back of her hand to his forehead. "Yes," she said. "It is a blood fever."

"Can you fix him?" The smaller, younger man had

backed away until he stood at the doorway, folded tarp in his hand, shifting from one foot to the next.

"I have this skill. But much of it will be up to him."

"Well, he'll be fine, then, won't he, Poussin?" Chunk smiled and glanced back at the young man. "Cap'n's strong as a whale, mean as a shark. He got the will, all right."

Poussin smiled, too, although not as broadly as his friend.

"I will send word with Captain Derya when he can return to your ship." Ruhee gestured toward the door.

"Wait—we gotta leave him here?" Poussin asked.

Ruhee folded her hands. "Yes. This will take many days."

"Come along, boy." Chunk's hand was at Poussin's back, encouraging him to leave. "The girl needs time to work her magic."

Ruhee watched the two men step out onto the beach. Chunk's hand continued to steer his young mate although Poussin kept looking over his shoulder toward her.

Yes, I can work my magic.

Once the men were in their dinghy and rowing back to *L'Implacable*, Ruhee turned to her patient. She ran her hand across Rocco's forehead, brushing his dark curls aside. A dark silken cord lay around his neck, pulling to one side. She lifted the cord and found a charm had fallen to the pillow, a small gold hand with its fingers folded down and a ruby heart in the palm. Placing the amulet on his chest, she straightened the cord.

"So, you wear protection against the Evil Eye?" She let her fingers trace the hand. "You will find no such demon here—I swear."

Rocco opened his eyes, his lids heavy and fluttering, giving her a glimpse of azure between black lashes. Once, and for a mere moment, those blue eyes had glanced in her direction, and she'd forever wanted more.

"Relax, Captain." Her voice softened. "I'm certain you do not remember me, but we have met on many occasions."

"Where's Lisette?" he asked, before passing into unconsciousness again.

Ruhee sighed. "Yes. Lisette. She crewed with us on the *Dişi Aslan*." She went to the fireplace and chose a jar from several on the mantle. "Lisette is a good woman. She is also beautiful. I can see why you love her."

After scooping some dried herbs from the jar into a bowl, she added a touch of hot water from the kettle, and mashed the liquid into the herbs, making a paste.

"But Lisette is gone. We do not know where, only that she disappeared." The girl returned to Rocco's bed, carrying the bowl.

Ruhee scooped some of the herb paste and laid it on his open wound. His back arched and he groaned, sucking air through his teeth. Nodding, she untucked her shirt and tied it under her breasts, exposing her midriff.

"I know the medicine is painful, but it will help." She pressed another handful into the wound, before wiping the residual paste across her own bared flank. Leaning over him, she whispered, "Now. Give me your pain."

Ruhee pressed her side to his as he groaned and hissed. Pain, sharp as a blade and hot as a firebrand shot through her, and she yelped, doubling over in agony. Rocco sighed once and fell into a deep sleep. She lingered, her face close to his, before slowly straightening and pushing away from him.

Crawling to the other bed, she collapsed. As she curled under the silken covers, she reached up to the gold chain around her neck and wrapped her fingers around the charm that hung from it. A thick golden cross with a teardrop at the top, the ankh was weighty in her palm.

I can always use this but not yet. The wound is deep, and there is much anger in it.

Many times, she had escorted Rocco to Captain Derya's cabin on the *Dişi Aslan*. Many times, she had served the dinner and poured the drinks while the two captains discussed galleons and riches and their plans of attack.

He may not have seen her, but she had seen him.

"I did not plan this," she whispered. "I was instructed to heal the captain and send him on his way. It is not my fault that I should love him. And it will be his choice, to stay with me."

Lisette rose early from a restless night. She stood to stretch and looked down, rubbing her stomach. It seemed rounder and harder as if Alara was expanding in all directions.

Was I this big yesterday?

"Lamya?" she asked in a quiet voice, then louder. "Lamya? Where are you?"

The Ancient One walked up the path from the opposite side of the lagoon, a bowl in her hands. "Calm yourself."

"Lamya, look at my stomach. I am only halfway to my date. I think it's grown too much."

Lamya regarded Lisette, her head cocked in study, and smiled. "Do no worrying. It is this way the first time. Your body does not know what it is doing."

"Neither do I." Lisette frowned as she walked to the fire and lowered herself to a sitting position, still running her hands across her stomach in disbelief.

Lamya handed her a bowl of food. Lisette hesitated.

"Eat," Lamya ordered. "You are not going to make it go away by starving."

Lisette rolled her eyes and took the bowl. Shrugging, she put a piece of fruit in her mouth.

"Very well," she said. "I'm eating."

"Finish your breakfast, and you can have a morning swim." Lamya stood. "It will prepare you for the day."

Once Lamya was satisfied, they walked from the grove to the lagoon, Lisette still focused on her ever-expanding stomach. The day was warm and humid, making her cotton dress cling, even on this quick stroll. As they walked, she pulled her dress away, attempting to air herself. Her mind was as burned as the rest of her, and each step felt like one step too many.

The water awaited, inviting her in. Lisette slipped out of her dress and draped it over a rock, wasting no time in slipping into the sparkling blue. The lagoon enveloped her like a comforting hug.

Floating on her back, she closed her eyes and let herself drift in and out of the trees' shade. The lagoon was not large or deep, and she relaxed into restfulness, propelling her body lazily with an occasional sweep of her arms or paddle of her feet.

If I fell asleep, I might drown, but it is tempting to relax and think of nothing.

A vision of little Alara floated beside her. "Mama, I cannot wait to be born. We will do wonderful, difficult things together!"

"Oh, Alara, must we?" Lisette asked. "Let's do fun things together."

Her daughter looked puzzled. "But Mama, it is why I am here. I want to do what is difficult because it will be wonderful."

"All right." A tear ran down Lisette's face and she reprimanded herself for being so emotional. "But let me at least rest here for a little longer. I've already done a lot of hard things."

"Yes, Mama, get some rest." She felt Alara's small hand in hers. "But not too long. We have a lot to do before Father comes home."

Lisette turned and swam to the far side, tiring herself before once more floating on her back, and kicking lazily to propel herself to the beach. She watched the clouds above, considering Alara's words, and Lamya's insistence that she chose all this. Who would choose to be a dragon in love with a pirate, having a child with magical powers who is already planning difficult tasks from the womb?

As if in response to her thoughts, the water dipped away from her, causing her to sink, then rushed over her head. She spluttered, flailing about the pool, until the waves subsided to ripples and she could paddle toward the beach. Was the water trying to tell her something?

"I realize I made choices," she told the lagoon. "I didn't think they were these choices."

The water lapped at her, pushing her away from the shore. Breezes rustled the palm fronds above. The wind whooshed—a yes—at her. She frowned and swam for the beach, kicking hard. A sudden swell launched her forward, depositing her on the sand.

"Oof, the baby," she huffed, pushing against the ground to keep her stomach from hitting the shore.

A laugh caught her attention and she looked up to see Lamya relaxing against a tree, mango in her hand. Lisette struggled to her feet and reached for her clothes.

"It was as if that water was talking back to me," she said, tugging the dress over her head.

"It was," Lamya said with a chuckle.

Lisette pointed. "I realize this place is magic, but that

is still just water.”

“No. That is the Lagoon of Becoming. The water tells you the truth about yourself.”

“There must be a mistake.” Lisette lowered herself to the sand beside Lamya, who handed her a piece of fruit. “All it did was try to drown me.”

“Yes, and when did it do that?”

“When I said I didn’t know my choices would lead me here.” She turned to Lamya. “How does that help me become anything?”

“When you understand, you will know what you’ve become.”

Lisette frowned. “What if I’d rather become something else?

Lamya shot her a glare and Lisette put her hand up to ward off her displeasure.

“Yes, Lamya, I made my choices, my choices got me here, and I shall see this through.”

“Good. You can say the words.” The Ancient One rose. “Even if you do not believe them—yet. Finish your fruit. We have much to do to prepare you for your next task.”

“To be a mother?”

“Hmm, yes, that. But also, to be a moon dragon.”

“I thought this child was the reason I am a moon dragon.”

Lamya looked down at her and gestured. “You have finished. Come.”

Sighing, Lisette stood. “Yes, Lamya.”

They walked around the lagoon to the far side, where another path led them into a thick jungle of vine-covered trees. Birds called to each other above the canopy and Lisette could hear the rustling of small animals through the brush. The air was warm and moist, without much breeze, and the sun shot darts of light and heat through the leaves. Soon all she wanted was another lagoon.

Several times, she spied a clearing ahead, but Lamya steered them around the open spaces, keeping to the narrow sandy trail. At last, they arrived at a large sparse area, one of less sand and more soil that sloped down to a small basin. Ferns and a few vines scattered across the space, but not enough to impede movement, or even require a path.

Lamya pointed. "To the bottom."

Lisette nodded and followed, marveling at the way Lamya strolled down at a slight angle, her thin legs wobbling with each step, knobby knees bouncing and catching as she descended. The slope was steep and within two steps, Lisette halted, leaning back until she plopped onto her backside. Lamya continued down the hill without looking back.

"I don't think I can get down," Lisette said.

"Don't be silly. One foot in front of another."

"I have no balance. The baby—"

"Do not blame the baby." Lamya had reached the basin and now looked up at her. "You have gotten soft. This weakness will not suit you. Now, come down the hill."

Fire shot up in Lisette, and she stood, wobbling, and took one sideways step. Her weight pulled her forward, so she angled her body back to compensate before taking another. She continued in this way, one struggling step sideways at a time, until she joined Lamya at the bottom. Gazing around, she saw a large square blanket of moss. In the center stood a stone altar, surrounded by a ring of polished, marbled rocks, all larger than a hand but smaller than a head.

"I thought I was supposed to rest, to be calm for the baby, to get soft. Am I instead going to push boulders and climb mountains?"

Lamya's expression remained stern. "You must learn

what you are."

"A moon dragon—you already told me. I am here to help my daughter learn about what she is." Lisette shrugged. "What else do I need to know?"

"Only everything." Lamya fixed her with an intense stare before reaching into her bag and taking out a small bundle of cloth. "Put this on."

Lisette studied the sky-blue material Lamya handed her, running her hand across it. It was light but substantial, a familiar weave of silken threads. "Another robe for my travels?"

"Your black robe did not survive your time as a blood dragon." She gestured. "Blue is more soothing to a mother-to-be. Put it on, then choose a rock and place it on the altar."

Lisette did as she was told, selecting a large stone with veins of white, tan, and blue. Setting it in the center of the altar, she turned to Lamya who pointed to a spot on the moss.

"Now take a seat facing the rock."

Lisette raised her eyebrows but walked to the indicated place. She sat, gazing at the Ancient One, running shaky fingers across her forehead.

The sun glared back at her, bright and unyielding except for Lamya's dark silhouette.

"Do no worrying," Lamya assured her. "It is not like before, full of burning and pain."

"I know I should trust you, but the unknown is a frightening thing."

"Yes," Lamya said. "It is a frightful thing to be a human in the world of magic. As much as you accept its existence, it is difficult to embrace. You cannot truly trust it. But once again, you must gain another skill."

Lisette nodded. *Who am I to reject this path, even if I could?*

"You could choose another path," Lamya said. "But it is not recommended for you or your child. Now then, focus on the rock and breathe deeply."

As Lisette followed the instructions, her body relaxed.

"Listen to my words." Lamya's voice drifted in, low and soft as a cat's purr. "Close your eyes and notice your breaths. Let them take their time. Count them slowly."

Lisette took a breath, her chest moving out, then contracting in slow motion, and counted through the numbers in a hypnotic state. The shiny stone appeared in her mind, rolling back and forth with her breath.

"Repeat after me." Her words rumbled in Lisette's bones. "One river, many streams. Paths are chosen, feeding dreams."

Lisette repeated the words, seeking their meaning.

Lamya spoke the chant again, and Lisette repeated. After the third time, Lamya said, "Now, look into your heart, Lisette. You know what you are."

A calling bird caught Lisette's attention. *Look into my heart, where's my heart? Do I know what I am? I was a lady in a castle. I was a pirate on a ship. I was a blood dragon. I was a killer. What am I now?*

"You know." Lamya's tone was impatient.

Lisette sat, her eyes squeezed shut, pursing her lips, and exaggerating her breaths in and out. Tears gathered at the corners of her eyes, and she inhaled, trying to call them back. When her lips trembled, she surrendered. Opening her eyes, she pounded the ground with her fists, sobbing. "I don't know. I'm going to be a mother, that's all I know."

"Lisette—"

"No! I will not listen. I know nothing, except putting one foot in front of the other and doing the next thing that has to be done. Eat this, drink that, bathe here, be a dragon, have a baby." She dropped her eyes to her hand, balled into a fist, and opened it. Her weeping quieted to soft sniffling. "I'm so tired."

She collapsed, head in her hands. The sunlight that had been her bane all day now softened to golden threads, a warm mantle over her shoulders. Cool wind pressed against her like a gentle fan. She swayed in its rhythm until she was rocking. As her tears dried, she discovered she was in Lamya's lap, being rocked, with the Ancient One's strong arms wrapped around her.

"I know I have asked much of you."

Lisette brushed tears from her face. "No, it is my fault. I must perform this task, to raise this child. It does not matter whether I wanted to be with child—I wanted Rocco, and that was my consequence, just as being a blood dragon was my consequence for wanting revenge against Eric and Mercedes."

"You did not know about blood dragons when you vowed to seek vengeance."

"Perhaps." Lisette sat up and looked at Lamya. "But I wanted revenge at any cost. Had I known about blood dragons I would have chosen that path anyway."

Lamya smiled. "And now that you are beginning to understand, let us try again."

She gently scooted Lisette back onto the moss and stood, her back to the sun. Lisette sat, upright, facing her and the altar.

"This time do not think," Lamya said. "Do not try to be what you think you are. Do not try to be anything. Close your eyes, open your heart, and breathe. Whatever comes will come."

Lisette closed her eyes, her ribs expanding for a deep breath, then contracting. She spent a few long moments in this space, breathing and emptying her mind.

The first thing she sensed was a protective shield of feathers around her stomach. The feathers increased as her bones lengthened. Unlike the uncontrollable transformation to blood dragon, this was purposeful, and Lisette was controlling the process. Neck stretched and tail grew, talons extended, and wings unfolded. At last, she stood before Lamya, her dragon mind as calm as her human one.

"Go now, discover your talents." Lamya looked up into the heavens. "But do not stray too far. The moon dragon transformation can be fragile, and you do not want to be over the ocean when your wings disappear."

Rocco slept, his pain ebbing, like the tide pulling away from the land. He was aware of the girl who came, who put something hot in the wound and brought the fire back to his flesh, then cooled it with her own. Each time she tended his wound, he watched her scrutinize his face, smiling.

His mind was restless. When he was not awake and wondering where he was, he was locked in endless dreams of searching for Lisette. It seemed nightmarish, that he could find love again with Lisette, just to lose her. Not only her, but the baby she carried—his child.

He awoke in the middle of a bath. The girl had removed his clothes at some point and was wiping his body with a cool cloth. His skin prickled in the fresh air. The way she studied him as she ran the wet towel down his chest to his hips worried him.

Embarrassed, he coughed a bit.

"Ah, Captain, you are awake." Her eyes were calm, unashamed. "You have been ill for a long time. I thought a cooling bath might break your fever."

Rocco nodded.

"Would you care for soup? I should like you to eat if you can manage it."

He nodded again. "And I should like my clothes."

She brought his breeches and shirt and attempted to dress him, but he pushed her away and managed to pull them on himself. Being clothed helped to relax him, although he feared not even armor would protect him from her soft, needy hands.

"My apologies," he said, "my illness has prevented me from knowing your name."

She lowered her lashes, gazing at the floor. "I am Ruhee Vaishya, of the *Dişi Aslan*. Captain Derya sends her wishes for a quick recovery."

"I shall have to thank her." He chose his next words with extreme care. "And thank you, Ruhee."

Ruhee's large dark eyes shone bright with her desire. She gave him a grateful smile and turned to stir a pot bubbling on the fire.

I must get well and leave this place. If I remain here, she will swallow me with her yearning. Rocco ran his hand down his side to his wound, wincing slightly. "When will my ship return to pick me up?"

"That I cannot say." Ruhee set down the ladle and turned to him. "The *Dişi Aslan* will be here within a week and can get word to *L'Implacable*."

"The *Dişi Aslan*? It will be good to see Begum again. Perhaps she could take me on—we could rendezvous with my ship early."

Ruhee returned to her cooking. "What is the rush, Captain? You require time to build your strength."

"It sounds as if I'll have a week, which should be enough. I need to find…someone." He wanted to say Lisette's name but something in him urged caution.

"Lisette?" Ruhee's back was to him, but he could see the tension in her shoulders. "You have been asking for nothing else."

"Yes. I need to find her. She carries my child."

"A child?" The girl dropped the ladle into the pot and stood, looking at the fire. She sighed, reached to her belt, and untied a small pouch. Pouring some of the contents into a clay bowl, she took a smooth stone and ground whatever she had poured, whispering to herself.

Rocco watched her unfasten a necklace and pour some of the liquid from the pot over a golden charm, onto the herb paste. Replacing her necklace, she smiled, then stirred the paste into the pot.

After breaking pieces of dried meat into a bowl, she added the liquid, blew across it, and carried it to Rocco.

"This will strengthen you, so that you may be well enough to leave when Captain Derya comes—if that is your wish."

He took the bowl in both hands and stared at her. "What strange potion is this, that you speak to it and stir it with gold before serving me?"

"Merely a prayer in the custom of my village." Her eyes were soft and her expression somber. "Wishing for good health and a long life in the arms of the woman you love."

He took a cautious sip. It tasted salty and sweet and a bit like having too much rum. He sipped again, and again. Before he realized it, he'd consumed the entire helping. "I hope your wish comes true, Ruhee."

"As do I." She took the bowl from him. "I've prepared a seat for you outside. Perhaps you would like to see the sun."

He swung his feet to the floor and pulled his weight

up. His legs shook, wavered, and dropped him back down. "I'm afraid my legs have lost their mettle."

Ruhee stepped forward and wrapped his arm around her shoulders. "Lean on me."

He pushed himself away from her as much as possible as he shuffled to the door, aware of where his hand and arm pressed on her warm skin. Beyond the foliage surrounding the hut was white sand and open sea. He focused on the outdoors and trundled across the warm ground to a chair that faced the water. As soon as he reached the seat he collapsed, pulling his arm away from the girl's shoulders.

"It will be good to be on a ship again." The sun was warm and uninterrupted by clouds, and he turned his face to receive the brunt of it. "By the way, what island is this?"

"Île des Oiseaux." She bowed. "I must do my chores, but I will return for you."

He barely heard her, already busy testing his strength, wanting to be ready when the ship arrived. Digging his toes into the sand, he wiggled them, lifting his legs from the knees, one by one, then repeating the motion. His arms followed, up and down, splaying fingers and gripping the chair. At first, he did not have strength to lift himself using his arms, but he practiced until he was successful.

The sun was a cheery companion, raising his spirits until the clouds rolled in and a gentle breeze drifted across the water. His body cooled and the pulsing whoosh of the ocean waves and wind whispering through the palm trees relaxed him to the point of nodding off.

Lisette came to him in his sleep, caressing his face with her hand, tender yet strong. In his dream, his daughter rose up between them, turning into a dragon and flying from her cradle. He transformed and followed her to Île des Anciens.

As the island's name stamped itself in his mind, a blackness descended, separating him from his memories, from the knowledge of being a father, and from Lisette. He fell into darkness, curtained by blood red rage. A name wrote itself across his anger: Tempest.

He awoke to the setting sun, disoriented, a fiery anger still pulsing in his heart.

"How was your nap?" A strange voice asked him. He stood, legs buckling, leaning on the chair, to see a lovely young woman walking toward him, carrying a cup and bowl on a tray.

"Who are you?" he demanded.

Her eyes widened, before her expression softened to a smile. "My name is Ruhee. You have been very ill, and your memory has been taken from you."

"You lie. I am Tristan de Rocco, captain of *L'Implacable*. I have not forgotten anything."

"No, Captain, you have not forgotten all, merely the last few days." The girl continued to advance, holding the tray toward him. "I am your wife. I will help you to remember."

He glared at her. "My only wife is Tempest, and she is dead." A familiar burning in his bones made him look up as the last ray of the sun disappeared.

There was a flash of pain, and Ruhee's beautiful pirate was no more. In his place stood a red feathered dragon, its glowing eyes fixed on her. Screaming, she dropped the tray and ran into the hut.

Rocco watched her flee, his dragon mind interested in her as prey, but his human mind dismissing her as unworthy of his time. She was of no consequence. Pushing up from the sand, he fanned his wings and set out in search of those who deserved his teeth and talons.

Lisette glanced down at herself and saw pale blue feathers, tipped in sapphire. She spread her wings and lifted away from the earth.

It was a fine afternoon for flying, sunny with a light breeze that fluttered across her face. Accustomed to flying in the dark of night and worried that sailors could see her, she scanned the horizon. There were no ships to be seen. but she flew close to the island in case she needed a quick landing.

She soon found herself enjoying her daytime flight. It reminded her of sitting in the crow's nest on *L'Implacable* and watching the sea below. She had wanted to break free of the ship, to spread wings as a bird and fly. Little did she imagine she would get the opportunity— twice.

She stretched her wings and pushed up through a layer of clouds until the island was lost to her. Hovering atop a thick puffy tower of white, she put her front paws out where she could see them. Soft and round like a cat's until she splayed her fingers and claws extended from the tips. They were not as imposing as her blood dragon talons, but they looked sharp as needles. She grabbed her left arm with her right paw, attempting to sink her claws to the skin as a test.

Her feathers expanded against the sharpness, preventing her talons from sinking further. *Hmm, I am even protected against myself.*

The cloud she had been using for cover had begun to thin and dissipate with the growing trade winds, so Lisette sought shelter from another cloud. Hidden again, she tested her fire-breathing skills by opening her mouth and forcing the air from her body. There was a rumble at the base of her neck that worked its way up her throat, and she held her mouth wide to allow the fire to escape.

No flames appeared.

Instead, she exhaled a thick fog-like mist. As it emerged, it formed a large chain of clouds that rolled with thunder. Lightning bolts lit from within, shooting from one side to the other. Lisette fanned her wings backward to distance herself while regarding her handiwork. While impressive, it was not as lethal as setting a victim aflame.

Luckily, she had no one to hunt. Her goal was not vengeance but motherhood. It was nurture and love, and perhaps a little discipline.

The sunlight had faded away when she turned and descended below the clouds. To her surprise, she was no longer over Île des Anciens. Open water lay to her right and another shoreline to her left. Curious, she flew closer. That's when she saw landmarks she recognized. It was Île des Oiseaux. She'd come home.

The shock of seeing her home island soon gave way to fear—how long would it take her to get back to Lamya? It was already dark. She cursed herself for flying so long.

Her wings were already fatigued, and she was hungry.

Still, the island called to her as a place she once loved. Her heart trembled with joy, sadness, anger—with everything she could feel about her old home and the family she missed.

The moon was a mere sliver, bringing the darkness quickly and making the village torches pierce the night. She paused in midair, studying it all and willing herself to calm her human nerves and think of what to do.

It would be easier to find her way back in the daylight, and she yearned to stay here longer, but Lamya had warned her not to stray.

Stupid girl, to wander like this. Looping back, she turned toward Île des Anciens. *It does not matter if your wings are tired. You must lie in the bed you made.*

She heard a rush of wings and spun in time to see a red flash ram her side, propelling her toward the open water. Flapping wildly, she was able to stop her sideways motion and launch her body upward, looking for whatever had accosted her. She was surprised to see a red dragon rearing in the starlight, glaring at her before charging again.

Again, he dove at her, this time with talons splayed and seeking flesh. She flew up, sideways, left and right, attempting to outmaneuver him. As he reached out to grab her, she curved her body away, rising upward to escape. His talons grabbed one of her back legs and squeezed.

She felt nothing except pressure. The feathers on her limb had puffed and hardened like a shell against his claw. He was focused on her feathers, a look of confusion on his face. Lisette tried to pull free, but the red dragon held on. Glaring up at her, he opened his mouth and unleashed a stream of fire.

Instinctively, she opened her own mouth to answer. The mist she had experimented with this morning erupted as a deep fog, cutting the flames. The red dragon released her, and she backed away into the thick cloud she had created. He dove into her private storm and was stung on the nose by a small bolt of lightning.

She watched him retreat then return, searching for her, flying into the cloud, being hit by the flash, and backing away. Each time he attempted to find her she could see another burn mark on his face.

The cloud that enveloped her dissipated and Lisette whipped about, trying to find the red dragon and fly away from him. She was surprised to see him in the distance, traveling toward the open sea. Even without a common language, she knew where he was bound.

He headed toward Île des Anciens, which is where she needed to go. Was this Rocco? She saw him change to his human form after he killed Count de Medina. He swore on that night his blood dragon curse was over, as was his desire to kill her.

The sliver of moon was now at the western horizon, leaving even less light available. She flew a few strokes toward Île des Anciens and stopped. Following the red dragon so closely might end in another fight with him. Her feathers and clouds protected her, but what if she had some unknown weakness in her defense?

She had a baby to protect.

Looking back, she could see the outline of her old castle. *Surely, I can afford one pass over my home, merely to see it before heading back to Lamya. And it will greaten the distance between myself and the red dragon.*

She turned and flew toward the island. Hovering over the turrets and stone walls of her old home, she could see men in uniform at the gate, and a well-tended courtyard. Someone had moved in, replacing her late family. She wanted to cry. She also wanted to dive down and snap the necks of these intruders.

Instead, she took one more pass around the boundaries of the wall before departing. She had just turned toward the beach when she felt the familiar warmth. Dismayed, she headed down to land before the transformation took her wings away. Bouncing down into the brush behind the castle, she stood and adjusted her clothes.

There was a small thicket a few steps away where she and her brother used to play and hide. She indulged her memories of their games together as she crawled into the vines and bushes. The ground cover was as soft as she remembered, and she nestled into the velvety moss. Through the vines, she could still see the castle.

Now all I have to do is figure out how to change back into a dragon, then return to Lamya.

Gold and pink beams grew from the edge of the eastern skyline. Lisette watched the sunrise, thinking of a time when she and Rocco transformed together and fell into a frenzied state of lovemaking before parting. There would be no physical release today.

Lisette watched the light grow across the sky, too anxious for sleep and too tired to move. Exhaustion eventually won and when she next opened her eyes, the sun was well toward its halfway mark.

No one was around, so she slipped out of the thicket, far enough to transform but still remain hidden. She closed her eyes and breathed slowly, rhythmically, trying to conjure an altar in her mind. What were the words Lamya had her repeat?

"One river," she whispered. "Something about dreams. One river. Stolen dreams. No, that's not right."

She opened her eyes and looked around. *Maybe I'm not facing the correct way.* She scooted to face the sun. *I still don't know the words. Perhaps if I tried whatever I did last. I closed my eyes and didn't think.*

Very well, Lizzie, you can do this. Don't think, just

become the dragon. I am a dragon. I am the dragon, dragon, dragon, dragon. Wings and feathers and dragon.

She opened her eyes and huffed. "This is foolish. Whatever I did, it was not what I am doing now. I shall have to find a boat. And money. And perhaps some more modest clothes." Shaking her head, she chuckled. "Should be easy for a pirate."

Standing, she brushed the dirt and leaves from her robe before gazing around at the landscape, green and rolling. Île des Oiseaux was lush and rippling with vines that snaked through low ground cover. It would take at least two days to reach the village and the port which would do her no good with no money.

Looking at the castle wall and the turrets that rose behind it, she allowed herself a moment of grief. *Papa, Mama, I don't even know where you are buried.* At the back wall, there was a wooden door that the servants would use to access the path leading further inland, to bring wild yams, mangos, and other island fruits back to the castle. It was always locked, but Lisette knew how to jiggle the handle loose. Not needing a key made it easier to lie to Mama and swear she hadn't ventured outside.

All she needed was enough coin to get her back to Lamya. Of course, a few clothes would be helpful, too. Enter unseen, grab a few things from the laundry line, and a few coins from the tins the housekeeper kept in the pantry should all be easy. Her stomach growled.

And maybe a biscuit.

At the wall, she stopped, listening intently for voices on the other side. The stone was thick and high, making it difficult. She heard no one stirring and reached her hand out to try the latch. The door opened, causing her to jump back and wish for her dagger.

A petite young woman stepped out, carrying a large, empty basket. Lisette recognized her at once.

"Pinar." It was the clever girl from the Duke de

Martinmas' castle on Isla de Pimienta, who had helped Lisette escape the duke. She had also inked the first half of the lioness tattoo Lisette wore on her wrist, marking the beginning of her life as a pirate aboard the *Dişi Aslan*.

Pinar gasped before smiling and embracing her. "M'lady Lisette, how are you here?"

"It is a longer tale than I dare say at the moment. Right now, I seek enough coin to leave this place and travel to Île des Anciens—and perhaps food and a few more clothes. How are you at my family's home?"

The young woman closed the door and motioned for Lisette to accompany her. "I suppose you heard of the terror on Isla del Lagarto, yes? At the wedding of Marquess d'Auguste and Marquise de Medina, two dragons descended—*two of them*—and proceeded to kill or injure everyone there. The duke and his son were mercifully spared, but the upheaval on the islands has been great. The king sent the duke to assume command of Île des Oiseaux, as all in the Medina family were slain, and the d'Auguste family was never on firm footing with Spain or France."

"Such is the price for lukewarm loyalty," Lisette said. "Did the d'Auguste family survive the attack?"

Pinar nodded. "Yes, apart from Eric, although their grief has been great. Most of the servants here are from their house—they tell me that the count and countess returned to their castle only long enough to pack before returning to France on the first boat. Their former home sits empty."

"What about their younger son? Did he return with them?"

"I was unaware of another son." Pinar shrugged. "The servants did not mention him."

"That bodes ill for their house." Lisette had always suspected Eric's younger brother Willem was the brightest one of the lot but the way his parents ignored him did him no favors. His intelligence was wasted on mischief, manipulation, and mayhem.

They walked further up the path before veering into a grove. Pinar set to searching the ground, so Lisette joined her, looking for dark heart-shaped leaves which held their sweet secrets under the soil.

"What of Isla del Lagarto and Isla de Pimienta?" Lisette asked. "Who rules there?"

"The duke's son has remained on Isla de Pimienta to rule. As for Isla del Lagarto, it is currently at the mercy of pirates and brigands, or so says the rumor. The truth is that pirates are more merciful than any crown. So far, no toady has attempted to take the count's place. They shall have tough times trying to rein in the island now that the people are free from Spain's tyranny."

"Am I to assume that the *Dişi Aslan* is among the new citizens of Isla del Lagarto?"

Pinar smiled. "The captain keeps her wits and does not follow the crowd. But it is a new and different world when the *Dişi Aslan* does honest business with island merchants."

"Might she come close enough to this island to grant a *Dişi* sister a ride?"

"Oh, yes, that can be managed." Pinar pointed to her basket. "We have enough. Let us return and I shall get you some food and see where I may hide you away from the duke."

"How is the duke? I saw him quite a lot in my journeys."

Pinar stopped and looked at her, wide-eyed. "Oh, dear. He raged so when he awoke from the drug, did he harm you?"

"Dear Uncle Oscar." Lisette laughed. "I found him quick to get over his temper. Let us say we came to an agreement, and he held up his end admirably. His surprising loyalty to me is what saved his life in the end."

They had returned to the gate and Pinar put her finger to her lips. "You stay, m'lady, and I will return when it is safe."

"Pinar, m'lady is so formal. I'm just Lizzie to the crew."

"As you wish…Lizzie." She smiled.

The young woman slipped onto the castle grounds, leaving Lisette to lean against the wall and wait. She wanted to sit down, but if she needed to move quickly, her baby bump did not allow her to spring into action the way she used to, so she alternated between pacing in front of the door and leaning to the side of it.

The minutes ticked by, and Lisette grew impatient and hungry. The sun inched toward noon, and her clothes clung to her with perspiration. Lamya would have fed her twice by now and taken her to swim in the lagoon.

At last, the door opened, and a small hand motioned her forward. As soon as she walked in, Pinar grabbed her wrist and scurried across the courtyard, Lisette running on her toes to keep up. They headed toward an arch Lisette recognized. It went into the kitchen to the right, and the servants' quarters to the left. She waited for Pinar's tug to tell her which fork they would take.

Pinar whipped her toward the kitchen and into the larder, shoving an armful of material into her hands. "Put this on and stay here. I'll get you when Amoy goes upstairs with the afternoon tea."

Lisette fumbled in the darkness to find the front of what turned out to be a muslin shift with a cotton skirt and blouse. The shift was tight around her middle and about a foot too long, so she gathered the material as best she could and folded it into the waistband of the skirt. Her blue robe gathered the blouse until it sent ruffles from her cleavage. As she worked, she heard footsteps clomping back and forth, and dishes rattling.

She smelled meat cooking—it must be for the

evening supper. The aroma awakened her stomach and it begged for food. Lisette reached about the shelves, hoping to find something to quiet her complaining belly. Sacks of grain, flour, salt were of no use to her. She moved her hands slowly, praying not to encounter any vermin that might also need sustenance.

Her fingers found a cold, hard cylinder with a lid. As soon as she opened it, the aroma identified it—her mother's special herbal tea. Back on Isla del Lagarto, Nan had prepared it for her when Alara first visited, and she found out she was pregnant.

Although it was a delicious drink, the leaves were inedible in their dried state, so she moved on.

Her fingers found a sack whose contents felt firm. She gingerly opened the top, put her nose toward the middle and inhaled. Rum cake! She tore a small piece and nibbled at it. It probably needed one more soak, but to her starving stomach, it was heaven. She pulled a section out of it and gobbled, relishing every bite. When that section was gone, she helped herself to another.

Amoy, whoever she was, would think they had rats as big as dogs when she saw what Lisette had done. *Now if I only had some cider.*

The door cracked open, and Lisette saw Pinar beckoning once more. "Up the back stairs to the left," Pinar whispered. "At the top is an empty room. Here is the key."

Pinar pressed cold metal into Lisette's hands. Lisette nodded and scurried across the kitchen to a familiar staircase. She was on her way to the tower, a place she used to play in as a child. It was a delightful hideaway, but a miserable climb of tall, narrow, winding steps.

"Too bad I can't fly up there," she told herself. "But then, I'd be able to fly back to Lamya."

Halfway up the stairs, Lisette paused to catch her breath and let her racing heartbeat slow down. She wondered how she had been able to bounce merrily to the top in her childhood. Looking down at her continually growing belly, she remarked, "I suppose I'm walking for two now."

Continuing on, she climbed with less haste, taking small rests several times. At last, she reached the landing and stopped to take deep breaths, happy to be finished with the trek. She placed the key, damp and warm from her fist, into the lock. As she did, the door swung open. Stepping into the room, she met two dark eyes that were as surprised as she was.

"What are you doing here?" asked the Duke de Martinmas.

7

The sun was already beating down on the island, bringing steam from the leaves, when Rocco woke. He was nestled into a moss bed at the base of a balsam tree, with vines creeping around the trunk and reaching out as if to tap his shoulder.

Pushing himself upright, he immediately grabbed his head to contain the fire in his brain. He closed his eyes and tried to recall the last evening, the last day, the last anything. Where was he and how did he get here?

This place looked familiar but stirred a sourness in the pit of his stomach. His body was as sore as his head, and his arms and legs were covered in scratches and bruises. His breeches and shirt were threadbare and torn, and there was a stain around a tear on his shirt. He lifted his shirt to see a scar. Frowning, he ran his fingers along the ridge of skin, attempting to retrieve the memory of how it got there.

A low, purring voice startled him. "When you are quite able, join me at the fire and receive sustenance."

Rocco staggered to his feet, leaning against the tree for support. He looked around for the source of the voice.

"I am to your left, just down the short path to the lagoon," it said. "Come, refresh yourself in the water, then eat your fill."

Within a dozen steps, he arrived at a crystalline blue body of water, bubbling from the center, and inviting him in. He walked straight into the lagoon and submerged himself. The water refreshed him, lightening his aching head, and soothing his scratches and bumps. He swam here for what seemed like a long time.

At last, his stomach reminded him of his need for food, so Rocco kicked his way back to shore. To his right a small fire blazed, tended by a woman who looked familiar. She was hunched over the fire, yet he could see how tall and muscled she was under her green robe. Long copper hair was loosely tied at the nape of her neck, revealing angular cheekbones. She lifted her head to look at him, fixing him with large eyes of burnished gold.

"Good day, Tristan de Rocco. I am Lamya de Sang." She held a bowl out. "Come. Eat."

He walked, dripping, toward the fire, glancing down to his torn clothes. "I'm afraid I'm not dressed for polite company."

"Humans and their bodies." She shrugged. "I will supply you with new clothing. First, you must eat."

He took the bowl, which overflowed with fruit, roasted root vegetables, and flowers. "Is there no meat or fish to accompany this?"

"This is what you need."

"Is there no rum?"

"You have much to do. Rum will not help you achieve it."

He opened his mouth to protest, but she made a motion for him to pick up food and put it in his mouth. Her expression told him not to argue. Reaching into the bowl, he picked up a piece of sweet yam and ate it. Each time he tried to speak, Lamya stopped him with the same gestures. Soon, the bowl was empty.

"Good," she said, taking his bowl, and throwing him a bundle of fabric. "Put these on and we will start work."

Rocco stepped into a pair of breeches and tied them around his waist with a crude belt made of hemp. "Before we start anything, I have questions. This place looks like I should know it. You are familiar, but I can't remember why. Even your name—it rolls around in my mind like a fish I can't catch."

"What is the last thing you do remember?"

He ran his hand over his face, combing down through his beard. "I have a dim memory of a young woman." He touched his scar. "She was tending to my wound."

"And what do you remember about who you are?"

He glared at the ground, his brows knit in frustration. "My name is Tristan de Rocco. I was married to Tempest, but I know she is dead. I desire revenge on the man who murdered her. But…somehow…I think he is also dead." He turned to Lamya. "I still have this anger, it consumes me…but anger at whom?"

Lamya stepped over to him and took his hand. "I know it is difficult, but I will ask for your trust. A large segment of your memory has been, hmm, how to say, locked away from you. To find the key, you must do the work."

"Can't you just tell me?"

"It is not enough for me to give you the facts." She placed her palm on his chest. "To recover what you have lost, you must feel it in your bones."

"You are most likely correct." He frowned. "But I am a man of action, not feeling."

"Then come." She gestured inland. "Use your body."

The landscape of the island disturbed him as they walked toward a tall, slender butte, standing alone amidst the island vegetation, ablaze with red and yellow foliage. It was familiar yet strange.

Rocco stopped and pointed. "That looks like something I've seen before."

"It is possible." Lamya handed him a machete. "You are going to climb it."

A vision passed through his mind of forging a path through the heavy brush and tangled vines and pulling himself up the mountain by any rock or root he could find. The memory was awash with physical and emotional pain, and he turned away from it before holding out his hand and accepting the blade.

"Let us to it, then."

The sun hammered him relentlessly as he hacked a path to the butte. His hands slickened with sweat until he could not swing the blade, and he'd stop to wipe his palms on his breeches. Soon his breeches were so wet, he had to dry his hands on surrounding leaves.

He stopped and turned to Lamya. "Why am I doing this?"

"You say you are a man of action." She pointed to the butte. "It must be done."

Rocco grumbled a curse and swung the machete, letting his back and arms fly wildly to and fro, half-hacking and half-pushing the brush out of the way, then shoving his legs through the poorly carved path he created. He could hear Lamya's scolding sigh behind him and turned to snap at her.

One glimpse of her expression warned him not to say a word. Wiping his hands carefully, he took a breath and resumed a proper path-clearing, swinging with purpose and cutting through the brambles.

Once they were at the base, Lamya took the machete

from him and pointed to the top.

"Up."

"I need a moment to rest," he panted.

"You do not." She put her foot in the bend of a vine and pulled herself up. "Climb. You must be tired for tonight."

"I am tired."

She glared at him. "Not tired enough. Climb, now. It is necessary."

The vines were full of thorns and the footholds in the rocks were sharp. It was not the place to be climbing without shoes or gloves, yet here he was, pushing himself from one end and pulling from the other, pouring sweat from every corner and certain that his lungs would burst at any moment.

Rocco thought of himself as a strong man in his prime, but by the time he collapsed at the top of the butte, his muscles were limp rags. He lay for a moment, resting his head on his hands and closing his eyes. A vision passed through his mind of a previous time when he was in this position. His eyes sprang open, and he sat up.

"This place is called Dragon's Breath."

Lamya smiled, standing over him and holding out her hand. She pulled him to his feet as easily as setting a chair upright. "Good. Come quickly, we are almost there."

"Almost where?" He marveled at her strength even as he groaned with pain at his sore muscles.

"To the fire. To the meal." She led him to a clearing near the middle of the mountain, where a small rock pit cradled a fire. Taking an animal-skin sack from her belt, she warmed it over the flames, then handed it to him. "Drink this."

Rocco held the sack up. "Drink? Where is the meal?"

"Drink."

Holding the sack to his lips, he squeezed the contents

into his mouth. It was rich and hearty, strangely satisfying. The bag felt perhaps halfway full, yet he drank from it for several minutes. When at last he had drained the last drop, Lamya stood and gestured.

"It is time."

8

The duke gawked at Lisette, his eyes wide and mouth slack.

"Sire!" She hid her gasp with the word. "How nice to see you once again."

"Yes, it has been a long time. What brings you to my castle?" He gestured to her hand. "Especially in this tower with that key?"

"This key? Oh, well…as you know, my family used to reside here." Her mind raced to find a version of the truth. "I am recently returned and in need of shelter. I knew where the key was kept to this space and—managed to avoid your staff. I was hoping for rest, and perhaps a small meal."

"The last time I saw you, you were—not quite yourself." The duke apparently also struggled with the correct words. "I hope you have been cured of that particular malady."

"Yes." She nodded. "My health has been restored."

"And what ship brought you back?"

She glanced down, unprepared for the question. "Let us say that it was an unusual trip."

The alarm on his face told her more than any words.

"Uncle Oscar." She used the name he had adopted on Isla del Lagarto. "I am no longer a threat to those around me, but the…magic has left its mark." She moved into the sunlight, smoothing her clothes down the front of her body. "I am with child. For my child's sake, I need rest and food, followed by passage to Île des Anciens to receive proper care."

"A child?" He grinned and slapped his sides. "Wonderful! I doubted you and Connie that night, but you *did* consummate your meeting!"

"No, this is not your son's baby." She placed her hand softly upon his arm. "She belongs to another."

"*She*? How do you know? It could well be a son."

Lisette tried again. "Did you hear me speak of the magic? I know I am having a daughter, but she is not your son's child. You were correct, we did not consummate anything, other than a plot for us both to escape our bonds."

"Well, even if it is a daughter, you and Connie can try again for a son." He stepped forward and took her hand. "Come, you cannot stay in this drafty space. I'll have the maids prepare your old room. Are you hungry? Pinar can put together a plate of meats and fruit. Rum. Rum is what you need."

He steered her back toward the stairs, while she attempted to protest. At last, hunger forced her to give up. She could argue better on a full stomach.

They descended from the tower, the duke leading each step, his hands upon her forearm to protect her from falling. The man who had refused to row their dinghy when their ship was sunk by pirates surprised her with his attention.

Once at the bottom, he clapped his hands and launched a whirlwind of activity. Women were dispatched to arrange Lisette's old room, pulling dust covers from furniture, knocking down cobwebs, and freshening the linens. In the meantime, Lisette sat in the great room, being served roasted venison and potatoes.

"I do not need this amount of fuss, really," she protested. "I can eat in the kitchen easily."

"Nonsense," the duke said before ignoring the rest of her arguments.

When at last she was ushered into her old bedroom and left alone, Lisette stood for a moment gazing around, soaking up the familiarity, and feeling her heart shatter. She picked up the little red ceramic dragon that had long graced the mantle and opened its body to find her trinkets undisturbed.

The two gold pieces her father gave her on her sixteenth birthday. *For luck.* A white shell she'd found on the beach the day she and her brother Jules had escaped the castle and hitched a ride with one of the buckboards that delivered sacks of grain. Her first pearl comb, placed in her hair one morning by her mother in a hurried moment as she swept through the room.

Clasping the comb to her chest, Lisette sobbed. It was the only gift her mother had given her—just from her. They were never as close as Lisette would have liked, but perhaps this baby would have bonded them. Her father would be all bluster about her choices, but he'd protect her with his last breath. As for her brother—well, she could imagine his joy at being an uncle.

There was a faint knock, followed by the creak of the door opening. Pinar appeared carrying a tray of more food.

"I must apologize," Pinar said, placing the tray on the table and uncovering a plate of small cakes and a pot of tea.

"Think nothing of it." Lisette swiped the tears from her cheeks. "You could not have known the duke would be in the tower. I am surprised he even attempted those stairs." She sat beside the table and reached for the tea. "And now I cannot convince him that this child is not his heir by Constantine."

"A child? I did not know."

Lisette stretched her clothes again as proof. "She is the child of Tristan de Rocco."

"I see," Pinar said. "When does the child come?"

"She is not due for five more months. Wait…four months."

"Then we have time. We must take care—if the child is born while you are here, the duke may attempt to take possession of her. But for now, eat and rest. Restore your body. I am at your command whenever you are ready and able to escape. With God's help, the ship will be here within a fortnight, and you will be away."

"Tell me, are any of the old servants still here?"

Pinar shook her head. "From what I hear, the Medina family took the servants into their own households, either here or on Isla del Lagarto. Most of the people working here came from the duke's castle, except for the housekeeper, Amoy Simone. All I know about her is that she is stern, likes to be in control, and does not reveal much about herself."

Lisette smiled. "So, you don't trust her."

"I trust no one, m'lady—I mean, Lizzie."

"Understood. And thank you." Lisette nibbled on a cake. After a few bites, she put it down. "I cannot possibly eat more."

"I imagine you need rest now." Pinar smiled. "I shall wrap some of these cakes and leave them with you. The duke will otherwise send me back to encourage you."

"Thank you." Lisette walked to her bed, telling herself to take care of her body and her child. After she was rested, she could attempt to change into a dragon. If she could remember the steps and work at it more calmly, it might still be possible.

When she had awakened from her nap later, she found a note on the mantle. *Please join me for dinner this evening at 7. It was signed, Your Erstwhile Uncle Oscar.*

She gave the note a wan smile. Opening her wardrobe door, she looked through all the clothes she had once worn. It had been little more than a year since she lived here, but it felt like her life in this castle, as well as her youth, were long ago and far away. She found a lovely brown silk brocade and held it up to her burgeoning figure.

It might fit. She slipped out of her robe, stepped into the skirt and pulled the cap-sleeved bodice up to her chest. The overall looseness of the garment surprised her—although her stomach grew more each day, her body was still sinewy from a year of pirating, not to mention exacting vengeance as a dragon. The waist on this dress was cut high, which accommodated her condition.

She tightened the back lacings as much as she could before ringing the bell to summon help from a maid. Pinar answered the call, stepping into the chamber within moments.

"Could you help me into this dress?" Lisette asked.

Pinar gestured to the vanity. "Perhaps you'd like to freshen up first. Have a seat, Lizzie, and I'll do something with your hair. Then you may have a soak in the tub. There is plenty of time before dinner."

Lisette looked in the mirror and handed Pinar a brush. "Thank you, a bath sounds lovely. And it's been a long time since I cared about this bird's nest on my head."

Pinar rang the bell again and instructed the arriving maid to fill the tub. While buckets of hot water were being emptied, Pinar took Lisette's hair from its braid, and gently brushed through the auburn curls.

Once her hair was untangled, Lisette stepped out of

her clothes and into warm scented water. She submerged herself, coming up at last when her curls were heavy with water. The time passed as she scrubbed the weariness from her bones. Soon, the other maid reappeared, this time with buckets to rinse her and a large sheet for drying. Pinar dried her hair, fastening her gown and arranging her curls and tendrils into an elegant updo.

"Have you any combs to wear?" she asked.

Lisette handed her the one from her treasure trove. "Use this one." Her eyes misted as Pinar placed the comb over her right ear, the same place Mama had put it all those years ago. Mama had stuck it against her scalp in a quick, dismissive stroke, but Lisette treasured it as if it had been presented on a silk pillow.

The duke was awaiting them in the great room, dressed in velvet and sweating like a fountain in the tropical evening heat. He extended his hand, so Lisette took it and curtsied.

"Good even', Uncle Oscar," she said with a tease in her voice.

"I am pleased to have your company at dinner, Lisette. Usually I am alone." He led her to a chair and held it for her.

The servers moved slowly, but with efficient grace to serve the first course, a cold soup that tasted of lemongrass and spice.

"You look lovely this evening," he told her. "That dress becomes you."

"Thank you. It is pleasant to be in my own clothes again."

"I do hope you'll not hold it against me, being in your family home." He gestured at the space. "One is often at the mercy of the king."

"I understand, but I am curious." She reached for her wine glass and sipped. "The house of Medina has a castle on this island. Was that not to Spain's liking?"

The duke opened his mouth to speak but shut it quickly as a servant appeared to clear the table for the next course. He sat silent until they left.

"This is not for common ears," he said. "And I do not want to add to the servants' wagging tongues."

He stopped speaking while the meat was served, until the man was gone.

"There is something amiss at Castle de Medina."

Lisette put down her fork. "Amiss how?"

"I have been assured that a member of the familia de Medina resides in the castle, however, I have not met this person, nor do I know anything about them, apart from rumors."

"Does no one investigate?"

"I have sent a contingent of my guard to present my card and request their presence at dinner. The gate remained closed, without even the courtesy of being rebuffed. All I know is that there is a light in the evening, one that travels from room to room."

Her eyes wide, she took a larger drink of wine than she had planned. "Tis a pity they do not want to dine with you. It does not sound as if they want to present a united front for Spain."

"No, which worries me. After the incident on Isla del Lagarto, the islands tremble with murmurs and unrest. The nobility need to stand together, or this will all be taken back by the natives."

"Yes, that is a concern. Do tell me what happened after the unfortunate wedding. I trust you and Constantine were unharmed."

"We managed to escape with our lives, although Connie got a few bruises from the Count de Medina's guards, who were trying to enter against his wishes." The duke watched the servant prepare for the last course before continuing. "Fortunately, there was an available carriage, so we took it straight down to the village and made arrangements for passage home immediately."

"Your son is a valiant fighter."

The duke nodded. "Little known fact." He looked at Lisette intently. "When we arrived, we saw a ship in the harbor, one of unclaimed country. From my vantage point, I could see three people in a dinghy, rowing toward the ship. Two people were seated, one lay across a lap."

"Your eyes did not deceive." She pushed at the roasted meat on her plate. "The crew tended to me until I found that I was with child. I was then offloaded to receive care from someone skilled in magic."

"Ah, yes." His eyes widened. "Of course, my son would have a magical heir!"

Lisette frowned at her clueless faux-uncle. "I fear I cannot take another bite, Sire. Might I be excused? It has been a day of much excitement, and I am overcome with weariness."

The duke blustered and stood, helping Lisette out of her chair, and ordering the servants to escort her to her room. "We will dine tomorrow, then, yes?"

"Yes." She wondered how many meals it would take until he was convinced of the truth—if he could ever be convinced of it.

As Lisette walked up the stairs to her room, she was aware of heavy footsteps behind her. She waited until she had reached her door to turn and look. A tall, big-boned woman approached, light-skinned with islander features, her black hair slicked into a tight bun.

"Who are—" Lisette began.

Her bedroom door flung open, and Pinar stepped out. "M'lady, I was sent here to help you prepare for bed."

The woman stopped at the door. "I will attend to her, girl. You assist the kitchen staff."

Lisette lifted her chin and pulled her shoulders back, assuming the haughty stance of nobility. "And you are?"

"I am la gobernanta, Amoy." Her accent was from the island, but she used a particular Spanish term instead of *ama de casa*. Lisette guessed that she was the child of a Spaniard and an island woman. She was clearly accustomed to giving orders, perhaps even to the duke.

"Thank you, Amoy, but the duke has assigned Pinar to attend to me."

"The duke cannot be bothered with unimportant decisions." Amoy moved as if to enter the room.

"But I can." Lisette stood firm, blocking her way. "Pinar has attended me many times when I was a guest on Isla de Pimienta. She will attend me now that I am a guest here." With a small nod, she ended their conversation. "You are dismissed, Amoy."

The woman folded her arms over her chest and scowled. "Pinar is required—"

"Pinar is required to attend to me." Lisette said, her tone quiet but menacing. "If the duke disagrees, I will speak with him. If you disagree, well, we'll see if a marquise has more sway in this castle than *una ama de casa.*"

Amoy dropped her hands to her sides and backed a step before turning slowly to walk away. Lisette slipped into her bedroom and shut the door, bolting it.

"Does m'lady require help in undressing?" Pinar asked, loudly enough to be heard by anyone listening nearby.

"Yes, thank you." Lisette answered in the same grand timbre.

Pinar's eyes were round as she gestured to move away from the door. She put her finger to her lips and said in a lowered voice, "I'm afraid you've made an enemy."

"At least I shall recognize her," Lisette whispered. "And I shall not turn my back."

It took no time to unlace the dress and slip into a nightgown before Lisette sat at the vanity, reaching up to her hair to remove the pins and combs that held it aloft.

"Let me do that." Pinar pushed her hands away and smiled in the mirror. "Lizzie."

Lisette put her hands in her lap and waited as Pinar took out each pin and brushed through her curls.

"Who was your lady's maid when you lived here?" Pinar asked.

"Her name is Genevieve. I last saw her on Isla del Lagarto, where Count de Medina took her," Lisette closed her eyes, enjoying the bristles of the brush against her scalp. "But it is well. I rescued her and sent her back to France to join her husband."

"Ah, yes, I remember she rode with us on the *Dişi Aslan*. It was the voyage after the dragons attacked."

After the dragons attacked. Lisette wondered if that was the way the islands would now refer to time. Before the dragons. After the dragons. For things few claimed to have seen they were in front of everyone's minds.

Her preparations for bed complete, she dismissed Pinar and walked to her balcony. The moon was still waning, another sliver of light stripped from its arc. The blood dragon would be hunting tonight. She recalled meeting the dragon Rocco on this balcony. He visited every year of her childhood, intending to kill her. He always intended to—until the day he fell in love with her.

Lamya had told her that she could become a moon dragon at any time, so she decided to attempt her metamorphosis again. She tried to remember everything that had happened. It seemed like weeks ago.

What do I need besides myself? A rock? Maybe it was simply something for me to focus on.

Her ceramic dragon sat on the mantle, so she retrieved it and went back outside. Setting the dragon on a bench, she sat across from it on the stone floor, wishing it was the tender moss of Île des Anciens. Now all she had to do was focus on the dragon, breathe deeply, recite the spell.

Lisette focused on the dragon, letting each breath ebb and flow in her ribcage. All the while, she wracked her brain for the words to the incantation, making it difficult to maintain her focus. She stopped and uncrossed her legs, rubbing the cramps from them.

"What are the words?" She begged her mind to dig them up. "One river…streams and dreams…one river, different streams. One river, crossing streams. One river…ugh, by the gods!"

She stood and paced the balcony, looking up at the night sky. "Lamya! Can you hear me? I cannot do this without you—not yet. Please give me a sign."

The silent sparkling sky offered no help at all. Lisette picked up the dragon and returned to the chamber, where she slipped into the freshly made bed. From her pillow, she could still see the stars and wondered if Rocco was looking at them, too.

She closed her eyes and gave one last prayer for Lamya's words to return to her before falling asleep.

The morning's warmth woke her and for one small space of time, Lisette believed she was again living with her parents and brother, on the verge of turning twenty and marrying Eric. As she rolled to her side, her hands made contact with her ever-expanding belly, and she remembered everything. She brushed a tear from her cheek and sat up.

"Harden up, Lizzie," she told herself. "You can't waste your time weeping, not when there's a baby to have and a spell to conjure."

She wrapped her robe about her and rang the servants' bell. While she was braiding her hair, Pinar entered, carrying a breakfast tray.

"The Duke says you're to rest during the heat of the day, and join him for dinner."

Lisette frowned. "Rest as in, stay in this room? What am I, a prisoner?"

"I guess he's used to holding women hostage," Pinar said, wearing a wry grin.

"Once I figure out—" Lisette stopped, wondering if she should share her secret. She lowered herself onto the chaise and lifted her saucer and cup, taking a small sip of tea. "That is, once the ship arrives, I will be free again."

Pinar gave her a sideways glance. "Lizzie—the captain has kept your secret safe from all. However, the rumors are strong."

"Rumors?"

Pinar sighed. "Since childhood, I've been told stories of dragons and how they come to life. It is part of our legends. My mother would use the blood dragon tale to bring me into the house at night. 'Do you want the blood dragon to spear you with his mighty claws?'" She laughed. "I had just signed on with Captain Derya when she took her turn breathing fire and hunting the night skies."

"The captain never discussed it with me. Do you know what indignity she had suffered?"

Pinar nodded. "Like most of us, she was not always a pirate. She grew up in a small village in Turkey, and was betrothed to the son of the agha, a very important man. It was a marriage for power, not love—before the ceremony, a kind foreigner offered to help her. They fell in love, but he was already married and was ordered to return to his home. She found that she was with child and tried to flee, but the agha's son caught her. He and his father broadcast her shame and drove her entire family from the village."

"Sounds familiar. So, she became a blood dragon to kill this foreigner."

"No, not him. Just the son and the agha. I do not know why she did not hunt the foreigner."

"What happened to the child?"

"No one knows." Pinar shrugged. "She never speaks of it."

"Lamya was right."

"Who?"

Lisette pursed her lips, wishing she had not said the Ancient One's name aloud and wondering if that was a punishable offense. "My—teacher. She told me that the captain's curse burned quick and hot, then passed forever."

"Yes." Pinar moved to the bed and straightened the bedclothes. "We knew of this teacher, although we never saw her."

Lisette studied the young woman as she attended to her tasks. "I suppose if you are comfortable with your captain growing wings and talons, I can trust you with my tale. In any case, I'd rather you knew the truth and not the rumor."

Pinar fluffed Lisette's pillow and turned to her. "I'm listening."

"Sit." Lisette gestured to the stuffed chair across from her. "Help me eat these cakes and I will tell you all."

The young woman put down the pillow and joined Lisette in the sitting area. She reached for a cake, smiled shyly, and sat, nibbling on her prize. Lisette poured tea into a spare cup and offered it to her. "I'm not certain why you brought two cups, but please have some."

"The duke requires that I bring an extra cup or goblet at each meal, so that he may join you if he wishes."

"What about what I wish? Never mind, I shall attend to that man. Sit back and let me tell you the story—of dragons and violence and love. It is a long tale and I hope the duke understands that this time together is a part of you being my maid." She winked. "If he wants me to produce a happy heir, my need for company must be met."

Pinar settled into the chair with her food and drink. Lisette recounted her last year from her betrothal to her betrayal, her blood dragon curse, and the battle for Rocco's heart. She recounted the events of the last few weeks as well and revealed her current status as a moon dragon.

"I must get back to Lamya before this child is born," Lisette said. "I confess, I am anxious about her birth…I fear meeting her for the first time. Flying back in my moon dragon form would solve my problem immediately—if I could but remember the spell!"

"It does no good to worry." Pinar gave her an understanding smile. "Granted, I have never been in your position, so perhaps my words have no weight. I do know that worry and fear are not good partners and lead to bad endings. Until our ship arrives, I think it would be best if you relaxed and helped your baby grow, without constantly plotting your escape. I've found that resting my mind sometimes causes it to think afresh and remember what I thought I'd forgot."

Lisette nodded. "You are right. Lamya said this child would require my love, and my confidence in her. Worry and fear will not give that to either of us. The ship will be here in less than two weeks, yes? Surely, I can wait until then."

After breakfast, Lisette dressed and went downstairs, only to find a tall, gangly young man in uniform barring the door to the gardens outside.

"Pardon me, m'lady, but the duke would prefer you stay in the castle." His voice was as melodious and charming as his body was awkward and angled.

Coming home reminded Lisette of who she was—at least, who she used to be. She raised her chin and declared in a voice both sweet and commanding, "And I would prefer to get some sunshine and enjoy the flowers."

"That may be, m'lady, but I take my orders from the duke."

"And I take orders from no one," she replied coldly. "That leaves us with a problem."

The guard flinched, his eyes worried, before stretching himself taller, almost comically so. "The only problem," his voice crackled, "is that you may not leave."

She opened her mouth to see if she could overrule the duke's command. *Wait—there are other exits in this castle, secret doors.* "You are correct, I may not leave." She turned away from him and walked toward the great hall. "Or maybe I will."

Like most great rooms in castles, the walls of the great hall were adorned with large tapestries depicting everything from Biblical scenes to the nobility themselves. Lisette was hoping that the duke had not yet replaced her family's décor with his own. It was not something she noticed last night when she dined here. She had become too passive about her surroundings.

I must be sharper.

She was heartened to see familiar artwork hanging on the walls and scurried across the room to a particular scene of two white doves in an olive tree. It was an enormous work, reaching up past the arched windows and down to the floor, being perhaps half as wide as it was tall, and weighing heavily. Lisette's father used to tell her it took twelve strong men to lift and hang it on its brackets, which had been fortified to hold its weight.

At one side of the tapestry, she used both hands to pull it away from the wall, revealing a small alcove with a bench large enough for two people. Behind the bench was a small door that led to a ground-floor balcony. Genevieve had told her the servants referred to it as Lovers' Cupboard. Lisette had never used it and now wondered why she hadn't taken advantage of its secrecy.

Passing quickly through the alcove, she went straight to the small door. It pushed open silently and she looked through the crack. No one was in sight, so she shoved harder and stuck her head out. The balcony was empty. Stepping out quickly, she closed the door behind her and flattened herself against the wall—or tried to. Little Alara was getting more pronounced each day.

Lisette stayed quiet for a moment, listening for

voices or footsteps. Hearing none, she scampered across the stone, down the steps, and around the castle until she spotted the back gate. Deliberate strides took her across the court and to her objective. Soon she was outside the walls without detection.

And she knew just where to go.

The red dragon thrashed about the mountain top, flapping his wings in an attempt to escape. Lamya held one end of the woven cords that bound him, snapping him down each time he pulled against her. In frustration, he opened his mouth and roared a firestorm at the ground, engulfing his captor.

It did no harm, not even to her temperament. She stood tall, arms wrapped in his restraints, wearing a placid expression.

"Tristan de Rocco." Lamya's voice was strong over his flailing. "Who do you hunt?"

Them. The ones who killed my Tempest.

For a second, a different image flashed before him— a young woman with auburn hair. A name flew on the wind, but he could not hear it. Then the young woman was gone, and the face of Juan de Medina taunted him anew.

He growled, roared, spit fire, and pushed his body into the sky again, only to be restrained by Lamya.

Why do you keep me here? I must go—where? Where is Juan de Medina? He relived piercing the count's flesh with his talons, hearing his screams, setting his limp body on fire.

The Count de Medina is dead. Who am I to kill?

His wings lost their grip on the wind, folded, and sent him crashing to the ground. He lay there as light peered over the horizon, feeling the fire in his bones. Exhausted, he sank into unconsciousness.

When he opened his eyes, Rocco found himself at a campfire on the banks of a lagoon, covered in silks. Across from him, Lamya sat at the fire, poking at the flames, and humming to herself.

"You are ready for breakfast." She had a way of making it sound more like a command.

He sat upright, groaning quietly through his teeth. "How did I get here?"

"I carried you."

"You?" He squinted his eyes at her.

"Do not ask stupid questions. You are not a stupid man." She handed him the warm skin full of liquid. "Drink."

He took the bag and tipped the opening into his mouth, wondering if he would be able to eat an actual meal today.

"No." Lamya answered his thoughts. "You have forgotten much about the first time we trained, yes? This broth serves your need for nourishment and prepares you for the evening task."

"Task of what? Writhing around, hallucinating that I'm some kind of beast?"

Her golden eyes flashed an anger he could read. She stood and towered over him—had she grown taller?

"Drink every drop. When you are finished, join me on the plateau. You can *hallucinate* your work today."

She snapped her attention away from him and strode off.

Rocco tipped the bag again and drank. How did he get here? He had not asked enough questions yesterday, while he was climbing Dragon's Breath.

"Dragon's Breath—I'm on Île des Anciens!" He closed his eyes and images flooded him, of flying through a castle, raining fire, striking with talons, and of a black dragon by his side. His heart quickened, hammering within him until he thought it might burst forth.

Squeezing the last of the broth from the skin, he tossed it aside and leapt up, determined to get answers from Lamya.

He found her in the center of the stone circle, sitting in front of four long ropes growing up from the ground, woven of various materials. Her arms were extended, palms up to the sky, and she held her chin up, her face angled into the sun. As he approached, she flipped one palm toward him. He stopped.

After a few breaths, she exhaled a single note, one that grew in intensity until it was a bell, echoing across the island, after which it shrank down to a whisper. Opening her eyes, she lowered her arms and beckoned him.

"Come, sit by your gaoler. Feel the heft. Ask what you must, believe what you will."

Rocco sat on the ground where the ropes were embedded. Dark green in color, the cords were soft as silk but when he tugged on them, they were unbreakable. At the end of each cord was a large loop like an animal snare.

"These held me last night." He ran his fingertips across the collar, his skin prickling at the touch. "Or held my nightmare."

"Yes." Lamya gave him a wry grin. "They controlled your hallucination."

"Forgive me." He frowned and shook his head. "I am trying to accept what is, but I have holes in my memory, and what I do remember is in tangles. Did I fly with a black dragon yesterday, or long ago? I hunted Juan de Medina—some force is drawing me to keep hunting him, but another memory tells me he's dead."

"Do no worrying." Lamya sat, nodding. "It will come."

"It needs to come faster." He fell silent, fingering the weave of the rope. "When I first changed on Île des Oiseaux…I remember being full of rage, frustrated, wanting to kill. There was another dragon, a blue one."

"It is time to rise and work." Lamya leapt to her feet. "By the time you leave here, you will remember more, and we will have much to discuss."

The day was spent rolling a boulder across the plateau, stopping to climb a palm tree, and rolling the boulder back. Rocco's muscles weakened and trembled, and he desperately wished to stop, but he refused to complain. This goddess would have no pity for him, he knew.

"I am no goddess," Lamya said, "but you are correct. I cannot afford pity. You must be well tired before the sun sets."

"If you are so gifted that you can insert yourself into my thoughts," Rocco puffed as he shoved the boulder another few inches. "Why can you not fill in my missing pieces for me?"

She glared at him, her golden eyes burning with the sunlight until he had to look away. "Come, the sun is waning. You must drink before we begin to train again."

Rocco stood and rubbed his shoulder, breathing heavily. "Yes, Lamya."

They were quiet by the fire, Rocco sipping his bagged elixir, and the Ancient One drawing circles in the dirt in a meditative motion. He watched her, letting his mind devote itself to the constant circles.

"Mercedes." His voice startled him.

Lamya continued to draw. "Yes, what about Mercedes?"

"I remember. She was Tempest's daughter, by the Count de Medina." He frowned. "She is supposed to be dead, but I think I was following her scent on Île des Oiseaux."

"So now you are convinced that you are not dreaming?"

He shrugged. "The pain and the anger feel real as it is happening. When I awaken it seems too fantastical. But I do recall Île des Oiseaux and being called by a scent. Then the blue dragon appeared, and I was distracted."

Lamya nodded and looked up. "Do you recall anything about the blue dragon?"

"Only that it was there, and I attacked it because I wanted to kill everything."

"So, it fought you?" She leaned toward him.

"No." He shook his head and downed the rest of his broth. "It evaded me. My talons could not pierce its feathers and it hurt me with—" He ran his hand across his face, feeling rough strips across his cheek and nose. "Lightning?"

Lamya turned, but not before he caught the glimpse of a smile.

"What do you know of this dragon?" he asked. "It does not appear to be a blood dragon."

"It is not." She was silent for a time, gazing at the sky as if in conversation with the clouds. Finally, she looked back at him. "It is a moon dragon. It does not destroy. It nurtures and protects."

"Nurtures and protects what?"

"Itself. New life. The weaker ones." The soft glow of sunset crossed her face. "We should prepare. It is time."

Lamya rose and walked toward the altar of cords. He allowed her to fasten the loops around his wrists and ankles.

The last of the sun fell into the ocean and set his bones on fire. It would be another night of learning to control this demon he'd become. The previous night he'd been too full of anger to pay much attention to Lamya's voice. She was a tormentor, preventing him from hunting down his prey.

Tonight, he rose with intention. He needed to gain Lamya's trust, so that she would lighten her grip. The desire to kill still burned strong in him. Be a good lad, he told himself as he rose into the sky, flying within his boundaries and taking care not to pull against his captor. Be good and Lamya will reward you with your freedom. *Then I will leave for Île des Oiseaux and find Mercedes— and the blue dragon.*

The Castle de Medina was at least an hour's walk if one used the road, but only half that time using the footpath that ran behind both castles. Lisette strode down the trail as rapidly as she could but halfway down the path, her legs grew sluggish, and her heartbeat raced.

She slowed her pace. *Child, I love you, but you are an extra weight I wish I didn't have to carry today.*

As she got closer to the castle, she moved to the edge of the brush. The three castles on this island had been placed strategically on hills, with the surrounding trees cleared away to keep marauders from sneaking up to and over the walls. Of course, the jungle had a way of creeping back into the neighborhood, but the castle's location still allowed it to be guarded successfully.

The ring of brush at the bottom of the hill provided moderate cover for a single spy, allowing a partially restricted view of the back wall, including the gate. It took Lisette several minutes to wind back through the grove of trees, fight the underbrush and vines to the north, and steal up to the edge again. She found a bower inside a clump of young mahogany trees, no longer saplings but not quite adult. Nestling herself into their midst, she found a comfortable position to sit and watch.

The sun was overhead, making this the normal time for mid-day rest. Perfect timing. When good people nap, the rest come out to play.

A small breeze floated by at intervals and the afternoon heat had silenced most of the birds. Soon, Lisette's eyes grew weary, and she longed to nap along with the rest of the good folk of the island. One long sigh drew her eyelids down to sleep, only to pop open with the sound of movement in the brush to her left. The quick clunking rhythm of the steps did not sound like any animal.

Lisette couched lower into the space, pulling vines around her blue robe as camouflage. The tromping got louder, accompanied by a wheezing sort of breath. A small, tubby man appeared in the trees, carrying a basket, his eyes fixed on the castle as he pushed his way through the foliage. She held her breath as he passed her, so close she could have kicked him.

At the edge of the glade, he stopped and leaned against a tree, huffing. He remained there briefly, panting, wiping the sweat from his face. With a large sigh, he took the final few steps to a wooden gate set into the stone wall and knocked five times. He was rewarded with the creak of hinges as the door opened.

Lisette was glad she was positioned where the gate opened toward her. A dark hunched figure pushed the door open a mere crack, just enough to receive the basket from the little man. She could not see the figure clearly, but they were wearing black from head to toe. Even their face was covered by a heavy veil, making it impossible to tell if it was man or woman.

The pair were talking, but she could not make out their words. The figure loomed large above the man as he slunk backwards, his hands in supplication. *Whatever he has done he fears punishment.* The dark figure threw the basket at him and pointed toward Lisette.

A gravelly, yet somewhat familiar voice screamed. "The purple ones, you fool! These are not even ripe!"

The gate shut and the little man grabbed the basket from the ground and set off toward Lisette, mumbling all the way. "How am I to know what's ripe and what's purple?"

Lisette waited for him to pass by her, watching him trudge back down his own path. When he was far enough away, she stood, shook the vines from her robe, and followed him, being certain to walk quietly.

He kept moving further into the brush, mumbling about the indignities of trying to find something he'd never seen. Lisette stayed a respectable distance behind while she decided when to reveal herself.

At last, his wanderings brought him to a small pond, where he stopped and sat, mopping his face again with his sleeve. Lisette gazed around. The water in the pond was dark and green with algae. Lilies floated on the surface, and a pleasant carpet of ground cover swept down to the water's edge, round, vibrant emerald leaves with spiky pink flowers. Across the water there were small trees Lisette recognized—sea grapes.

She glanced skyward. The sun had made significant progress, so much so that she wondered if she'd get back to her castle before dinner. Stepping out of concealment, she strolled over to the man, who still sat, catching his breath.

"Could I lend any assistance?" she asked.

The man fell over, jumped up, and backed away from

her. "See, where'd you come from?"

"I was wandering near the castle," she lied. "I saw the black figure throw the basket, heard the screeching, and decided to follow and see what you're unable to do."

The little man studied her up and down, pausing to note her bulge. He sighed. "Her Ladyship requires ripe sea grapes, only I can't tell the ripe ones from the greenies. I'm colorblind, you see. Only way to tell's to eat them, but I can't bring back grapes I've already et, can I?"

"I should say not." She shook her head. "Although even ripe sea grapes are not the tastiest of fruits. Why not mangos? Those you can at least tell by their softness whether they are ripe."

"I don't know that she eats them, only that she needs them ripe. I stripped a whole branch of its fruit, so I lucked out with some ripe, some green. She yells about the waste and tells me nothing but ripe fruit or it's the whip."

Lisette looked at him. His clothes were tattered but wore the markings of a holy man. "Are you a priest? What is your name?"

"Tumas, and I was a priest, till it happened—you know, the kidnapping of the marquise. The decent nobles were killed, the so-so ones disappeared, and the mean ones have taken over. I serve where I can."

She remembered his name—he was always speaking up for the benefit of the village. Her father treated him kindly, inviting him into his study where they would discuss a solution to whatever complaint the priest made. She had met him a few times, but as a child. It was long ago. She remembered Count d'Auguste joking with Father about him, saying, "You allow the gnat to pick at your arm instead of swatting it away."

"Well, Tumas, I'm not colorblind, so I could help you find ripe berries. I only ask two things in return."

He cocked his head. "What might those two things be?"

"One is merely that you tell me everything you know about the person in black who abuses you so." She smiled, hoping to look friendly. "The second is that you take full credit for finding the ripe sea grapes and don't mention our meeting. Ever."

Tumas smiled.

Ruhee sat in a far corner of the hut, shivering and rocking. Her screams had not stopped entirely, they had merely decreased to the high whine of a boiling kettle each time she exhaled. The early sun lightened the room, but she took no notice of the gentle rays.

There had been talk when she first crewed on the *Dişi Aslan* of Captain Derya's curse. A few women claimed to have seen the transformation, although they argued about the details of it, which made the rest of the crew doubt their stories. Ruhee definitely doubted.

People did not become other things, certainly not dragons.

Mixing herbs into potions, along with the use of her ankh—that was as much magic as she could believe in. And it was the properties of the herbs themselves that held the key. She whispered the spell into each potion, but that was tradition. The herbs would work, whether she told them to or not. At least that's what she believed.

It was not like I made a love potion, only a forgetfulness one. His love for me must be real, not based on leaves and roots. I only helped it a little, cleared an obstacle, made him forget Lisette.

She closed her eyes and saw him again in her mind, twisting and stretching, feathers popping from his skin, shrieking in agony as his body grew talons and tail and wings. He glowered at her, his wide nostrils flaring before growling and rearing on his hind legs.

Gasping as if drowning, she opened her eyes and shook the memory away.

She crawled from the corner and stood on shaky legs, walking unsteadily toward the dying fire. The cool morning air made her wrap her arms tight until she could pick up a shawl and bury her shoulders in it. She checked the kettle and saw there was enough water for tea, so she put a log in the pit and stirred at the ashes until the embers caught the wood and sparked to life. Once the fire was strong, she picked up the kettle in both shaking hands, and hung it over the flames.

As it heated, she opened a small pouch and poured the contents on a small table. Leaves, seeds, and small green branches fell out. She combed through them, looking for anything that she should not have used.

"I don't understand," she said. "All I picked was sea grape leaves, valerian, plumeria. Nothing else. It shouldn't have turned him into a…" She could not say the word aloud.

Her musings were interrupted by sounds coming from the beach. A boat's hull was being scraped on the sand as oars hit against the wood. Ruhee ran to the doorway and paled, her heart and stomach looking for somewhere to hide.

Two dinghies approached, one already on the sand

and another closing in. Captain Derya leapt out of the first dinghy, into the surf.

The second boat slid in beside hers. A large man, familiar to her, emerged from that one—Chunk, from *L'Implacable*. They waved and approached, with long, quick strides. Captain Derya was a slender woman, her legs perhaps half as long as the big sailor's. Still, she kept pace with him, smiling as they grew nearer.

Ruhee pulled herself up and walked toward them. The dragon may have spared her life, but she doubted if either of these two would.

"Ruhee." The captain's dulcet voice held a note of excitement. "How has our patient fared?"

"Well, Captain." Her voice trembled as she watched the pair fix their gaze on the hut. She could not let them go in. "But…there have been…complications."

The captain and Chunk stopped walking.

"Compli-what?" Chunk said. "Like, a problem?"

Ruhee ran the back of her hand over her forehead. There was no sweat to wipe, only the trembling of her fingers. "I barely know where to start," she muttered, before the world darkened and she fell to the sand.

She opened her eyes to see the inside of the hut from atop Rocco's bed. Looking down at her were two faces with worried expressions.

"Welcome back," Captain Derya told her as Chunk lifted her head to offer her water.

"Thank you," she said between gulps, trying not to drown with Chunk's good intentions.

"Now then." The captain pulled a chair close to the bed and sat down. "Why don't we start with the obvious. Where's Rocco?"

Ruhee pushed herself into a sitting position, clasped her hands, and lowered her head. "I made a mistake, my Captain."

Chunk stood next to her, his arms crossed. "That don't answer the question."

Captain Derya shushed him and turned back to Ruhee. "One step at a time. I'm listening."

Ruhee sat, staring at the floor, her cheeks blossoming into cherry-red flames. The silence pushed at her from all sides until she couldn't breathe. At last, she cried out, "I just wanted him to love me as I love him!"

"What the devil?" Chunk said, scratching his head.

Captain Derya stood and lifted Ruhee's chin in her hand until the girl's eyes met her own. "What did you do, Ruhee?"

"It wasn't a love potion. I know better than to do that." Ruhee took a breath. "I thought, if he forgot Lisette, he might…he might see me instead."

The captain nodded, encouraging her. "And what happened when you did this?"

"It was fine until last evening as the sun set." Ruhee's eyes widened and she trembled at the memory.

Captain Derya sighed. "You saw him change."

Ruhee was crying now. "I swear I didn't do it. I wouldn't know how to make a potion to do *that*. And he flew away, and he never came back, and I'm so scared of what I did."

The captain paced across the hut, shaking her head. Chunk walked toward her, scowling. "Fool girl!"

"We have a problem." Captain Derya held her hand at his chest. "We need to figure out where he went, and what he might do."

Chunk looked at Ruhee. "Has no one ever told ya not to meddle with the past?"

Ruhee gazed up at the two, tears glistening on her cheeks. "It was only one memory."

Captain Derya spun toward the girl. "Only one memory? Even you are old enough to understand that if you pull one end of the thread, the garment unravels. That *one memory* was a guard for so much more. You knew of Lisette, but you did not know Tempest, Rocco's first love, the woman who died, the reason he became a dragon to hunt those who killed her."

The more the captain spit words at her, the more Ruhee wept.

"Now he is stuck hunting people who no longer live," the captain added.

"Meanin' no one's safe," Chunk said. "He be huntin' everyone."

Captain Derya rubbed her temples and turned to the girl. "Show me the potion you used."

Ruhee pointed toward the table, where she had dumped the contents of the sachet. "I swear I didn't use anything that…anything that…"

The captain shushed her stuttering and went to the table. For several minutes, she combed through the assortment of plant cuttings, examining each sprig with care, pinching leaves in her fingers and sniffing at the odor. She shook her head.

"The good news is that I don't see anything here that would harm the captain's memory, only stifle it for a while."

"How long a while?" Chunk asked.

"That is harder to say. He may awake tomorrow with his full senses intact, although I suspect he will gather his memories slowly, and only when tapped." She gave a sharp glare at the girl. "Have you ever used this potion?"

Ruhee shook her head vigorously. "No, my captain. I've only been taught to assemble the contents. I did see my nani use it once."

Chunk towered over her. "Wha' happened that time?"

She shrank from him and looked at the ground. "A young man was infatuated with me. After the potion, his heart forgot to love me, and he was able to love another."

"Did you not love him?" Captain Derya asked.

Ruhee shrugged. "He was a nice boy. I liked him and could have married him, but I was not unhappy to not marry him." She looked down at her hands, picturing the pirate with wild dark curls and eyes like the sea. "He wasn't Captain Rocco."

"Girl, you listen to me." The captain's voice was stern. "Rocco is not for you. The young man could forget his love for you—he had very few years of memories. Rocco's life was not for you to meddle in."

Ruhee burst into tears again. "I meant no ill!"

Chunk scowled and walked out of the hut. "I can't stand cryin'."

The captain approached Ruhee and stroked her shoulder. "I understand, he is a handsome man, strong, brave, confident. It is difficult. You will hurt for a time, but one morning you will awake and your heart will be light. And perhaps you will love again."

Ruhee reined in her tears until they were sniffles and nodded.

"Your orders are to remain here and wait for Rocco. If he returns, tell him that *L'Implacable* is heading toward Isla del Lagarto, and *Dişi Aslan* is on its way to the pirate's port on the other side of this island. The *Dişi* will return for you at the end of the new moon's cycle."

"Yes, my captain." Ruhee watched Captain Derya stride from the hut and join Chunk at the dinghies. She waited for them to vanish around the point before she sank down on the hut's dirt floor, screaming and pounding her fists.

13

Lisette stood below the tree and plucked deep purple sea grape berries from its branches. "How did you come to this place, Tumas? It seems that your priestly duties are being wasted."

"I have been blessed," said Tumas, holding the basket, "to be able to read people and adapt to their needs. It is, I believe, the only reason I am still alive."

Lisette pulled another dark fruit from its stalk and placed it in the basket. "Why don't you just go live in the village, or perhaps appeal to one of the other castles?"

He shook his head. "I had been installed at the Castle de Medina by the Duke de Lille, in an attempt to discover any plans to remove France from the island's rule. The duke chose me because I could listen well under the cover of serving the family. The Count de Medina was rarely here, and the countess was indifferent about political intrigue. To my dismay, their daughter, Mercedes, not only guarded her father's interests, she suspected my fidelity to the duke. She distracted me with an imagined plot to replace the d'Auguste family. Had I known the Lady Lisette would be taken…" He lowered his head, crossing himself.

"Yes, it was a shock for many." Lisette turned away to hide her blush. "So, who lives in the castle now? There is a rumor that it is a cousin of the Count de Medina, but no one knows for certain."

"The lady of the castle has kept her identity a secret from all. However, I have my suspicions. She dresses in black, including a shroud over her face. Only one person in the castle has seen her, and she is a deaf-mute woman, devoutly Christian and sworn to fealty."

"And who do you think this lady is?"

"In truth, I cannot say." Tumas put his finger to his lips and peered over his shoulder at the glade, brows knitted. After some seconds, he whispered, "Mercedes, the count's daughter."

"Mercedes?" Lisette's fingers opened, dropping the berries she just picked. As she bent down to retrieve them, she whispered, "But she is dead—or so I was told." A vision of Mercedes flitted through Lisette's mind, face down in the garden, her white dress crimson and blackened with flames.

"She was set aflame by some evil force, but she survived." He bowed his head. "Horribly scarred and in such constant pain she lashes out at all."

"She was never a fount of kindness." Lisette raised an eyebrow then collected herself. "Still, it is a harsh punishment for one so young."

"Yes, may God have pity on her." Tumas took the basket from her arm. "Well, it has been a delightful afternoon. I do enjoy company when I'm on these outings."

"I suppose I need to get home as well." Lisette regarded the late afternoon sky. She had enough time to return and change for dinner, but not much more.

"Farewell, miss—I never got your name."

She turned to him. "Father, I am Lisette de Lille."

"Little Lisette? I did not recognize you!" He bowed. "My apologies, I hope I did not speak out of turn about your family."

"Not at all." She smiled. "I wish I had known that my father was so concerned about the Spanish. I might have helped him."

"Yes, m'lady."

"Perhaps we can walk together again sometime when you are hunting sea grapes."

"I would like that. And do not hesitate to ask for my aid."

They parted, and she pushed through the underbrush as quickly as possible until she emerged near the path to her castle. Once free of vines and brambles, she ran to the door at the back wall and slipped inside, stopping to catch her breath. No one was in the gardens, so she hastened to the balcony, where she could enter the Lovers' Cupboard.

Lifting her skirts to run up the steps, she was stopped by a large pair of boots, attached to long legs, and an unhappy guardsman.

"M'lady, I believe I was clear about my orders."

"And I was—" She frowned at him, holding her hand above to shield her eyes from the sun. "Excuse me, but this is impossible." Pushing past him, she climbed to the top step and turned to face him again. "I was clear that I am not under any such order."

"That is not my concern. I have an order from the duke."

Lisette sighed. "We could have this argument until we both die of hard-headedness. I am dining with the duke this evening. I will get this settled without getting you in trouble."

"Why should I be in trouble?" His expression was of shock. "You were the one who disobeyed the order."

"No. I had no order. You will be in trouble for not performing your duty." She grinned and patted his arm. "But don't worry. Your secret is safe with me."

He was still frowning and spluttering when she crossed the balcony and disappeared into the great room from the arched door.

Back in her chambers, Lisette needed a cool bath and conversation with Pinar, so she pulled the velvet cord. To her surprise, one of the other maids, a tiny older woman arrived.

"Yes, I'd like a cool bath drawn," Lisette said. "I thought Pinar would be attending me."

"Ordinarily, yes, m'lady." The wiry dark-haired woman's French was spoken with a Spanish accent. "I am Maria. I have not seen Pinar today."

"That seems odd." Lisette sat at the vanity and brushed her hair while the water was being prepared. It was possible that Pinar was occupied elsewhere—Amoy was probably exerting her will. Still there was an uneasy knot in Lisette's stomach.

"The duke had your dresses let out a bit, m'lady, because of the *niña*." In the mirror, Lisette watched the woman's eyes go large at her gaffe. "I mean, because of the *bébé*."

"Thank you. That will be all."

"Do you not wish me to help you dress?"

"No." Lisette dismissed her, watching her close the door.

The maid seemed friendly enough and the duke was Spanish, so it was natural that he'd have help from his own country. Uneasy, she locked the door and bolted it before undressing.

The water was delightfully cool and scented with lavender, one of her favorites. Mama had to order it from France, as she had no luck in growing the plant on their tropical soil. Lisette sank down into the tub, relishing the goose-pimples that rose on her arms and legs. As she soaked, she considered who to ask about Pinar.

She had just leaned back and closed her eyes when she heard a key in the lock. Sitting upright, she listened intensely, as the metal rattled, the key being jiggled within. The door was not going to open, due to the wooden bolt holding it shut. Still, someone on the other side worked the door, attempting to open it.

Lisette rose from the tub and grabbed the sheet to dry herself. She threw on a shift and her blue robe, irritation rising. Drawing herself up to royal wrath, she stomped over, lifted the bolt, and threw the door open.

"Who interrupts my bath?"

Tall Guard stood at the door, shoulders back, expression stern, and a blush deepening all the way to his ears. "M'lady, the duke is asking for you to join him. It is the dinner hour."

Her eyes narrowed as she glared at him. "Tell Monsieur le Duke I shall join him shortly."

"He said to tell you he'd rather you not be late."

"Tell him I'd rather not be with child. I'll be down presently. And do not *ever* unlock my door or enter my chambers *uninvited*." She slammed the door, allowing the bolt to fall into its cradle with a bang.

After slipping into a teal gown, she sat at the vanity and pinned her hair into a braided roll off her neck, mumbling the entire time about the waste of a good, scented bath. She gave herself one last look in the mirror, pinching her cheeks for a little color.

"It will have to suffice," she told her reflection. "The duke certainly doesn't deserve better."

14

The air cooled somewhat as she descended the stairs, reminding her of the night of her birthday. She was turning twenty and there was so much to look forward to. Her engagement to Eric d'Auguste would be announced to everyone. The mead had been excellent. Instead, it was used against her, to render her unconscious and sell her to a pirate.

My birthday, my betrothal, and my betrayal. At least the wine was good.

The duke sat at the head of the table in the great room. As she approached, he smiled. "There is my lovely niece—or should I call you my daughter?"

"No, Uncle Oscar," Lisette sighed as she sat in her place beside him. "Please do not call me that. Lisette, or Lizzie, is fine."

"As you wish. I cannot wait for your child to call me

Grandfather."

She opened her mouth to protest but instead grabbed her goblet and took a sip of cider.

The servant appeared with the first course of chicken empanadas. Although her stomach nagged from hunger, Lisette's mind was awhirl.

How is Mercedes still alive? And where is Pinar?

"You seem preoccupied this evening," the duke said. "Is there something troubling you?"

"Much, Sire, and most of it at your hand." She scowled and picked at the crust of her fried pie.

"Me?" His eyebrows raised in astonishment. "How could I possibly trouble you?"

"Your guard denies me a walk in the sunshine among the flowers. He also feels free to unlock my chambers and enter when I am in the bath!"

"I did ask my captain of the guard to assign someone to keep you safe, but I did not mean only within the castle." He frowned. "And entering your chamber—Dios mío, that shall not be tolerated."

"You will remedy this?" She held up a fork full of potato.

"Yes. Please eat," he implored.

Lisette took a bite and put her fork down. "Now we come to the matter of Pinar. Your housekeeper Amoy and I had a disagreement about whether Pinar was to be my attendant. Amoy said she wasn't. I appeal to you as your guest—Pinar is to attend to me."

"Ah, yes, Pinar. I am surprised. Amoy said that you had released Pinar and required a midwife to attend to you. I sent Pinar into the village to procure one." He kept eyeing her plate. "Please, do eat."

Lisette frowned. "A midwife? I am but halfway to my due date. A midwife will not be required for months."

"Oh? I did not know. No matter, it will be good for

you to have a midwife to depend upon. Pinar is just a young girl with no training in childbirth."

"But I prefer Pinar's company." Lisette's backbone stiffened in anger.

"Don't be silly." He chuckled between mouthfuls. "One maid is easily swapped for another."

"Not for me." Lisette pushed her plate away. "I have lost so much already. My parents, my brother, this home…to lose my maid is more than I can tolerate."

"Why, Lisette, you can still live in this castle as if it were your own. I regret your family's untimely demise, although I was not the cause of it. But soon you will have my grandchild—that will surely lighten your heart."

"I have appealed to your kindness to grant a pregnant woman's simple requests." She gave him an icy, knowing glower. "If you cannot be kind, I cannot be…responsible for the consequences."

He dropped his fork. "You assured me that part of your life had ended."

"All I said was that the magic had left its mark. You asked no more, and I did not volunteer." She turned her nose up at her still-full plate and gestured to the servant who had just entered the room. "You may clear this. I no longer have an appetite."

"But the baby," the duke sputtered. "You must stay healthy to keep my grandchild—"

Lisette stood, her back steeled and straight. "There is nothing I must do at this moment, except excuse myself to my chambers. I prefer to be alone." She strode from the table.

"It barely matters what you prefer," he called after her. "You cannot escape this place."

Heat shot up her cheeks, as she whipped about to face him. "I grew up in this castle. I know all of its rooms, its hiding spaces, its nooks, and secret exits. You cannot guard them all, even if you could find them." A part of her regretted her outburst—he could easily add more guards to her every move.

He stood from the table, napkin in hand. "You would not take my son's child away!"

She shook her head. "For yet another time, I tell you this child is not Connie's. And secret exits are also secret entrances. I might not leave, but who knows who—or what—I might let in."

His face flushed, then paled. "Lisette, I…"

"Sire, I have no desire to do battle with you." She sighed, softening her tone. "Having my baby here would be lovely, were it not for the unusual circumstances of this child. My mamha is well acquainted with my particular—malady, and I must go to her for assistance. It was my hope to return here once the baby is able to travel."

He turned from the table and paced a few steps. "You are certain—it is not Connie's child?"

"She is not."

He tugged at his beard. "If I let you leave here and have the baby, would you agree to return and present the baby as my heir?"

Lisette frowned. Her plan was to find Rocco, and then…what? Marry a pirate? Sail off with him and his crew? Raise their daughter on L'Implacable? She ran her fingers over her burgeoning belly. "Let us say, I am not opposed to it under the right circumstances."

The duke's face brightened. "Then it's settled. Tell me where to find this—what did you call her, a mamha? Tell me where she is, and I'll have one of my guards fetch her."

"I don't think you understand. I must go to her."

"Nonsense. This castle is a much more comfortable place for childbirth. What island does she live upon?"

She stood staring at the duke, who now seemed like less of a mountain of a man and more like a stone wall—a thick stone wall. "My child will require a special place with a special midwife to control the magic. A place far from people who are not magic.”

“All this talk of magic wearies me.” He frowned. “At least finish your meal.”

She sighed. “You have fed me amply since my arrival and I am certain the baby is content. May we discuss this in the morning? I am tired.”

As if snapped from a dream, he blinked, looked at her ever-expanding middle and exclaimed, “Of course, you must be exhausted! Do you need assistance up the stairs?”

“No. But I do require my maid to wait upon me. My maid, Pinar.”

“Yes, of course. I will find her and send her right away.” He rang the bell for the servant, barking orders as the woman entered. “Find Pinar! She will attend to the mistress.”

“Your lordship.” The woman bowed deeply. “Pinar has not returned from her errand.”

Lisette looked out the tall window at the night, a coldness in her gut warning of danger.

Back in her room, Lisette paced across her balcony, trying to recall the chant that turned her into the dragon.

"Many rivers…rivers and streams…streams and dreams…argh!" She threw her arms upward at the stars. "Stars! Moon! Can someone please get a message to Lamya? And where is Pinar?"

She collapsed on a stone bench, hating the tears that rolled down her face. *A cup of tea might relax me and allow me to think more clearly.* Going inside, she rang the bell for a servant. Maria appeared at the door.

"Has Pinar returned yet?" Lisette asked.

"No, m'lady." Maria's voice sounded unconcerned.

"Oh." Lisette did not try to hide her disappointment. "In the kitchen pantry, there is a blue crock with sachets of tea. I should like a pot brewed, please."

"Yes, m'lady." The maid gave a slight bow and left.

Lisette watched her go. There was nothing she could criticize the maid for, yet she sensed a troubling insolence about her. Even if Pinar could not be located, she would discuss having a different maid with the duke.

She removed her clothes, down to her slip, and wrapped herself in her blue robe. It was lovely and still fit, and she hoped that wearing it might jolt her memory. Sitting down near the fire, she ran her fingers over her baby bump, softly humming a song from her own childhood.

"Mama used to sing this to me," she told her stomach.

A light rap at the door preceded its opening to reveal Maria with a tray. "The Duke also sent some cakes." She set the tray next to Lisette and stood waiting.

"Thank you, Maria, you are dismissed." When the maid was gone, she opened the teapot and checked its contents. It appeared to be fine. Pouring herself a cup, she sat back and stared at the ceramic dragon on the mantelpiece. "I used to be just like you, little dragon, except I was black. Rocco was red."

She recalled the blood dragon that fought with her on the first night. Whoever it was, she had not seen it again. Strange, considering the moon was still a slender crescent.

Could Mercedes be the blood dragon? What if she'd found one of our feathers? Lisette shuddered. She had firsthand experience with their magic.

The tea tasted a little stale, which didn't surprise her. Tomorrow she should get fresh leaves from the garden and prepare a new batch. Her eyelids were drooping so she decided to get some sleep. As she placed her cup back on the saucer, she noticed how weak and shaky her hand looked. She stood and turned to her bed, clutching the chair to keep from falling down.

There was only one other time she had been this wobbly, and she had awakened in a pirate ship, frightened yet full of righteous anger. This time there was nothing but wrath in her heart. She staggered to the desk and picked up a slender letter opener—not particularly sharp, but useful. Shaking her head, slapping at her face, she fought the drug's effects and struggled to stay awake.

With effort, she focused her eyes on the door and could see it was unbolted. As she moved to lock herself in, the door opened. Maria entered with the tall guard. Lisette grabbed at the desk, holding herself upright and keeping the letter opener close to her body.

"I think we'll have no more arguments about my assignments, *m'lady*." The guard sneered the last word and walked toward her. He lowered his shoulder to fold her across and carry her. As the last of her consciousness slipped away, she thrust her weapon at him. It found flesh and he dropped her. "Gods dammit!"

Those were the last words she heard.

Cold awakened Lisette, a damp chill that seeped into her bones. She opened her eyes and saw a ceiling of dark wooden beams, ragged and chipped with time. Rolling over, she pushed herself into sitting position to discover she was on the floor of a castle dungeon.

This was not her family castle. Of the two remaining castles, there was the d'Auguste family and the Medina family, both of whom had their reasons to dislike her.

A small square window let in a pinpoint of daylight, and would let in whatever weather there was, since there was no glass. Lisette stood on tiptoe and looked out. It was much too small to try to escape, but she could clearly see a familiar stone wall, and a forest beyond.

This was the Medina castle.

The door to the cell was thick iron bars, so she leaned against them to see the dungeon's layout. Two other cells graced each side. The cell to her left seemed empty, but she recognized the man in the one to her right.

"Ah, my tall bodyguard. It does not look like you

were paid well for your treachery." She sneered at him. "Does the mistress of the castle have no trust in you?"

He flushed and touched his left arm. "You stabbed me."

"What did you expect? You were kidnapping me."

He turned and threw himself backward against the bars, one hand rubbing his forehead. "I was so smart. Do the job, get the money."

"So, no allegiance to the duke for you?" she asked.

"The duke is a satisfactory noble, no more demanding than any other, I suppose." He turned back to face her. "They're all Spanish. What does it matter if I earn coin from both?"

Lisette shook her head. "It matters enough that you keep your duties to the Medinas secret from the duke. What is your name?"

"Pierre Tournier."

"Nice French name. You are unfamiliar to me, so you must have been a guard in the d'Auguste house?"

He nodded. "Then the young master was killed, and the count and countess sailed back to Toulon. They did not return here, nor did they send for any of their staff or guard. We were left to find new stations where we could."

"Can you tell me what happened to the guard of the Lille castle?"

His mouth set in a grim line. "When the duke and duchess died, the Count de Medina swept in with his soldiers. Most of the guards were executed—your father's people were foolishly loyal. Some escaped to the village, where they were hidden until they found passage on French ships."

"I am glad some lived." Lisette turned her back and leaned against the bars, muttering, "How do I escape this hellhole?"

"Hellhole?" A low, raspy voice interrupted her. "And

I have struggled so to make my guests feel welcome."

A figure stepped from the shadows. Lean and angular, she wore a long black dress with high collar and a cape flowing behind. Atop her head was a wide-brimmed black hat with a veil so dark as to hide her features completely, and black gloves covered her hands.

If this was Mercedes, Lisette did not recognize her. The young woman she knew had been tall and voluptuous, swaying with each step as if listening to music. This woman was shorter, hunched as if with age, and moved with a limp.

"Countess," Pierre addressed her, "I owe no allegiance to the Duke de Martinmas. I should not be in this gaol cell. I wanted merely to pay for passage away from this island."

"Shh." She waved her hand at him as if shooing a fly, while she approached Lisette. "Buenos días, my old friend. Much has happened since last we spoke."

"Yes." Lisette stood tall, her expression grim. "The last time we met, you were trying to kill me, the way you killed my parents and my tatie. I suppose you also had a hand in my brother's death."

"You have a fair amount of blood on your hands, my dear. Or should I say, your *claws*?"

"A chain of events begun when you sold me to a pirate." The old rage built again in Lisette's bones, and she wondered if she might return to her blood dragon form.

Mercedes shrugged a small, crooked shoulder. "A calculated risk taken for king and country."

"I'm quite surprised you survived the flames," Lisette told her. "But I suppose witches are used to fire. I should have doused you with water instead."

Mercedes clawed through the bars, but Lisette quickly jumped out of her reach. "We'll see how sharp your tongue is after a month in this cell. I doubt that your dragon form can escape these walls."

Lisette grinned. "I was wondering if you saw the red dragon that hunts the skies."

"Yes, and I know it's you."

"You are most mistaken." Lisette laughed. "Have you forgotten that night? I wore black to the party."

The gloved hands that had tried to reach Lisette withdrew, folding into tiny fists. Mercedes stretched her body up, quietly groaning as she did. "You and that baby will die here."

"The Duke de Martinmas will discover what you've done." Lisette glared at the black veil, her expression somber. "You will pay for killing his grandchild."

Mercedes huffed. "Maria heard you tell him it was not Connie's child."

"Maria heard me say a lot of things, no doubt. She is a simple woman and does not understand negotiations between nobility."

The door to the dungeon opened and a tall, broad soldier entered. Lisette noted his thick neck and island features.

"Countess," he said. "The guard is ready."

"Countess?" Lisette asked. "I didn't know El Rey had bestowed that title on you."

"It does not matter. My mother was a countess, she is dead. Now I am a countess." Mercedes clipped her words before turning her back on Lisette. She hissed and put her hand to her hip before sinking back into her crooked shape. Limping past the soldier, she said, "Come, Captain Simone."

"I believe you are mistaken about being a countess," Lisette called out as the pair left the dungeon. She leaned her forehead against the bars and sighed. Mercedes was a conniving, manipulative, ego-driven woman before Lisette set her on fire. Now, she was cruel, too. *I have to find a way out of here before she does something horrible to pay me back.*

"What's this about a red dragon?" Pierre asked.

16

It was Rocco's last night on the island and Lamya had prepared real food, including meat. He had never tasted anything so delicious. His senses were sharpened by this dragon curse, and the aroma of charred fowl, the creaminess of cooked grain, and the salty bite of vegetables combined to make this meal better than any he'd ever had.

"I haven't had food in so long," he said. "It's quite delicious."

"I am glad you are satisfied." Lamya picked at her own meal. "Tonight, you will fly without restraints. Tomorrow night you will be but a man again."

"Yes. I wish I knew who I was hunting. I am stumbling in the dark." He ate a few more bites. "And I cannot forget the blue dragon. I have many questions."

"You will find answers." She put her bowl down and

rose. "If you are willing to open yourself to the possibility."

"What possibility?"

"The possibility that nothing is as you believe." She gestured. "It is time."

Rocco stood and followed her to the ropes. "I thought tonight we didn't need these."

"We do not. But you will change here because it is the custom." As Rocco took his place, she added, "You will meet a young woman on your journey. Give her a message for me. Tell her, 'The words do not matter. Close your eyes, open your heart, and breathe.'"

He repeated her message. "How will I know this woman?"

"You will know."

Rocco knelt on the platform as usual and watched the sun disappear into the sea beyond. Fire shot through his blood and his bones, and soon he rose over Île des Anciens. He took a final look at Lamya, standing with her face to the sky, her golden eyes illuminated by the stars. Giving her a small nod, he banked right and flew toward Île des Oiseaux.

"Godspeed, Tristan de Rocco," the Ancient One told the sky. "May you find Lisette and bring her back to her mamha."

Words do not matter. Close your eyes, open your heart, and breathe. Rocco went over the message again, wondering how he was going to find this young woman.

Île des Oiseaux was still asleep when he arrived at its coast, but the dawn would soon arrive. Already his dragon sense of smell had detected the person he needed to destroy. The scent drew him inland, to a trio of castles. As he flew, he checked constantly for the blue dragon, but saw nothing except the night-hunting seabirds, all of whom gave him a wide berth.

The dark castle at the northern end of the island both

attracted and repelled him. It was like going into a battle, wanting to leap in with both feet and sword slashing, and also wanting to push away from the blood and the stench. He flew around the high towers and stone walls, letting his sense of smell direct him to his prey, wishing he didn't feel so damned blindfolded.

Something caught his attention at the balcony on the far side, a shadowy figure leaning against the rail and searching the grounds. By the clothing, Rocco guessed it was a woman, although her shape was obscured. As he hovered over her, she turned and went inside, allowing him to fly lower.

The castle interior was darkened, but his dragon eyes could see easily, given any small reflective object. A sliver of light brightened one of the windows, as the figure lit a small candle. Whoever she was, she was a dark shadow, malformed and limping. She was also the source of the scent he followed.

Capturing his prey in an enclosed room was a dicey proposition. His size did not allow him to maneuver in close quarters, and his victim could easily escape through a door too small for him to follow. Hoping she might stroll out to the balcony again, he landed on the stone railing, taking care to let the pads on his paws touch the stone first, lest his talons announce him with their clicking. He perched behind a tall shrub with a painted screen in front of it, hidden from the room's view but able to watch from the shadows.

The figure in the room did not increase the light—she went about her nightly routine in relative darkness. Rocco watched as she removed her cloak, then her long black overskirt and blouse. Stockings and shoes were next, followed by several layers of undergarments and slips. He found it curious that she still wore her hat, veil, and gloves.

At last, with a sag of shoulders, she removed all and

sat, completely naked at a dressing table. The table held no mirror and Rocco understood why. The figure was obviously female, but scars obscured the normal curvature of a woman's body. Wrinkled skin ran from her ankles to her neck, lumpy and misshapen. There were black and gray patches splayed all over her back and legs, as if her skin was tattooed in a hideous pattern.

Only one side of her face bore scars, but it left her mouth and eye drooping. She picked up a bottle and poured something into her gnarled hands. The heavy aroma of honey overwhelmed the light scent of aloe, mingled with sea grape, although he could smell it all.

This was Mercedes de Medina, the daughter of Tempest de Rocco, his eternal love, and Count de Medina, his sworn enemy. A vision of flames consuming a white gown rushed his memory and he slipped from the balcony's edge, catching himself in mid-fall by extending his wings.

Had he set her on fire that night?

A scream to his left distracted him. He whipped about in mid-air, and saw an older woman, wiry and dark-haired standing on a balcony, staring at him, and shrieking as if mad.

Mercedes now stood at her doorway, her mouth opening. He heard a shallow cry from her to her guards, but it sounded too weak to travel far. She disappeared into the room.

If he did not catch and kill his prey tonight, it would be at least fourteen days before he could try again. He longed to wait where he was and hope she came out to the balcony to attempt to shout for the guard from there.

But the screaming…

This woman on the far balcony distracted him, piercing his ears. At last, dragon instinct overruled, and he flew at her. Terrified, she backed against the wall, where he swooped her up and dispatched her with his talons.

Tossing her to the ground, he rained fire down upon her body.

A small flash of light from a building to his right caught his attention and he flew closer. Lowering himself cautiously, he approached the source of what he'd seen. It was a small window to a dimly lit room. The bars told him it was a dungeon. He peered inside, his nostrils flaring, smelling something familiar.

Two small hands appeared at the sill, followed by a woman's face. She gazed at him without fear. Curious, he landed near her, wishing he could ask her name. A raspy scream from the balcony startled them both. He spread his wings and heard the woman at the window call out.

"Rocco? Is that you?"

He turned to face her, curious.

"Guards!" Mercedes had finally found her voice. "Gather your weapons!"

If dragons could smile, Rocco was grinning ear to ear. None of these puny weapons could pierce his feathers, let alone his skin. Still, he had no time for fighting these men. With a final look back at the small window in the dungeon, he snorted an angry puff of smoke, and lifted himself into the clouds as arrows bounced against his legs.

The eastern skyline was growing rapidly paler. Rocco recognized the approach of sunrise and flew to the brush behind the wall, searching for a sanctuary to land, change, and get some rest. Mercedes would have to wait for the next waning crescent.

He spied a rivulet winding through a glade of sea grapes. It seemed as good a place to settle as any, far from the beaten path and with at least something edible nearby. He folded his wings and nestled himself under an elephant's ear plant, allowing the large leaves to shield him. A burning flash put him back into his human form, and he fell into immediate sleep.

Fitful dreams made it difficult to rest. His mind leapt

through disparate scenes that made no sense. Between memories of being with Tempest, a young blond nobleman sat at a table inquiring about a job. Now, Tempest was with the Count de Medina, and then his ship was anchored off Île des Oiseaux. He was kidnapping a woman. He didn't want to do it, but he wanted the woman. She was—

A black hole opened before him, and he fell into darkness. It jolted him into consciousness, and he sat up, sweating and panting, regarding his surroundings. It took a moment to recognize the glade and recall last night's journey.

He stood and walked to the stream. The water flowed at a quick pace, bubbling over rocks, and crashing against the banks at each turn. Rocco put his fingers into the coolness. Laying on his stomach, he drew water up from his cupped hand and drank, splashing his face when he was full. Food was his next goal, so he gathered ripe sea grapes from the nearby trees, along with a fat mango. Meat would have been preferable, but he was without weapons.

Settling at a bunching of small, silver-barked trees, he took the first bite of ripe mango, and heard a shuffling sound in the brush. He shifted his body behind the trees and peered through the branches at the clearing.

A man of short stature and round belly fought his way through vines and bushes, pushing himself out to the clearing with a comical hop. He wore the robes of a priest, though they were old and tattered. A small basket hung on his arm, and his face was set in an aggravated frown.

Rocco looked down at himself for the first time and saw that his clothes were no better than the priest's and possibly worse. His breeches and shirt were not only stained with dirt and sweat, they were shredded to the point of immodesty.

Still, if any man might help me, it would be a priest, no matter how disheveled or unhappy.

"Priest, could you help me?" He stepped out, making certain to round his shoulders and hunch over, pleading. "I have been waylaid by robbers. They took all from me."

"My son, are you hurt?" The priest rushed to his side. "You are so scratched and bruised."

"Not badly injured, except for my pride." Rocco bowed his head. "They tried to drown me in that stream. I held my breath and went limp, and they left. No doubt, they believed I would not live to tell the tale."

"You are very wise. My name is Tumas. I used to be the local priest."

"I am Tristan," Rocco said.

"Well, Tristan, we might first find you some better clothes." Tumas put his basket down and pulled the hem of his robe up. "I do have shirt and breeches under this robe, both of which I suspect to be too small for your shoulders and wide for your belly. You are however welcome to them, to at least be able to walk about in public."

Rocco smiled. "I humbly accept your offer, Priest."

Tumas reached up and shimmied out of his breeches, handing them to Rocco, who stepped into them. As expected, they threatened to fall around his ankles, except for the leather belt the priest included. Rocco gathered the pants at the waist and tied the belt as tightly as possible.

"A perfect fit!" Tumas laughed and lifted his robe in order to take off the shirt underneath. A low moan on the opposite side of the stream stopped him. "What was that?"

"It sounded like a person."

"Were you alone when you were attacked?"

"Yes," Rocco said. "At least, I assumed so."

The moan repeated, and Rocco glanced at Tumas as he listened for the source. Tumas started off, through the stream, so Rocco followed. The noise sounded louder here. After nodding to one another, Rocco swept left while Tumas went right, each working back toward center. They moved slowly, brushing away at the ground cover while they searched underneath. Rocco had just arrived at the base of a large palm when he heard Tumas cry out.

"I've found her!"

Rocco ran to him and helped him turn the girl over. She was young, dark-skinned with black curls, and pretty, despite the dirt and the blood on her mouth and nose. Moaning again, she raised her arms to fight, her eyes struggling to open.

"My dear," Tumas said, his voice low and soothing. "We are here to help you."

She managed to open her eyes and focus on his face. "I must get back."

"Back where?"

"To the castle." She tried to sit, grabbed her ribs, and sank down again. "Lisette needs me."

At the name *Lisette*, Rocco felt a sharp pain in his chest. "Who is that?"

The girl shifted her gaze to him. Her eyes widened. "I know you." She held up her wrist, revealing the lioness head. "My name is Pinar. I sail with the *Dişi Aslan*."

17

With Pierre's question about the dragon still hanging in the air, Lisette heard a woman scream, followed by the familiar soft whoosh of large wings. She ran to the window and peered out. A red dragon circled the courtyard. The woman's constant shrieking made his tail whip angrily. Within moments, the shriek became a terrified yelp, followed by silence.

A body dropped from the sky, a woman Lisette recognized. Maria would not fix another cup of drugged tea. A stream of fire from above quickly obscured the corpse's identity. Lisette grabbed the bars of the window and pressed her face against them, to get a better view.

The dragon turned toward her and descended, landing outside her window. Silver crescent eyes met hers. For a moment, she remembered her nights of fighting

Rocco as a blood dragon, only to indulge in coupling with him when they transformed into humans. Her hand drifted to her stomach. He spread his wings and turned away.

She called to him. "Rocco, is that you?"

His head snapped around to focus on her, his wings still. Lisette opened her mouth to ask him to nod his answer when she heard Mercedes scream for the guards. The dragon looked toward the noise, snorting a puff of smoke. She watched him lift off and fly over the wall.

Lisette left the window, suddenly aware of Pierre's voice.

"Answer me!" His tone was that of a small child—a combination of frustration and whining. "What's happening?"

From her barred door she could see him pressing against his own bars, as if to squeeze out of his cell.

"You want to know about the red dragon?" she asked, then gestured at the window. "That was him."

Pierre backed from the bars, a half-chuckle in his throat. "You don't mean to say a real dragon. Dragons don't exist."

"There are many who say that," she said with a shrug, a twinge of her mother's memory stinging her heart. "But they are wrong. Blood dragons are cursed humans who hunt for revenge, although they might take an innocent life, especially one who won't stop screaming."

With each of her words, his mouth hung open wider. She worried he had gone catatonic when he finally spluttered, "How can this be?"

"Magic exists in our world, though we do not acknowledge it—"

The dungeon door flew open, and Mercedes rushed into the chamber, struggling to make her scarred body keep up with her fury. Her cloak was wrapped around her, and a scarf wound around her head, exposing only one eye. "What do you want with me? Wasn't ruining my life enough?”

Lisette held her hands out. “What have I to do with that dragon?”

“Obviously you have set it upon me.”

“If I controlled that dragon, why wouldn’t I enlist it to free me?” Lisette frowned, noticing Mercedes’ ungloved hands, and realizing the extent of her injuries. “I do not know why the dragon is here or what it wants.”

“I think she’s lying,” Pierre said.

Lisette whipped about to face him. “What?”

“That *thing* landed outside her cell. I think she knows it.” Pierre pointed. “Release me, m’lady. Release me and I’ll hunt down the creature and bring its head back as proof.”

Lisette couldn’t help but smile at his naivety. “Yes, it landed. It looked at me. And it flew away.”

“She called it Rocco.”

Mercedes glared at Lisette, one eye narrow and her body tense.

Lisette wished she could become a blood dragon and run Pierre through with her claws. “I thought it might be the red dragon I knew. It didn’t respond. I don’t think it was him.”

“We shall see,” Mercedes told her. “Tonight, you’ll be chained to a stake, a pretty sacrifice for the beast.”

Lisette kept silent and looked away, knowing he would not come tonight. Ever since her own experience, she was acutely aware of the moon, and still felt a pull when it was in its crescent-to-crescent phase. Tonight began the moon’s first quarter. There would be no dragon.

Mercedes scowled and disappeared, slamming the door behind her. Lisette moved to the small window and looked out to the yard. Being outside, even chained might afford a way of escape. If only she could remember that chant—dragon wings could lift her away from here, away from Mercedes and her treacherous fellow prisoner.

"I hope you do not hold my words against me," Pierre said. "I was hoping to gain her trust and be freed, so I could return to the duke and effect your escape."

"I wouldn't worry," Lisette said, scowling. "When I return to the duke, I shall tell him just how *helpful* you were to me—and his unborn grandchild."

Pierre blanched. "I doubt if you will beat me back to the castle, as you will be a morsel for tonight's dragon dinner."

"We shall see," she told him and turned to the low flat stone that served as a bed. It promised to be cold, hard, and miserable, but she needed some sleep. At least she still wore her cloak to wrap around herself.

The morning light was in full bloom when she awoke, stiff and aching. The first thing she heard was a harsh voice shrieking—Mercedes. Lisette looked out the window and saw her browbeating Tumas. No doubt he had once again gathered unripe sea grapes.

Mercedes pushed him out the back gate and threw the basket after him. That meant he'd be returning. *Perhaps I can attract his attention. He might be able to help me.*

She was still watching for his return when she heard the door open and footsteps descending into the dungeon. Lisette turned to see a servant with a tray holding two bowls.

The woman held a bowl out to Pierre through the pass-through on the door. He grabbed it and retreated out of Lisette's view, although she could hear his slurping as he ate. She watched the woman pick another bowl up and walk toward her.

"Buenos dias," Lisette said.

"Buenos dias." The woman spoke the words with an island accent. She was dark haired, dark skinned, dark eyed.

Lisette took a calculated risk, and extended her arm,

slightly raising her sleeve, so her lioness tattoo would be visible if one looked for it. The woman gave her the bowl with no expression. Either she did not see it or did not know its meaning.

"I hope m'lady enjoys the food," the woman said, pulling up her own sleeve. A matching lioness decorated her wrist.

Lisette made no motion of recognition, nor did she smile. She allowed herself one small upturn of her chin, which the woman returned.

"I will be back in the evening," the woman said. "I am Ghreta."

"With more food, I hope." Pierre flung his empty bowl out of his cell, breaking the pottery.

Ghreta picked the pieces off the floor. "Yes, with more food…for anyone who still has a bowl."

She left as Pierre sputtered angry epithets. Lisette couldn't remember the last time she'd laughed so hard.

18

Rocco kept watch over the girl while Tumas scurried to the stream's edge to fetch water. He returned with a cup and a rag he had moistened. Rocco lifted her head gently and held the cup to her lips. She drank a few sips and relaxed her head back into his hands, waving the cup away. He laid her back down and softly dabbed the wet cloth around her face, cleaning the dried blood and cooling her brow.

"Pinar from the *Dişi Aslan*?" he asked. "I assume Begum Derya still captains it?"

"Yes, Captain." Her words came slowly, whispered.

"Captain?" Tumas asked.

Rocco frowned. "My full name is Tristan de Rocco. I am captain of *L'Implacable*."

Tumas crossed himself. "Only God judges."

"The *Dişi Aslan* will be in harbor tonight." Pinar squeezed Rocco's arm. "I was supposed to get the message to Lisette before I was waylaid."

Again, he blanched at the name, and wanted to ask her about it, but she was in no shape for conversation. He looked at Tumas. "We must get her to the ship, where she can be attended."

"There is a physician in town," Tumas told him.

Rocco shook his head. "It would be a death's sentence for her. The tattoo on her wrist confirms her as a pirate."

"Understood." Tumas rose. "But we cannot carry her to the harbor. The villagers will certainly see and ask questions."

"The *Dişi Aslan* will not drop anchor at the village harbor." Rocco smiled. "Pirates in these waters use another beach on the windward side. The trade winds are fierce, but once we get through, there's a small cove that's both deep and quiet."

"What is our plan, then?"

"I am grateful, priest, that you are a willing helper, but I don't wish to trouble you." He gestured toward the castle and Tumas' basket. "You were sent to gather something, and you will surely be missed."

"True. It won't be the first beating I've got." Tumas shook his head. "I cannot leave you half-clothed and carrying a young woman across the island."

Rocco looked up at the sun. It still had not reached the midpoint. He glanced at Pinar, who had closed her eyes. "If we leave now, I imagine we'd reach the cove by late afternoon. The ship arrives tomorrow." He looked at Tumas. "If someone could bring us a little sustenance and perhaps a shirt and shoes for myself, we could leave later and still be at the cove by dark."

Tumas smiled. "If you could assist me in picking ripe sea grapes, I can return with your requested items."

Rocco turned to Pinar. "I'm leaving you for a moment, but—"

She waved him on with a small motion of her hand.

The two men quickly found their trail back to the grove, where Rocco stripped the ripe berries and filled the priest's basket. "I hope you are not punished for taking so long."

"As long as there is a basket of the correct color in her hand, she is placated." Tumas turned and shuffled out of the clearing and back to the path that led to the castle.

Rocco returned to Pinar and knelt beside her. "Rest now, girl. Soon you will be aboard the ship and receiving good care. I only wish I could help you in the meantime."

She beckoned him closer. He leaned his ear to her mouth.

"There is a plant. Look for broad shiny leaves and white blossoms that spread like a fan." She stopped to take a few breaths. "Bring it, boil it in water. The tea will soothe my wounds."

Rocco nodded. "I'll do my best to find it."

"Look for it near palm trees." She sank back, closing her eyes.

By the time he found the plant she described, Rocco was drenched in sweat and had nearly decided this flower didn't exist. Pinar had neglected to mention the long thorns attached to the shiny leaves. Gathering a bunch of flowers to turn into tea resulted in scratches over his arms and hands. Not having a knife to cut the stems was a disadvantage.

"These had better work," he mumbled as he carried his treasure back to the girl. "They were not easily gained."

When he returned, Tumas was approaching, both hands full. "I come bearing gifts."

"As do I." Rocco held up his bouquet, and his bleeding arms.

"I suspect my lot was easier to harvest," Tumas said.

"Perhaps, but mine do not carry a penalty if I am caught. I am grateful, Priest."

In addition to dried meat, bread, and potatoes, the priest had brought a flask of rum, a small metal cup, and a complete change of clothes for Rocco, including a dagger.

"It's not much as a weapon goes, but I thought you needed something."

"Thank you." Rocco handled the dagger, turning it over and feeling its weight. "I only wish I had it while picking these flowers."

Tumas gathered water while Rocco built a small fire and followed Pinar's instructions to strip the petals from the flowers and scrape the underside of the leaves. Soon the tea was steeping, and Rocco was changing into the clothes Tumas supplied.

"I also brought these strips of cloth," Tumas said. "We can wrap Pinar's ribs and keep her more comfortable on the journey."

"I was going to use these." Rocco pointed to the priest's breeches he had been wearing.

"If you don't mind, I'd rather keep those," Tumas said, taking them from Rocco and pulling them on under his robe.

Rocco laughed, sat down, and helped himself to a chunk of meat. He downed it quickly, along with a swig of rum, before turning to Pinar. "Can you eat something? I believe your tea is cool enough to drink."

Tumas sat down and propped her against his chest. She reached for the cup, sipped a little, made a face, and drank. When the cup was empty, she leaned back with a sigh. "I believe I will have some food."

While Tumas fed Pinar, Rocco tested the blade on his dagger.

"Pinar, weren't you on Isla de Pimienta?" Rocco asked.

"Yes, but the King sent the Duke de Martinmas here, to inhabit the de Lille castle and reinforce Spanish rule." She nibbled at a roll. "His son now inhabits the castle on Isla de Pimienta."

Rocco frowned. "De Lille…the name is familiar, but I do not remember."

Pinar opened her mouth to speak, but Tumas interrupted. "The Duke de Lille and his family were the primary nobility a year ago, when Île des Oiseaux was under French rule. Then their daughter was kidnapped, their son set out on a journey to find her, and the duke and duchess died." Tumas bowed his head. "It was the beginning of a nightmare for us on the island."

Rocco listened, nodding. His body was restless and churning, as if the words disturbed him. He changed the subject. "We should wrap Pinar's ribs and be on our journey. Even as small as she is, it will be an arduous trek to the coast."

Working together, the two men lifted the girl, winding the strip of muslin up and down her ribcage, until there was no more fabric to wind. It provided several layers of padding and stiffness to hold her body steady.

"Captain," she said, "I believe I can walk, for at least part of the way."

Rocco was skeptical. "Perhaps, but you will be slow. We can go faster if I carry you."

"At least let me try."

He frowned and nodded. "You can try. If you are slowing us down, I carry you. Agreed?"

"Yes, Captain." She put her arm around his neck. "If you could help me stand, I would appreciate it."

Once she was standing, Pinar bent over for a moment, holding her ribcage. Taking a few breaths, she straightened, both hands still supporting her body, and walked forward. Smiling at the two men, she said, "Shall we be on our way?"

Tumas turned to Rocco. "Here is where I leave you, my friend. Take care of Pinar and yourself. Are you sailing on the same ship?"

"I do not know," Rocco said. "I should like to be reunited with my crew. In the meantime, I am not quite finished with my task here."

"Know that I am your friend," Tumas said. "And that if you need, I will come to your aid."

"And my sword is yours, Priest." Rocco turned to Pinar. "Let us go. We do not dare waste the light."

Lisette paced her cell, busying her mind by counting the steps, memorizing the stones in the walls, and peering out the window to catch Tumas' return. As she walked, her hands drifted to support her back, which was feeling the strain of the baby pushing further forward. She wanted to lie down again, to rest her muscles, but she didn't want to miss Tumas.

"Why do you not relax?" Pierre asked. "Your constant shuffling is distracting."

"What are you so busy doing that I distract you so?"

"Sleeping."

"Poor lad," she cooed. "Are my footsteps so heavy? Is my clomping keeping you awake? My apologies." She faced the door and sang *"Ah! Vous Dirai-je, Maman"* in as full a voice as she could manage. The song from her childhood was the only one she could remember.

Pierre growled, cursed and stomped. Between the notes, Lisette heard him flop upon his stone bed, groaning as he did.

She reduced her song to a quiet hum. It comforted her, and perhaps would comfort Alara. A wrinkle of worry crossed her brow. Alara used to come to her so often but was strangely silent of late. She caressed her stomach, wondering if Alara's voice had been quieted as she grew.

As if in answer, something punched her hand—from inside her stomach. Lisette gasped.

"What are you on about?" Pierre asked, sounding irritated.

She had no time, nor any desire to respond. The screeching sound of Mercedes' voice distracted her, and Lisette went to the window to observe. She saw Tumas coming into the garden with his basket. Mercedes grabbed it and pawed through the contents. With a dismissive gesture of her black glove, the woman turned and limped back toward the castle. Lisette was certain the basket didn't please her, but evidently it was good enough to spare Tumas a beating.

Lisette waited until Mercedes' back was turned and waved her arms crazily at Tumas. She wanted to call out but was afraid her enemy would hear. Tumas was watching Mercedes while creeping toward the castle himself as if he was planning to do something that would get him into trouble if caught.

She waved more furiously, adding a high birdlike whistle, hoping it would be less conspicuous. Tumas lifted his head. Lisette whistled again. This time, he looked side to side. When he turned toward her, she practically threw her arms out of the cell at him.

Looking both ways as he scurried, he came over to stand at her dungeon window, making a show of examining a bed of flowers nearby.

"Lisette, what are you doing here?" He kept his voice

low.

"Mercedes paid mercenaries to kidnap me. She wants to make me pay for her suffering."

"Surely you did not cause her such grievous harm."

"It is a long story, Father, and I cannot tell it here." She glanced over to see Pierre's hand at the closest bars, the rest of his body hidden in the shadows. "The walls of this gaol have ears."

Tumas nodded. "Perhaps you require the services of a priest."

"Yes. Tonight, I shall be chained in the garden as a sacrifice to the red dragon."

She expected a cry of disbelief or confusion from the priest, but he stood quietly pulling dead leaves from a stalk. "Does she believe your sacrifice will make it go away?"

"I don't know. I don't think she knows. I think she hates me so much that after the dragon kills me, she'll weep because she can't bring me back to life and let him kill me again." Lisette patted her stomach to calm her kicking baby. "I'm surprised she hasn't tortured me herself."

Tumas reached down to squeeze her hand through the bars. "I am so sorry, but I cannot remain here, as I have a mission to complete. I'll return when I can to give you absolution."

"Yes, Father." She watched him move along the wall, until he disappeared into a side door. Lisette guessed it was the larder. She whispered, "Good luck," and lowered her body onto the stone slab.

The baby kicked out again, hard enough to fluff her gown. She massaged her stomach, trying to soothe her restless child. After some moments, she closed her eyes and rested her hand atop her belly. As she drifted into a nap, the pressure of a tiny hand pushed up into her own.

"Mama, it's going to be all right," Alara told her.

"You need to be safe," Lisette whispered. "And I don't know the words to turn into the dragon that keeps you from harm."

"I am safe with you." Alara's hand pressed harder into her palm. "You will find a way."

"I hope so."

"You hope what?" Pierre asked.

Lisette's eyes popped open, aware that she'd been talking aloud. She lay silent, hoping Pierre would leave her alone. It was too much to hope for.

"Who are you talking to in there?" He was louder now. "Is that dragon back? Are you talking to your dragon friend?"

She sighed, heavy and audibly, allowing herself a small groan at the end. "It is of no concern to you. Go back to—whatever you were doing."

"The Duke de Martinmas is going to hear of your mad ramblings."

As if that was a threat. "Please do tell him." Smiling, she decided to have a little fun. "Did the duke tell you how he and I met? He hired me to assassinate a count." It was only a slight exaggeration. "He doesn't like to get his hands dirty. I was able to dispatch the gentleman and leave the duke's name unblemished."

Pierre had no response. The silence was heavenly.

The sun was making long shadows when the dungeon door opened. Ghreta entered with a tray. On it sat a bowl containing roasted meat and potatoes, and several pieces of broken crockery with the meat and potatoes perched in their shards.

The servant pushed the chunks of pottery into Pierre's cell. "Mind the points, dear. They cut the mouth and destroy the innards."

"Hey!" He banged on the bars once, but Ghreta ignored him and shuffled toward Lisette.

"Serves you right," Lisette said.

Ghreta passed the bowl inside, using both hands. "Make certain you have a good hold, m'lady. It's a heavy bowl."

Lisette put both hands around the dish and felt something jagged against her palm. Ghreta gave her a knowing look, so she glanced down. A long key pressed into her hand. She pulled the bowl back into the cell. "Thank you, Ghreta, it smells delicious."

The servant idled by Lisette's cell. "M'lady is sending in a priest, seeing as you'll be *locked* into chains tonight to be sacrificed to the dragon."

Lisette understood at once what the key was for.

"Pardon, Ghreta," Pierre interrupted. "What would be the price of helping us escape? Or maybe just one of us, since I'm sure I'd rescue Lisette, and she'd rescue me."

"That is a large assumption," Lisette told him.

"You mean, you wouldn't at least alert the duke to my circumstance?"

Lisette looked at Ghreta, raising an eyebrow in contempt. "Oh, he'd soon know where you are, and what you did. After that, I could not be responsible for his actions."

Footsteps echoed outside, and there was a knock at the dungeon door. Ghreta welcomed Tumas and gestured to Lisette. "There she is, Father."

Lisette smiled at the familiar face.

"My child," he said, "let us take this time to reflect and pray for God's mercy." He knelt at the bars and gestured for her to join him. In a graceful motion, he made the sign of the cross and held his hand to her through the bars. "We shall pray."

She took his hand and felt paper. Glancing over at Pierre, sitting against the bars, she saw he was acting disinterested, but his head was cocked her way to eavesdrop. She gave Tumas' hand a squeeze.

"Please, Father. Pray for my immortal soul."

The priest recited the words she had heard from infancy. *Our Father, who art in Heaven.* They were as well known to her as her own name, yet how long had it been since she'd spoken them? Lisette was again aware of her heretical position—a blood dragon who had killed in revenge, now a moon dragon created to protect a bastard child.

If I could only remember the words. She frowned and listened intently to the priest. *Yes, Lord, deliver me from evil. I do not understand where the Ancient Ones fit in with Moses and Abraham, but I just want to find Rocco, have my baby, and live to tell the story.*

Tumas stood and placed his hand upon the top of her head. "Go in peace, Lisette. God watches over you."

She made the sign of the cross and rose to her feet. "Thank you, Father. You've been a great comfort."

Tumas left, and Lisette returned to her meal, sitting where Pierre could not see her before silently unfolding the paper the priest gave her. She chewed on a chicken thigh as she read:

I came across two strangers in the forest. The girl Pinar was sent to tell you her ship arrives tomorrow. She was beaten, but lives. A pirate, Tristan de Rocco, is helping her to reach the harbor. Ghreta is giving you a key to the chains. Unlock them and run for the back gate. A horse will await, to take you to the ship.

Lisette tore the note into small pieces and added them to her bowl before finishing her meal. No doubt the juices of the food would make the paper more palatable. She hid the key in the cuff of her sleeve and prayed it would be convenient enough. Reclining on the stone again, she practiced retrieving the key until she could dig it out one-handed and not drop it. There would be only one chance to get it right.

At last, she closed her eyes. There was nothing left to

do except wait for someone to open her cell and lead her to the garden. So much was at stake—she had to escape, find Rocco, and make her way back to Lamya. Somewhere inside her head, a voice said she didn't need to find Rocco, she needed to return to the Ancient One.

"Silence," she whispered. "I need his protection and partnership to help me with this child."

"Who are you talking to?" Pierre shouted.

"Myself." Lisette scowled.

"It bothers me."

"My apologies, but I needed to discuss things with someone intelligent."

It took a few seconds before she heard the groan of understanding from his cell. If she was still a blood dragon, that stupid guard would be marked for death. Perhaps she could put in a word with the red dragon.

Rocco steadied Pinar with a hand around her ribs as they walked. She took small steps, but did not limp or struggle, for which he was glad. He was certain they would make the harbor by the setting sun. A night's sleep would be good for both of them.

She did not make conversation on their trip but seemed intent on simply getting to their destination. This suited Rocco as he mulled over his predicament. It was almost two weeks until he would fly as a dragon and could hunt Mercedes. Did he attempt to rejoin his ship, or remain here until the deed was completed?

A woman's face crossed his mind. Green eyes and auburn curls seen through a barred window. She had shouted his name. Who was she and how did she know him?

Lamya told him this spell would not last long, and he

would have his memory back soon. It was not soon enough. He remembered her message, the one she instructed him to give to a young woman. *Words do not matter. Close your eyes, open your heart, and breathe.*

Which young woman? *You will know.*

"I know nothing," he said, startling himself and Pinar.

She glanced up at him. "What is it that you wish to know?"

He shook his head. "My apologies. A part of my memory has been locked away—or perhaps erased—by a spell cast upon me." He looked at her, so young and darkly pretty. Could she be the young woman?

A soft light shone in her eyes. He opened his mouth to say the words, and the light diminished. Her face gave him the answer. *I am not the one.*

"I am sorry, Captain," Pinar said. "I will pray that the gods restore you."

They found a small path through the brush, allowing them to quicken their pace toward the harbor. The terrain soon pushed up into a small peak, making travel more strenuous. Halfway up the path, Pinar stopped, panting, and pulled on Rocco's arm for attention.

"Apologies, Captain, but I must rest briefly."

"Yes, of course." He looked to the top of the bluff. The harbor lay on the other side, after a narrow, winding trail down. The sun had just passed its most torturous point in the sky and was heading toward that boundary between late afternoon and early evening. "I realize you must be tired and sore. The harbor is on the other side, and I would like to gather wood and build a fire before the sun sets. Would it be permissible if I carried you the last few steps?"

She nodded. "Thank you. My legs could use the rest, and I, too, am anxious to make camp before the sun disappears."

Rocco secured their bag of food over his shoulder and leaned down to pick her up. Pinar put her hands lightly around his neck. He was aware, in their closeness, how stiff she held her body.

"If you are concerned that a pirate might take liberties in such intimate circumstances," he said, "please do not be. I wish only to get to the harbor and deliver you to Captain Derya."

She quickly reached down and pulled his dagger from its sheath with a smile. "A pirate is prepared to defend herself in any situation."

He chuckled. "Understood."

The climb to the top of the cliff was strenuous, and Rocco was glad that Pinar was so petite. It was not much harder than carrying a full knapsack. At the crest, he could see the inlet of calm water, protected by cliffs on two sides, and a small beach below. The trail snaked its way down to the sand, worn by travelers who did not relish the idea of a steep ascent, or a rolling descent. Soon they were on the shoreline with plenty of late afternoon sun.

Rocco gently placed Pinar against a large boulder, which she leaned against for a few moments while holding her ribs and breathing slowly.

"Are you in much pain?" he asked.

"I have felt worse," she said between long breaths. "But I shall be glad to be in Oleta's care."

While she rested, he gathered dried sticks, leaves, and driftwood from the area and knelt in the sand. It took him mere moments to dig a small pit, line it with the sticks and leaves, then stack the driftwood to catch and keep a flame. There were boulders piled behind the fire, and he pulled out the cape Tumas had brought to attempt a shelter. He took the rest of the dried leaves to spread under the cape for bedding, saving a few for himself.

As he worked, Pinar made her way to the camp, walking slowly but standing straight, as if to defy her bruises. Rocco gestured to the boulders and the cape.

"That is about as much shelter as you will have tonight. We will pray that Begum keeps her appointment tomorrow."

"It is passable, Captain, thank you. I have no complaints."

He reached into the bag and brought out the food, plus the implements to make more of the tea that she desired. They were again silent, Rocco tending to the evening meal and Pinar leaning against a smooth boulder, eyes closed. He decided not to wake her when the tea was ready, but she opened her eyes and sat up.

"This will soothe me," she said, reaching for the cup.

Rocco divided out half of the food, storing the other half for the next day. "We don't know when *Dişi Aslan* will anchor."

Pinar accepted a roll with her tea. "I would estimate they will be here when the sun is cresting the ridge behind us. I know their route well, even if I am not currently sailing with them."

"Are you the only *Dişi* crew here on the island?" Rocco pulled a wing apart and stripped the meat with his teeth.

"No. Our captain has many of us stationed on all the islands to learn of political intrigues, and to exploit opportunities…empty a few larders here, lift a few coins there." She sipped her tea. "The only island we are not permitted to be on is Île des Anciens."

"Ah, yes," Rocco studied the potato cooking in the fire. "It's small, and uninhabitable."

"Something lives there. It is important that Lisette return."

"Who is this—" It surprised him that he could not push the name from his lips. "This woman you speak of?"

"Lisette de Lille." She paused, looking confused. "She is a…a noblewoman. I was her personal servant, until I was assaulted. I hope the priest can get her the message, although I am doubtful that she can join us here before the ship arrives."

Rocco nodded. "Hope is always a good thing to have."

They finished their meal with no more conversation. He was consumed with pondering, attempting to force his mind to fill in the holes.

"You seem to wrestle with a problem, Captain," Pinar said. "If there is anything you wish to say aloud, I promise to keep your confidence. One of the reasons I am kept on islands, spying on nobility, is that I do not give up secrets."

"I appreciate your camaraderie, Pinar. I have a task on this island to perform, and memories to unlock. It is impossible for me complete my task until the moon has moved past the last quarter. My struggle is whether to ask Captain Derya to return me to *L'Implacable* or remain here for the entire time."

"Understood." Pinar leaned against the boulder. "I do not know how many memories you have lost. What do you remember of Begum Derya?"

"I met her when the *Dişi Aslan* came to our aid—we were attempting to take a large galleon, the largest we had ever attacked. It was the only time I underestimated the Spaniards. They fought viciously. I believed we would find the usual plunder aboard—a few coins, powder, perhaps a jewel or two. It held a much larger prize—one hold was filled with jewelry and gold, a tribute to the king from the Spanish nobility in all the islands."

"Yes, I remember. We fought hard that day."

"Begum jumped to our defense, doubled the amount of cannon we aimed, and we brought the ship to its knees." Rocco stopped.

"Is that all?"

"No." His brow furrowed. "I was in need of, well, a

special kind of aid. Begum introduced me to someone who could help me."

Pinar smiled. "I recall Captain Derya having to seek—aid from someone special. If your need for the moon's shadow is what I suspect, I believe you'd be better staying on this island. It would help to study your goal, in order to best complete your task."

"Yes, that is also what I think." He tipped the flask, taking care to save a few swallows of rum for tomorrow. "Pinar, I suspect you are both an excellent servant and an excellent pirate."

She lowered her eyes. "Thank you, Captain."

The day had passed into night long ago, and now the quarter-moon climbed up from the horizon.

Rocco patted down the leaves he'd gathered for Pinar's bedding. "Use this night's sleep to rest. Tomorrow you should be in good hands."

Pinar eased herself into the space and closed her eyes, as Rocco stood and walked toward the shore. He stopped at the edge of the waves that were gently rolling up the sand and folding back into the sea. *L'Implacable* would be here tomorrow, and he would be reunited with his crew. Would he sail with them?

Lisette tried to nap, but her nerves were like dry twigs on the fire, waiting to spark. It was almost sunset when the door opened, and Mercedes entered. She held herself tall, and Lisette could almost feel the heat of her pain. Lisette found her heart softening, and a small piercing of guilt for having scarred the young woman so horribly. The feelings dissipated as soon as Mercedes spoke.

"I can't decide which will be better," she said. "To see you run through on the beast's talons or set on fire."

Lisette shrugged, expressionless save for one arched eyebrow.

Mercedes leaned toward the bars and lifted a corner of her veil, whispering, "Would you like to know what it feels like to be burned alive?"

From the little bit of scarred face that she saw, Lisette knew how much pain Mercedes had endured. She had been but twenty when it happened, twenty and beautiful. There was no way to undo the damage.

"I take no joy in your disfigurement," Lisette said. "But I am not sorry that I tried to kill you. You murdered my family. It was my duty to avenge their deaths."

"I did what needed to be done!" Mercedes' gravelly voice strained to shout. "My king demanded this island for Spain. I am loyal to El Rey."

Lisette narrowed her eyes. "You are loyal to Mercedes."

Mercedes shook with rage. "Guards! Take her!"

Two large men stomped into the room and waited as Mercedes unlocked Lisette's cell. They reached for Lisette's arms, but she backed a step, out of their way.

"You do not have to drag me. I'm capable of walking myself to the chains." Folding her hands in front of her, she walked between them out of the cell and over to the bottom of the stairs, where she turned and looked back. "Are you coming?"

At the top of the stairs, one guard opened the door and allowed her to pass before ordering her to stop.

"Wait here," he said and turned to his partner. "I'll lead, Bruno. You follow."

"You always lead," Bruno told him. "What makes you such a leader?"

Lisette stood waiting as the two continued to bicker about their positions. She was peering around, eager to spot a chance to sneak away, when she heard a commanding voice.

"Maybe we should feed the two of you to the dragon." Captain Simone, who had accompanied Mercedes earlier walked up and slapped both guards' heads. "I'll lead. Diego, you stay behind her with Bruno." He gave Lisette a quick glance. "This one should not give you any trouble."

"Beware, Alwan." Mercedes stood in the shadows at

the door. "She is capable of more trouble than you imagine."

Lisette bowed her head and stepped forward with a docile countenance, mentally putting Alwan Simone on her list of people she could kill without guilt. Alwan Simone…wasn't housekeeper Amoy also named Simone?

I shall keep watch over those two. It might be a coincidence, but they do resemble one another.

She believed they would chain her in the garden where she would have to maneuver her way through the trees and flowers to the gate. When she saw what they had done instead, she nearly wept with joy.

A large fig tree stood outside the castle on the corner where the wall widened to allow a sentry to stand. One long thick branch reached over the wall before heading skyward. They had placed a heavy chain over the limb, with an iron cuff at either end. Two ladders were set up against the wall.

The guards led her to the ladders and stopped. Alwan pointed up. "Well? Get up there and chain her to the tree."

"Do we have to climb up and chain her?" Diego asked. "I don't like climbing on things."

"The wall's quite wide," Bruno told him. "I'll go first and help her up. All you need is to climb up, pop her hands in the cuffs, and down you go again."

"Aww, all right, but I'm not liking it."

"Would you like to be chained up there instead?" Alwan asked.

"No, Captain." Bruno pushed his partner forward. "We know what to do."

Diego gestured for Lisette to climb. She put her hand up.

"If I could but tuck in my skirt, gentlemen, I should be able to climb the ladder without tripping."

"Tripping…" Diego said. "I didn't even think about

tripping."

Lisette pulled the back of her skirt between her legs and tucked it into what was left of her waist, stretching the fabric taut across her belly. Diego stepped back and pointed.

"You're with child!"

"Yes," Lisette said. "I'm not certain what it says about your mistress, that she is going to feed a poor mother to a dragon."

Diego turned to his partner. "We can't do this."

"We have our orders," Bruno said. "And if we don't obey, she'll have our heads."

"And I shall swing the axe," Alwan told them.

Lisette grabbed the ladder and put a foot on the first rung before looking at Bruno. "Up we go, yes? I'll race you to the top."

Even having to round her back to keep her stomach from hitting each rung, she managed to scurry up the ladder almost as fast as when she crewed. Bruno was still three steps behind her when she reached the top and leapt from the ladder to the wall.

"My, this wall is wide," she said as she looked around. To her horror, she realized the wall was higher on this side by at least five pied. Below, she saw two pointy ears, which could only belong to a horse. On the ground was the hem of a tattered priest's robe.

The sun was fading, and Lisette had to be quick. Moving further along the wall, she called out to the guards. "It will be dark soon. We better get on with this."

Atop the wall, Bruno picked his way slowly toward her as Diego reached the top of the ladder, trembling.

"Don't shake so," Lisette told him. "You're going to make the ladder fall and take you along."

Bruno glanced over at his partner. "Look, just climb back down. I can cuff her."

Diego looked down at Alwan, who was glaring at him. "No, I'll come up."

Lisette held out her arms, taking care to push her sleeves out of the way, and slipping the key into her palm. The guard took one cuff, placed it around her wrist, and shook his head.

"This isn't right," Bruno said quietly.

"No," Lisette said. "It is not. But do not abandon hope. I do not."

He clicked the lock and put the other cuff on her. The chain was loose and allowed her arms plenty of movement. They obviously did not think she could go anywhere.

"I hope you escape," he whispered as he patted her head, "but it doesn't look good."

She watched him climb down the ladder and turn to see her. He and his partner made the sign of the cross before leaving. Alwan slapped their heads again.

As soon as they were out of sight, Lisette stretched her right hand across to her left sleeve. Under a pretense of stretching her arms, she deftly unlocked her left cuff. Leaving it loose around her wrist, she repeated the action on her right cuff. Now freed, she surveyed all the balconies. Mercedes would want a front row seat to this spectacle.

She spotted her emerging from a chamber in the corner, a balcony closest to the tree. Lisette kept the cuffs on her wrists, pretending that she was still bound. Night crept in.

The bushes rustled and Lisette glanced down on the other side of the wall. She could see the priest leading the horse right underneath where she stood. It was a good fifteen-pied drop—could she jump? What about the baby?

It's that or be dragged back to the dungeon, or worse—maybe Mercedes will beat me to death in a rage when the dragon does not appear tonight.

Mercedes leaned over the balcony toward her, turned, and went inside, screaming something about night falling. It would soon be too dark to see clearly and watch the carnage. Mercedes would need torches to light the way for the dragon who was not coming.

"Merciful God in Heaven," Lisette prayed, "Lamya and the Ancient Ones who tend this land, if anyone hears me, I need your aid."

She took a breath, slipped from the cuffs, and wrapped her hands around her belly for protection. As she jumped, she experienced the familiar heat in limbs and back, and landed softly on four padded feet.

Lisette landed softly as a cat falling from a fence, tucking her wings close to her body to keep them from getting caught on branches. She looked around and saw the horse the priest had led galloping across the hill, its tail high and waving.

Tumas was on the ground to her right, on his back, eyes wide and mouth gaping like a fish. She bowed her head to him. He sat up, still tense, and whispered, "Go with God—I think?"

Lisette nodded, wishing she could smile. She walked a few paces away from the castle wall, extended her wings, and rose into the night sky, exhaling an impenetrable barrier of cloud and mist to keep Mercedes' forces from finding her.

As she flew, she heard blustery shouts and general chaos. She hoped Tumas was not in trouble for trying to help her. He could possibly invent a reason for being out there, but did priests lie to save their own skins?

She remembered Father Felix on Isla del Lagarto. She had exchanged a few chickens for his aid in giving Tatie Elena a proper burial, chickens he would have to hide from the Count de Medina. He was willing to lie by omission. Of course, the chickens would help his own flock of followers, and the count did not live long enough to discover his deception.

Still, she hoped Tumas invented a brilliant and believable excuse to be there.

The night air was sultry, and she was glad to be immune to its sticky heat. Her wings caught a draft of warm current heading northwestward, where she remembered the pirate's cove being. The bay's use was known to her father, but he did not attempt to pursue or capture the brigands who used it. His philosophy had been to do what was needed to keep the island safe. Pirates could be useful if you did not harass them.

She wondered if her kidnapping had changed his mind. A tear for the dead ran down her feathered cheek, surprising her. She didn't think dragons could cry.

As she neared the cliffs that protected the small beach, Lisette slowed her flight. She landed quietly on the ridge and peered down at the inlet. To one side, there were boulders that had tumbled from the cliffs and been smoothed by years of water. A light glowed from within a group of three large white rocks.

Fire.

Lisette spread her wings to fly down. Rocco had to be there. She had missed him so much. Her mind was full of all the things she wanted to tell him, to ask him. She glanced down at her feathered chest. There would be no conversations while she was in this form.

She folded her wings and sat. *How am I supposed to turn back into a human? I don't even know how I turned into a dragon.* She recalled asking all the deities for help—perhaps one of them heard her prayer. Not knowing how to transform was quite inconvenient.

If she didn't turn human by the time the *Dişi Aslan* arrived, she couldn't travel on the ship, or ask Captain Derya to drop her off at Île des Anciens. She could attempt to fly over the sea back to Lamya now, but what if she changed halfway to her destination?

"Argh," she huffed, forgetting her dragon form. The sound was more like an osprey's screech. Her enhanced senses detected movement from the direction of the fire. Lisette ducked behind a circle of brush, twisting around to peek past one leafy corner.

A head popped up from the near side of the boulder, followed by the rest of a man. He was tall, broad-shouldered, with dark curls and a goatee. Rocco.

Even in her dragon form, Lisette could feel Alara bouncing in her womb. She, too, wanted to fly down immediately and embrace the pirate she adored. *I'd like to see him, too, Alara, but he wouldn't know it's me in this form.*

She sighed, placing a soft paw on her stomach, and found a spot in the brush that had been trampled to softness, probably by deer. Curling up, she closed her eyes. There was nothing else to do until the ship came. Hopefully, she'd be back to her human self by then.

If I could remember the words, maybe saying them backwards would reverse the spell. Human. I am human. I am a woman. Woman, woman, woman.

She drifted to sleep, the word *woman* on repeat in her mind.

She woke to sunrise and the sound of voices she recognized. Pinar and Rocco stood at the shore, looking outward. A ship was pulling in, one with the flag of a lioness. Captain Derya and the crew were coming into harbor. Lisette looked down.

Feathers. Still feathers.

She watched the ship anchor and launch a dinghy. Soon the boat arrived at the shore and she heard excited greetings being exchanged. Captain Derya was commanding, as usual, ordering Pinar to be escorted to the *Dişi Aslan*. Someone else got out of the boat and stood before the captain, receiving orders. She looked familiar, but Lisette was uncertain.

From what she could hear, this must be Pinar's replacement on the island. As the girl moved and spoke, Lisette recognized her—Marisha, the girl from Isla de la Ballena, who helped her when she was stuck in Madame Marchand's brothel.

A distant noise behind her grew louder, catching her attention. She backed into the bushes, peering inland. The jungle undergrowth was being pushed aside and hacked down by more than one person.

A man's voice, unknown to her, spoke in low tones as if explaining to someone. "We can definitely see some creature carries her. See how the large footprints are now the only ones, and they are deeper?"

The flash of white uniforms in the brush beyond told her that Mercedes' guards had followed her. Moving further into the hidden grove, she strove to remain unseen. The ship would be far out of reach by the time these guards arrived, and there could not be many of them.

Lisette could hear both the guards advancing toward her and the ship sailing away. She could still detect voices on the beach, but the heavy rattle of chain told her the ship was pulling up anchor. After several minutes, the rustle and whack of bushes being trampled came close enough for her to see the group.

She only recognized one face among them. They were dragging Tumas along. He tripped and fell as they prodded him forward, no doubt looking for an avenue of escape. His gaze stopped at the underbrush where Lisette hid. She closed one eye in a wink, and his eyebrows lifted in surprise before giving her a small nod.

The soldiers reached the ridgeline and stopped to catch their collective breaths. Lisette counted. Six young men of varying sizes and fitness stood ready to fight someone, anyone.

"Good thing we interrogated that de Lille guard last year before we killed him," one of the guards said. "We'd never've found this place."

Lisette's blood rose in anger, but there was not much she could do. Her new dragon form was for nurturing and defense. Apart from her run-in with the red dragon, she had not tested her battle skills.

She watched the crew disappear over the crest, listening to them trying to find the path, and stumbling down the thorny groundcover. Moving out again, she peered over the ridge.

Her heart sank at the scene. The ship was already far away, but on the beach stood Rocco and Marisha, swords in their hands, looking up at the guards coming down.

The guards picked up their pace, leaving Tumas and running down the zigzag trail, taking leaping shortcuts when they could. Rocco ran forward to start the melee early. The six men quickly surrounded him, ignoring Marisha. Her sword pierced the smallest man's back, causing him to scream in agony as he fell. Two of the remaining five turned to dispatch her.

Lisette gave no thought to whether her claws were long enough or teeth sharp enough. She extended her wings and launched herself over the cliff.

Marisha lay on her back, sword upright as her two attackers brought their swords down upon her. In a flash, their blades clanged on something white and broke in shards. Lisette's wing covered Marisha, feathers puffed against the onslaught of metal.

Fear drained the soldiers' faces of all color. They ran

backward, stumbling, falling, rising again just to repeat the process. One of them opened his mouth to scream but gurgled instead as if drowning. They headed back to the cliff, ignoring the path, and heading straight up, clawing at the spiny underbrush.

Lisette turned to find Rocco. He had run two of his attackers through and was on to the last man standing, who had just seen Lisette. The guard stood for a moment, sword out, before rushing toward her. Lisette raised her front paw and caught his blade, snapping it in half.

Her front paw stung and she pulled it back to see a scrape across her pad and drops of blood appearing. In a burst of pain and anger, she reached with another paw and swept the guard off his feet, throwing him against the rocks, where he crashed, silent and still.

Marisha stayed on the sand looking up. "I have seen too many dragons in my short life. But thank you for saving us, whoever you are."

"Lisette?" Tumas approached her, wearing an expression of disbelief as before. "Is it so?"

She tucked her wings and bowed her head.

"How is this possible?" he said.

Rocco looked at her, his eyes narrowing. "You! You're the one who—"

Lisette cocked her dragon head. So, it was him that night, trying to knock her out of the sky. His curse was over. How did he return to being a blood dragon?

"Priest, did you say her name was Lisette?" Rocco asked.

Marisha got to her feet. "Lisette, my friend? Last time, you were black. You tryin' out all the colors?"

"Tell me about this Lisette." Rocco touched Marisha's shoulder. "I feel like I should know her."

Lisette shook her head, her eyes wide. How is it that Rocco did not remember her? It had been barely three months. She wished desperately to pop back into her human form. One more time, she raised her head to the heavens and begged for help.

The gods weren't listening, or they had some reason to keep her a dragon. Or perhaps they were all capricious and enjoying a laugh at her expense.

She was aware of the trio looking at her—not merely looking but studying. It was forgivable. Dragons were a rare sight. She sat, curling her tail around her, and regarded her paw. The cut was not deep, and the bleeding had already stopped. *Feathers may protect me but my paws are vulnerable.*

She sighed, which came out as a puff of white mist, startling Tumas and Marisha and making Rocco laugh. Reuniting with Rocco was all she wanted.

I have to change back sooner or later. I'll just stay here until I do.

A vigorous kick from Alara reminded her that what she wanted was not what she needed—at least not at the moment. She was going to have a baby and for that she needed Lamya's help. Reuniting with Rocco would have to wait a little longer.

Flying to the island could be dangerous if she accidentally turned human. Of course, if she could catch up to the *Dişi Aslan* and follow them, she'd be close enough to be picked up if she lost her wings.

The *Dişi Aslan* was nearly out of sight by this time. Lisette walked to Rocco and stood, staring into his blue eyes. Stretching her neck toward him, she touched his chest gently with her nose. To his credit, he did not turn and run.

Unfolding her wings, she ascended, banking toward the sea and the ship she would follow. The flag of the *Dişi Aslan* was already at the horizon, but it was a small jaunt for a dragon. Lisette rose on the warm current and pushed her wings down and back, propelling herself forward. She would be near the ship in a few moments.

As she flew, Lisette allowed herself a glance back at Île des Oiseaux. She had rounded the island and could no longer see the pirates' cove. The village and port were visible along with her home, standing to the west of the other two castles, north of the d'Auguste home and south of Mercedes. She allowed herself to dream of her return—tending Alara, spending her days and nights with Rocco, finally being able to relax in their love and enjoy their lives…

The familiar burning crept through her bones. She was at a fairly high altitude and still too far from the ship to hail it. The only fortunate thing was that the water would cushion her fall. She folded her wings and descended as quickly as possible. In mid-fall, she felt the flash and the sting of the water as she hit.

Trying not to panic, she kicked and swept her arms in frantic motions, while trying to rid herself of the robe that weighed heavy and cumbersome in the water. She looked around. The port was far away, but it was the only place she could go.

Once her fear subsided and her robe was thoroughly soaked, she discovered it had buoyancy, enough to keep her head above water. After comforting her unborn baby with a caress, she kicked her legs and stretched out more skillfully with her arms.

She reached the tidal range well before mid-morning, where she was able to relax and use the tide to pull her in. Aiming for the pier, she managed to wash up underneath the wooden support pillars. She crawled away from the waves, up the beach, where she could dry, thankful that no one was around.

When she was younger, she often came to the pier with Father to see the ships come in. He held her hand as they walked to the end and met the captain. Father would talk business and weather—asking about the trip, and if they had brought the spices he ordered, or the fabric, or the wine. Resting in the sand, she placed one of her hands in the other, trying to imagine his strong, weighty fingers folded around her own.

Papa, I'm having your granddaughter.

Would he approve of Rocco? He wouldn't mind that he was an honest sailor before all this happened.

Mama would no doubt be suspicious of her pirate. He was not nobility, even prior to his life of crime on the high seas.

It was all a noble's fault, Papa. You can't blame him. And Mama, we will be married and happy. Trust me.

Would they be married? Lisette assumed when Rocco proclaimed his love there would be a proposal behind it, especially with a child on the way. He would not want Alara to be nameless. Would he?

More importantly, was marriage what she wanted?

Watching the dragon disappear out to sea, Rocco glanced over to find his two companions doing the same. When at last the trio turned away, they stood as if lost.

"Can someone direct me to the castle where the Duke de Martinmas resides?" asked Marisha. "I am to work for the household."

"Certainly," Tumas said, and gestured toward the path. "It is a bit of a walk."

Marisha turned to Rocco. "Where are you bound, pirate?"

Rocco shrugged. "I have a task to perform, but I cannot begin for a fortnight. In the meantime, if I may walk with you, I intend to get acquainted with this island."

The trio made their way to the top of the ridge and down again to the south. At a large clearing, three wide and distinct roads lay before them.

"The one to the right is where the castle de Lille—I mean, the castle de Martinmas—is found," Tumas said.

"Where do the others go?" Rocco asked.

Tumas pointed. "The center road leads to the village and its port."

Marisha prodded. "And to the left?"

"The castles of d'Auguste and de Medina." The priest frowned. "I am employed by the young countess, Mercedes de Medina—or I was. She delighted in finding things for me to do at which I failed and then beating me when I was unsuccessful at them."

"Like picking ripe sea grapes when you are colorblind?" Rocco asked.

He nodded. "And now she is convinced I am in league with her sworn enemy Lisette de Lille and wants me to lead her to Lisette and then kill me for being so helpful. Even a priest values his life more than that."

"Are you in league with Lisette?" Marisha asked.

Tumas shrugged. "I am a priest. I help all who require my assistance. In that way, I suppose I am in league with everyone."

"It is not a bad thing to be in league with Lisette," Marisha told him. "She is a fine woman, strong and smart."

"Not to mention being a dragon," Rocco said. "Shall we take the path to the right?"

They walked toward the duke's castle slowly, as if none wanted to reach the destination. Rocco took notice of his surroundings, not only potential hiding places, but food and water sources.

"Marisha," he said, "What did you mean when you said Lisette was black before?"

"A very few months ago, I was a servant at Madame Adelinde Marchand's brothel on Isla de la Ballena. That is where I met Lisette." She told them of the night the young man died, describing the chaotic scenes of the black dragon hunting down and killing Madame before disappearing into the moonless sky.

"Still gives me chills to think of it." She rubbed her arms.

"The young man who died?" Tumas asked. "Was he a tall, lanky lad with dark curls and green eyes?"

"Yes, Father. He'd come in on some ship, down on his luck. The owner of the store in town gave him work and a place to sleep."

Tumas crossed himself. "No doubt that was Julian, Lisette's younger brother. We knew the duke and duchess died, but no one knew what happened to the boy. Dead, too, eh? That's a pity."

Soon the castle loomed in front of them. Built of stone and wood in the European style, it was massive with balconies and turrets and everything undesirable for the Caribbean yet necessary for French and Spaniard nobility to feel at home. The roofs of smaller outbuildings peeked above the stone wall that stood guard around the whole affair.

"Well," Rocco said, "I suppose we part here. Priest, where are you bound?"

"To the port. I have a bit of coin, so I hope to find a ship that will get me off this island. That is, if Mercedes does not find me first."

Rocco patted his shoulder. "Good luck, and God be with you."

"I have an idea," Marisha said. "Rocco, you could take a job here with the duke's guard. That would put coin in your pocket, clothes on your back, and allow you to settle into the island while you await your task."

"The duke and I have met," Rocco told her. "Although I don't know that he would recognize me. He was fairly terrified."

Marisha nodded. "You'd at least have to change your name."

"How about his guards?" Tumas asked. "You've waylaid a fair number of Spanish ships."

Rocco smiled. "Yes, but no one has lived to tell of our encounters."

Tumas nodded. "Only God can judge."

Marisha regarded Tumas. "You know, Father, perhaps you could also find a place in the duke's household, at least until there is a ship and you have enough coin to be on it. We have just met but you deserve better than to be a pawn in Mercedes de Medina's game."

"I would be pleased to stay, as long as I am out of Mercedes' employ. My life has been pledged to give spiritual aid to those in need."

"I must report to the housekeeper, she is headmistress of the servants," Marisha said. "Stay close. I will make the proper inquiries—at the very least, I shall return with food."

"That is worth waiting for," Rocco told her.

Marisha walked around the wall, toward the center gate and its guards. Rocco watched her disappear before turning to Tumas.

"Shall we take our rest, Priest? Whether food or employment, it will not come quickly."

Tumas snuggled into a leafy bed and closed his eyes. As the priest snored, Rocco reached into his pocket and pulled out the feather he'd discovered on the beach. Pale blue with dark edging, its shaft was solid as a steel blade, and its tip as sharp. It had obviously come from the dragon but was unlike his own. Soft, gentle, yet strong and impenetrable. Not even his dragon talons could pierce this.

He remembered fighting another dragon, in another time. They scraped and stabbed and burned one another, battling for dominance. That dragon was black. The memory was almost in his hand, but every time he closed his fist, it slipped away. In Marisha's story, Lisette de Lille became a black dragon. Why couldn't he remember her?

Rocco put the feather back in his pocket and leaned on a boulder. Lamya said the answers would come.

25

Lisette heard voices above her on the pier. She looked out to see a ship rounding the bluff and heading into port. The large vessel sat low, meaning it was laden with goods to deliver. That meant staff from the castles coming to gather their purchases. Sitting up, she pulled her robe around her legs and listened with more focus.

I hope I recognize someone. I can't run around like this, not even after dark.

Turning her left hand over, she examined her palm. An angry red stripe ran across the middle, and a small shiver of fear rippled through her. *If I need to defend anyone again, I shall have to take care not to play catch with sharp objects.*

She rubbed her belly, feeling Alara stretch out and then curl into another position. The duke had promised to secure her passage to Île des Anciens before she was unceremoniously kidnapped. With no money, no decent clothes, and no hope to transform into a dragon, she'd have to return to the castle and make him keep his word.

Rocco was still on this island. She longed to be reunited with him and cursed being a dragon during their last meeting. *Why couldn't I change back when it was so important? And why didn't he recognize my name?*

"M'lady?" A female voice interrupted her thoughts.

Lisette turned with a gasp. Ghreta crawled under the pilings and plopped next to her.

"What are you doing down here?" Lisette wrapped her robe tighter. "Could you see me?"

"No, not from the pier," Ghreta said. "Not where most folk are. I like to come down to the sea on the days I meet the ships and sit here for a bit, feel the sand in my toes." She looked out at the sparkling blue and nodded. "I confess, I long to be back on our ship."

"I understand," Lisette said, gazing out to sea. "I, too, miss the creak of the wood and the roll of the waves."

"I got another thing to confess—when I saw you in the mistress' dungeon, I recognized you at once."

Lisette turned and studied the woman's face, blushing. "My apologies, Ghreta. There were so many faces on the *Dişi Aslan*, and I had so little time to meet everyone."

Ghreta smiled. "Well, ya stood up to Mar, so you were okay by me. Then when we heard how you found the gold and give it to us—why, you coulda been a rich woman."

"Don't think I sacrificed too much. I still held enough back to get vengeance on the people who killed my family…at least, I thought I did."

"Mercedes?"

"Yes—I believed I had killed her."

"Will you try again?"

Lisette looked at the ground. "No. Living with her scars and disfigurement is a worse fate than dying. I even feel pity for her."

"Not too much, I hope." Ghreta huffed. "She mistreats everyone at the castle with her screaming, her impossible demands. She's flogged more servants than I can count because they put too much salt or too little fat or left dust on the table."

"Well, she was not a pleasant person before the incident. But pain begets pain, I suppose." The murmur of voices above distracted her. "I am curious as to Pierre's fate."

"Who?"

"Pierre, the guard in the cell next to mine. The yappy, two-faced man-child who betrayed me for money."

"Ah, he was set loose again, to return to the duke."

"What?"

Ghreta shrugged. "With Maria dead and you missing, the mistress still needs her spies."

"What does the mistress think happened to me?"

"It is barely to be believed," Ghreta said, chuckling. "When two of the five guards finally returned from trying to find you, they told of a trio of ruthless pirates and a blue dragon what helped them. Mistress screamed with such rage the entire castle rang. She was certain you sent your dragon to aid the pirates."

"So, she believes I have a dragon at my beckoning," Lisette said, shaking her head. "Or I suppose two, since she also thinks I keep the red dragon as a pet."

"Which I know couldn't be true," Ghreta told her. "It's not the right cycle of the moon."

"How do you know about dragons and moon phases?"

"By being on the *Dişi Aslan*, of course." Ghreta looked up at the pier, while heavy footsteps marched above them. "I need to get back to the cart. No doubt the flour and sugar are loaded. Where will you go now, and how can I help you?"

Lisette sighed. "Would you have the means to fetch me a few more clothes? I have only my nightclothes and I need to get back to the duke's castle. He promised to secure my passage to a safe place for me to have my baby."

"Easily done, m'lady." Ghreta leaped to her feet and disappeared.

Lisette waited, listening to conversations above her. Some goods were paid for in advance, but the ships were fond of carrying a few more items to entice their clientele. She could hear the haggling, the offers, voices raised and lowered, until "Sold" was pronounced. Her father used to bargain this way for something that caught his attention.

Alara rolled around again, distracting her from her melancholy.

"Yes, my baby," Lisette whispered. "We will walk these roads together and I shall tell you stories of my mama and papa, and my dear silly brother Jules."

Moments later Ghreta reappeared with a bundle in her arms. "A few clothes to get you amongst decent folks, and a little coin for a meal at the inn. Sorry, I wasn't able to get food."

"I am grateful for whatever help you can give. I hope someday to be able to sail with you again. And if you require aid while you serve Mercedes, my sword is at your service."

"You have more pressing needs at the moment." Ghreta pointed to Lisette's round belly. "But I appreciate the offer."

Lisette watched her spring up and away, until all she could see were the woman's leather boots scurrying under her simple frock and petticoat. She scooted into a more hidden grouping of timbers, ones that had no gaps to let in light or prying eyes, where she could put on the clothes Ghreta had procured.

A camisole, a slip, blouse, and skirt, along with a pair of servants' booties—leather anklets with laces. Lisette made quick work of unfastening her robe and slipping into the garments. The long skirt would not tie around her middle, but if she fastened high, under her breasts, it gave room to the baby and was short enough to match her stature. Putting her robe back on, she crept from under the pier, staying out of sight for as long as possible, until she could blend in with the crowd.

A tall, broad galleon stood at the end of the pier. Most islands required a ship to anchor away from the dock and carry goods by dinghy, but this island's port had been chosen for the depth of water close to shore. Sailors needed only to lower the crates down the gangplank.

Lisette noticed the flag, Spanish, and turned toward the pier, planning to inquire about passage. But passage to where? This was not a ship to dock at Île des Anciens, and she could not imagine it passing close enough to send a rowboat.

Her stomach rumbled, followed by a firm kick. *Yes, Alara, eat first and think of a plan to get to Lamya later.*

She strolled to the inn, head high and shoulders relaxed, attempting to look as if she belonged there. The people who passed her by did not pay her much attention—she gave them each an acknowledging nod with an open expression, and no one's gaze lingered.

The inn was as she remembered it from years ago, whitewashed adobe with large windows. She stepped inside and looked around. Six tables and a bar with stools.

"Help you m'lady?" The innkeeper approached. He was a large, dark-skinned man, soft-spoken and agreeable, but with an imposing presence. He smiled, showing one gold front tooth among the whiteness.

"Have you bread and cheese?" Lisette returned his

smile. "And perhaps a little cider?"

"Ah, a woman of simple tastes." He gestured to a table. "Make yourself comfortable and I shall return."

The table was against a wall. Lisette pushed it out slightly, so she could slide the chair around and face the interior. She grinned at the habits she had acquired, such as not sitting with her back to the door. The innkeeper nodded as he placed a plate before her.

"I included a few slices of salted fish," he said, almost apologetically. "In case m'lady needs a little more for her meal. Caution can take its toll on the stomach."

She met his gaze and saw two impenetrable black orbs, set within yellow-tinged whites. They seemed to be sending her a message of safety. She held out several coins. "Thank you."

He took one and waved the rest away. "Ghreta's friends are never charged strangers' prices." Leaning in, he dropped his voice to a low rumble. "I do not require your name, but I am Horace if you need anything."

Lisette took a breath and relaxed, realizing how tense her body had been. Horace returned to the bar, where he wiped down mugs and gazed at the crowd outside. A group of men entered and sat at a large table near the windows, calling him over immediately for rum and whatever the kitchen was serving.

They appeared to be port workers from their dress, but they made her uneasy. The two that faced her spent too much time glancing in her direction then looking away. She ate her meal, marking the distance to the door if she needed a quick exit. Reaching down to her thigh, she regretted losing the dagger that had been strapped to her leg. She fingered the coins in her pocket and wondered if she had enough to procure a new blade.

The jingle of silver made one of the men turn his head. His eyes scanned the room, settling on her where they lingered much too long. Lisette glared at him until he turned back. He leaned into the group and Lisette heard low rumblings of conversation. She put both hands around the jug of cider and poured herself another mug, concentrating on not spilling while her peripheral vision kept track of the room.

"M'lady." Horace was before her, his back to the men. He was frowning, rolling his eyes to the left toward the group even as he kept his voice light. "Is everything satisfactory? You look as if you are in discomfort."

Heeding his meaning, Lisette rose, holding her stomach. "I am feeling unwell…perhaps I can make it home. I'm staying at the castle of the Duke de Martinmas."

"Ah, the old de Lille castle." Horace helped her to her feet. "I have a cot in the back where you can lie down. I will send for a carriage."

She remained bent and shuffled forward, allowing the innkeeper to escort her behind the bar. As he parted a curtain for her to enter the back room, he looked over his shoulder and told the men, "I will return shortly, good gentlemen, as soon as I get this woman settled and send my boy for help."

Behind the curtain was a combination of kitchen and living space. It was obvious there was no cot. There was also no boy to send for help.

"Can you drive a cart?" he whispered.

Lisette nodded and straightened. Horace led her to the back door of the inn and out to an alley. A fat gray pony stood tied to the rail, harnessed to a light buckboard.

Horace's mouth was at her ear. "Be quick now and do not worry. I shall reclaim my property at the castle when it is safe."

"Thank you." Lisette untied the horse and pulled herself into the driver's seat with Horace's help. Reaching beside her, she released the wheel brake. She slipped the reins between her fingers, and bounced them on the gray's back, encouraging him forward with a cluck of her tongue.

The pony stepped into the weight of his harness, and they proceeded down the alley to a narrow backstreet that would lead them to the main road and ultimately the castle. As they got to the end of the alley, Lisette saw a shadow in a doorway to her right. Her pulse quickened. She slowed the pony's pace and steered him away from the shadow, hoping to make a quick, smooth left turn that would avoid any interaction.

They were almost to the corner, Lisette shifting her body to balance the wheels, when the shadow jumped at her. It was one of the men from the inn. He leapt into the seat and grabbed her by the shoulders.

His voice was high and nasally. "I'll have that silver in your pockets, putain!"

Lisette pushed back, screaming for help. The man clamped one hand on her mouth and reached down her body with the other, searching for the coins. She grabbed his throat with both hands and squeezed. He paused his search to try to pull her hands away.

"Get off my cart," she yelled. "Thief!"

That's when she felt a blow to her stomach. She wrapped her hands around her body and tried to catch her breath. The man grinned and resumed his probing. She raised her head and glared at him, the heat of a protective rage building in her.

The rage exploded and she saw one blue-feathered paw wrap around the man's throat, while the other snapped his head until it faced backwards. She tossed the body to the side of the street before noticing that the pony had spooked and was galloping toward the wide boulevard, the cart bounding and jumping behind him.

As quickly as she had become a dragon, the warmth returned, and she saw her own hands again. She reached down for the reins and pulled back gently but firmly as she murmured, "Here, here, whoa, little horse," slowing the gray to a trot, a walk, and finally to a stop. She hopped from the cart and went to the pony's head where she stroked his neck and whispered to him.

"Good boy, it's okay." She looked up and down the main road. They had long since left the scene of the attack and no one was nearby. A horse and rider were approaching from the opposite direction but were still distant. "Let us go to the castle, little gray horse. You shall have extra grain tonight."

She pulled herself back up onto the seat and picked up the reins again. While they rolled on, Lisette replayed the attack over and over, trying to understand how she turned into a dragon and back again in mere moments. That it had to do with protecting Alara was obvious, but was this out of her control or did she say or think something that made it happen?

The man had wanted her silver—it wasn't even hers—why didn't she give it to him? *Because he tried to take it by force, and I might need it for my baby.* This answer came as if from a stranger, one who lived in some hidden place inside her. It was the moon dragon's answer.

Lamya wasn't teaching her to transform. She was introducing her to something that had taken up residence in her. She was teaching her to open the door and let the moon dragon out.

This realization was so exciting Lisette wanted to try

it immediately. One glance at the pony trotting down the road convinced her not to attempt anything yet.

Poor little horse has already been frightened out of his wits once today.

They came to the fork that pointed three directions to three castles. Lisette lifted her reins and signaled the pony left. She could see the turrets peeking above the soft rise of hill. The pony kept trotting although the uphill slowed him a little. Lisette clucked at him to keep his legs moving. Soon they were at the top and the castle was in view.

Lisette sat back and kept herself from urging the tired pony to go faster. Inside, she was excitedly planning a solitary evening on her balcony, communicating with her inner dragon.

First, a reunion with the duke, and a discussion about Mercedes de Medina. He would no doubt want retribution. Lisette admitted she was fond of the large man although not fond enough to go along with all of his schemes.

They were almost to the front gates when Lisette saw them open, and the guard change his watch. To her dismay Pierre stepped out to take his place. She halted the pony and sat, staring at him. Pierre looked at her, squinting for a moment before a look of recognition crossed his face.

Now what? He will no doubt try to keep me from entering the castle, and he will definitely run to Mercedes with the news that I am alive and have returned. I suppose I could kill him, but that will anger the other guard, so I'll have to kill him, too. What a mess.

As she sat weighing her options, she heard wheels on gravel behind her. Lisette turned to see a fancy cabriolet pulled by a shiny chestnut horse flying up to pass her. As the rig got next to hers, it stopped, and a familiar face popped out of the window.

Lisette grinned. "Connie, I am so glad to see you!"

Rocco heard soft footsteps and looked up to see Marisha strolling toward them, carrying a basket. Rocco stood, stretched, and kicked the priest's foot, startling him out of slumber.

Marisha handed the basket to him. "I am supposed to be cleaning the master's bedchambers, but they gave me enough time to retrieve both of you. You are to come with me immediately. Captain Rocco will be given a uniform and training as a castle guard. The captain of the guard asked your name. I hope you don't mind being Julian Santiago."

Rocco grinned. "I've been called worse."

Tumas stood and rifled through the basket, pulling out a hard roll and some slices of dried meat. "And what of my fate?"

"You have a most special place in the castle."

Marisha gave him a mocking curtsy. "The duke has requested that you perform religious ceremonies."

"Sounds like softer work than I get," Rocco said. "Wonder what sins the duke has to confess?"

"I know not and care even less." She gestured toward the castle. "We must enter at the back gate. You will get no meal until evening, so I brought you this bit of food. Eat as we walk."

Tumas again reached into the basket, but Rocco was quicker and grabbed the last roll.

"Let me have a bite, too, priest."

"My apologies, Sire, I believed you had already taken your share." Tumas patted his substantial yet grumbling stomach. "I can certainly wait until the evening sup."

The trio walked northwest around the wall to the back of the castle. The sun was still high and trained its heat upon them. Rocco rolled up the sleeves on his muslin shirt and wiped his brow, wishing for a little ale to wash down his meal.

Once at the wooden gate, Marisha knocked. A short, stocky guard answered, and she introduced herself and her assignment.

"Captain Delgado, may I present—" She gestured to Rocco and Tumas.

Rocco stepped forward. "Julian Santiago. I am here to provide my service to the duke."

The guard studied him and nodded. "You look fitter than most. We'll see how skilled you are." Looking at the priest, he asked, "And what are you here to provide?"

"The services of comfort, wisdom, and spiritual aid," Tumas told him.

The guard frowned so Marisha added, "He was requested by the duke to perform rites and ceremonies."

"All right, priest," the guard said, standing aside to let the trio in. "But I'll warn you, the duke is not the sort of man who needs comfort or spiritual aid, and he'll spit you out into the streets if you try to offer him wisdom."

Tumas bowed. "I am also a man who knows when silence is the best course."

Marisha led Tumas to the main house while the guard stared at Rocco and gestured toward a set of barracks next to the stables in the northeast corner.

"My name is Luis Delgado," the guard said. "I served on *El Gallo Blanco*."

Rocco's eyes met his. His memory, though spotty, recalled the ship—the one time he had left most of the crew alive—why did he do that? Someone softened his resolve. At the moment, it didn't matter. There was no way Luis did not recognize him.

He smiled. "So, we've met."

"Let us speak frankly," Luis said. "I know you are Tristan de Rocco, a pirate feared and hunted throughout these islands. I count it the luckiest day of my life that you spared us when you burned our ship."

"What do you intend to do with me?"

Luis shrugged. "Nothing. This is a job to me like any other. Although I did not enjoy having to jump ship and row a dinghy until my arms fell limp at my sides, the captain of *El Gallo Blanco* was an enormous ass with no sailing mettle. I might have been happy to see him fall. And the duke was gracious enough to offer me this post as part of his gratitude. According to him, it was partially his fault for giving his traveling companion passage."

"His traveling companion?"

"A young woman—I do not recall her name. She was a pleasant traveler, fond of talking with the crew about the ship as if she had crewed herself." Luis stepped up to the door of a low, white L-shaped building made of stone and adobe. "These will be your quarters."

Rocco stepped inside. Small windows let in enough light to see, but not much more. The large room held ten bunks, a long table with mismatched chairs, and a cabinet filled with broadswords, rapiers, and daggers. The bunks varied in their degrees of neatness, some being tidy enough to eat from and some appearing to still have a body in them. The room had the familiar smell of maleness, tobacco, and rum.

"Where do I bunk?" Rocco asked.

Luis pointed to a bed in the far corner. "We lost a man last week. That was his."

Rocco nodded. He liked being in the corner, where he could keep an eye on everyone else. "That'll do fine."

"You'll need a uniform and arms," Luis said. "Go to the stables and look for Quince. He'll assign you a uniform and a horse. When you're dressed, report to me at the guardhouse in front of the castle. I'll give you your orders." He turned and walked toward the door, waving over his shoulder as he left. "Pick your weaponry from the cabinet."

Rocco looked over the selection of blades. Most of them were rejects, rapiers with ornate hilts and etched blades, beautiful and useless. Dull edges could be sharpened, but many of these were ill-weighted. He wondered what swordsmith slapped these together and called them weapons. On the middle row, a sword hung to one side, plain and dull to look at.

Rocco picked it up. As he suspected, it was light in his hand and quick to move. He tested the blade and found it honed and ready. Searching the bottom of the cabinet, he found a dagger that matched his new rapier, both in precision and sharpness. Scabbards for both were procured, belted, and he marched off to receive his uniform.

Quince, a slender old man with a bad leg, limped around finding breeches and a jacket that fit Rocco as precisely as he could. Each time Rocco protested that this uniform "fit well enough" Quince scowled and told him that "well enough was unsatisfactory." At last, he was happy enough to let Rocco keep his clothes on, and they moved to horses.

"The last guard rode this fine beast." Quince patted the nose of a big chestnut mare, who snaked her neck out at him, teeth bared, and ears flattened. "She managed to unseat him at least once every outing and bit him every time she saw him. I wish you better luck with her."

Rocco walked over to the horse, large enough to carry a man twice his size. He stood and looked into her eyes. She stretched her neck out to sniff him. Her nostrils grew round, and she perked her ears forward, snorting once. Rocco stood quiet and held the back of his hand out to her. She pressed her muzzle to his knuckles, licked them, and dropped her head.

"We shall get along, I think," he said.

He arrived at the gatehouse to the sounds of an argument. Luis stood at the opened front gate, hands on his hips, giving orders to a tall lanky guard who appeared to be refusing.

"She is in league with the dragon," the guard was yelling. "She calls to him by name. If we let her back in, she will betray us all."

Rocco could see through the open gate a decorated carriage and high-bred horse accompanied by a simple buckboard pulled by a shaggy gray pony. A handsome young man leaned out the window of the carriage, his brows knit in frustration.

"What is the holdup?" the young man asked. "Do you know who I am?"

"Yes, m'lord." Luis held his hand up in supplication before turning to the guard. "Pierre, I shall say this once more. The marquess is the duke's son and will be given entrance and as he has requested the young lady behind him to also be allowed to enter, we shall obey."

"But captain, I am to protect the duke," Pierre protested.

"Captain," Rocco interrupted, "may I be of assistance?"

Luis glanced at him, looked down at the weapons he'd selected, and smiled. "I see you found suitable blades. Yes, open the gates for our company. If you are given any resistance, you have my permission to run the offender through."

Pierre's face boiled crimson as Rocco stepped past him to open the gates, trapping the guard against the stone wall in order to allow the carts to pass. The buckboard was driven by a young woman with wild auburn curls and green eyes that burned with hatred at Pierre.

Rocco turned to Pierre to see his reaction. The young guard's face had paled, and Rocco could see the cold sweat of his fear. He looked back at the young woman who was now staring at him, lips parted, her face a mix of recognition and confusion.

She took a breath as if to speak to him, before turning to address Luis. "Captain, may I have a word?"

The captain approached the buckboard and looked up at her as she leaned to whisper something in his ear. Whatever she told Luis, he did not acknowledge it physically except for one small twitch of his mustache. While they whispered, Pierre puffed his chest out, his eyes narrowed.

At last Captain Delgado stepped aside for the cart to enter and turned to the guards. "Guardsman Santiago, please escort Guardsman Tournier to the barracks. I will be along to speak to him."

Rocco withdrew his rapier, saluted his captain, and addressed Pierre, gesturing with the point of his blade. "Shall we?"

Pierre scowled. "What's to keep me from drawing my own weapon in disagreement?"

"It is of course your choice," Rocco said. "It does not matter to me whether I take you to the barracks dead or alive, unless the captain has a preference."

"I will leave it up to you." Luis turned to Pierre. "I've

seen this man fight, Tournier. You would not stand a chance."

The young guardsman blanched a purer white than before, put his head down, and walked toward the barracks. Rocco followed at a safe distance, sword at the ready.

As they strode, Rocco struggled to keep his mind focused on the task. The way the young woman stared both worried and excited him. There was an aching in his memory as if he was supposed to know who she was and why she was significant.

"That woman seemed to hate you, Pierre," he said.

"The feeling is mutual. We were both kidnapped by Mercedes de Medina. That woman bribed and coerced her way to freedom, even employing a red dragon to kill the servants. She left me to die in the dungeons."

Rocco's mind whirled but he kept his expression blank. "How did you escape?"

"I whittled a rock in my cell until it had a sharp edge. When the old hag came to deliver my meal, I held her and threatened to slit her throat if she didn't unlock the door."

"Ah." Rocco nodded. "So, the servant had the dungeon key with her?"

He saw a blush sprout up the back of Pierre's neck. "Yes, all the keys were on one ring."

When they arrived at the barracks, Rocco gestured for him to open the door. "Get comfortable. I'm certain Captain Delgado will be along soon."

The two men entered the room. Pierre unbuckled his scabbard and tossed it on one of the beds, so Rocco returned his own rapier to its scabbard and turned to leave. From the corner of his eye, he saw Pierre pull out his dagger and spin to thrust the blade at Rocco's side.

Rocco brought his left forearm down on Pierre's wrist, loosening his grip and knocking the dagger to the floor. His right fist found the young guard's face, smashing his jaw and snapping his head around. The pirate had just enough time to pick up the dagger before Pierre's wobbling legs finally gave way.

The door opened and Luis entered. He looked at the scene before him and raised his eyebrows at Rocco. Rocco shrugged.

"I warned him," Luis said.

"He isn't dead, just unconscious." Rocco handed Pierre's dagger to his captain. "The fire isn't hot until you touch it."

The lump of guardsman moaned and stirred. Luis pointed to Pierre. "He'll probably need rum. Think he deserves any?"

Rocco walked to the table in the corner and held out a jug. "I suppose he can have whatever we don't drink."

Luis joined him at the table where they poured two mugs and sat, watching Pierre crawl to a sitting position, holding his jaw. Eventually, the young guard looked around the room. When he stopped at the two men, they raised their mugs.

"Come join us," Luis said. "I'd like to hear the story of how you've been working for the lady of the castle on the hill. How much has Mercedes de Medina paid you to betray the duke?"

Pierre's eyes widened. He stumbled to his feet and ran to throw open the barracks door. The sight of two guards with swords drawn encouraged him to stay. He slammed the door shut and turned to face the captain and Rocco.

"Lies! That woman lies! I told you, she is the one who is a friend of the Medina woman. She is the one who had me kidnapped—why, I was on my way here to warn the duke! Lies, lies, it's not me, it is all lies!" He sank to his knees, covering his face in both hands.

"Youth." Luis lifted his mug in a mock-toast and took a drink. "So overwrought."

"You have to admit, his lies were energetic," Rocco said. "What to do with him now?"

"Well, of course, I could hang him," Luis said. This brought a wave of weeping protest until the captain held his hand up. "Stop your blubbering, knave. The master has the final say on your fate. He is not by nature a ruthless man, but he will not take kindly to the facts. You did kidnap Lisette de Lille, and you are still working for Mercedes."

Pierre glared at him. "You have no proof."

"Haven't I? Wouldn't the duke take the word of Lisette herself, plus a priest?" Luis grinned. "Who doubts the word of a man of God?"

Pierre's body sagged as he sat back on his heels, defeated. It was like watching a wineskin empty. Rocco tossed the rest of his rum back and set the empty mug on the table.

"As much as I have enjoyed this, Captain Delgado, I wish to be given some duty. I am unaccustomed to being idle."

Luis nodded and strode to the door. Opening it, he turned to Pierre. "Guards, you will escort Pierre Tournier to the dungeon and lock him there. Guardsman Santiago, you will accompany them, so you know where the dungeon is. Then report to the front gate to relieve Guardsman Bellefleur."

"Aye." Rocco rose and stood aside for the two guards, who lifted Pierre by his arms and dragged him out of the barracks and into the light.

Lisette pulled the cart behind Connie's cabriolet and got out. She explained to the servant that Horace the innkeeper would call for his rig and gave the gray a pat on the neck before she walked up the steps. She turned at the door.

"Oh, and give the pony extra grain," she told the man. "He deserves special treatment."

How different it was to walk into the grand hall from the front gate—different and yet familiar. She steeled her heart against breaking when she looked up at the portraits of her family that still hung by the entrance.

And Rocco was here. Lisette had nearly leapt from the buckboard at the sight of him. The only thing holding her back was his cold stare through her. He had not remembered her name back on the beach, but did he really not recognize her face?

The captain of the guard had called Rocco

"Guardsman Santiago." He had obviously not wanted to use his real name—clearly the duke did not recognize him. She hoped that she would not accidentally reveal his identity.

Sighing, she wiped a tear away. She rubbed her stomach and told herself it was approaching motherhood that kept her on the constant verge of weeping and had nothing to do with Rocco's indifference.

Lisette looked around the hall for the duke's son Connie, but he had vanished. Turning left, she walked through the corridor that led to her room at the top of the turret. She was halfway up the stairs when she heard a smooth baritone voice.

"There you are!" Connie stood at the bottom of the stairs, gazing up. "And ye gods, you are blossoming with motherhood. Come down here and let us go to the kitchen. You look like you need sustenance, and perhaps a shoulder to cry upon."

"I have missed you." Lisette smiled. He was still as handsome as the first time they met. "Yes, let us have a chat, somewhere that I can put my feet up and feel at home."

They wandered through the halls to the kitchen. The staff were preparing the evening meal, making the space quite aromatic. Lisette breathed in deeply.

"It's so surprising that when I was first expecting, I could not endure the smell of spices or meat cooking. Now it comforts me."

"How much longer until the blessed event?" Connie asked, holding a chair out.

"A couple of months." She cradled her stomach. "It is happening so quickly, and I confess I am frightened. Childbirth is a dangerous thing, even in normal conditions."

The maid set a teapot and two cups on the table next to them and Lisette was keenly aware of her presence, as if the young woman might be interested in their conversation. It made her aware of how many ears were listening to what she and others might discuss.

Lisette put her hand out to stop Connie from pouring. "Perhaps we should take our tea somewhere else. I wouldn't want to bother the servants."

Nodding, he stood and helped her to her feet. "A tray, please, and some cakes," he told the woman who'd brought the teapot. "We will take our tea in the library."

Shutting the door behind them, Connie set the tray on a small table beside two large chairs and checked the contents of the pot before pouring.

"Thank you," Lisette said. "I've become sensitive to prying ears."

"I shouldn't wonder." He sat down with his own cup. "I'm curious, Lizzie. What conditions will this baby be born into?"

"The last time I saw you, I believe you were made aware of my circumstances."

"Yes, quite unusual." His eyes widened in knowledge.

"I was unable at the time to thank you for your assistance." She sipped her tea. "It was life-saving."

He bowed his head. "You are most welcome."

"It seems I was in this condition during that episode." She shook her head. "I am supposed to be on Île des Anciens, getting proper instruction from a mamha. Instead, I accidentally ended up here, discovered by your father who still has dreams of being a grandfather. To make matters worse, I was kidnapped by Mercedes, but I escaped and have crawled back to the duke in the hopes that he will take pity on me and send me to my mamha for a proper birthing."

"Oh my." Connie drank his tea.

"There is a part of me that is happy to be in this place. But it's all been so…soiled. Darkened by death, and what

I've become." Lisette's voice broke and a she let a sob escape.

Connie put down his cup and rushed to cradle her in his arms, offering her a silk square. "Dear, dear, we can't have you so heartbroken. You are right, it is a horror what happened to your family, and do not think it is lost on me or my father that the Medina family was behind it all. We may be sharing this island for Spain, but we are willing to take any opportunity to rid Île des Oiseaux of their taint.

"But do not degrade yourself. What have you become? A strong, resourceful woman, a soon-to-be mother. I have seen you prevail, and I will continue to applaud you. And if I desired women, you are the one I would seek out."

Sniffling, she leaned back into her chair, dabbing at her eyes with Connie's kerchief. "My apologies. I seem to cry at everything these days."

"Nonsense. If you cannot cry at missing your family, what is left to cry over?" He patted her shoulder. "Feeling better?"

"Much." She nodded.

He returned to his own chair and sat. "Would the tears start again if I asked where the baby's father is in all this?"

Lisette frowned. "That is my biggest frustration. If you recall our last meeting, there was someone else in the great hall having an unfortunate event."

Connie squinted at her before understanding crossed his face. "Ah, yes. He wore red."

"Yes. He is on this island, but he acts as though we've never met. How is it that he does not remember me?"

"I confess, I cannot say. Have you asked him?"

She shook her head. "I have not had the opportunity."

"Then take the opportunity." He stood up and offered his hand. "After you have rested. You should have a nap, and perhaps a soak in the tub before supper this evening.

Dear Father will want to know everything, and you know how he is."

Lisette accepted his aid and rose from her comfortable seat. They moved to the door and Connie opened it briskly, causing a young servant girl to stumble into both of them. Connie grabbed her arm and set her upright before he took her face in the other hand.

"Spying at doors, my girl?"

The girl's eyes revealed her terror. "No, m'lord, no! I was checking if the room was occupied—yes! I was tasked with cleaning the library and wanted to know if anyone was in there."

"You could knock." Lisette's voice was flat yet menacing.

"Who are you spying for?" Connie's hand squeezed the girl's face tighter.

"No one!"

Lisette tapped Connie's arm until he relinquished the maid, then took the girl's face in her hand, and glared at her. The old burn of her blood dragon days returned, when her eyes would glow crescent moons in anger. "Who?"

"Amoy," the girl squeaked like a mouse.

"Why don't you go up to your chambers and rest?" Connie asked. He tightened his grip on the servant's arm. "I'll attend to this matter."

She nodded and released the girl's face. Heading upstairs, she glanced over her shoulder to see Connie leading the servant out of the room, his mouth close to her ear. Whatever he was telling her, the girl looked as if she was being led to the gallows.

Once in her room, Lisette reclined onto her bed and watched the day's light through the window. The afternoon sun was forging long shadows. She replayed the events of the day, her on-and-off transformation, and her plan to try changing here on her balcony.

Waiting for nightfall was unnecessary. She raised her

arm, to lift herself from the bed. Then she remembered the duke. He expected to dine with her and for the first time, she wanted to tell him everything that happened.

What if she couldn't change back? He wouldn't talk to a dragon, and she couldn't talk to him.

She relaxed back against the pillow and closed her eyes. Nap now. Dinner next, then find Rocco and get answers. Working on transforming could wait.

The sun had almost disappeared when knocking awoke her. She turned her head to see the door open, and smiled when Marisha entered, carrying a pail of steaming water.

"I have come to prepare your bath, m'lady."

Lisette rose from her bed and rushed toward her. "Marisha, I am so glad to see you. Tell me all that has happened to you since that night."

The young woman rolled her eyes as she poured water into the tub. "I don't know I have that much time."

Shuffling steps in the hall made them both look toward the door. Two more servants entered, both stout dark-haired island women, each resting a yoke on their shoulders that supported a bucket at either end. They went to the tub and proceeded to add each bucket's water to the one supplied by Marisha.

Lisette frowned. "Why are these women carrying water like oxen in the fields? This was never the way my bath water was prepared."

"It is well, m'lady." Marisha's tone was that of a subservient. "The women do not mind."

"I'm certain they do mind, breaking their backs for my comfort." Lisette addressed the women. "This is enough water, thank you. You are dismissed."

The women looked at her in confusion. Marisha spoke to them in an island tongue Lisette did not understand. The women answered, so Marisha interpreted.

"They say the duke has given orders for two more

trips."

Lisette stretched into her no-nonsense nobility pose. "Tell them I decide how I like my bath, and that I shall discuss it with the duke if he disagrees."

Marisha explained and sent the women away. Their faces wore expressions of relief.

"They are happy to not carry more buckets," Marisha said as she helped Lisette undress. "But they are frightened of the duke. He is large and likes to roar when he is displeased."

"He is quite substantial and blustery." Lisette slipped into the warm water, enjoying the scent of roses. "However, he should be more agreeable to my suggestions. He hasn't quite given up on claiming this child as his heir."

"Which it is not, I assume?"

Lisette shook her head. "Let us say his son Constantine and I are incompatible. But tell me, have you been asea since I saw you last?"

"Yes." Marisha loosened Lisette's braids and massaged the soap through her hair. "We managed to take a fine haul just south of Isla de Pimienta after loading the gold you found for us. Being so flush with treasure, the *Dişi* was able to stop at the islands and give the crew some much needed shore leave. We saw family, and some sent money and goods back to their homes."

Lisette closed her eyes and listened to Marisha's news, relaxing and sponging herself.

"...about a month ago, we met up with *L'Implacable*." Marisha had just poured water over Lisette's head to rinse her hair.

"What?" Lisette sat up, sputtering from the dousing.

"My apologies, Lizzie, I didn't mean to drown you."

"No, I am fine. What did you say about *L'Implacable*?"

Marisha leaned forward as if relaying a secret. "Captain Derya received a message that the captain of *L'Implacable* was in need of help. We met them on the northernmost point of this island. Our captain set out early with supplies and Ruhee and came back alone. I was curious, so I watched. Soon a dinghy carrying three men launched from the other ship—an older man, a young one, and the third barely visible. Rumor was their captain was injured and Ruhee was to heal him."

"Then what happened?"

"Their dinghy left the beach without the third man." Marisha gathered a sheet and wrapped it around Lisette as she stood. "But it gets more interesting."

Lisette wanted to reach down Marisha's throat and drag the words out. "Tell me, please."

"A fortnight later, we returned to the island to pick up Ruhee. *L'Implacable* was also there, I assume to pick up their captain. When Captain Derya returned with Ruhee, it did not look like things went well. Captain was angry, Ruhee was sobbing." She held Lisette's slip to help her dress. "I do not know what was supposed to happen, but Ruhee kept blubbering, 'I didn't know,' and the captain kept snapping, 'This is why children do not play with magic.'"

"Magic? I thought Ruhee was a healer."

Marisha shrugged. "When I was a child, I saw the women of my village use plants in magical ways. Who is to say what Ruhee concocted? All I know is that two men rowed to the beach from *L'Implacable*, and two men rowed back."

Lisette let Marisha dress her, mindless of the activity. It sounded as if Ruhee had tried something she shouldn't, but what?

"At any rate," Marisha said as she directed Lisette to her dressing table. "Captain Rocco is here now, although he pretends to be a common soldier named Julian

Santiago. He appears in good health, so whatever Ruhee did, it is not something that is easy to detect."

"No." Lisette watched in the mirror as Marisha combed and styled her hair. "Magic is not easy to see sometimes."

"Speaking of magic," Marisha said, giving Lisette a knowing look. "What is it that you are doing now?"

"It is a long story. I hope I wasn't as frightening as when you saw me at Madame's."

Marisha shook her head. "The fight alone had my blood up. I did not have time to be startled. I do thank you for the assistance, and no, you were not frightening. You reminded me of a mother hen protecting her chicks."

Lisette chuckled before growing serious. "That seems to be correct. I am no longer a blood dragon seeking revenge. I am a moon dragon seeking to protect, especially this baby. And I worry about what kind of baby is conceived in a vessel of vengeance and born into one of peace."

Marisha put the last pin in Lisette's bun and laid both hands softly on her shoulders. "No matter what happens, your child will inherit your goodness."

Lisette stood and faced her. "I hope so. And I am glad to have such friends."

Marisha turned her attention to emptying and cleaning the tub, while Lisette left the chambers and strolled down the stairs to dinner. She wondered what to tell the duke and what to leave out. Certainly, the topic of Rocco should be left alone.

The duke's offer was tempting, to accept her child as his heir and allow her to reclaim her family home. She and Alara would be safe in this castle from everything except Mercedes.

Something had to be done about that woman.

30

The duke was already there when she arrived in the great hall, standing by his seat at the head of the table. The candlelight threw shadows across the tapestries and paintings on the walls, giving the faces in them a look of judgment.

"My apologies if I kept you waiting, Sire," Lisette told him.

"Nonsense, my dear." He smiled and motioned to the chair on his left. "I do not expect haste from a woman in your condition, and we are still waiting on my son. But sit and rest yourself. I will have the servants bring the food."

Within moments, Lisette was sitting before an array of bread and cheeses, and a large terrine of stew. She took a roll and nibbled at it, trying to maintain her manners. *If I was on the ship, I'd be tearing through this meal like a starving dog.*

"Girl!" The duke clapped his hands until a servant appeared. "Where is the rum? M'lady requires fortification."

"Stop screeching at the servants." Lisette scowled. "I mean, I'm certain the girl was on her way to fetch the drink. She can carry but one thing at a time."

The duke appeared shocked and slightly offended by her scolding. "My apologies. I was unaware of my *screeching*."

"You are unaware because it is your natural form of speech around servants." Connie strode through the hall and slid into the chair across from Lisette. "Good even, Father. Good even, Lizzie."

The duke frowned. "I am the master of this castle. I am accustomed to giving orders and being heard."

"Everyone in the village can hear you," Connie said, and held out his hand to Lisette. "Hand me your plate and I shall ladle some of this fine stew for you."

The girl reappeared with a pitcher and three goblets, which she filled and set at each place. Connie glared at his father until the duke told the girl, "Thank you." She returned a nervous smile with a curtsy before vanishing back into the kitchen.

"Wasn't that better?" Connie asked.

"You shall have them laughing at my weakness." The duke turned to Lisette. "But I am beyond happy to have you back. When you disappeared from the castle, no one could tell me what happened. I sent guards out looking for you, but they reported nothing."

"Too bad you couldn't send Pierre Tournier," Lisette told him. "You remember, the guard you assigned to keep me in this castle? Or perhaps Maria, my new lady's maid?"

"I could not find either of them. I will take them to task for failing their assignments."

"Fail is an interesting word, Sire." Lisette took a sip

of rum before continuing. "Guardsman Tournier actually did not fail. Neither did Maria. They simply weren't working for you."

In between bites, she told the men of being kidnapped and escaping from Mercedes' plan to have her killed by the red dragon.

"The red dragon? Is it here?" The duke's knuckles whitened as he gripped his goblet, his eyes wide.

"Yes," Lisette said, "but that is a trifle. He will not appear until the beginning of the new moon's cycle. The problem—"

The duke interrupted her. "When does the cycle start? We must be prepared!"

"Not for another two weeks." Lisette's voice rose. "The problem is that not only did Pierre and Maria work for Mercedes de Medina, Pierre works for her still and has returned to this castle, although why he would still trust her, I do not understand. I would not be surprised if there were not more servants and guards spying on you for Mercedes' coin."

"Such as that lovely young servant we encountered this afternoon," Connie said.

"Ah, yes." Lisette nodded. "How did you resolve that?"

"Young servant girl is on a ship." Connie took a sip of rum. "And Amoy is being watched."

"What about Maria?" the duke asked.

Lisette shook her head. "I fear the red dragon took care of her. She should not have been screaming so loud and for such a long time."

"We need a plan against this dragon—" the duke began.

"Father." Connie's voice was sharp. "Lisette is correct. Spies in your castle are your first and worst worry. Lizzie, is the dragon hunting someone specific?"

"The good news is, I believe he is hunting the last of the Medinas. I'm not certain, but when I was in Mercedes' gaol, it seemed obvious he was hunting her."

"How do you know the origin of his curse?" the duke asked.

Lisette was silent for a moment. Revealing too much might point him toward Rocco. "At the wedding, the red dragon was specifically hunting the Count de Medina. His other victims were unfortunate people in his way."

The duke nodded. "And he would not seek out anyone who had simply attended the wedding and witnessed what happened?"

"No." Lisette smiled and put her hand on the duke's arm. "That is not how the curse works."

He blushed. "Perhaps, dear girl, we would feel less threatened if we knew more of your past."

She looked at Connie, who shrugged.

"Very well," she sighed. "Sire, you recall our conversation about Eric d'Auguste and Mercedes, what they did to me and to my family."

He nodded. "Wicked people, all."

Taking care to choose her words, she told them of the curse of the blood dragon, that it lasted from waning to waxing crescent, and only from sunset to sunrise. She also explained the dragon's feathers and their impenetrability.

"So, nothing can pierce them?" Connie asked.

She looked down at the red line on her palm. "Only another dragon's teeth or talon."

The duke sat quietly, drinking his rum. After a long silence, he said, "When I first saw you here, you said that this magic had left its mark. I should like to know what you meant."

Lisette swirled the amber liquid in her goblet. There were already people here who knew what she was. Pinar knew, but she was safely aboard the *Dişi Aslan*. Tumas the priest had seen her change—where had he disappeared to? As a rule, priests were required to keep the secrets of their parishioners. Lisette hoped that was true of her new friend.

She regarded the two men at the table. Connie seemed worthy of a secret, but could the duke keep one? He might betray her out of complete accident. There were people who would consider her magic a blasphemy, punishable by death. And unfortunately, she could not protect herself by transforming—yet.

"I have my reasons for not answering at this moment," she said at last, "however, I assure you that when I am able to discuss it, I shall tell you, both of you, freely."

The duke sat back, studying her. "I see. Would it make it easier if I arranged passage to wherever this special midwife is?"

"Yes." She smiled. "I'd rather stay here in my castle with its comforts and its familiarity. However, I know my baby will require special handling, due to my magic. This midwife knows how to help me."

The duke nodded. "Very well."

"And let me assure you," she added, "I will return with my daughter as soon as I possibly can. Perhaps the same arrangements that you make to get me to the island can retrieve me?"

"That would be marvelous." The duke's features brightened. "My offer still stands, you can return here to live as my daughter-in-law and raise your daughter as Connie's."

"Wait, I did not agree to this," Connie said.

"You do not need to," the duke told him. "A marriage of convenience to satisfy the curious. What the two of you do separately is your own concerns."

"Marriage?" Lisette said. "As in, an actual ceremony? You said we could tell people I was your daughter-in-law. You said nothing about me officially becoming so."

"A mere formality." The duke brushed at the air. "How else do you expect me to document the legitimacy of your child's right to this castle and my estate?"

"Some other way." She shook her head. "Any other way."

The duke smiled. "Do not worry, Lisette. The de Lille castle will ultimately be yours again."

Connie slammed his goblet on the table, creating a sprinkling of rum to fall on the duke. "Father, you know there are other ways to ensure the safety and comfort of Lizzie and the baby."

"Perhaps I do not want the castle," Lisette murmured.

31

Two astonished faces turned toward her. "What?"

Lisette looked up, surprised. "I may not want to live here. Despite its comforts, each time I walk the halls I am reminded of my family, who is no longer here."

The duke patted her arm. "My dear, your sadness will give way to pleasant memories, given time. Why, when the duchess died, I was inconsolable for days until the king sent me to Isla de Pimienta with a full household. That cheered me tremendously."

Lisette frowned and looked over at Connie, who looked unhappy as well.

"I suppose some people are able to push their grief aside," Connie said. "I was only four when she died, and I missed her for much longer. Now that I am grown, I grieve the fact that I barely remember her."

"Exactly! You barely remember her." The duke sat back with a smile as if proving his point.

Lisette took a deep breath. *I am weary with this conversation.* "If you will excuse me, gentlemen, I have had an arduous adventure. I feel the need to retire."

"Yes, of course." The duke rose and assisted her from her chair. "You need to be well rested for the wedding planning."

Connie and Lisette voiced their objections at the same time, their words tripping over each other.

"My child has a father," Lisette snapped. "If I am to marry anyone, it will be him."

"You cannot force us into wedlock to serve your fantasy," Connie said.

The duke maintained a steady smile. "I'm certain the father of your child can be easily dealt with, Lisette. And you, my boy, know what I am capable of—I *require* an heir to my title."

It was obvious to her that the duke was willing to push Rocco out of the way by whatever means necessary. Banishment, prison, or death were all on the table once he knew who the father was. Which was all moot when Rocco didn't even remember he was a father.

Lisette gave the duke a small, sharp curtsy, whipped around on her heel and strode from the hall. She knew he would not flinch at her unhappiness, but she would not pretend that he would prevail without a fight.

Back in her chambers, she fussed with the buttons on her gown, wanting to rip them off if it meant getting out of her clothes. Marisha entered with a tray of tea and cakes, setting them on the small table and moving to attend to Lisette.

"Calm yourself and allow me to help," she said, loosening the gown and holding it for Lisette to step out of. "Now, what has you so riled?"

Lisette repeated the duke's plan. "I should not be

surprised by his audacity and boldness, and yet I am struck by his stubbornness. After escaping from Mercedes, I returned here thinking it was my haven. I was mistaken."

"Is the duke going to let you go have your baby on Île des Anciens?"

"I don't know." Lisette shook her head. "He had been agreeable to it, but this evening may have changed his mind. I'm afraid I was too argumentative. And to be honest, although I know it's for the best to have the child where the magic can be contained, I have a strong desire to stay."

"Because this castle is so comforting to you?"

"No." Lisette shook her head. "At this point, if I could I'd give it to you, to the people of the village. It is not about the property."

Marisha seemed to read her dilemma. "Because you wish to stay close to someone here?"

Lisette looked into Marisha's eyes and ran her fingers over her tattooed wrist. She remembered her days on the ships, fairly smelling the salty water and feeling the spray on her cheeks. She hadn't been a noblewoman then. She had been a pirate and Marisha was her sister.

"Yes. Tristan de Rocco is the father of my child, though he does not remember that fact, or me. I dare not let the duke know, as he is prepared to do anything to push the father out of the way. You see my dilemma?"

Marisha held out her nightgown. "Get yourself comfortable and have some tea. I shall help you in any way that I can."

Lisette was quiet as she pulled the gown over her head and wrapped her special robe about her shoulders. She sat at the small table and poured a cup of tea, holding it up toward Marisha. "Come sit with me. I need a friend and you are my sea sister."

Marisha joined her in the sitting area, and Lisette prepared a cup for herself. "Tell me about your life,

Marisha. What led you to join the *Dişi*?"

"Sometimes I barely remember." The young woman took a cake from the plate at Lisette's insistence. "I was a very young girl, living with my family on Isla de la Ballena. We lived on a hill near Bec de Baleine, the Whale Spout, with goats and a small garden where we grew what we could not find wild. There were Frenchmen living on the shore, sending and receiving ships, but they left us alone, and we rarely went to the village for anything."

"That didn't last, though, did it?"

Marisha shook her head. "I heard my parents talking about it. The Spanish had come. They were fighting the French for this island. I don't know why, except that if one country has something, another country wants to take it away. One day, out gathering wild yams for dinner, I hear many voices. Soldiers sweep across the island like a blanket of insects, killing and stealing.

"I drop my basket and run toward home, but I am stopped by a woman dressed like a warrior. She is a tall island woman, and her features are so fierce, I cry. She reaches down and says, 'Be strong, Child. There is an enemy at work, and they have taken your home. Come with me and you will survive.'" Marisha stopped to take a sip of tea. "That was our old captain, Dayana Cruz, who fought courageously. She took me to the *Dişi Aslan*, where I was adopted into the life."

"Do you ever regret it?"

"No. I miss my family, some days worse than others. But I am proud to belong to no nation, to be a pirate. Nations are messy things, too full of their own pride."

Lisette nodded. "Yes. I, too, miss my family, but my happiest days since have been sailing under a flag of undeclared country."

"What do you intend to do now?"

"I barely know where to start." Lisette put her hand to her forehead. "I need to speak with Rocco, find out whether he is unable or unwilling to remember me. I need to have this baby—well, she will come whether I need it or not. I need to keep the duke from manipulating Connie and me until we wake up married one morning. Oh, and it would be helpful if I knew how to transform into a moon dragon—and back again."

"I thought it was like…the other kind, dependent upon the moon or the earth or something out of your control."

"I wish it was. The spell seems to work when the baby needs protection, but I cannot conjure it on demand, nor can I release it when the danger has ended." Lisette recalled her encounter with the robber. "Sometimes I flash into the beast's body, defend myself, and become human so quickly I am left dizzy. Other times, I remain a dragon until the most inconvenient moment."

"Which is why you did not transform on the beach, after coming to our aid," Marisha said.

"I didn't know how!" Lisette sank her head into her hands. "Sometimes it feels like too much."

"You have more sea sisters here than you realize. We will all do our part to help you. Perhaps we can talk the priest into slowing down the wedding plans." Marisha rose. "And now I have duties to attend to. Please get some rest. The answers will come."

Lisette watched Marisha leave and bolted the door. On her way to the balcony, she glanced at the ceramic dragon on the mantle. It hadn't done a thing for her last time but maybe she wasn't trying hard enough. She grabbed the figurine and headed outside.

Rocco accompanied the two guardsmen as they escorted their prisoner to the dungeon, a low-roofed stone building away from the castle. The prisoner protested the entire way, proclaiming innocence of all wrongdoing, to the point of declaring himself pious as any priest.

"I've known my share of priests, Tournier," Rocco said. "Their virtue often depends upon landing a soft spot within a noble's house."

"You know nothing," Pierre told him. "All I did was try to guard that wench and she evaded me every time. Then when she gets kidnapped by Mercedes de Medina, I run after to help her, and she accuses me of being a spy for Mercedes."

The two guardsmen gave each other a glance.

Rocco smirked. "It's a sad tale, indeed. Unfortunately, there are witnesses that back up the *wench's* story—a maid, I believe."

"That's not possible. Maria was killed by the—" Pierre closed his lips and tightened his jaw, a scarlet glow rising up his neck.

The guards frowned. One of them, a clean-faced older man, prodded him forward. "Once a weasel, always a weasel, eh, Henri?"

Henri, a young guard, ran his fingers down his trim beard and nodded. "Always, Philippe."

"I don't understand," Pierre said. "Medinas or Martinmas—they're both Spanish. What does it matter if I share information between their households? It's an easy job and pays well."

Rocco scowled. "It's not about the money or the king they swear allegiance to. Who do you serve? Even Spanish nobility have their little wars—will you defend the duke against Mercedes?"

"I don't know why I shouldn't work for both."

Henri tapped Pierre's shoulder. When he turned, the guard punched him in the face. Pierre fell to the ground where Henri kicked him repeatedly. Rocco and Philippe stepped up to pull him off.

"Traitor!" Henri screamed at him. "You would get us all killed just to jingle silver in your pocket!"

"Calm yourself," Rocco said, patting his shoulder. "This worm needs a proper execution. Kill him now and you don't get to beat him every time you deliver his gruel."

Philippe turned to Rocco. "We've had trouble with this one since we were in the Count d'Auguste's service. When the Duke de Martinmas hired us, we were rid of him, but he squirmed his way back in here. We are certain he sent two of ours to their deaths at the Medina castle. He cannot die soon enough for our tastes."

"Understood." Rocco watched the traitor pull himself to his knees, collapse with a groan, holding his ribs, and attempt to rise again. "Let us agree, gentlemen, that Tournier will not leave his cell alive unless it's to visit the gallows in the courtyard."

They nodded. Rocco picked Pierre up by the collar. "Get up and walk or we'll drag your carcass from here."

Pierre pushed to his feet, aided by Rocco's yank upwards.

"Mes amis," Pierre said between moans. "Please. I can be a great help. What would you like to know about Mercedes de Medina? I am willing to share what I know."

"For a price, I assume." Rocco threw him forward.

Henri chuckled. "Always for a price. Tournier never gives away anything he can get coin or advantage for."

"No, I swear," Pierre protested. "Not a centime!"

"Allow us to guess, then." Henri looked at Rocco. "Information in exchange for keeping his neck away from the noose."

They'd arrived at the large wooden door of the dungeon and Philippe stepped forward with a key to unlock it. Once inside, Rocco saw two separate cells, both with locks. Philippe again unlocked one of them, and Henri kicked the prisoner in the back to push him inside. Pierre landed on his hands and knees.

Philippe drew his dagger from its scabbard. "I do not know why we delay the inevitable. Let us slit his throat and be done."

Rocco held up his hand and walked to the bars. "You have nothing to tell me, Tournier. Mercedes was the only child of the Count and Countess de Medina. They are both dead. She was set on fire and presumed dead, but she lives, horribly disfigured by the flames."

Pierre pulled himself up to a cot and sat, a strange smirk on his face. "That is not half of what I've gathered. I can give you names of all the servants and guardsmen who are working for both houses."

Henri waved his dagger toward the prisoner. "Trust

him to betray all around him if it saves his own skin."

Rocco glanced at the guards. "Give us the names. If they are truly spies, we will dispatch them. If even one person cannot be proven to be a spy, you will die immediately."

"I shall not fail you," Pierre said, relaxing onto the cot. "Bring pen and paper and you will have names."

Philippe frowned at Rocco and opened his mouth to speak, but Rocco stopped him.

"Lock the cell. You can return with paper to record the names, while your partner finishes showing me the layout of the castle."

The trio walked out of the dungeon and came face-to-face with a tall, surprised servant.

"Amoy, what are you doing out here?" Henri asked.

Her face registered a flash of red before she drew herself up with importance. "I am housekeeper of this castle. I go where I am needed."

"Needed at the dungeon, are you?" Rocco asked.

She glanced at him, her eyes narrowed. "I don't believe I'm required to check in with the guards. Have you nowhere to be now?"

Rocco looked at his companions, both of whom were scowling. "I don't believe we're required to check in with a servant." He nodded to the other two guards, and the three men walked away.

"Sometimes I'd like to toss her in the dungeon," Philippe said.

"Who is she?" Rocco asked. "Besides the housekeeper."

"Amoy Simone. In charge of everything, including the air we breathe, according to her." Henri spat. "Runs the servants into the ground doing useless tasks and tries to run us. We don't take it from her and she's mad about it."

"Something tells me she holds a grudge," Rocco said.

Both guards looked at one another and at Rocco. They nodded, and Philippe stepped inside the castle to retrieve something to write on.

"Why didn't you volunteer to find writing implements?" Henri asked.

"I am barely a day on this assignment," Rocco said. "Why should you trust me with a traitor? Besides, I need to know my way around any property I am to defend."

"I believed we were clear that Tournier was not to live. How do you possess the power to pardon him?"

"I don't. And I didn't promise to." Rocco smiled. "We will kill him. I simply said we'd kill him immediately if he fed us false information."

They continued on their journey, Rocco pointing at different areas of the castle, the walls, and the outbuildings and asking about their use.

"In all truth," Henri told him, "None of these castles has ever been attacked as far as I know, apart from the night the young lady was kidnapped by pirates."

"Yes, this Lisette de Lille I keep hearing about. I do not know her."

"I am originally one of the guards from the castle d'Auguste, so I did not know her well. She was supposed to be betrothed to the son of the count I served. Instead, she was kidnapped, and nearly a year later, he was dead."

"Ah, pity. She is in mourning?"

The guard shook his head. "Not that I've seen. She is back at this castle and grows heavy with child."

"Wait—the young woman in the buckboard today, that was Lisette de Lille?"

"Yes." He looked west. "The sun is low. We should hurry to the gate so that you may relieve the man on duty."

They strode along the wall to the front of the castle. Arriving, Rocco shouted to the guard in the small turret to the right of the gate. Footsteps tapped down the wooden stairs and the man burst from the door.

"Julian Santiago?" the guard asked.

"Reporting for duty," Rocco told him. "Anything I should know before I take my post?"

"Yes," the guard took off his hat and wiped the sweat from his face. "The night is long and boring, and it's hot as hell in that shack. Don't fall asleep."

Rocco climbed the winding staircase to the top. The guardhouse was an enclosed cylinder made of stone, with an opening tall enough to see anyone approaching and aim an arrow or two, if need be, yet narrow enough to prevent any hostilities in response.

Looking about the small enclosure, he saw a crossbow and a quiver of arrows. He picked up the bow and steadied it against the crook of his shoulder, aiming it at the horizon. The wooden shaft was sturdy without being cumbersome. He stepped into the stirrup and cocked the string. The lathes stretched back equally. Looking through the sight again, he decided the aim was good, if a little skewed to the left. Nothing he couldn't compensate for.

He put down the bow and leaned against the wall, gazing outward for signs of visitors. The man he'd relieved was correct. The odds of receiving anyone were not high. And it was hotter than hell in this stone sweathouse.

Lisette de Lille. The name danced across his mind, teasing him, almost bringing up a memory but conjuring nothing. She'd looked at him with such expectation as she drove through the gate. Was she someone he was supposed to know, or someone he was supposed to forget?

It didn't matter, he supposed. She was a marquise, daughter of a duke. As the duke was now dead, she might now be the Duchess de Lille. Even before he became a pirate, Tristan de Rocco was a commoner who earned his keep as a sailor. His mother was a seamstress for the local nobility. He never knew his father but was told he was a sailor in the Spanish navy.

I may be a commoner, but I'm not a fool. There would be no circumstance where I kept company with a noblewoman. He reached up to the charm at his neck, fingering the delicacy of the gold hand holding a heart.

Hooves on gravel alerted him to someone leaving. He peered out the back and saw the buckboard with the little gray, the rig that had delivered the woman. A beefy black man handled the reins. The guard manning the gate exchanged a few words of cheer with the driver before lifting the wooden bolt and swinging the gate outward.

The dappled gray horse walked out onto the path, the wagon jostling behind him. Once they were clear, the gatekeeper walked out and around to swing each half of the large wooden gate shut. As he pushed the first half, quick footsteps crunched the rock and a man ran past the gatekeeper, the gate, and the walls of the castle.

Rocco looked down and recognized Pierre Tournier, whose awkward limbs seemed desperate to cooperate in order to run faster. He glanced back as he ran, confirming his identity. Philippe ran along after him, calling for him to stop.

There was only one option. Rocco picked up the crossbow and yanked the string back. Loading an arrow, he took aim at the young man, adjusting the sight to the right. One pull of the trigger and the arrow hissed down its path, nicking Pierre's ear. The fleeing man grabbed the side of his head and looked back.

"A little more to the right," Rocco told himself and reloaded.

The next arrow shot true, lodging in Pierre's back. His momentum carried him another couple of steps before he pitched forward onto his face.

Philippe slowed to a walk, panting, and stopped at the body. He knelt down, gave Pierre a brief exam, and stood, announcing, "Dead."

Rocco descended the tower and met the gatekeeper and other guardsman at the steps. Together, they walked out to the body, picked it up and carried it back inside. As they neared, Philippe held a piece of paper out to Rocco.

"He's finally silent, but I got names."

Lisette sat on the cool stone of the balcony, her ceramic dragon before her. She focused on the figurine, counting her breaths, and willing herself into transforming. The words Lamya had given her refused to return but she tried anyway.

"One river," she whispered, "many dreams. No, streams. One river, many streams."

She rubbed her temples. "Why can't this be easy like before? Night falls and poof. Sun rises and poof again."

The thief she had killed in the village—the transformation had been quick and thorough. Threatening man? Turn, kill, turn. She conjured the scene again in her mind, trying to relive the fear. His hands were on her, mauling her, trying to take her few coins away. She felt a small measure of guilt. It was a heavy price for him to pay for so little money.

But he shouldn't have hit her.

She closed her eyes and focused on Alara, placing her hands lightly on her stomach. The baby was actively pressing outward with hands and legs. Lisette pressed back and felt the connection between them. She wrapped her hands around her body, tenderly hugging the baby who could soon be held in her arms.

"Alara," she breathed. "I can't wait to see you."

The burn came slow and easy, stretching her limbs and growing her spine. The nubs on her shoulders reached out into wings. Within moments the blue dragon stood on four legs looking up at the moon which was nearing its fullness. She climbed upon the ledge, extended her wings, and flew.

The night sky was clear, inky, and pricked with thousands of stars. She rose high, hopefully out of the view of most prying eyes. Her plan was to fly to Lamya if she could maintain her form.

The moon and stars had plenty of light to see the outlines of buildings and garden paths below. She whooshed silently as any barn owl, dipping lower as there was no one to see her. As she banked around the front, she noticed the gates open.

Three guardsmen were carrying something limp—a body. They held him with his head facing down, which looked odd until she saw the arrow protruding from his back. One of the guards held a piece of paper in one hand, the other one holding the dead man's feet.

"He was always the type to play both sides against the middle," said one. "We could never've trusted 'im."

"Remember when he took Philippe's watch and sold it? Claimed he found it in his own pocket and was on his way to return it when thieves robbed him."

"I remember. I also remember the merchant in town who swore Pierre was the one who sold him the piece."

Pierre Tournier, the traitor. Lisette was not surprised

he had been killed—he'd been tempting fate on both sides. It was the manner in which he was killed that surprised her.

"That was a good shot, Julian," one of the guards said.

"Thanks, Henri." A deep, melodious voice answered.

Lisette glimpsed a mass of dark curly hair and well-muscled shoulders. It was Rocco. He walked along, carrying his share of the corpse.

"Can you read the list in this light?" Rocco asked the guard with the paper.

"Nah, I can't read t'all."

Lisette wanted desperately to talk to Rocco before leaving. *I can transform back, then return to my dragon form and go to Lamya.*

She flew back inside the walls and landed in a garden in the front, close to the gate but hidden in the bushes. She closed her eyes and pictured her human form, hands and legs and fingers and toes.

Nothing changed.

She tried again, thinking of how it felt when she killed the thief and had rid herself of the danger to her child. Her dragon form remained.

Very well, I'll fly to Lamya. Talking to Rocco will have to wait. Spreading her wings, she lifted back into the sky and turned toward the beach.

As she flew over the wall of the castle, the familiar burn came to her body. She managed to light beside the wall in time to flash back into her human form.

"By the gods," she muttered. "Why couldn't I have done that earlier?"

She turned around to return to the side gate and looked down. There was nothing but gravel all around the perimeter, and she was barefoot. The side gate was the most private, but the front gate was closer. After two steps toward the side gate, she turned, deciding to risk the guards at the front gate and save her feet.

Lisette crept gingerly to the front, expecting to be addressed. None of the guards called out to her, so she shouted, "Guardsman," several times, until at last a voice responded.

"State your name and purpose."

She recognized Rocco at once and tried to contain her excitement. "Guardsman, I am a guest of the duke, and I have gotten locked outside the castle."

"How is it that you are outside?"

"I went for a stroll after dinner and walked through a gate to admire the moonlight." She looked up to the small turret and saw his face in the shadows.

"Is your name Lisette de Lille?" Rocco asked.

Her heart raced. "Yes."

"And this was the de Lille castle?"

"Yes, this was my home."

Rocco leaned forward into the light. "Then how is it you don't know how to find the gate to lead you inside again?"

She made fists that dug into her hips. "I am outside of the castle walls. I need to be inside the castle walls. I don't think I need to justify it to you."

"And I am tasked with keeping the castle safe for the duke, so you do need to justify it."

Lisette sat back on her heels, shifting her weight quickly as the rocks dug into her feet. She crossed her arms over her expansive stomach. "I know where the gate is and would easily return, except that I have no shoes and this ground is coarse."

"Why were you strolling in the garden with no shoes on?"

A blush of anger rose up Lisette's neck and heated her face. "Open the gate, Rocco!"

"How do you know that name?" Hard, quick footsteps sounded on wooden boards, then gravel. The gate opened and Rocco appeared, scowling. "Who are you?"

She fought every desire to run and throw herself into his arms. Instead, she took slow, deliberate steps toward him, looking for any sign of recognition.

"Well? Do I get an answer?"

"I…I am a woman you knew long ago."

He pointed to her stomach. "I hope it wasn't that long ago."

Tears poured from her eyes, and she pushed at him, trying to get past to her room, where she could cry in private. He caught her by her shoulders and prevented her from moving.

"Dry those tears, little mother—I was but jesting." He picked her chin up in his hand and looked her in the eyes. "My apologies. Perhaps you do look familiar to me."

She wept harder at his cavalier attitude, sinking her head in both hands. Rocco pulled her close and embraced her. His arms were so familiar. A multitude of memories tripped through her mind, from the first night they met on *L'Implacable*, to the last time they embraced on Isla del Lagarto, before the battle that was supposed to end their curses.

"There, there, m'lady," Rocco soothed. "As soon as my partner returns from his assignment, I shall escort you to your room. Come in and have a seat. You must be weary of carrying the niño."

His tenderness made the tears start again, but Lisette strengthened her heart and wiped them away with her sleeve. She allowed him to lead her to a stone bench, and sat, pulling her feet next to her, and covering them with her robe.

Rocco pointed to her clothing, a wry grin on his face. "Your clothing is rather scant for an evening's stroll."

"I quite forgot myself. When my family lived here, I often took a walk around the garden at night. I find it soothing." She let her thumb roll down the small scar on her opposite palm, turning it over to see its progress.

Rocco took the injured hand in his own. "How did you acquire this wound?"

"A sword." Lisette did not think about her answer until it had escaped her lips. She glanced about for anyone who might be listening, before standing and lowering her voice. "In truth, I was not strolling tonight. I believe you met a certain—defender—on the beach recently."

His left eyebrow arched as he whispered, "A feathered one?"

She nodded. "I may have discovered how to turn dragon but turning human still seems to happen at the most inconvenient times and places."

Rocco stared at her until she thought he might have fallen into a trance. She reached out to touch him, break the spell. The crunch of boot on gravel awakened him and he looked past her down the path.

"Here is my replacement," he said, and offered his arm. "Shall I deliver you to your quarters?"

Lisette laid her hand upon his forearm and was transported back to the night he delivered her to the Viscount Barragan. He had lifted her as easily as a bird and escorted her, first to the dinghy, and finally to the viscount's apartment.

She had made many choices that night, killing the viscount, taking his gold and his jewels, and finding her way back aboard Rocco's ship. At the time, it did not feel like choosing at all. It seemed more like feeling around a darkened labyrinth and always moving toward the path that was open.

They took their time walking to the entrance, as Lisette's feet were not accustomed to the gravel path. After a few mincing steps, Rocco turned to her.

"M'lady, perhaps I could save your feet if you would allow me to carry you."

Lisette hesitated. It would be both thrilling and painful to be held, and she had long abandoned her pampered lifestyle. But her feet did hurt with each jabbing rock. Alara suddenly kicked her so hard it made her grab her stomach.

Apparently, her daughter had an opinion.

"Are you in distress?" Rocco asked, concern on his brow.

"No." Lisette smiled. "The baby is being active. Yes, thank you, I would accept your help. My feet are not normally so fragile, but the baby is putting extra weight on them."

Rocco reached down and swept her into both arms with one fluid motion. Lisette wrapped her hands around his neck for stability.

"My apologies," she said. "I require you to carry two of us."

"It is not the heaviest burden I've ever borne." His expression was blank, that of a servant doing his job.

She was again reminded of the trip to Isla de la Soledad. A large sailor had picked her up, much like this, to put her into the dinghy.

"How are Chunk and Poussin?" she asked.

Rocco stopped walking. "How do you know them?"

"I know all on *L'Implacable*, captain—or I did when I sailed with you." She watched the confusion on his face. "I do not know why you don't remember me, but I remember all."

Rocco looked away, toward the front door to the castle. He resumed his walk, increasing the pace until he stepped upon smooth stone, where he set Lisette back on her own feet.

"I trust m'lady can see herself to her room."

"Yes." Lisette's heart dipped a little. She had hoped her memories would prod his own, but if they did, he was fighting them.

Alara stretched out within her, diverting her thoughts. *Keep trying, Mama. You've planted the seed.*

Lisette entered the great hall and turned to the stairs. She climbed slowly. As well as her feet complaining with each step, Alara was using her as a punching bag, kicking and striking out. She put a hand on her stomach and massaged it gently.

"Dear daughter, I am trying my hardest to make him remember. What would you have me do—shout at him that we fought together, made love together, and that you are ours?"

One sharp push with both feet was the answer.

"Alara," she cooed as she reached the top step and walked to her bedroom door. "I love you and your father and want our lives to be together and happy. Stop scolding me."

Once inside her chambers, Lisette soaked her feet in cool water, dried them, and headed to her bed. Exhaustion dragged her limbs down into the mattress, but her mind was awhirl.

She had successfully turned into a dragon but turning back did not go as planned. Her daughter was showing signs that she would like to make the rules from within the womb. Lisette desperately needed Lamya's instruction, as well as the safety of Île des Anciens.

But Rocco was here. She did not know why he did not remember her, although she suspected it had something to do with whatever magic the girl Ruhee had attempted. If she could give him enough clues to their past, she was certain he would recall their love. He could then come with her to see Lamya and help her with their child.

She smiled at the idea, until a shadow crossed the moon. A night bird, flying low, swept across the balcony. *Rocco is somehow still a blood dragon, apparently hunting Mercedes. If I could but hold out here until the crescent moon, Rocco could end his curse.*

The night was long, and she passed it without much sleep.

It was a steady, constant knocking that made her finally rise, dragging her weary frame to the bolted door and opening it. Marisha stood, holding a tray laden with food and drink.

"I am accustomed to ringing for my meal," Lisette said, yawning.

"I understand and apologize," Marisha told her as she entered. "The duke is worried. According to him, you did not eat enough last night. I am to stay here and *encourage* you."

"Let me guess." Lisette closed the door and shuffled to the table, where Marisha was setting out the plate of cured meats and roasted vegetables, along with a basket of rolls and a bowl of papayas and mangos. "These plates are to be completely emptied when you return."

Marisha nodded. "It would take two sailors after a

full day's push against the wind to finish all this."

Lisette looked at the feast on the table. "Well, take a plate and let's do what we can."

"Lizzie, I was supposed to help with mopping this morning."

"Who is giving you tasks? You are supposed to be my personal maid and attendant."

Marisha shrugged. "Amoy Simone the housekeeper. She delights in throwing her weight about."

"Ah, yes, we've met." Lisette shook her head. "I shall leave you the choice—go about your mopping, or stay and have breakfast with me, after which I shall pay a visit to Amoy and inform her of your duties."

The smile on Marisha's face widened to display her magnificent white teeth. She picked up a plate. Lisette laughed, and they sat down to eat.

"I hear a rumor—maybe you were outside last night, wandering in the gardens," Marisha said between bites.

"My evening was spent trying to find magic if you understand my meaning. It did not quite go as planned."

Marisha nodded. "And a certain guardsman helped to see you safely back to the castle?"

"Yes, Rocco. I suppose I should call him by his other name here—it is Julian something."

"Santiago."

"Guardsman Santiago," Lisette said. "There are few people here who would recognize him, although I do hope the duke does not see him close, as he must remember his face. He did commandeer *El Gallo Blanco* and shove *el grande duque* into a dinghy."

"That he left him alive is a miracle." Marisha helped herself to another roasted potato. "Was there any sign that Rocco now remembers you?"

"That I cannot say." Lisette shrugged. "There was a moment that he seemed to be struggling with something.

Within an eye's blink, he was stone-faced and cold."

"Struggling is good. We shall continue to make him struggle."

Lisette pushed her plate away. "I cannot eat another bite, or I shall burst. Can we perhaps sneak some of this food to the rest of the servants?"

Marisha smiled. "If you can resolve my problems with Amoy, I can make it so."

They rose from the table and moved to the dressing area, where Marisha helped Lisette into a pale green day gown that accentuated her eyes. Lisette sat at her mirror to arrange her hair, but Marisha was behind her in a moment to take the brush from her hand, braid and pin the auburn curls into a manageable shape.

"If you will direct me to Amoy," Lisette said and pointed to the table. "I will attend to her while you make this disappear."

"Like magic, m'lady. Amoy will be in the kitchen, yelling at the girl to wash the dishes faster yet leave no crust of food."

Nodding, Lisette left her chambers and made her way downstairs. The scene was exactly as Marisha had described. A broad-hipped island girl stood at a large tub, scrubbing a plate furiously while Amoy screeched.

"That is not clean—scrub it with some strength, Girl! Why are you not finished yet?"

Lisette walked to the center of the room and into the large woman's view. She made certain to stand tall and lift her chin. "Good morning, Amoy."

Amoy quieted and stood back, wiping her hands on her apron. She regarded Lisette with a suspicious squint, her expression one of contained contempt. "Good morning, *m'lady*. As you can see, we are quite busy with our chores. How may I help you?"

"Please continue with your morning tasks," Lisette told the girl, ignoring the sneering use of *m'lady* and turned to the housekeeper. "Amoy, I am certain your voice could take a brief rest from screaming."

Amoy's jaw flexed in annoyance, but Lisette continued. "I'm afraid there has been some miscommunication. The duke has assigned Marisha to be my personal maid. I believe we had this discussion with Pinar. You may believe my maid has time for other household chores, but as you can see, I grow larger with child each day and find that I require her more than usual."

"There is always extra time," Amoy countered. "For example, you are currently here, taking up my time. Marisha could be doing something else."

Lisette glared at the stubborn woman. "She *is* doing something else. She is cleaning my chambers."

"And after that?"

"After that, Marisha's duties will be whatever I require. If you need reassurance, I'm certain the duke will agree that I need full-time care." Lisette turned to leave and stopped. "And do not refer to me as *m'lady*. I am the Marquise de Lille."

She walked toward the door, feeling the heat of Amoy's rage but not wanting to turn and look. An argumentative servant was not of interest to her unless they were armed with weaponry. Lisette was banking on witnesses to stay Amoy's hand. She did make a note to herself, to never be alone with the woman unless she had a dagger.

Having a dagger sounded like a good idea, so Lisette stepped out of the castle. Most of the better blades were found near the soldier's barracks. The morning was pleasant, so she strolled down the peaceful garden path and enjoyed the scenery. Frangipani was in bloom and the perfume was delightful.

An older man stood at the furnace outside the livery, pumping air to build the fire, his tongs holding what appeared to be a horseshoe. Sweat ran down his face but he did not attempt to wipe it away. Lisette watched from a distance, not wishing to interrupt his task and risk injury. At last, he pulled the tongs out, stepped to the anvil and pounded the red-hot metal before him.

He glanced up at Lisette, but she gestured for him to keep working. Once he dropped the shoe into a bucket of water, she approached.

"Good morning," she said. "I am Lisette de Lille, a guest of the duke's."

The blacksmith smiled, yellowing teeth shining through his sooty features. "I recall you well, m'lady. Name's Quince, I came across with your father to this castle."

"Oh, yes, Quince. I'm sorry I did not recognize you. I'm happy to see you are still here."

"Aye, it was hard fought, but I lasted." He wiped a rag across his face. "Got steel run through my side in the battle."

"Battle?"

"The night your mother died the Count de Medina's soldiers swept through our grounds. Most of the household were taken as slaves. The guards were all slain, as it was well known they were loyal to your family, those that didn't escape. The rest were allowed to live if they agreed to become indentured to the count." He shook his head. "I'm a free man, willin' to die a free man."

"You survived, though."

"I lay still when I was stabbed, playin' dead. Island folk found me, healed me. I was workin' in the village when the duke came. He asked me to work for 'im." Quince smiled. "I was hopin' you or your brother would return and take the castle back."

She sighed. "Sadly, Julien is dead, just as my parents are. I am back, but with no power to take this castle for my family."

"Ah, that's all right, m'lady. Lifts my heart just to

have you here."

"Quince, I'm here because I'd like to have a dagger. A woman must be able to defend herself. Have you any extras?"

He grinned. "Got a beauty. I was makin' it for Pierre Tournier, but let's say he won't be needin' it where he's going."

"Or where he's gone," she said. Quince looked at her, squinting, so she added, "He was killed trying to escape last night."

"I did not know. I heard shovels this mornin', but I paid it no mind." He disappeared into his back room and returned with a leather scabbard the color of honey, holding a handle inlaid with iridescent oyster shell. Laying the scabbard across his hand, he turned the handle toward Lisette, inviting her to draw the dagger from the sheath.

It was a beautiful blade, ice-blue and honed to a sharpness that would leave a slender but deadly wound. Enemies would not even feel their demise.

"It's beautiful," Lisette told him.

"He'd ordered some etchings on the blade, but I had not time to finish them. You may have this as-is, or I can add some flourish."

He was a friendly man, but she did not trust him with the one etching she would put on any blade. She'd have to ask her sea sisters where to engrave a lioness' head.

"I prefer it unadorned, Quince. It's just what I need."

35

Rocco returned to the barracks at sunrise, having been relieved at the gate. Despite blocking all light in the room, he slept fitfully. He had not expected to be so disturbed by the woman Lisette. She said she was someone he knew long ago. He had known many women, but most had been the ones who frequent the ports and gladly accept coin to provide a night's entertainment. Most, except for his Tempest.

Lisette de Lille did not look like that kind of woman. Nor did she resemble Tempest, an innkeep's daughter with no guile, used to hard work. This was a noblewoman born to luxury.

And yet, there was about her a certain…not-nobility. There was a strength about her as she handled the buckboard, a willingness to dig in and get her hands dirty if that's what the job took. She was not prissy or demanding if he overlooked her insistence at coming in the gate.

He did not know why he was so obstinate about her entering—he knew that she belonged inside. If the duke had appeared, he would have let her in with a bow and salute.

For some reason, he enjoyed arguing with her, especially when she stomped her little bare foot.

It was a shock when she shouted his real name, and yet he wasn't as surprised as he might have been. Somehow, he knew. The visceral memory of her body in his arms triggered feelings. He had held her before.

Each time he reached into his past to pull her out, it was like fishing for an eel in the dark. Slippery, evasive, and with not even enough light to throw a shadow. An eel bite was one of the nastier things he'd ever endured—he nearly lost a finger. Trying to recall this woman felt like he might get his hand wrapped around the memory, only to be sliced open, swallowed up.

Better to put it away, lock it up. He was a guardsman now. In a few days, he'd be a dragon again, hunting Mercedes. Hopefully, it would be over soon, and he could return to *L'Implacable* and the life he'd chosen.

But he could not stop his mind from focusing on Lisette—she knew Chunk and Poussin. How? According to her, she had spent time on the ship with the crew. This was something no putain ever did. But if she was a part of the crew, how could he not remember her?

Just before midday, he fell asleep. His dreams were of being lost and trying to find his way back to the ship. He was in a dinghy, rowing toward *L'Implacable* but when he looked up, he was rowing toward shore. A figure waved to him. A girl with long black hair. It was Ruhee.

"You've forgotten her," she said. "You are free to love me now."

He opened his eyes and sat up. This was Ruhee's

doing. Lamya had told him of the enchantment. She had also assured him his memory would return. What she had not told him was how this spell worked.

As he dressed, he reached back in his memory, to the night of the wedding on Isla del Lagarto, when he killed the Count de Medina.

He was a dragon at night, attempting to capture and kill the count, and one more person. Mercedes? His nighttime flights were spent hunting at the castle, avoiding detection, and fighting a black dragon. Rocco stepped into his breeches, running his hand up his leg to his hip.

I remember the wounds and the fights. I remember the night I killed Juan de Medina. The black dragon killed Medina's wife and set Mercedes ablaze. Rocco knew he had arrived at the gala as a human. The black dragon was also human—he confronted it, tried to kill it, but a wave of forgiveness washed over him. The memory of bowing his head, stepping aside, letting the black dragon complete their task, washed over him. *Who was that dragon?*

"Guardsman Santiago?" Luis' voice commanded his attention. "You are due at your post. Today you are at the back gate. Grab some hardtack and see that you report."

Rocco nodded, adjusting his belt. "Yes, captain."

"And be prepared for special duty tonight. I was told we'll have visitors—some count has been sent from Spain to take over the d'Auguste castle."

"Spanish, eh?"

"Antonio de Mendoza." Luis mocked the name with a grand bow. "He and his family are coming to dinner, and the duke has something planned. Do not ask me what, just be ready."

"Aye." Rocco gave a mocking salute and left the barracks to take his post.

The old guardsman at the back gate smiled as Rocco approached. "Good to see you, my boy. I am in need of feed and rest."

The wide wooden gate, gray with weather, sat anchored in the thick stone wall. Vines crept up the stones from the garden inside, and tall trees peeked over the wall from the wilderness beyond.

"Is this gate always guarded?" Rocco asked.

"Not usually," the older man said, rubbing his graying stubble of beard. "Orders came down yestereve. We're to tell the captain who comes and who goes." He reached into his pocket, pulling out a crinkled piece of paper and a small pencil. "We was supposed to write them down, 'cept I don't know how's to write.'"

"Did anyone come in or out?" Rocco asked. "I can write them down for you."

"Nobody." The guard shook his head. "Well, 'cept for that headmistress."

"Who?"

"That woman from the castle. Amoy." He scowled. "Disagreeable wench. Always treats me like a cockroach."

Rocco considered the list Pierre had provided. That name wasn't on the list. If Pierre had lied, Rocco would dig up his body just to kill him again. "I'll put her name down for you. Now get some food and some sleep."

The old guard gave him a quick nod and sauntered toward the castle where he would no doubt try to score a meal. Rocco watched him, wondering how accurate Pierre's list of spies was. There would be no opportunity to torture the truth from him now.

A familiar figure strode down the path toward him. As Luis came closer, Rocco stood at attention, a habit he picked up in the Spanish navy.

"You needn't salute, Guardsman," Luis said with a wry grin.

Rocco relaxed. "Old habits die hard."

"You were once in the king's service?"

"All good pirates started in a navy." Rocco smiled.

"Do you always check up on the gates?"

"No." Luis pulled paper from his pocket. "I wanted to discuss this list with you."

"You know, captain, I have not been here long enough to know anyone, spy or no."

Luis nodded. "I know. I wanted to discuss the plan of attack."

"Have you presented this information to the duke yet?"

"No." Luis looked about and lowered his voice. "The duke, I have learned, is a man of quick decision, tending sometimes to impulsiveness and near panic."

"So, presenting this list would result in the names being rounded up and executed?"

"I believe so. I would prefer to present him with a plan for exposing any spies."

Rocco smiled. "I was rather hoping you had a better idea. Spies can be useful in their way."

"Agreed. Feeding them false information, paying them to get information for us—I'd prefer to find every rodent before I send the cat in."

They read the list together. There were two guards and three servants. One name Rocco recognized. Marisha. It did not seem possible that she would work for Mercedes. Pierre could have seen her as suspicious in general. Or Pierre could have added her out of some kind of spite. One lie damned the whole list.

"How well do you know these people?" Rocco asked.

"Most I know from the d'Auguste household," Luis told him. "Except for this girl, Marisha. She is new. Could she be Maria's replacement?"

"Marisha is the one name I do know," Rocco said. "For reasons I should not expose you to, I can say that she may not be loyal to the duke, but she is no spy for Mercedes."

Luis nodded. "I get your meaning, Pirate. How would you approach this?"

"The guardsmen are simple. You pair them with guards you trust, and they keep watch. At some point they will need to get information to Mercedes and receive payment. That is your proof that Pierre named them correctly."

"Yes." Luis tapped the paper against his wrist. "How can we capture the household staff?"

"I only know the one who is on this list." Rocco shrugged. "But perhaps we give false information to each and see who tells what."

Luis looked at the ground, nodding. "Yes. It may be the only way."

"Very well, captain, when I am finished with my post, I shall pay the kitchen a visit. First, I must concoct a fable small enough to be harmless but large enough to be noticed." As he spoke, a dark cloud rolled across the sun.

Luis regarded the sky. "The rains will be here soon. We'll have enough on our hands keeping the men active without hunting down Mercedes' paid lackeys."

The captain left Rocco to his post and returned down the path toward the guardhouse. Rocco watched after him, thinking about the rain. He had not considered the monsoon season in his plans. Flying through sheets of rain and trying to work fire up from his belly was a challenge.

Rattling of a key in the gate caught his attention. He stood near the hinges, so that he could see the visitor before they saw him. A semi-familiar face peeked through the opening. She did not look toward the hinges, but out at the courtyard. Rocco stood very still and in as much shadow as he could while she entered and turned to lock the gate behind her.

"State your name and purpose." He growled the command.

The woman jumped, hissing, and spilling the

contents of her basket on the ground. "I am Amoy Simone," she declared with venom. "How dare you sneak up and question me!"

"I was put here in charge of the back gate, at the captain's orders."

"Captain." Amoy spat the word. "Pfft, he's an imbecile. And you made me spill my yams." She leaned down to pick up her fallen crop.

A couple of yams had rolled to Rocco's feet, so he picked them up to put them in her basket, noting that they had no dirt on them. He held them out, and she snatched them from his hand. Looking in her basket, he saw that all of the yams looked freshly washed.

Perhaps he would not have to wait to feed the household a lie.

"Terribly sorry for frightening you, Housekeep," he said, "but captain's under the duke's orders, of course. It all rolls downhill, as they say."

"The duke's afraid of his own shadow." She straightened her posture, repositioning the basket on her arm. "Why does the back gate need defending?"

Rocco glanced both ways before leaning toward her. "You are preparing the castle for visitors tonight, yes? The Count de Mendoza and his family. The duke's spies have told him that the visitors have been sent by King Charles to assess the island and report weaknesses to him."

"So? What is that to us?"

"Nothing, if you do not consider that the Mendoza family has a history of ruining other nobility in order to advance themselves. And the king has provided a large contingent of guards to assist them in their conquest." He sighed and raised his brows. "Good thing the duke is seen as more politically stable than whoever rules the old Medina castle."

He watched Amoy's eyes widen slightly and her hand press against her collarbone. She showed no emotion, but her body told the story—she was hooked.

"Please do not spread this information." He stepped back toward the gate. "And go with God."

She turned down the path, striding toward the castle.

Rocco looked after her, a small grin playing on his lips. *Now, we wait to see if we catch a bigger fish.*

36

Lisette placed the sheathed dagger in her pocket and stepped out to the gardens. The day was bright, but the air had a denseness to it as if she could tear off a piece and hold it in her hand. She looked up at the sun. It was at a lower angle as it streaked from east to west. Monsoon season would be here shortly.

She did not mind the rains, but it was going to be miserable flying with wet feathers. Still, it would postpone any wedding plans the duke might have. No one would attend a gala in the kind of rain these islands produced.

The heaviness of the air brought the smell of flowers closer. She walked down the path that led to large planters of orchids, mixed with passionflowers. The nobility tried to bring their aesthetic to the Caribbean, but the flora was not easily tamed. The orchids had refused to remain in their planters, preferring to escape into the ground around the pots. Bright passionflower vines wound around everything, exuding a sultry aroma, and making a slippery mess of the walkways.

Lisette strolled through the colorful arrays, inhaling the mingled scents until she was nearly giddy. She managed to find a bench away from the blooms and sat down to catch her breath. Closing her eyes, she leaned back into the seat.

A large drop of water hit her forehead.

"You might want to find shelter, m'lady," a low voice said.

She opened her eyes to see Rocco standing there, holding out his arm. Another drop hit her shoulder and she looked up at dark clouds rolling across the sky.

"We may have to run for it," she said, extending her hand.

Rocco removed his jacket and held it over Lisette's head as he ushered her toward the cover of a small pavilion in the center of the garden. The rain came down in earnest, so they quickened their strides, running to escape the pelting drops. Lisette stood in the middle of the structure, breathing hard and shaking the water from her skirt.

"Thank you, Roc—I mean, Guardsman. I appreciate your gallantry."

"I could not allow your ladyship to drown like a ship's rat."

She laughed. "I assure you I have been that wet. Remember the time my arm got caught in the line during the squall? I nearly drowned before I cut myself free."

He looked at her, blank confusion in his eyes.

"I'm sorry." She frowned, taking his hand to comfort him. "You really don't remember?"

"It's not your fault." He looked at his hand in hers. "I remember many squalls aboard ship. I remember someone having to cut the line to escape. I just don't remember you."

Lisette nodded, fighting tears.

"My apologies if I trouble you." Rocco turned his hand around, to place her palm into his. "It is not my desire."

Dabbing at her eyes, she smiled. "Well, at the very least you could call me Lizzie."

"All right…Lizzie."

They stood, holding hands, looking into each other's eyes, taking the heavy air in with slow, quiet breaths. Lisette saw his focus dart away, just as a ray of sunlight pierced her vision.

"It appears the storm has passed," she said.

"Yes." He resumed his thoughtful gaze. "I should return to my post."

"Yes." She kept her hand in his.

"I presume m'lady—I mean, Lizzy, I presume you can return to the castle safely."

She nodded, making a small curtsy before stepping close to him. "Thank you, Rocco. I am safe."

As it had the first night they met, the heat from his body engulfed her, and their breaths moved in rhythm. She was certain that if she reached her hand to his chest, his heart would be beating in time with hers. That night she had been his hostage, wildly afraid of what he might do to her, yet boldly demanding that he keep his hands to himself and return her home.

Now it seemed they had traded places.

"What do you fear, Tristan?" she whispered, reaching out for him.

He caught her hand in his own, pushing it down as he released her other hand. "Remembering."

Turning abruptly, he strode from the pavilion back toward his post. Lisette watched him go, waiting until he was out of sight before she took the path toward the castle.

Her heart was filled with hope and disappointment and impatience.

"Have courage, Lizzie," she said to no one. "He is an honest man and brave. He will have to confront his fear because he cannot live this way forever." Baby feet pounded at their confinement, so she cradled her stomach in her hands. "*He* has to remember, Alara. My memories are of no use to him."

As she approached the kitchen, a large shadow popped out of the trees, heading toward the door. Amoy took a few hurried steps before spotting Lisette and stopping.

"Amoy, where have you been this afternoon?" Lisette asked, taking careful study of the woman's face and wet clothes. "I see you got caught in the rainstorm."

Amoy's cheeks flushed as she looked away. "The larder was almost out of mangos."

Lisette cocked her head. "Seems like a mundane task for the housekeeper. Why not send one of the kitchen underlings?"

"If you must know, *Marquise de Lille*, they are in the middle of preparing the feast for tonight. I know where there is a patch of ripe fruit growing and could make a quicker trip of it."

The sneer attached to her name was not lost on Lisette. "There is a feast tonight? More so than our normal dining?"

Amoy shrugged. "All I know is that his lordship has demanded venison, quail, pork and goose, with enough dishes to feed fifty people, even though there may be at most ten."

Lisette kept her expression haughty but neutral, although she wanted to gape in surprise and ask a million questions. Better to ask the duke—or Connie.

"I'm certain the duke always wants more," she said, and entered the castle, making certain to walk in ahead of the woman.

Once inside Lisette went on the hunt. She usually did not care where the duke was and certainly did not go looking for him. Today, there was a bad feeling in her gut. A feast usually meant guests, and guests usually were not invited without a special occasion, and special occasions could be anything from a holiday to a birthday…to a wedding.

She was on her way through the great hall to the chambers above when she spied a black robe scurrying across the marble floor. Tumas the priest was on his way somewhere in a brand-new frock. Lisette called to him. He hesitated, took another step, and turned.

"I suspect you did not want to see me," she said.

"That is untrue, m'lady. I was thinking and did not hear your call."

Lisette propped her hands on her hips. "Do not jest with me, Father. I see you have a new robe. I've also heard that there is to be a feast tonight. What are we celebrating?"

Tumas squeezed his palms together, his head lowered. "M'lady, you know—"

"Call me Lizzie. And remind yourself of when we were friends and I helped you escape Mercedes' beating."

He looked her in the eyes, and she saw his face relax. "Yes, Lizzie. I hope you will agree the duke is an intimidating fellow. It is difficult to not be swayed into his confidence."

Lisette smiled. "Yes, he likes to have his way. Now, what do I need to know?"

Tumas stared at the ground. "The duke has learned that there are new inhabitants on the island, a count and his family from Spain who are to occupy the d'Auguste castle. He has invited them to dine with us this evening."

"Us?" Lisette's stomach turned sour. "You do not normally break bread with the duke."

The priest raised his gaze as he spoke. "I do when I'm invited to perform a marriage ceremony."

"Marriage?" She scowled. "I hope you do not mean my marriage. That will not occur tonight."

"In my defense I was not given names. But the marquess was in the room when the duke spoke to me and he stomped away, cursing."

"Connie and I will not be married, now or ever," Lisette said.

"Lizzie my dear, I understand your hesitance." Tumas laid his hand on her shoulder lightly. "But think of what this would mean for your child—a name. Title and breeding give you a certain advantage, but having a bastard child is a black mark on any woman."

Lisette pulled her shoulder away and turned to face him, stretching her spine regally. "You, priest, do not get to lecture me on children, as you shall never carry one, birth one, or even father one, if you uphold your vows. My *bastard* child has a father. We will marry if it is my wish. But not if I am already married to Connie."

Tumas bowed his head. "Of course. I only offer advice. You have free will to choose."

"A free choice, Father, as in confess or go to the gallows?" Lisette lifted her chin and glared, letting her gaze move disdainfully from his face to his feet. "I hope you get to keep your new clothes when the duke's plan falls apart."

She turned and strode toward Connie's room. They needed both of their clever minds to find a way out of the duke's snare.

37

Lisette's knock at Connie's door resulted in an angry, "Go away!"

She cracked the door open. "Do not yell at me, this was not my doing."

"Oh, Lizzie, come in." The tall, handsome marquess was throwing clothes into a large portmanteau. "I am on my way to the port. Join me?"

"I would love to. I just spoke with our priest." She walked to his bed and looked at the array of clothing. "Are all those shirts going to fit in one bag?"

"No, those go in the trunk." He pointed to the ornate wood-and-leather chest at the end of the bed. "Father asked me to come here to visit, not to get married. No offense, dear, but we've had this conversation."

"Many times," Lisette said with a smile. "Is there a

ship in port?"

"I do not know, but I will stay in the inn rather than here while I'm waiting."

She laughed. "No, you wouldn't. You enjoy your luxuries. I think we both need a plan that does not start with a hasty retreat."

"You know I am fond of you, Lizzie, but I know my father. He is a stubborn bull and manipulative to his very soul. If we both stay, we shall be married by the morning. And I fear, if you stay, he might just marry you himself."

"Oh no." She could not prevent her cringe. "What would it take to stop this madness?"

Connie tossed a pair of silk stockings in the bag. "Hiding the priest might delay things. Of course, if the child's father stepped up and claimed his rights, married you…"

"Getting married to the father is currently difficult. Hiding the priest might be easier, but not by much." She relayed her conversation with Tumas.

"What did I tell you? Father is a manipulative man." He closed his trunk. "Come with me. We can find a way to hide in the village until our ship comes in."

"It's tempting." Lisette again considered her choices. Stay and force the duke to honor his promise to get her to Lamya. Go with Connie and try to find a ship that might get close enough to Île des Anciens to drop her off. She shook her head. "No ship lands where I need to go. As long as you can escape, your father will not be able to marry us."

Connie shrugged and rang for a servant. "God be with you, then, Lisette de Lille. I shall pray you remain safe."

"God be with you also." Lisette hugged him, walked to the door, and opened it. She shut it quickly. "Connie— the servant might not arrive."

"Why not?"

"There are guards outside."

Connie joined her at the door, where four guards stood.

"Four of you, for me?" he asked. "I'm honored."

"No, m'lord," Captain Delgado said. "Only two for your door. The other two will escort the marquise to her room. It is the duke's wish that neither of you miss dinner tonight, as there will be guests."

Lisette looked up at Connie, then at the guards. She recognized Luis Delgado. The guard standing next to him was the other guard from the gatehouse. They had called him Philippe. The last two guards stood well back of the door, in the shadows. Captain Delgado gave orders to the men, causing them to open a path for her to step through.

As she walked forward she recognized a young, bearded guard—Henri, who had congratulated Rocco on his marksmanship. The last guard was Rocco. She kept the smile from her face but could not keep the sparkle from her eyes. Alara fussed inside her, so she massaged and cradled her baby to keep her from kicking her opinion.

"Good evening, gentlemen," she said. "Guardsman Santiago, is it? And Captain Delgado, it's lovely to have you for an escort."

"Thank you, m'lady," the captain said.

The trio walked down the long hallway that connected the rooms, the captain leading and Rocco bringing up the rear. Lisette slowed her pace slightly to walk closer to Rocco.

"I hear we are to have guests at dinner, a Spanish nobleman and his wife. Any idea who they are?"

"I only know it is Count de Mendoza, his wife, and their daughter and son-in-law," Rocco replied.

"Truly, I'd love to meet them, but I fear the duke expects the evening's entertainment to consist of my marriage to his son."

Rocco frowned. "Should you not marry his son?"

"I should not." Lisette chose her words carefully. "Connie and I are friends but are not anxious to marry, not even in name only. And as the father of my child is alive and I believe wants to marry me, I cannot make this match."

"You are not certain that he wants to marry you?"

"It is—complicated. But I shall not marry Connie even if that means I must flee this place."

Captain Delgado interrupted. "Are you encouraging her to escape, Santiago?"

"No sir. We have our orders to stop her if she attempts to run."

They turned the last corner and stood at her door. She pushed it open and stepped inside, followed by Rocco.

"I've been thinking about your magical condition," he said, closing the door. "An—elder—gave me a message for a stranger, a woman. She said I'd know her when I met her. I think it's possible she meant you."

Lisette's heart beat faster. "What did she say?"

"She said, 'The words do not matter. Close your eyes, open your heart, and breathe.'"

"Thank you, Lamya!" Lisette threw her arms around Rocco's neck and kissed him.

His lips were as warm and inviting as the first time, and she had no problem melting into him once again. He stiffened at first but quickly joined her passion and took her face in his hands, cradling her head with his fingers. They stood in the embrace. Time drifted away.

Rocco opened his eyes, pulling his lips from hers. She stood still, letting him go but leaving herself open to his return. His brow furrowed and she could see the confusion and pain in his body.

"M'lady—" He backed toward the door. "The captain and I shall be outside to escort you to dinner."

He left, leaving a smile on Lisette's face. She gazed

after him, pressing her lips with her fingers, reliving every nuance, every touch of his skin, his mouth on hers. When Marisha came in to prepare her bath, she was still glowing from the encounter.

"What happened?" Marisha asked. "You look all dreamy-eyed."

Lisette told her.

"He kissed you?"

"I admit, I did kiss him first, but he joined me wholeheartedly before his confusion stopped him." Lisette chose a burgundy brocade for the evening. "And he gave me a message from the Ancient One, the mamha who will deliver my baby."

Marisha looked suspicious as she poured a bucket of hot water into the tub. "Did this Ancient One tell him to give a message to you?"

"In a way, yes. She sent a message and said he would know who to give it to."

Four women entered, each with one bucket that they added to the tub. Marisha stood, supervising, her hands on her hips. When they left, she spoke again.

"What makes you think he does not tell the message to every woman he meets?"

Lisette shook her head. "It doesn't matter. I know what the message means."

"And what does it mean?" she asked, helping Lisette to lower herself into the hot fragrant water.

"It means I know how to transform now." Lisette smiled. "Now, while I soak the day from my bones, I need you to make a few modifications to my gown and undergarments. I procured a dagger today and will need access to it."

38

Rocco stood at his post, attempting to stay focused and becoming increasingly distracted. As long as Lisette de Lille was near, he would wonder why it felt like firecrackers lighting his skin when she touched him, why her hand felt like it was supposed to be in his. When she spoke about being on the ship, he could almost see her there.

Tonight, she said Lamya's name as if she knew the Ancient One and her magic, and her kiss was like coming home. He knew her lips, knew her arms and her hands and her face. He knew her. Why couldn't he place her?

This spell had gone on long enough. Whatever Ruhee had done to him, it was time to break the enchantment. He needed to push fear aside and learn the truth.

"So." Delgado broke the silence. "What were you doing in the marquise's chambers?"

"I had a matter to discuss with her about Marisha."

"Ah, yes, did you find any proof of Marisha being a spy?"

Rocco shook his head. "The marquise does not know anything beyond Marisha's excellent care as a personal maid.'

"Did you observe the maid leaving the grounds today?"

"No, but I did stop Amoy Simone," Rocco said. "I know she is not on the list, but she goes out of her way not to make friends."

Delgado nodded. "What was her excuse for leaving the grounds?"

"To bring back yams for tonight's dinner, which she did. I noticed that the yams were very clean and not like they had just been harvested. I took a chance, captain, and fed her a piece of gossip."

Delgado leaned forward. "What kind, and how did she react?"

"That the guests at tonight's dinner are planning to overthrow the duke and Mercedes, take over their castles, and install their own lackeys to rule Île des Oiseaux." Rocco smiled. "And she ate it all with gusto."

Delgado laughed and slapped Rocco's shoulder. "Very good! Now we wait to see what your lie produces. Does this mean we give up on Marisha, or should we tell her a different lie to see which one makes it back to Mercedes?"

Rocco shrugged. "Whatever the captain orders. I might suggest we see what this evening holds. The duke has plans, but we do not know the guests, and we do not know what our two unwilling lovebirds will do to stave off this wedding."

"Tis truth, I cannot think of two people less willing to be joined together, and I have seen many marriages based on what was good for Spain."

"I believe a marriage for the good of a country is possibly a better incentive than a marriage for the good of a duke."

"Perhaps, although the duke seems to believe that the marquise's child might belong to his son." Delgado shook his head. "I do not know why he formed that idea."

"I do not know either," a voice behind them said.

Rocco and Delgado whipped about. The marquess was standing behind them with an echo of quick footsteps bursting down the hall. His guards Philippe and Henri caught up with him, panting, hands on the hilts of their swords and ready to draw.

Delgado bowed. "My apologies, Sire. I spoke most out of turn."

Connie waved his apology away. "You are forgiven. My father's delusion was something that the marquise and I created many months ago, and now we pay the price for it. Is she ready?"

"We have not checked," Delgado replied.

Connie pounded on the door. "Lizzie? Are you dressed and ready? We must go thwart Father's plan."

Lisette's voice was faint but clear. "Patience, Connie. I am arranging my hair."

He leaned against the wall. "As you can see, gentlemen, we are most incompatible."

Rocco stifled his laugh but could not avoid a small grin, which elicited a laugh from Connie.

"I realize that you four have been given your orders," Connie said, "but they end at keeping Lizzie and I from running away, yes?"

"Yes, Sire," Delgado replied.

The tall, dark noble studied the guards before approaching Rocco. "You seem like an honorable man."

Rocco gestured to his fellow guards. "No more than these men and possibly less."

"What I mean to say is, you are here to do your job and take your coin. And if I give you a job that does not interfere, accompanied by coin, you might be interested?"

"I cannot help you escape." Rocco's voice was low and firm.

"I would not ask it." Connie looked at all the guards. "I will never ask you to disobey your orders."

Rocco exchanged glances with Delgado and the others. They all shrugged with the exception of Delgado, who nodded.

"What is on your mind, Sire?" Delgado asked.

"Let us be honest men. We know what is on the duke's mind tonight—to marry me off to the marquise, and we know how much Lisette and I are resistant to the plan. One of the guests at dinner is the priest, Tumas, who will perform the ceremony." Connie paused and dropped his voice to a whisper. "I would pay heartily and heavily for the priest to be occupied elsewhere instead of available to fulfill my father's request."

The men stood silent, eyeing each other. They shifted from foot to foot, reluctant to say anything in front of the marquess.

At last Rocco spoke. "So long as you and the marquise did not use it as an opportunity to flee, it might thwart the duke's goal, but it would not be against his orders to us."

"You do realize," Delgado said. "This will not be a final solution. We cannot kill the priest."

A woman's voice interrupted them. "It does not need to be the final solution, good sirs."

They all turned to see Lisette standing at the doorway, the burgundy of her dress lighting her skin and catching dark highlights in her auburn hair. Her green eyes reflected the depth of the dress' hue and gave them the look of emeralds on fire.

Rocco stifled a gasp as a memory hit him, of Lisette

in a golden gown on a balcony, her chin lifted in regal confidence as she faced Mercedes and a young man he didn't recognize. *She was at the wedding when I killed the count.*

"As I was saying, you do not need to make the priest unavailable forever," she said. "Only for this evening. We need but a night's diversion."

Connie took a bag from his pocket and jingled it. It looked and sounded heavy with coin.

"What keeps us from taking your coin and doing nothing?" Henri asked.

Lisette turned to him her expression cold. Her hand slipped into her pocket, through her clothes, to the dagger strapped to her thigh. "If you do, I shall kill you."

The men's eyes widened, although Connie and Rocco smiled.

"Thank you," Connie said, his smile broadening, "for defending my honor."

She shrugged and gave him a small grin. "We shall not wed tonight or any other night, no matter what I have to do."

Connie stepped to her and kissed the top of her head. "Gentlemen, make no mistake. If you agree to this, you swear an oath on your life to carry it out."

Delgado motioned for the others to come close, away from Connie and Lisette.

"We must agree as a group. What say you?"

Henri spoke up. "We could take the money and tell the duke."

"You saw the look on the marquise's face," Rocco said. "And judging from the way she stuck her hand into the folds of her skirt, I should think she has weaponry to back up her promise."

Delgado nodded and turned to Philippe. "What say you?"

Philippe glanced at Henri, and back at Lisette. "I say we cannot take the job, nor the money. There is madness is attempting to kidnap a priest, even sacrilege."

"I must agree." Delgado nodded. "It would result in chaos, and possibly the noose."

They rejoined the couple, and Delgado gave them the unfortunate news.

"It is not unanimous," Delgado said. "If we cannot promise to a man, we dare not attempt to do as you request."

Lisette and Connie looked at each other. Connie shrugged. "Have any other ideas?"

"Just one," Lisette said. "Shall we go to dinner?"

She walked past the group to the stairs, glancing out the window as she went. The evening star was still visible, even as the moon was on the ascent. The guards scurried after her except for Rocco who remained near Connie. His gaze followed the young woman even as he escorted the marquess.

"Lizzie's quite the firebrand, isn't she?" Connie asked.

"If you say so, Sire." Rocco kept his voice even despite the roil of emotions running through him.

"I certainly pity her as a mother." Connie put the bag of coin in his pocket as they walked. "Her child will no doubt inherit her stubborn passion."

"Perhaps the child will take after its father," Rocco suggested.

"I don't know that's much better. According to Lizzie, the baby's father is a blood dragon."

Rocco stopped at the top of the stairs as numbing chills washed over him.

Lisette took a deep breath before making her way into the great hall. It had been decorated gaily, using candles, mirrors, and blooms from the garden. She remembered this room on the night of her birthday, betrothal, and abduction. The last time she was with her family and had a plan for her life—a nice, boring, normal plan. At least the room was not as grand tonight. To see it any more festive than this would rend her soul.

Mouthwatering aromas wafted in from the kitchen, making her stomach gurgle. The growl of her hunger made the baby shift and push out, as if trying to get away from the noise.

Six people stood at the large fireplace, goblets in hand. The duke stood facing the arched entrance to the hall and called to her as soon as he saw her.

"Lisette! Come meet our new neighbors."

She strolled toward them, using her swollen belly as an excuse to slow her feet and delay the inevitable. The visitors turned to look at her. Three of the four appeared to be very high-bred Spanish nobility, with long chins, narrow noses, high cheekbones, and rheumy eyes. The fourth was tall, blond, and blue-eyed. She recognized him at once.

Willem d'Auguste, Eric's younger brother. Of all the d'Auguste family, she always suspected he was the brightest and had the most potential. It was unfortunate that the count and countess fawned over their older son and left the younger to his own devices, although perhaps that was why he was so much smarter.

Standing apart from the group, Tumas kept his eyes down, staring at his goblet.

Lisette walked into their midst, giving them a polite bow of her head accompanied by an apologetic smile. "I'm afraid my balance does not permit a proper curtsy."

Looking at Willem for a hint of recognition, she found none. If he held any animosity toward her, he did not reveal it.

A young girl, well fed in a green-gold gown oversewn with lace and baubles, clutched Willem's forearm, leaning into him. Her expression was one of territorial politeness.

The Duke de Martinmas stepped forward. "Lisette, this is Count Antonio de Mendoza, his wife, Countess Catalina, their daughter Renata, and her betrothed, Willem d'Auguste. And of course, you recall Father Tumas."

"Charmed," Lisette said.

"I understand this is a very special evening," the countess said. "Where is your novio?"

Lisette shot the duke a look of rebellion.

"My Constantine does like to make an entrance," the duke laughed. "In the meantime, Lisette dear, would you like some rum?"

"No thank you, Sire." She placed one hand delicately on her baby bump. "I believe cider will be better for me this evening."

"My dear," the countess said, moving to her side. "Are you well? The duke told us of your condition. It's a pity you and the marquess had to marry under the French flag, but I am honored to witness your lawful ceremony tonight."

Lisette let her hand drift to the dagger at her thigh as she smiled at the duke. "I'm sure Uncle Oscar has told you much. He does like to keep everyone informed."

"I didn't wish to betray your secret." The duke waved his hands as if he conjured a spell. "But why should they not know that you were married asea, on a French galleon?"

Lisette stayed her hand from grabbing her blade and carving him like a suckling pig.

Amoy appeared with a tray containing a single goblet, which she offered to Lisette. "Cider for the marquise?" Her voice dripped with false obeisance.

"Thank you." Lisette took the cup and waved the housekeeper away.

"If my son would make his way here, we could sit down to dinner." The duke looked toward the archway again, frowning.

"Then let us begin." Connie's voice exuded mischief as he appeared behind the group. They turned to see him, and he raised his goblet. "Sorry for the delay, but I passed through the kitchen for a little refreshment."

"So good of you to be here." The duke's mouth twitched.

One of the servants appeared at the large mahogany table. "Dinner is served."

"Excellent," Connie said and held his arm to Lisette. "Shall we?"

As they walked to their places, the duke spoke with

the count. "So, you have lived in Spain your entire life? Lovely. How was your trip down to our island?"

If the count answered, no one was listening, not even the duke.

Connie leaned down to Lisette's ear and whispered, "What's the plan?"

She looked into his eyes and rolled her gaze down to her hand, which still rested on her stomach. "I'm afraid the baby is very active tonight."

He patted her arm. "Poor little mother. Don't overdo it."

"Nor you," she whispered through gritted teeth.

She had taken her seat when she looked up and saw the shadows of guards on the balcony. No doubt the duke had all the exits covered. While she studied the darkness, trying to find Rocco's shadow, she heard voices conversing around her. At some point, she was aware of someone saying her name. She looked to her left, where the duke was staring at her expectantly.

"My apologies," she said. "I am distracted tonight. I fear the baby is restless."

"Of course. I was merely asking if you wanted more potatoes."

Lisette looked down to see her plate heaped with food. "Oh! No, this is adequate, thank you."

The countess sat across from her. "My, yes, m'lord, I doubt if she will be able to eat so much. There is not much room when you are with child."

Lisette smiled at her. "Thank you, countess."

"Please, call me Catalina."

"And you may call me Lisette."

Lisette picked up her fork and regarded her plate. She remembered being in the castle on Isla del Lagarto, having dinner with the Count and Countess de Medina. Her stomach was sick with pregnancy, and she had to force herself to eat the rich meal they had prepared. Now that everything smelled heavenly and her stomach craved it all, she had to pretend that she was too sick to eat it.

She raised a tiny forkful to her lips, nibbled at it, and put it down. Taking a long drink of cider, she looked at everyone eating.

"Marquise Renata, when are your nuptials planned?" she asked.

The young girl lifted her head, looking startled. "A year this summer. There are so many preparations."

"Yes, indeed," Willem added. "I remember my brother's wedding. Everything so organized, so planned."

"Were you at his wedding?" Lisette asked.

His expression grew dark. "No, sadly, or I could have helped him, or at least tried. I had been sent to Versailles to serve in the king's brigade."

Lisette saw no pointedness to his remarks. If he was trying to upset her, he was not trying very hard. She knew he was smarter than that.

"We were there," the countess said, and lowered her eyes. "It is difficult to get the images out of one's head."

Lisette glanced at the duke, who seemed at a loss for words.

"Yes," Connie said, "my father and I attended. It was a day I shall never forget."

The party grew silent, a pall in the air.

Tumas spoke up, his voice light and happy. "Let us look to a better future. Marquess Willem, are you and the marquise being married on the island? If you require a priest, I'd be happy to perform the rituals."

"We aren't certain," Renata said. "We may have sailed back to Spain by then."

Count Antonio looked at his daughter and frowned. "Do not make any such plans, daughter. We have been sent here by the king, and here is where we shall stay."

"You have been sent here, Papa," she countered. "Willem and I still await El Rey's orders."

"So, Willem," Lisette said. "You will now be a part of the Spanish navy?"

Willem's face grew flushed in the candlelight. "My conscription is coming to an end, and as my feelings had grown toward Renata, I thought it best to leave the military life behind and take my place as a nobleman, wherever El Rey assigns me."

"I'm of a certainty that we will all serve the king at his command," the duke said with a wide grin before turning to Lisette. "You need to eat. The baby needs it."

"It is a beautiful plate and smells wonderful, Sire, but I am unable. My apologies. I can barely swallow anything."

"Do not chastise her, m'lord," the countess said. "As a woman who has borne children, I understand her plight."

Lisette had never been so grateful for a stranger's help. "Thank you, Catalina. It is difficult to smell delicious food and yet be so opposed to eating it."

Connie touched her shoulder. "Should you go to your chambers and lie down?"

She rose from her chair gingerly, holding her stomach like it might roll from her body. "I would like to rest—"

"Before you take your leave," the duke interrupted. "Why don't you sit with your cider and wait for us to finish? Then we can have the ceremony before you retire."

"But Sire I—"

"I won't take no for an answer," the duke said. "Sit back and I'll get you more drink."

While the duke rang for the servant, Lisette shot a frustrated glance at Connie. He rolled his eyes in response. She glanced over at Tumas who seemed blissfully involved in eating another helping of everything. Resigned, she stabbed a potato and bit into it, then washed it down with Connie's rum.

The night was quite dark, and Lisette had attempted to leave thrice more times before the guests were ready to leave the table. With each attempt, she shoved one more bite into her mouth, followed by rum. At last, the duke stood.

"I would have preferred a true gala to celebrate my son's wedding, but with the monsoon season upon us and the need to give my grandchild a proper name, I am most grateful that we have new neighbors to join us for this occasion." He refilled his goblet and gestured toward the fireplace. "Shall we gather to witness the ceremony?"

Lisette was the last person to rise. Connie took her by the elbow to help her stand.

"Now what?" he whispered.

She gave him a quick glance before doubling over with a moan. No one paid her any attention—at that moment, there was shouting from the corner of the room.

"I can't find anything!" Tumas burst from behind one of the tapestries.

"What are you talking about?" the duke asked.

"My Bible, my rosary, my crucifix—I cannot perform the ceremony without them." He pointed toward the tapestry. "I had stored them on the bench in this alcove. They're gone!"

Lisette saw her chance and took it. Holding her stomach, she groaned again and clutched Connie's arm. "Sire, Uncle Oscar, please allow me to retire to my chambers. When you find what we need for the wedding, send a servant for me, and I shall return."

The duke frowned but nodded. "Captain of the guard!"

Delgado appeared from the balcony. "Yes, Sire."

"You and another guard, escort the marquise to her chambers and stand watch until you are relieved."

"Yes, Sire." Delgado gestured as he moved toward Lisette. "Guardsman Santiago."

Rocco stepped forward. With a guard at each side, they guided her to the stairs. She shuffled along, making her apologies to the visitors.

"Please forgive my manners. I believe I need to lie down for a while." She glared at the duke. "The rich food does not agree with the baby."

A shiny object caught her eye and she glanced over at Rocco. Tucked into his jacket, a small corner of silver crucifix peeked out. She looked over at the captain and saw the edge of a Bible in his jacket. "I'm certain I shall feel well enough for the ceremony when the good Father has found his items."

The duke opened his mouth to speak, but the countess interrupted. "Do rest, dear Lisette. Childbearing is an exhausting duty."

Lisette smiled and walked to the stairs, where the guards folded one of their arms behind her waist and steadied her hands with the other, supporting her as she climbed each step.

"Thank you, gentlemen," she said with a tiny smirk. "I am more grateful than I can say."

The guards kept their eyes forward without answering. When they reached her door, she turned to them.

"Although in truth you did not disobey the duke's orders, I do not think he will be happy to discover what you have done. You must put the objects back, perhaps in another alcove to avoid punishment."

Delgado patted his jacket. "Once they find these, they will recall you to fulfill the ceremony."

She smiled. "By that time, it will not matter."

An odd expression crossed the captain's face. "M'lady, we are to keep you from escaping, but I hope you are not considering anything…permanent."

"What? No!" She shook her head. "Captain, life is not always bright and joyful, but it is always worth living. As for keeping me from escaping—" She looked at Rocco. "There are some things you may not be able to prevent."

Opening her door, she bade them both a goodnight. The captain wore a look of concern. Rocco's expression was less clear. As she stepped inside, he pushed the door open.

"M'lady, I must have a word."

Lisette moved away from the door, and he entered, closing the door behind him.

"Yes, Santiago—or may I call you Rocco now?"

"It barely matters." He shook his head and stared at her. "Lisette—Lizzie—I have been placed under a spell, one that has caused me to forget what I believe to be people and events important to me. You tell me you have crewed on my ship, and you know much about me and my men. It's possible the spell made me forget you. Tonight, I learned that your child is fathered by a man who is a blood dragon. I must know—who is the man?"

Lisette opened her mouth to blurt, he is you! Instead, she studied him for a moment. He still had no memory of her. Telling him what he should remember might not produce the result she desired. She couldn't force-feed him stories of their love if he didn't feel it in his heart.

"I will put it to you this way." She took his hand and placed it on her stomach. "This is Alara. She may be able to answer your question."

Lisette watched Rocco's face as his hand touched her stomach. The baby shifted about, poking a hand toward her back, a foot into her ribs, until settling. She could tell that Rocco felt the baby's movements, but there was nothing special about them.

At last, Alara's hand reached for Rocco's. The sweet, high voice came to her as before.

Yes, Mama, I am holding Papa's hand, Alara told her. *He is still under the spell of that awful woman. I am angry with her.*

Lisette could feel a heat rising up in her that she could not control. It radiated from her stomach and the baby, quickening her heart, and stifling her breath. She looked up at Rocco, perspiration at her temples, her legs growing weak. Rocco still stood caressing her stomach, pushing back against the small hand that reached toward him. He did not appear to notice Lisette, as a look of troubled understanding washed over his face.

"I was on a balcony." His words did not seem to be aimed at anyone. "There was blood. My hand was on a gown, and I heard, 'Here is your child.'"

He's remembering, Alara told Lisette.

The internal heat subsided as Lisette reached for Rocco's arm, attempting not to collapse. He helped her to the chaise, and she laid back, her arms wrapped around her stomach. Rocco knelt by her side.

"The baby…" she whispered.

"Is the baby all right?"

She nodded, wondering how much to tell him. "She is fine, but I must have Lamya's care. This baby is not like other children."

"I have my orders," he said.

Lisette looked outside. The moon hung bright, almost to the point of fullness. "The moon will not allow you to follow me. I am not bound by the waning crescent."

Rocco stood and reached into his pocket. He withdrew the feather. "I had not heard this story."

"Nor had I." She looked at the plume and pointed to the sharp end. "Do be careful with the tip. I believe there is magic in the shaft, at least there is in a blood dragon's feather. I discovered it the hard way."

He studied the feather, twirled it, and stuck it back into his pocket with a little more care. "What are we to tell the duke?"

"You and the captain will not hang. I will leave him a note." Lisette sat up. "I am better now. Let me escort you to the door. You have work to do, and so do I."

He helped her up from the chaise. She smiled and walked to the door without trouble. As she touched the handle, he put his hand on hers.

"Lamya told me I would regain my memory," he

said. "Tell Alara that soon I shall remember all."

Lisette stretched up, laying her cheek against his. "I know," she whispered as she let her lips brush his face.

He gazed into her eyes, and she drank it in, committing every detail of this moment to her memory. At last, he smiled and nodded, removing his hand from hers. She opened the door.

"Thank you, Guardsman Santiago. You've been most helpful."

After shutting the door behind her, she removed her gown and threw a simple cotton skirt and blouse over her slip before adding the robe Lamya gave her. She strode to her writing desk and sat, inked her pen, and crafted a letter.

My dear Uncle Oscar,

I do apologize for my exit, however I wish to be clear—my guards could not have prevented my escape unless they grew wings. You made me a promise to return me to the mamha to deliver my child. I fear the hour grows close and I cannot delay any longer. I also made a promise to return to Île des Oiseaux with my child, and I plan to make good on my word.

If you absolutely must have more explanation than this, I suggest speaking with Father Tumas. He is a wealth of information, and you can show him this letter if he is hesitant.

As always,

Lisette de Lille, Marquise

Sealing the letter with her crest, she left it on the mantle and took her ceramic dragon to the balcony. The night sky was cloudless, but the stars and moon kept it from being dark. She sat upon the hard stone and recalled Lamya's message from Rocco.

The words do not matter. Close your eyes, open your heart, and breathe.

Lisette stared at the dragon in front of her, breathing. Her ribs expanded, narrowed, expanded again. Closing her eyes, she allowed her love for Rocco and Alara to swell within her. She would do anything for them. They were her very heart.

Warmth flooded her limbs when she heard a knock at the door, followed by the creaking of hinges. She glanced back and saw Rocco and Luis enter. Too late to stop the process, the heat of change came like an explosion sparking in her body. Audience or no, she was now a dragon. Spreading her wings, she wanted to circle back and say farewell to Rocco, but time was precious. She was still wary of changing back in the middle of the sea. If she wanted to get to Lamya, she needed to fly now and fly quickly.

Setting out in a southeast direction, Lisette lifted herself as high as possible, finding drafts of air to save her strength and move her along. Île des Anciens was between Isla de la Soledad and Isla de la Ballena. She decided to fly south toward Soledad before turning east to Lamya. If she changed into human form, it would be best to be close to land.

The night air was cooler than normal. The temperature of the islands was always on the tropical side, but she had lived here so long, even a slight drop was noticeable. A steady breeze brushed against her, and she wished it was blowing her toward Lamya instead of away from her.

As she flew, she wondered about the baby inside her. Had she turned into a dragon as well, or was it still a human form that grew?

Alara's anger at Ruhee frightened her. Conversations with her unborn daughter might be hallucinations, but physical heat that threatened to roast her like a goose was not all in her head. Lisette would have to convince her dear girl to forgive.

Of course, she'd have to forgive as well. She wasn't certain what Ruhee had done. Lisette did not believe she acted with malice, she was such a sweet girl and valiant fighter. But sometimes even sweet girls made unwise choices.

Soon she recognized the coast of Isla de la Soledad. The last time she visited here, she had killed Viscount Barragan and escaped back to *L'Implacable*. It was the first of many detours that dropped her off at this place, pregnant, unwed, and a dragon. One river, many streams. Her eyes popped wide.

One river, many streams,

Paths are chosen, feeding dreams.

The words—she remembered the words that Lamya chanted. Lisette finally had the key to her transformation. Even if she accidentally turned into a human, she had the words to transform back again.

She flew a little lower, to look at the island. It was much like the others in this archipelago, with a well-defined shoreline and verdant inland. In the moonlight, Lisette could see the pattern of a dark green center, lightening in hue as it spread outward to the whiteness of the sandy beaches. She readjusted her path to head east. It was her biggest risk of the long night, to cross the ocean between Isla de la Soledad and Île des Anciens.

Lamya, I am on my way.

She sensed the first damp cloud behind her. Turning her head, she saw a darkness rolling from the west. A squall raced across Isla de la Soledad. It would catch her well before she arrived at Île des Anciens. Her only choice was to rise higher and attempt to fly above the storm, or dip down, where she'd receive the brunt of the rain but survive if she were knocked out of the sky.

She stopped midair and looked at the oncoming clouds. They were high and rolling up as they advanced. Rising above them might not be possible.

Hang on, Alara. She dove toward the sea.

Her wings were aching from flying so far, but she

could not afford to rest. She swept them forward and down, folded them back, swept them again, trying to use sheer power to cut through the wind and stay ahead of the storm. The wind angled north and pushed her sideways. She fought to retain her bearings and stay on course.

In the far distance her eyes detected a dot on the water. This might be Île des Anciens. Lisette turned her body toward the dot and pumped her wings, rising and swerving in the wind to try to find a clear path without resistance. It was no use. The squall was coming, and it would blow where it would.

I shall have to ride it out. She sat herself on the water. Her wings remained open to provide stability to her body, and she dipped her tail down, hoping it might serve as a rudder. Although her feathers were waterproof, she was not as buoyant as a duck. She pumped her legs in order to remain upright as well as move toward the island.

The squall hit like squalls do—sheets of water that pounded her body as the wind whipped in every direction at once. The sea peaked around her, shoving her forward and sideways while the rain pummeled her from above. Flapping her wings was like trying to push them underwater, and for a moment she thought she had turned upside-down. The storm stalled, concentrating its fury on her.

Tucking her neck down, she wrapped her wings around her head so that she could at least breathe without taking water down her throat. Her legs slowed their pumping to just enough to stay afloat, and her tail swayed. Closing her eyes, she said a prayer to Mary for the safety of her child. A wave washed over her, pushing her under, how far she didn't know but she might touch bottom soon. Four strong limbs and two wings pumped desperately for air.

Rolling upright, she flapped her wings harder, attempting to lift herself despite the pounding water. The storm was too heavy to allow her flight, but she was able to pull to the surface and dog-paddle toward the island. She could finally see the coastline, and waves were drawing her closer instead of tossing her in every direction.

I'm almost there. Good thing I'm not human yet.

Within two strokes of her wings, the burning flash granted what she did not wish for. Lisette extended her arms and swam toward the large shadow, now backlit by the dawn.

She heard the wave before she felt it, coming behind her with a mighty roar. The impact pushed her into the sand below, and her leg scraped on something sharp. Kicking and thrusting, she swam toward the top, only to be pulled sideways by the undertow. She changed her course and rode with the current, still climbing for the surface.

Finally, her face felt the night breeze and her lungs brought in air. She righted herself and floated, looking for the island. The undercurrent had pulled her off-course so that she had to swim back to where the waves could help her. Her body was exhausted, and she just wanted to rest and breathe, but she had time to do neither.

With her last bit of strength, she swam at an angle back toward the island, calling to Lamya for help.

Rocco came out of Lisette's chambers and looked at Luis.

"She, uh, wanted me to move furniture," he said.

Luis stared at him. "You look as though you've seen a spirit."

"No." Rocco managed to shake his head. "I don't know. Maybe I did."

"In the meantime, we need to return these things to the priest." Luis patted his jacket. "Without getting caught, and without having the marquise slip by us."

"She won't slip by," Rocco murmured. "We'll know when she's gone."

"What?"

"I mean—" Rocco looked at him. It would be no use to tell him until he could see for himself. "Why don't you give me the Bible, and I'll put everything back while you stand guard?"

"I don't want you to take all the risk. It was my idea."

"Yes, but I don't want you to blame me when the marquise escapes. I promise I am not helping her to flee." Rocco held his hand out.

"Where would she go?" Luis chuckled. "She cannot climb over the balcony while she's so big with child. Unless there are secret entrances in her chamber…"

"It will be no secret," Rocco said and took the Bible from Luis. "I will return as quickly as I can."

Tucking the Bible away, Rocco hurried down the stairs and to the giant veranda outside the great hall. He slipped behind a large planter, drawing himself up to squeeze into the space. A small door behind the pot led to one of the alcoves. The problem was whether the alcove was occupied at the moment, something he would not know until he pushed it open.

Turning back to the planter, he cleared a spot in the foliage and placed the priest's belongings in the soil, against the trunk. Relieved of his stolen goods, he replaced the greenery to make it look undisturbed.

He reached for the door and saw the dirt on his hands and nails. It would be a pity to find this fine hiding place and be betrayed immediately by dirty hands. He returned to the hall, staying in the shadows, and moving toward the stairs while the rest of the guards combed through furniture. Tumas sat at the table, still eating while following the search with interest.

"Guard!" The Duke de Martinmas' call made every man in the hall stop and turn. "Not you, get back to work!" He pointed at Rocco. "You!"

Rocco stepped forward, "Yes, Sire."

"Aren't you assigned to watching the marquise? Why are you here?"

"That is my assignment, Sire. The marquise sent me

down with the message that she is feeling much better. She knew you were concerned about her health."

Rocco's answer seemed to placate him. "Yes, I am very concerned. But I don't want her left unguarded."

"No, Sire. My captain is on the lookout, and I shall return now to stand with him."

The duke narrowed his eyes and studied Rocco. "Come closer. You look familiar to me."

Rocco remembered the duke's bleating appeals to keep him alive on *El Gallo Blanco*. "Do I, Sire? I was a guard for Count Barragan on Isla de la Soledad. Perhaps that is where we crossed paths."

The two men stood, eyeing one another for a few moments. At last, the duke nodded. "Yes. Yes, that must be where I saw you. Very well, get back to your post. And thank the marquise for her message."

Rocco strode to the turret and ascended the stairs, making certain his dirt-encrusted hands were out of sight. He arrived at Lisette's door to see Luis watching for him.

"How did it go?"

"I need to clean up the evidence." Rocco held out his hands.

"Good. Perhaps the marquise has water and soap for you." Luis knocked on the door before taking the handle and cracking it open. "Marquise? M'lady?"

Rocco stood behind him, listening for Lisette's voice. All was silent. Luis glanced back at Rocco, frowning, and opened the door all the way. The two men stepped inside.

"Lis—" Rocco was startled by a flash of light on the balcony.

Luis fell back against the wall, as they both watched a pale blue horse-sized beast stand, look at them with a snort, and extend its wings. Pushing off the balcony with its hind legs, it ascended into the sky and flew away.

Rocco glanced over at Luis, still backed against the

wall, mouth hanging open.

"Captain?" Rocco tried to get his attention.

Luis lifted his hand, pointed his finger. "Did you see—did you see that? What was it?"

"That was a dragon, Captain."

Luis uttered a high hysterical laugh. "A dragon? There are no such things as dragons."

"Perhaps not," Rocco said, "but you just saw one."

"Did it eat the marquise?"

Rocco's laughter stopped when he saw Luis' horrified expression. "No, Captain. What you—what *we* saw was the marquise. If you are willing to believe your own eyes, I will explain it to you."

Luis lowered his hand and crossed himself. "I scarcely see how this can be explained, except through sorcery and the devil."

"It might be both or neither, I do not know. I know that this dragon has saved my life, plus the lives of others, so I am not quick to judgment."

"This is not something I have dealt with, as sailor or guard." Luis looked at Rocco. "What are we to do now? I do not relish telling the duke that the marquise has 'turned into a dragon and escaped.' He will declare us mad and throw us into the stocks."

"He may throw us in the stocks, but he will not declare us mad." Rocco walked past Lisette's bed to her washbasin. Pouring a bit of water over his hands, he picked up soap and scrubbed the dirt. "Let us say dragons are not unknown to him."

He had just dried his hands when quick steps were heard outside the room. Tumas strode in, holding his Bible out like a prize.

"Look, we found my sacred objects. Where's Lisette? We can begin the ceremony."

Rocco and Luis looked at each other. Luis sighed. "There's a problem, Father."

Tumas frowned.

"Do you remember our meeting on the beach?" Rocco asked.

A look of wide-eyed understanding crossed Tumas' face. "You mean she…"

"Transformed," Rocco said.

Tumas sat, hard, on the chaise. "I did not think I believed it when I saw it happen before."

"You saw it, too?" Luis asked. "I thought I was going mad."

"Yes, my son, it is an indescribable thing to see, an immense act of magic." Tumas lowered his head. "I should think she called on Satan, but she protected us against Mercedes' soldiers who were trying to kill us."

"She left a note." Rocco held up the sealed letter. "It is addressed to the duke."

"We must tell him," Luis said. "It is a task I do not relish."

"Let me make the announcement," Rocco told him. "If he takes his wrath out on anyone, I would spare you."

Luis smiled and patted Rocco's shoulder. "You are a good man, but I am the ranking guardsman. For better or ill, it is my job to do."

The trio exited the room and headed downstairs where the duke paced the great hall. The Mendoza family sat by the fire with Connie, goblets in hand, sharing conversation and laughter. Luis held his hand out to Rocco who nodded and gave him the letter. Setting his back ramrod straight, Luis strode to the duke.

"Sire, I have disturbing news to report." Luis said. "Guardsman Santiago and I opened the marquise's door to find her…she was…I saw her…"

"By the gods, man, spit it out." The duke's face reddened.

"Lisette de Lille has turned into a dragon and flown away," Rocco announced.

The duke's red complexion paled as his eyes bulged from his face. "What?"

The rest of the party stood when they heard the news, their mouths open.

"Here is a letter for you, Sire." Luis thrust it at the duke. "From the marquise."

The countess gasped and put her hand to her chest, falling backward. Her husband caught her, easing her into the nearest chair where he fanned her face and offered her drink.

Connie rushed to his father and read over his shoulder. He patted his father's back. "Oh, well, this isn't so bad. She's just gone off to have her baby and will be back as soon as she can."

The Mendoza family huddled together, the count attempting to calm his rattled wife, and Willem comforting a crying Renata.

"I think an explanation is in order," the count said, scowling. "What kind of noblewoman transforms into a beast? It is of the devil."

The countess crossed herself at his words.

Tumas held his Bible aloft. "It is certainly magic and like nothing we have ever witnessed. I, too, condemned it as witchcraft when I saw her transform with my very eyes."

"Of course, Father, she should be executed—" the countess began.

"But." Tumas interrupted and stared at the group until they quieted. "I am now less anxious to burn her at the stake, and more curious as to how this is and what it means. Yes, it is unusual, and some would say demonic to take another form, especially a dragon. I believe some of you have experience with a dragon that took lives and caused tragedy."

They all nodded except Rocco, standing cautiously at the edge of the group.

Tumas continued. "I was able to observe this incarnation of the marquise. The dragon was docile and defended me against Mercedes de Medina's guards, sent to capture and imprison me for helping Lisette de Lille escape. Not that the marquise needed my help."

"I can attest to the priest's account," Rocco said. "I, too, was attacked by the guards. The dragon did not defend us with tooth and claw as much as she used her body to protect us from their swords and daggers."

"But, Father, she is—unholy." The countess' voice carried the outrage of religious sanctity. "And to think I felt sorry for the girl!"

"The older I get the more mysteries I find in this life." Tumas smiled. "Unholy? Yes, by our Christian values. But her actions—protection, nurture—are not those of a demon. I have been given authority in the Church, but I choose not to use it now. I'll not judge Lisette de Lille."

"Sacrilege!" The countess huffed and stomped her foot. "Antonio, call for the carriage! I shall not stay another moment."

"Oh, please stay," the duke said. "Little known fact— I was aware that the child was not Connie's, but I took pity on the poor young woman. Her family is dead, and this castle was once theirs. She appealed to my sympathy and told me she was willing to raise her child as a Martinmas heir."

"Did you know of this—ability of hers to turn into a *dragon*?" the count asked.

"I did not." The duke's tone was firm.

Connie regarded his father with a questioning look. Rocco watched them both, smiling. The duke was certainly versed in telling a version of events that made him look best. In truth, he did not know Lisette could turn into this kind of dragon. He only knew her previous talent for transformation.

"Let me call for your carriage," the duke said with a smile. "While it is being brought, have one more glass of port. We all need something to calm ourselves." He nodded at a servant to bring another round of drink. Calling to Rocco, he said, "Guardsman…what is your name? No matter, inform the livery that the count requires his carriage."

Rocco saluted and left. He was relieved to be away from those people. Hysterical, consumed with religious hypocrisy. People who had never encountered the true wonders of this world, and priests who had perpetuated the belief that there was no godly magic left.

I guess no one is allowed to turn water into wine

anymore.

His thoughts turned to Lisette and their encounter in her room. When he placed his hand on her, he had no expectations. He and his wife had not wanted children immediately after their wedding—had he known Tempest would be taken from him so soon, he would have hurried the calendar, had as many children as they could.

Feeling the roll of new life within a woman was like nothing he'd experienced. He was entranced by the movement and wondered how it would be to lay his head on her stomach and whisper to this baby. The baby had other notions, however. The hand that pushed to meet his was firm and intentional. And when the spoken words formed within his head, he nearly jumped back in amazement.

Papa, it's me, Alara, a tiny girl's voice had said. *I know you don't remember, and you may not believe but I am your daughter and someday you will understand. Mama needs to visit Lamya, but we will return and help you.*

The memory made him shiver. Had Lisette heard the same voice? Was he going mad?

"Possibly," he said, surprised at speaking aloud.

"Possibly what?" Another voice startled him even more. He'd arrived at the stables. An ornate coach sat in front, and a pair of fine grays stood at the trough, comfortably asleep. Men in white breeches and blue jackets sat around a table, cards in hand.

"The count requests his carriage be brought around."

One of the strangers looked at the sky. "Seems like an early evening."

Rocco shrugged. "I couldn't say. I was just sent with the message."

The driver and footman rose from their seats at a speed known as dawdling. They strolled to the horses and made their way toward the harnesses and carriage. Rocco left them to their task and returned to the castle, going through the kitchen to find sustenance. Marisha sat at the servants' table, picking at a chicken leg.

Rocco found a plate and helped himself to what was on the table. A pitcher of cider sat near Marisha, but he rooted around in the larder and found rum. He poured two goblets and sat down, sliding one across to the young woman.

"You look like you need this," he said. "I assume you've heard the news."

She nodded. "I am still waiting for the duke to order my head on a stake."

"Why? You were nowhere near her chambers."

"No, but I knew she was going to do it." Marisha took a swig of rum. "Yes, this is what I need."

Rocco leaned forward. "How did you know?"

She glared at him. "This was your fault. You 'gave her a message' from someone. She told me that she knew how to transform."

"The duke does not need to know that." Rocco shrugged.

"She also told me you kissed her."

"She kissed me."

Marisha sat up straight, her arms crossed. "You kissed back."

"Why wouldn't a man return such a favor?" Rocco managed a small grin. The kiss had brought a stream of shadowy memories, pieces of dreams not quite put into their correct order.

"Santiago!" One of the guards strode into the kitchen. "Captain Delgado wants to see you in the great hall."

Obliging, Rocco rose and gave a small nod to Marisha. "Enjoy the rum, and do not volunteer what no one asks for."

43

Lisette awoke, sweating and aching in full blistering sunshine, and entirely human. Her robe draped across most of her body, saving her from sunburn but drenching her in perspiration. She pushed up to look around, pulling her robe up to check her leg. Whatever she scraped it on last night, did not leave more than a rash.

She was on a tiny patch of dark sand, cradled by heavy brush and mangrove roots. The sea stretched out in front of her, as blue and clear as if the previous night had never happened. Behind her was wild growth that seemed impenetrable. She had arrived at Île des Anciens.

"Well, I'm here," she told the water. "Now what?"

She stood and stretched, pondering how to find Lamya, and listening to her growling stomach. This was not the friendliest of isles unless you knew how to utilize its magic. The small cove she had entered with Begum

Derya was on the southeast side of the island. As far as she could tell from looking at the sun, she was on the northeast side.

"I'll fly up," she said, and sat back down, looking at the water. She knew the words now, and recited them, focusing on transformation. *One river, many streams...I am a dragon.*

Nothing happened. She closed her eyes and repeated the process over and over until she was dizzy from the heat.

"What is wrong with me?" she shouted. "I'm doing the same thing I did last night!"

Huffing, she stood and reached for a large mangrove root to her right, hefting her body across. She would have to find that inlet. Traveling with a baby could be difficult but traveling with a baby that was still inside her protruding stomach added more complexity to the problem. Still, she could not stay on the beach. She needed to at least find the trail before dark.

The sun was relentless and though there was brush, there was no shade. Lisette followed the coastline, stepping over roots, crawling under vines, and even paddling through water, exhausted and starving but determined to find the trailhead.

The last golden rays flickered on the sea by the time Lisette found what she was searching for. She almost missed it. The trail was a small slip of dirt between overlapping mangroves. Halfway across a tangle of roots, she looked back and saw it.

Being able to stand and walk was a relief. She stretched skyward for a moment, one arm caressing her stomach. The baby kicked at her hand.

"I know, Alara. I too am tired and hungry, but we must find Lamya."

Setting out, she made every stride count as she hurried down the path. She recalled her first trip, and the way Begum would stop and look for signs. At the first fork, Lisette thought she remembered going right, but that led to a dead end. She backtracked to the trail and went left, worrying that night was falling, and she hadn't found a place to sleep.

The sun was perilously close to gone when she came to the next fork. She raised up on her tiptoes, looking through the trees, trying to see something familiar. There was nothing. Closing her eyes, she heard something she'd heard before. Water running.

Lisette turned toward the water and picked up her pace. She was almost running when she saw the soft white sand and dark shine of a lagoon. Collapsing to her knees at the edge of the water, she scooped her hands in and brought them over her face, cooling herself and letting droplets hit her parched lips.

Shadows surrounded her when she went searching for firewood. The rising moon was full and would soon light her way, but the sooner she lit the fire, the sooner she could find and roast a yam or two for dinner.

Using her blade and a rock against dried grasses, she quickly had a cozy flame. Yams were easily found, and she relaxed while they cooked, trying to ignore her hunger pangs. The moon was peeking over the cliffs of the island when she was finally at peace, eating the sweet vegetables and snuggled into a moss bed.

She studied the stars, still visible as they competed with the moon for attention. Alara stretched and rearranged herself and Lisette patted her stomach to reassure her.

"Tomorrow we shall find Lamya."

"Why wait?" A velvety voice spoke out of the darkness.

Lisette sat up and saw the Ancient One strolling toward the fire. She was not as Lisette saw her last, a nurturing old mamha sent to coax a new baby into the world, neither was she the tall warrior-goddess of their first meeting. This Lamya was an island woman, wide-faced and wide-hipped, with sun-kissed skin, swaying to her own music. She carried a large hemp bag slung over her shoulder.

"I do wish you looked the same each time," Lisette said. "How do I know this is the real Lamya?"

"My, we have developed a sharp tongue since we last met. Perhaps you did not understand me the first time. I take the form required, but you are the one who chooses the form."

Lisette frowned. "I choose?"

"Not with your mind, child." Lamya sat at the fire and pulled out a skin bag to warm over the flame. She tapped her chest. "With your heart."

"Whoever you are, I am so glad to be here with you. I have been lost without your guidance."

Lamya smirked. "Have you really?"

"Yes, I don't know how to transform into a dragon."

"And yet you did, yes?"

"Well, mostly, but only after Rocco gave me your message, and I failed this morning when I tried to transform. And I still cannot control my change back into a human."

Lamya waved her hand dismissively. "That is not important."

"It's pretty important when I'm flying over the sea, and I suddenly pop back into my human body." Lisette scowled. "And what of Alara? I need you to help me with her guidance. I'm not certain if she will be a good person or an evil dragon."

Lamya laughed. "Has Alara been acting poorly?"

"Not horribly so." Lisette recalled Alara's anger. "She is quite opinionated and headstrong. If she is both willful and a dragon, I do not know how to mother such a child.”

“By being a dragon.”

Lisette sighed. “I do not feel up to the challenge.”

“Of course, you are not,” Lamya told her. “We are never up to the challenge until we meet it. Then we do it, and we look at it from the other side and can say, yes, we did this impossible thing.”

Lamya handed the warmed bag to Lisette. “Here, drink. It will soothe you and your baby.”

The bag was filled with the warm nourishing broth Lisette remembered from her torturous days of blood dragon training. She took it and drank heartily. It lifted her spirits as it filled her stomach. Alara also seemed to like it and settled to sleep immediately.

Lamya took the bag. “Sleep now. In the morning we have much to do.”

Lisette settled back into the moss and draped her arm around her stomach. She closed her eyes and nestled into the luxury of Lamya’s silken bedding. Sighing, she drifted away and dreamt of Rocco until morning.

By the sun’s first light, Alara was restless, and her movements made it impossible for Lisette to sleep. She sat up, stretched, and yawned.

Lamya sat at the fire, stirring something in a pot on the flames. “I would tell you to sleep more, but it does not seem that the child agrees with me.”

“Alara feels entitled to an opinion about much of my life.” Lisette stood and pointed to the pot. “That smells delicious. Do I have time to rinse the salt from my body before breakfast?”

Lamya kept stirring, keeping her eyes on the pot. With her other hand, she gestured toward the lagoon, a sly grin working at the corners of her mouth. “Refresh yourself, unless Alara thinks it unwise.”

“She can fuss if she wants,” Lisette walked to the lagoon, stripping her clothes off as she went. “But the little mother is going to wash up before breakfast."

Unlike the Lagoon of Becoming, this water didn't try to drown Lisette. It invited her in, promising renewal. She floated quietly from one side to the other, rolling over a few times to get wet when her skin got too hot. Alara remained quiet—clearly, she approved. Once she was sufficiently restored, Lisette climbed from the water, slipped back into her clothes and rejoined her mentor.

"Eat." Lamya held out a bowl which Lisette gratefully took. The roots and grains Lamya served were always filling, delicious, and unique.

"I cannot think of a single food from any kitchen that tastes anything like what you prepare," Lisette told her.

Lamya shrugged. "I am part of the ancient ways in all things. Even food."

"Seems very plain and yet it is very good."

"You are very hungry." Lamya put down her bowl and closed her eyes, chanting in a quiet voice.

Lisette finished her meal and put her bowl with Lamya's.

Lamya opened one eye and stopped chanting. "What are you doing?"

"My apologies for interrupting. I was merely placing our dirty bowls together."

Lamya frowned. "And why would I want your bowl?"

"You…always take my bowl." Lisette frowned at her, confused. "What else should I do with it?"

"You take both bowls and wash them out." Lamya's voice was stern. "You take the pot, too. You are a mother, not a house pet."

"Please, Lamya, I know I am treated as a house pet at the castle, but I have also scrubbed decks and foraged for food and built my own fire." Lisette was scowling now, her anger rising. "Ask me to clean the dishes and I shall. You of all people know how to give me a command, instead of scolding me for not reading your mind."

The Ancient One smiled so wide Lisette worried her face might split in half. "That is a good start. If you can scold me, someone who has the power to make your life better or worse, then you can be a mother to your daughter."

"Apologies for my outburst, although I don't know how you could make my life worse. It's not that wonderful at the moment."

"Pfft, do no scoffing at what you have. You are healthy. Your daughter is healthy. Her father is alive—and healthy. There are solutions to your problems."

Lisette nodded. It was of no use to argue with Lamya. "I shall clean the dishes."

She returned to see Lamya push her hand toward the flames of the fire, which immediately dropped to embers.

Another gesture from the Ancient One pulled sand from the ground and covered the ashes, dousing the fire for good.

Lisette smiled.

"What is so amusing?" Lamya asked.

"The use of magic. It is not something people see often, if ever."

Lamya huffed. "Their own folly. Magic would make them gods in their minds, and they cannot have gods if they worship the Holy Trinity."

"Doesn't magic make you godlike?"

"Of course. Why do people fear being godlike? Does not your creation story tell you that God made man in his image?"

"I am no one to discuss religion with." Lisette held up a hand and counted on her fingers. "I am a pirate and a dragon, I have killed more than once, I am a wanton woman who laid with a man not her husband and carries his bastard child. Perhaps most importantly, I have no shame or regret for what I've done. I am fairly certain a rosary would burst into flames at my touch."

"Come." Lamya packed her bag and slung it over her shoulder. "We have much to do."

Lisette followed her down the path toward the center of the island. It did not take long before she saw the Dragon's Breath, rising tall to the north and covered in bright red and yellow flowers. She looked down at her prominent belly, rubbing it.

"You do realize I cannot climb up there at the moment?" she asked.

"I am an Ancient One, not a Stupid One."

They walked towards the plateau, tall with straight sides and a flat top. As they got closer, Lamya chose a path to the left, around the back. Their trail went slightly uphill, curving a little, and was shaded by flowering trees that intertwined at the top. Lisette laughed.

"Our trek is funny?" Lamya asked.

"Our trek is funny," Lisette repeated, "because I climbed a mountain I could have walked up, except that I had to climb it at the time."

Lamya laughed.

Once they reached the top, they proceeded to the Lagoon of Becoming. Lisette unfastened her robe, preparing to take her clothes off.

"You are not going in the Lagoon today," Lamya said. "Come. We go to the other side."

She led Lisette to a clearing surrounded by orchids of every shade, blue to fuchsia, with scents of spice and freesia. The sand was almost black. Lisette looked about, trying to take in all the beauty.

"I keep thinking I have seen the most beautiful parts of this place," she said. "Is this the endless variety of the magic?"

"Nature is all magic," Lamya told her. "It is difficult for me to say which flower was wished for and which just grew."

She led Lisette to the edge of the clearing, and two wide shelves that faced one another, made of tree and vine and flower, as if the foliage had knitted itself together to form chairs. Lamya gestured to the one facing north, while she sat opposite. Lisette scooted awkwardly into the vast seat and tucked her legs around her as best she could.

"Now then," Lamya said. "Tell me about each of your moon dragon transformations."

"Even the one on *Dişi Aslan*?"

"Every. One."

"On the ship, I kept having visions of a small child who called herself Alara which disturbed me. Of truth I did not believe I was with child. I had nearly accepted the fact when she appeared to warn me, and I immediately changed. The next time…"

Lisette went in detail over each time. Lamya sat, silent until she was finished.

"And when you transformed back to a human?" she asked.

"Always at the wrong time and in the wrong place." Lisette described each time she needed to stay a dragon a little longer, or a little less, and either changed, or did not. "It's almost as if as soon as I hope I don't transform I do. Each time I want to transform, I can't."

"Each time?"

"Except for the time I was attacked by the robber." Lisette shook her head. "It happened so quickly I almost didn't believe it. He hit me and I turned, killed him, and turned back."

Lamya smiled. "That is the key."

"How?"

"The moon dragon appears when you need it." Lamya's tone was maternal, explaining to a child. "It is not something you think about, not something of the mind but of the heart."

"I transformed when I needed to protect someone, like my baby."

"Yes, but that is a small part of it. Hmm, how to explain...Your power is tied to knowing who you are, and what you want. You transform when you know you must be a dragon. You have learned to do this."

"But when I try to return to human form, I can't." Lisette frowned. "I don't understand."

"You are changing back at the wrong time because you are allowing yourself to doubt."

"Of course, I doubt—I never learned how to change back. Only how to become a dragon."

Lamya shook her head. "You do not learn to transform back. You transform back when the dragon no longer serves you."

Lisette rose from the chair and paced. "But I needed to stay a dragon when I was trying to get back here, and I didn't—I turned human."

"You are not hearing me," Lamya said. "What is in your mind when you changed?"

"That I wanted to keep flying."

"Do not lie. Was that your exact thought?"

"That it would be a bad time to become human, but that is the same thing."

"Sit down." Lamya's tone was not pleased. "That is not the same thing at all."

Lisette sat, frowning.

"You must commit yourself to who you are," Lamya said. "When you are a dragon, you think of being the dragon. When you are ready to change, you commit—"

"To being Lisette de Lille." Lisette finished her thought.

"No. You are always Lisette de Lille, no matter what form your body takes. You must know what you want to be and be that."

"It sounds so easy."

"Oh no." Lamya shrugged. "It can be hard for people to know what they want to be."

Rocco met Luis at the entrance to the hall, noting the grim expression on the captain's face. When Luis stepped back, a large figure emerged from the shadows.

"Ah, yes, Guardsman *Santiago*," The duke said. "I asked the captain to call you here."

"Yes, Sire," Rocco said, maintaining his distance and checking the room for others.

"Little known fact." The duke smiled. "Many things remind me of many things. I may not remember the faces of servants or guards, but I never forget a voice. Especially when that voice belongs to a pirate who was kind enough not to kill me."

"So, you called me here to thank me?" Rocco bowed. "You're most welcome."

"I called you here to have Captain Delgado take you

to a gaol cell. The hour is late, and I need to be fresh tomorrow for your hanging." The duke snapped his fingers. "Captain."

"You are not very appreciative," Rocco said. "Next time I shall not be so generous."

"I will make certain there is no next time," the duke told him.

The captain took Rocco's sword and nodded toward the arched door that led to the balcony. "Let's go."

As they reached the archway, Philippe and Henri stepped out, surrounding them. Philippe drew his sword on Delgado and disarmed the captain.

"Apologies, Captain," Philippe whispered.

"I'm afraid you'll be joining the pirate, Captain Delgado," the duke said. "As an officer who crewed on *El Gallo Blanco*, I would expect you to recognize this brigand."

The four men strode into the night, Rocco and Luis in front, being guided at sword point by the two guards. Rocco glanced at Luis.

"My apologies, Captain. I did not think the duke would remember my face. He seemed too frightened at the time to notice anything."

"We took a chance, my friend," Luis said. "How do you want this to go?"

Rocco glanced about at their surroundings. There were no trees or other opportunities to hide on the path and escape. He casually rubbed his side, looking at Luis and indicating his hidden dagger. Luis scratched at the back of his head, raising his arm to reveal a hilt-shaped lump in his own jacket.

"This is your fault, pirate," Luis said, loud enough for the guards to hear.

Rocco snapped back. "You told me the duke didn't remember you—or me."

"How was I to know he remembered you?" Luis shouted.

"I'm in this mess because of you," Rocco yelled and turned to push the captain.

The captain shoved him in return and soon they were brawling. The guardsmen tossed their swords aside to pull the men apart. When they did, Rocco let go of Luis and turned to the guard. One quick spin of Philippe's shoulders and Rocco had his arm around the man's neck, a dagger threatening his ribcage.

Luis disarmed Henri as well, stripping the keys from him.

"We do apologize, gentlemen," Rocco said as they dumped each guard in a cell. "I promise no harm will come to the duke, but I have a mission to accomplish and cannot be detained. And your captain has done no wrong. He does not deserve the duke's punishment."

"We quite agree," Philippe told him. "Godspeed and good health to you both."

Luis locked the cells and the outer dungeon door, and tossed the keys in a planter. He picked up a sword and handed it to Rocco before retrieving his own.

"Now what?" he asked.

"Now." Rocco pointed away from the dungeon. "I'm headed over that wall and down to the village to find less recognizable clothes." He looked up at the sky. The moon was round and bright. "And then a place to hide and observe my target."

The two men trotted toward the back wall. The moon's glow allowed them to easily find footholds in the stone and soon they were atop and over. Rocco strode toward the village.

Luis followed. "I shall make my way down and see if I can join up with another ship."

"You're a good man, Luis. Do you have family?"

Luis shook his head. "Never had time or use for one.

I always wanted to be at sea.”

“Anxious to get back to a Spanish ship?”

“At this moment, I want to be under sail. I do not care which flag the ship bears.”

Rocco smiled. “I know a ship that could use you. Of course, it sails without country.”

Luis looked at him. “I’ve seen that ship. I was impressed by its maneuvers.”

“Impressed enough to join us?”

“I’d be giving up the military, and possibly my reputation.” The captain studied the path for several minutes. “But I do not think I’d regret the choice.”

“By the time we get to the village, it will be dawning. Have you any coin?”

Luis reached into his jacket pocket. “A few. And you?”

“The same.” Rocco looked down at his uniform. “I suggest we stop at the merchant and procure less obvious dress. We can then make our way to the inn for a meal and information.”

Luis nodded. “Will our silver be enough for all?”

“I can vouch that it will,” Rocco said with a smile. “I am a pirate by trade.” He saw the look of alarm on Luis’ face, so he continued. “I never take advantage of an honest merchant selling at fair prices. But we may have to take our clothes now with a promise to pay later.”

“I suppose if I want to sail on your ship, this is the life of a pirate,” Luis said.

Rocco stopped on the road and took Luis by the shoulder. “Do not lie to me or yourself. If you cannot live this life, we shall part as friends and hope never to see each other in battle. But if you are a pirate, you are sworn to a new code of honor.”

“I understand.” Luis patted Rocco’s back. “The idea of pirating has come so quickly. It will take me time to adjust—probably the amount of time it takes us to get to the village."

They proceeded down the path again.

"Do we need to worry about the duke sending his men to look for us?" Rocco asked.

Luis shook his head. "They are the duke's personal guards and have no authority anywhere but at the castle. They could contact the island's peace officer, but he only oversees the village and typically does not provide much support to the nobility."

"I am surprised he does not bow to the duke."

"This island has been in turmoil for many years, being inhabited by Spanish and French, even the English trying to take over. Local constabulary refuses to help any one family in case it turns out to be the wrong family."

Rocco nodded. "Instability works out in our favor."

"You said you had a mission to fulfill here before you could join your ship," Luis said. "What keeps you here for so long?"

"Second rule of pirating, if you want to keep your head—do not give up information, not even to your mates. My mission is a dangerous one, of interest only to myself, although I dare say it will help others. When it is done, I shall make my way to the pirate's cove and await *L'Implacable*."

46

As Rocco and Luis neared the village, the sun's early rays lit the edge of the hills. Their path took a turn down, to where the sea sparkled with morning pinks and silvers. They could see a long wooden pier and some buildings.

"Which one is the store?" Rocco asked.

Luis pointed. "Clothing, shoes, dried meats, beans, fruits. The shopkeeper is not kind but not cruel. He does not appear to cheat his clients."

"That's unfortunate. I prefer to steal from jackasses."

"Must we steal from him?"

"We haven't enough coin for clothes and food," Rocco said. "Although, I suppose there is another way. Do the guards come often to the village?"

"Often enough."

"Does the duke have an account with him?"

Luis grinned. "I believe so."

By the time they reached the shop, their plans were made. As they rounded the corner, Luis stopped Rocco.

"Let us hide our swords under the walkway. I should like to keep my weapon."

"Good idea," Rocco said. "We can collect them after we've bargained inside."

"Good morrow, Señor Lavin," Luis greeted the shopkeeper as they entered. "My guardsman and I are in a most unusual predicament."

The man looked them up and down. "How may I assist?"

"Of a truth, we were making merry in the barracks when the duke called for us. I'm afraid my guard here and I were a little worse for rum and only realized as we were standing before the duke that we had forgotten our swords and caps. As punishment he sent us to the village to procure clothes to befit our next month's duties as cleaning crew."

A smile cracked the man's face. "That'll sure teach you to think before taking the next sip of grog. So, cotton shirt and pants? Down to the boots, I'm guessing."

"Down to the boots," Luis said. "He said we were lucky he didn't make us walk into town in our bare feet."

The man hustled around the store pulling out plain clothes and cheap leather footwear. Luis and Rocco insisted on trying them on for fit. At last, they were both outfitted in the simplest of garb suitable for a servant of low station.

"Will this be on the duke's account?" Señor Lavin asked.

Luis handed him their uniforms. "Along with whatever you can get for these. If we hadn't just spent all our coin, he'd have made us pay."

"And I'd agree that you deserve it except that I have been in your position, and it was enough that I regretted my actions and the sore head they caused."

Luis and Rocco bowed and left the shop. They immediately turned toward the inn, picking their swords up on the way and reattaching the scabbards to their belts. Rocco slung a carrier bag across his chest.

"Where did you get that?" Luis asked.

"I needed it and he was not paying attention."

Luis scowled. "We could have put it on the duke's account. You didn't have to steal it."

"I know." Rocco shrugged. "It was something I needed to do." He could see the irritation on Luis' face, so he changed the subject. "The duke may want our heads when he finds out."

"The duke will not even notice." Luis chuckled. "His costs to keep the marquess in fancy clothes make our purchases seem like a pittance, not to mention the money he spends to hide the marquess'—peccadillos."

"Since we still have coin," Rocco said, stopping at the inn. "Shall we have a good meal while we can?"

The two men walked inside where a large black man with a gold front tooth greeted them. "Good morrow, gentlemen, I am Horace. Do you wish a meal? We have an excellent fish stew on the fire."

Luis nodded and Rocco held up two fingers. "We'll have the stew and some ale."

They chose a well-lit table in the corner and sat with their backs to the wall. By the time Horace returned with the drinks there were two shiny coins on the table. He smiled and picked them up. When he delivered their stew, he'd added a crusty roll to each plate.

"Horace, do you know when the next ship is due to arrive?" Rocco asked.

"Tomorrow." A trio of men walked in and sat at a table near the door, causing the innkeeper to step away and greet them.

Rocco turned to Luis. "My ship won't arrive for two or three days. If you'd like to sail sooner there are no hard feelings."

Luis picked up his mug of ale and held it out. "I'd prefer to wait."

Smiling, Rocco met Luis' mug with his own and they both drank. It took half the bowls of stew before they were sated enough for conversation.

"Where are we meeting the ship?" Luis asked.

"There is another harbor. More private. It is northwest of the duke's castle, so it will take a goodly two-day trek, unless we have horses magically appear."

"Do you require horses?" Horace had returned with more ale.

Rocco shifted his eyes to Luis before settling on Horace. "No, my partner and I have business along the road. We travel light."

Horace bent down, glancing over at the men near the door, and lowering his voice. "I do not presume to know the contents of your coin purses, but those men are notorious thieves. Be aware."

"Yes, I would like more bread with my stew," Rocco told Horace, glancing at the table of men. He adjusted his sword, allowing the scabbard to click twice against the stone floor.

One of the men looked up from their table at Rocco. Rocco did not return the stare but turned to Luis instead. "We should leave here soon. I'd like to be at least halfway to our destination before the sun sets."

"I agree," Luis said. "Even if the duke is not looking for us, it occurs to me that he will be sending guards to look for the marquise. Neither the village nor the main road will be safe."

Rocco shook his head. "He will not look for Lisette here. I believe he knows where she has gone. And she did promise to return."

Luis chuckled. "You think that makes him a patient man."

"No," Rocco said. "But the only way he can get to her is to sail to Île des Anciens."

"And you think he would not do such a thing?"

"Not if he is the one who must brave that uninhabitable island to find her."

"You speak true." Luis took a large swig of ale. "He is not the man to lead the charge."

Rocco squinted at Luis. "Have you ever been to Île des Anciens?"

"Only to the very edge of the coast. It's nearly impossible to land a boat. There is no beach. Ashore, we were barely able to pass through the bushes and vines. We had only stopped to hunt the wild pigs that roam on the coast and left as soon as we caught two of them. And you?"

"Twice." Rocco nodded. "It is a mysterious place."

"How is it that Lisette would be on that island?"

Rocco looked at his stew. "It is magic. That's all I can tell."

"To see that beast..." Luis shivered. "How is it possible?"

"You'd have to ask the gods."

Horace was back with more bread. He leaned down again, speaking softly. "I heard you mention Lisette. Is she well?"

"She is, thank you." Rocco recalled seeing Horace drive the pony and buckboard away from the castle. "How do you know her?"

"I helped her, about a week ago. She was in here with enough coin to arouse the interest of the brigands by the door. I let her use my buckboard to get to the castle."

"With a gray pony," Luis said. "That was your outfit she left at our stables."

"Yes, I picked it up that evening." Horace stood and looked at the men. "Funny thing. When she drove off, the men left the table. Three returned, all with white faces and shaking hands, demanding drink. The fourth was found dead soon after—his neck snapped so hard his head faced the opposite way."

Rocco kept his expression one of mild surprise, avoiding Luis' eyes. "I wonder what happened."

"I don't know. The only one talking about it was a little boy. He kept repeating, 'big blue bird.'" Horace shrugged as he walked away.

"Did you hear—" Luis gripped Rocco's arm.

"Yes." Rocco stiffened and pulled away. "Calm yourself."

"Protective and nurturing, I heard the priest say. That doesn't sound like either."

"Actually, it does." Rocco gave a small nod to the table of thieves. "What would any mother do to protect her child? I am thinking the man tried to rob or otherwise hurt her."

"I suppose you are right. It still sounds brutal."

Rocco shrugged. "He tried what he should not."

Luis pushed his chair out. "We should go. The road is long and hot, and we cannot take the easy way."

Rocco stood, adjusting his sword and his dagger. Horace appeared from the back room with small packages and wineskins in each hand. He extended them to Rocco and Luis.

"I couldn't help but overhear. Here are rolls, dried meat and cheese, plus a little ale to keep you on the road. Godspeed to you both, and if you see Lisette, tell her I hope she is well."

Rocco took his package and stuffed it in the bag he'd stolen from the merchant. "Thank you, Horace. I hope to see you again."

They left the inn, Rocco flattening the strap on his bag and Luis holding his packages.

"Perhaps I could store my food in your bag?" Luis asked.

"Perhaps you should have stolen one of your own," Rocco told him, and laughed, holding the large sack open. "But I will share the space."

47

Lamya sat in the large jungle-chair, back straight and legs folded. "It is time for you to show me. Change into a dragon, then change back."

"Now?" Lisette unbent her legs and scooted toward the edge. "I don't have anything to focus on."

"What did you focus on when you were falling off the castle wall?"

"That was despair." Lisette shook her head. "I prayed to all the gods, Christian or otherwise."

"Did you know what you wanted to happen?"

"No…maybe…I just knew I couldn't fall that far without injury." Lisette remembered that night, her fear for Alara's safety, and her strong desire to escape. "At least not as a woman."

"Yes, but you knew a dragon could land safely. That

is the boldness you must have." Lamya stretched her arm out, palm up, lifting the air. "Choose what you want to be and be it."

Lisette frowned but eased herself to the ground and stood, hands clasped, and eyes closed.

"Do not be so solemn about it," Lamya scolded. "Look up at the sky. Do you not want to fly again?"

Lisette opened her eyes and lifted her head. The sky was bright and the clouds inviting. She did love flying. Opening her arms, she extended them upward and felt the spark of change. As she stood between the chairs, the baby pushed against her, stretching limbs and—was that a small fire in her belly?

She looked at Lamya, her dragon eyes wide, emitting a series of huffs, whines, and growls in her attempts at speech.

Lamya smiled. "Yes, Lizzie. Your child changes with you. You are only now able to feel it."

Lisette unfolded her wings, preparing to soar. Lamya held her hand out again, palm facing the dragon.

"Stop. You will not fly today. Change back to human form."

Lisette wished she could speak. The Ancient One sat expressionless and expectant. Lisette took a deep breath and closed her eyes.

"No!" Lamya scowled. "It is not a coronation, full of pomp and puffery. It is a simple change. You want to be the human Lizzie, whatever she may be."

Lisette folded her wings and stared at the lagoon, looking for a reason to turn human. What did she want as Lizzie the woman? Rocco, but he wasn't here, and being with him would mean life as a pirate. It was an exciting life, but did she want it all the time? She wanted to deliver her baby and love her and raise her, but she was frightened by what this child might turn out to be. In some ways, life as a dragon was easier.

It occurred to her that the water she was staring at was the Lagoon of Becoming. Lamya said the water can help. *If I am a human, I can bathe in the water and gain understanding.*

She looked down at her feathered paws and pictured them as arms, her talons fingernails. It took a few moments, but she finally felt the burning and collapsed onto the sand, human.

"That was too slow," Lamya said. "You must decide to be human and commit to it—and you are asking much of one little lagoon."

Lisette shrugged. "You once said, 'One river, many streams.' I have too many streams. I cannot seem to find the right one."

"There is no right stream. There are only choices."

"But surely there are bad streams. The Church talks about sins."

"Ah, sins." Lamya laughed. "Your church has worked hard to keep you, how to say…in a bottle? They tell you what is good, what is bad, as if good is always good and bad is always bad."

"But it is, isn't it? I mean, things like stealing and killing and coveting are wrong."

Lamya stared at her. "Was it wrong for you to kill Viscount Barragan?"

"He was trying to rape me and would have probably killed me."

"And you stole his money and his jewels."

"One of those jewels was stolen from me." Lisette frowned. "And he didn't need the rest anymore."

Lamya laughed again. "Good is always good and bad is always bad, yes?"

Lisette could feel herself grow crimson from her chest to her temples. "I have already admitted to God and myself that I have sinned mightily and am irredeemable."

"Sinned." Lamya spit the word into the sand. "You have survived. Why does God put you here if you are to die young?"

"I don't know, Lamya." Lisette covered her face with her hands. "I don't even know what I want in this life that I've *survived*."

Lamya's face softened, and she rose to put her arm around Lisette. "I understand. Most people have no choices in this life. They are born, either rich or poor, children of nobles or of slaves. You have been given a gift, to set your own course, but it comes with a challenge—what course do you want?"

"I want to be with Rocco, but I don't know if I want to be a pirate. I want to have this baby, but I am afraid of this responsibility. I want to live in my family castle, but I don't want to continually fight the intrigue of kings and countries."

"It is a puzzle." Lamya looked at the lagoon. "But I have an idea. Take the best of your desires with you into the lagoon. It may be able to show you what you want."

Lisette smiled and headed to the shore, dropping her clothes as she went.

Lamya called after her. "Don't forget to ask the lagoon about being a dragon."

As Lisette stepped into the water, she turned to answer Lamya and saw the Ancient One grinning. She said nothing and submerged herself under the welcoming water.

For what seemed like a long time, she floated and paddled back and forth, lost in her own thoughts. Her body still recalled the feeling of Alara turning into a dragon. She had begun this journey knowing only of blood dragons. Now she was aware of moon dragons—how many different kinds were there?

She dragged her mind away from dragons to the problem at hand. Her reason for this visit to the lagoon was to receive guidance about being human. Being a dragon was pretty simple.

Lisette turned again to float on her back and closed her eyes. *Take the best of my desires with me. What would be my best dream?*

To go back to that night and not be kidnapped. She would still be a respected noblewoman with a family. Without the kidnapping Eric would go through with the marriage and Mercedes would have to find another way to take the island—or leave it.

She felt a wave of nausea as the lagoon pushed itself over her head, causing her to paddle upright, coughing and shaking the water from her face.

"You're right," she told the lagoon. "That is not my desire, although I miss my family every day and wish they still lived. Marriage to Eric would be a drudgery at best and would not stop Mercedes from her plotting."

She compared Eric to Rocco. They were both attractive, but where Eric's looks had a fastidious preening quality to them, Rocco was handsome without fuss. Part of his attraction was his athleticism and intelligence. Eric could be charming if it served him and apparently intelligent enough to manipulate others. Rocco's charm was in the fact that he saw no need for it.

Honesty was neither man's strong suit, but somehow, she trusted Rocco the pirate more. He may have been brooding over having to kill her to remove his curse, but their battles—and their lovemaking—had been truth and not manipulations.

Eric had only been sincere once, on the dance floor when he revealed his desire for wealth and power. Lisette realized that if she'd married him, she would have spent her life looking over her shoulder in distrust. It was just as well that she killed him.

But Rocco's life was at sea. A ship would be her home. Would she ever yearn for a home on dry land? How would she raise Alara among *L'Implacable's* crew?

The water around her swirled, cocooning her in a warm nest. A vision came to her of living in a simple house, raising Alara and being married to Rocco, who still sailed *L'Implacable* but returned to his family at the end of each voyage. Just as she settled into that dream another vision came of Alara staying home with Pinar while Lisette crewed with her husband, handling sails, swabbing the deck, and sitting in the crow's nest.

"Yes," she said, "it is a nice way to fly when I am no longer a dragon."

The water again sucked her down into its depths, as she fought to the surface. *Why would you no longer be a dragon,* a voice asked. *You can remain a moon dragon as long as you wish.* The water spit her to the top, where she coughed and sputtered.

"It is perhaps enough for you today," Lamya called from the shore. "The lagoon might drown you with knowledge."

Lisette swam to her, awkwardly lifting herself from the water and grabbing her dress from the sand. She smiled as she gathered it around her shoulders.

"I know what I want," she said. "Should we try the transformation again?"

"In a little while. First, you must eat more. Then rest."

Lisette walked back to the chairs where Lamya had prepared a small fire. Her bowl was filled with roasted vegetables as well as what looked like meat.

"You do not serve me meat," she said. "Only once, we ate fowl and you spoke of its sacrifice to my becoming a blood dragon."

"This is wild boar. There is a colony of them on this island, here because some muddle-minded sailor decided to bring a few pigs over so they would always have an easy meal when they visited this place." She huffed indignantly. "Humans. Always thinking they will improve this world when all they do is make it worse. The pigs of course bred wildly and now there are too many. They uproot the flowers and trees, not out of malice but because they must eat."

"Wild boar? Were they here the first time I visited?"

Lamya took another bite of her meal and smiled. "I know what you are asking—why do I not feed you boar meat when you are learning to control the blood dragon, working so hard every day on a few meals of broth?"

"It would have been more filling." Lisette picked up a piece of meat and looked at it before stuffing it in her mouth.

"And more dangerous. Wild boar are not like the pigs you keep in your castle yard for slaughter. They are ferocious and attack anything unknown to them. Eating the meat of such a violent animal would have fed the violent side of you, making your dragon much harder for you to control."

Lisette nodded. "The first few nights I was angry at everything, just wanting to destroy."

"Yes, imagine that you were never able to go past that and hunt your enemies."

"I'd have been a blood dragon forever."

Lamya smiled. "And that is why you can eat the meat now. Your dragon is not one of destruction. The boar has no power over you."

"Why don't you use your magic to…shoo them somewhere else?" Lisette made a motion with her hands to chase them away.

"I have the magic to do this, but it is not always an easy solution." Lamya shrugged. "Remember this well, Lizzie—nothing can be erased. Not even magic can make something disappear. It must either be changed into something else or appear somewhere else. So, I send the pigs to another island. What do they do? Tear up the jungles there. I cannot give someone else a problem that is mine."

Lisette chewed slowly. "But they could be changed into something else, you said. Why not change them into something less destructive? Birds? Trees?"

"Again, this would be trying to 'fix' the world. I do not know the consequences, but I have seen enough chaos to know I do not want to add to it." She picked up a rib bone. "What I can do is give a pregnant moon dragon meat to feed her blood and strength. And I consider it an honor to share in the meal."

"I confess, the meat is satisfying in ways roasted yams are not." The baby turned over and stretched her limbs. Lisette placed a hand on her belly to enjoy the movement. "Alara seems to like the food, too."

Lamya sat back on the sand, putting her bowl aside. "Do you know what you want?"

"Yes. After I have the baby, I will return to Rocco. There is no reason that I cannot live on the island while he is at sea." She shared her visions. "The only thing I did not approach was my concern about Alara. What will she be, and will I be able to mother her?"

"That is the least of your problems, my dear."

"How? I told you my plans for everything else."

"Have you not heard that humans plan and the gods laugh?" Lamya chuckled. "It is good to have these goals. But do not become so focused on them that you cannot recognize when they do not serve you."

"Why wouldn't they?"

Lamya frowned. "You are going to have this baby and go find Rocco. What if the baby keeps you on this island? What if you do not know where Rocco is? What if Rocco does not want to marry you and put you in a house on Île des Oiseaux and visit you every six months? Every year?"

Lisette's heart felt like it had been crushed and tears

gathered in the corner of her eyes. "You're right. I can have dreams, but there is no expectation they will come true."

"Do no crying," Lamya said. "It is good to dream and to work toward that dream. But in all your steps, be content with where you are and do not wait for happiness to come only when you have reached your destination."

Lisette nodded, wiping at her face. "So, I should be happy now?"

"In addition to being given choices in your life, you have been given the blessing of happiness. Think of the people you know and have met. How many of them meet their obligations of toil or position, and do not dare ask, 'am I happy'? Because the answer is never yes."

48

Rocco and Luis walked off the main road at the edge of the jungle. There they would be less conspicuous to the common traveler and able to escape into the brush and vines should anyone want to detain them. By the time the sun had reached its peak and was starting its descent to the sea, they were halfway to the de Lille castle.

"Let us stop here for a bite," Luis said. "This trail is slow, and the sun is harsh."

"And we are used to our afternoon siesta," Rocco said with a grin.

They found a patch of moss in a grove of trees, so they sat in the shade and Rocco got out the food and drink Horace had packed.

"It was quite a surprise to hear that Horace knew the marquise," Luis said.

Rocco shrugged. "She is a marquise, but I believe she has not had the sheltered life of a noblewoman in a castle."

"Did you believe Horace's story about the thief?"

As Luis spoke Rocco envisioned a young woman in boys' clothes climbing the ropes on *L'Implacable*. The woman turned to face him, and he saw for the first time it was Lisette.

"…must have great physical power," Luis was saying.

"I'm sorry, I was distracted. What about the thief?"

Luis took a swig from the wineskin. "I was talking about the killing. Do you think Lisette did it? I don't know of any human with that kind of strength, but if she was the beast we saw on the balcony—"

A rustle in the bushes caught Rocco's attention and he lifted his hand to silence his friend. There were plenty of birds and small creatures on this island, but this had the distinct sound of a boot crushing undergrowth.

Rocco rolled silently to his feet and looked up at the tree he had been leaning against. The lower limbs were sturdy and climbable, so he gestured to Luis and hefted himself onto a branch where he could watch for whoever was intruding on their rest. Luis found his own tree opposite Rocco and pulled himself up into a similar hiding spot.

The three thieves from the inn crashed into the grove looking about the ground.

"Where'd they go?" one of the men asked. "I swore I heard them talking."

A second voice spoke. "They was talking about that witch what killed Claude. They know what she is."

"Maybe they're the same," the first man said. "I wouldn'ta believed it if I hadn't seen it."

"Maybe, but if they got silver, we deserve it." This was the third man. His voice was deep, his tone angry. "We deserve payment for Claude. She had no right to kill him. And once we're done here, we head to that castle and take care of that thing."

The men had now passed Luis and were standing before Rocco's tree. Rocco eased his sword from its scabbard and leapt in front of the men.

"She had every right to kill a thief." He kept his voice calm and his sword leveled.

The trio reached for their hilts but were surprised by a voice behind them. "I wouldn't if I were you, gentlemen," Luis said, his weapon drawn.

The men looked back and forth at their two captors. The third man smiled. "There are but two of you. I believe we are more."

"Yes," Rocco said. "The odds are poor. You will not even make a snack for my blade."

The thieves drew their swords, but before they could step into battle, Luis struck the shortest man across the back and through the middle, leaving him to moan in death while he pursued a second.

The third man engaged Rocco.

"What's your name, thief?" Rocco asked the man as their swords clanged together.

"What matter it?" The thief thrust forward, but Rocco stepped aside and clipped his shoulder, drawing blood.

"I should want to know how to label your tombstone."

The thief's face turned crimson, and he attacked Rocco a fury. Rocco's face remained placid as he countered each blow. This was not a finesse swordsman, but a slasher who won by bullying his opponents. Rocco had fought many of these on ships. He defended himself against each strike until the thief was tired.

The man made one more attempt, thrusting his blade forward. Rocco used his left hand to grab the man's wrist as he drove his sword through his opponent, down and then up, to slice the most organs with a single stab. The thief dropped his weapon and fell forward, shoving Rocco's blade even further into him.

Rocco pushed him to the ground, pulling his blade out as he fell. He looked up to help Luis, but saw his friend watching the last thief run from them, holding his side, blood marking his trail. Luis turned back to Rocco, holding out his sword. Rocco extended his own and touched blades before wiping it clean and returning it to its scabbard.

"I doubt the lone survivor will have much to tell in the village," Rocco said. "But we cannot stay here."

"Agreed." Luis sheathed his weapon. "Where's a good place to hide these bodies?"

They settled on a patch of elephant ear plants, large enough to contain two bodies at their base and give no clue.

"At least they'll be useful in death," Luis said, "as fertilizer."

Gazing around them, Rocco asked, "What happened to our sack of food and drink?"

"Ah, yes, let me retrieve it." Luis shimmied back up the tree he'd hidden in and slid down holding the bag. "They can steal my coin, but they can't steal my ale."

Rocco laughed, and they continued their journey north. As they trudged through the dense undergrowth, he saw Luis pull a strip of meat from the bag and eat while he walked, looking thoughtful.

"Something troubles you?"

"I was pondering," Luis said between bites, "how do you know that the marquise hasn't been shut up in a castle her whole life?"

Rocco frowned at him and reached into the bag, removing a roll.

"My mistake," Luis said. "Second rule of pirating and all that."

The two were silent as they walked.

"It is all come back to me," Rocco whispered. He gazed past Luis. "I kidnapped Lisette to sell her to a viscount. I wanted to kill her, had been trying for years but guilt stayed my hand. And then I came to know and admire her, and it was love that kept me from taking her life."

"If you'll pardon me for saying so, that seems a thing hard to forget."

"I didn't forget on purpose." Rocco shook his head. "A young woman gave me a potion that took away pieces of my memory—apparently, any pieces that had to do with Lisette. Perhaps she thought if I didn't remember Lisette, I would be free to fall in love with her."

Luis grinned. "I s'pose that's one way around it. But what would be so bad about this young woman? Isn't one about the same as another?"

"Forgetting Lisette caused surprising consequences. My love for her is a complicated thing, not a trifle to be used and cast off at the next port. And the child she carries is my child." He looked at Luis. "So much for the second rule of pirating."

By the time the sun was disappearing, they had reached the southernmost edge of the de Lille castle and could see the torches at the front gate.

"Let's find a place further back in the trees to bed for the night," Luis said. "If I recall, the guardsman likely to get my captain's post is a bloodthirsty, ruthless rule-enforcer. He will comb the surroundings for brigands on a regular basis until dawn."

Rocco nodded. "I'd hate to slice any throats I didn't have to."

They headed into the brush, pushing past the foliage until they were too far to be reached by anyone casually patrolling. There was no real clearing here, but they found a couple of barer spots where each man could settle.

"We will not be able to afford a fire, I'm afraid,"

Rocco said.

"The night will not be cold. Especially when I fold myself into this slight space."

Rocco laughed. "Of truth. Sleep now and I shall keep first watch."

Only patches of sky could be seen through the canopy of trees, but Rocco looked up anyway, attempting to see stars he recognized. He would much prefer to be at the helm and navigating toward some island. Intercepting a Spanish ship full of goods would be even better. He felt a lightness about his body that he hadn't known in a long time.

Lisette. He could see her face now and connect that face to so much of his past year. The knowledge that he loved her, and that she carried his baby gave his heart hope for the future. He couldn't wait to rejoin her.

Would she sail with him on *L'Implacable*? That might not be an appropriate life for a child. Lisette may not even want a life eternally at sea.

Perhaps he should not step forward as the child's father. The Duke de Martinmas was going to marry her to his son. It was not a love match, but what marriage of nobles was? She and the child would have a luxurious life under the arrangement.

More importantly, they'd be safe.

Rocco was still internally debating when he heard voices coming toward him. They stopped at the edge of the brush, but the night was so quiet their words carried.

"New cap'n sure makes us work," a high male voice said.

"True, but this detail is better than being at the castle." This was an older voice. Rocco thought it might be Philippe. "Duke's raging about the marquise going missing and how he's going to make the marquess marry the first girl he can ship from Spain."

"How would he make his son marry? At sword

point?”

"All's I know is he's got the young man shut up in his chambers with guards at the door.”

Footsteps came closer. Rocco could hear a sword rustling the leaves and vines.

"I don't see any footprints, Philippe,” the younger voice said.

Philippe's voice sounded as if he was walking away. "C'mon, boy, we done our job. 'Tween you and me, I'm not lookin' to find anyone skulkin' about.”

"Ain't we was supposed to be looking for Captain Delgado?” The younger guard's voice indicated he had not moved.

"We especially ain't lookin' for him. He ain't stupid enough to hang 'round here, and even if'n he did, he did nothin' wrong.”

A couple of footsteps walked, hesitated, and Rocco heard, "C'mon, boy.”

He sat and listened to their conversation which drifted further until he heard nothing except Luis' snoring and the nighttime creatures. He sat, leaning his back against a broad tree, regarding the sky. The moon rose into view, a little less full than last night.

He guessed it would be another five days, before the waning crescent. His returned memory had filled all the blanks about killing the Count de Medina. Lisette had fought beside him, to kill her ex-fiancé and his new betrothed, Mercedes. He had not wanted Lisette to kill her. Part of her was Tempest and he wanted to cling to that.

When I had no memory, I wanted to kill Mercedes. Do I still have that desire?

This was something to consider. A vision of Mercedes came to his mind—horribly scarred, frighteningly cruel. Lisette had tried to kill her and had apparently failed. Did she plan to finish her task?

A swift rustling of leaves interrupted him. He looked

up to see that the darkness of the night sky had grayed. A squall was moving through. Rocco whistled to Luis, who stirred, groaning.

"Time for my watch?" he mumbled.

"No, squall's coming," Rocco said. "I thought you'd appreciate a warning."

The two men found a low, wide-leafed tree to huddle under as the first heavy drops hit. Sheets of rain pummeled them, driving their bodies toward the ground. Rocco had been through many squalls, but this was a new experience, being on land instead of asea. On the ship, his focus was on keeping it upright and afloat. The rain hitting his body was no more than an annoyance.

Huddling against a tree trunk and pulling a large leaf over his head to detour the water kept his focus on him and his comfort. And he was not comfortable. The rain pounded him relentlessly as if someone stood over him with a never-ending bucket of cool water. This storm was going to take a while to blow through. He lowered his head and pulled the leaf down further.

Just as Rocco decided to curse the gods for their brutal storm, it stopped as squalls do, with a small shake of droplets like a dog coming out of a lake. He let go of the leaf and took a deep breath in, wiping his hands across his face.

"Thought that'd never end," Luis said. "Not used to a storm on land, it's enough to drive a man mad."

"Agreed." Rocco stood and surveyed the brush, battered down around them. "It is far from morning, but we should be on the move. This storm will make it harder to hide our tracks. I'd like to be well clear of here before the castle awakes and sends another crew to look for us."

Luis nodded and rose. "Perhaps a sip of ale would warm us," he said, squeezing the water from his shirt.

Rocco handed him his skin and took a healthy swig from his own, adjusted the bag, and led them westward, being sure to keep heavy brush between them and the castle. The moon had continued its path, casting less light as it approached the horizon. They might have a couple of hours of relative darkness before the sun crept up.

Past the castle, the heavy jungle to the southwest disappeared, leaving a rolling clearing that ended at cliffs. Beyond the cliffs was a small beach, impossible to get down to without using a rope. Rocco led Luis toward the cliffs, hugging them as they continued north.

"We follow the sea at this point," he said, "until we get to a ring of brush and small trees. In the midst of the boulders, there is a winding path that will take us to the pirate's harbor."

"Good to know but I will follow you."

Rocco frowned. "I'm telling you in case something happens, and you can't follow me. It is your escape route."

"Even better to know," Luis said, grinning.

They walked for several hours, watching the moonlight disappear and the dawn crawl toward them. By the time sun was up enough to throw soft morning shadows, Luis spoke.

"How much further, Captain Rocco?"

Rocco looked at the sky and the coastline ahead. "I anticipate we will be at the harbor when the sun is just past its midday mark."

"Will the ship be there?"

"I do not know, but I expect them to be there by tomorrow at the latest." Rocco kept walking. "If they do not stop to relieve any Spanish ships of their goods on the way."

Luis shrugged. "Then I shall not ask you to retrieve my leftovers yet, even if my stomach does beg for them."

Rocco laughed. "Tell your stomach there are more pressing matters, and bread saved now is bread you'll need later."

True to his estimate, they arrived at the path to the beach when the sun was barely past overhead. Rocco stood for a moment on the cliff and looked out. The bay was empty, as was the shore, but the outline of a ship could be seen in the distance. He recognized it at once.

L'Implacable was on her way.

49

Rocco gestured to Luis and headed down the path. They wound their way, zigzagging across the steep descent. Rocco nearly ran to see his ship and crew, but he restrained himself to a dignified stride.

They reached the shore well before the ship dropped anchor, so they found soft seating with tall rocks to lean against and finished their ale and food. Soon they watched dinghies being loaded and dropped to the water. The first one to land was led by a familiar face.

"Chunk, how goes it?" Rocco asked.

The burly man turned to see the captain and almost let go of the rope. The sailors increased their efforts and hauled the boat to the sand, after which they gathered around Rocco to welcome him back.

"It is good to see you all," Rocco said. "I have missed *L'Implacable* and the crew and being asea. These land-legs are strange to me."

"We took care of a few Spanish ships whilst you were away," Chunk said. "But we sure need you back wit' us."

"And I am anxious to return." Rocco patted him on the back. He turned and gestured to Luis. "Men, this is Luis Delgado. You might remember him from *El Gallo Blanco*, the one ship I allowed survivors. He's a seaman like us with no particular allegiance to anything except the sea life—and perhaps his share of the gold."

They laughed and greeted Luis. While the crew introduced themselves and helped the next dinghy through the surf, Chunk led Rocco to a more private area for conversation.

"We was worried about ya, Cap'n Derya and me." Chunk dropped his voice to a whisper. "How are ya—feelin'?"

"I have my memories back, if that's what you're asking."

Chunk sighed and clapped Rocco's back. "Thank the gods. Once we found out what the girl Ruhee had done to ya—"

"I was worried as well," Rocco told him. "I realized that there was something wrong with my mind. And when I became a blood dragon again, I was confused. But I have regained all that I lost, thankfully."

"Ah, that's good, Cap'n. We'll be takin' ya back at the helm."

Rocco frowned. "I can't go with you yet. When I lost part of my memory, my blood dragon tried to hunt down Mercedes de Medina."

"Ah, but she's dead."

"No, she survived." Rocco explained her wounds. "I have perhaps five more days until I would turn and be able to hunt her. With the effects of Ruhee's potion gone, I do not know whether I will still become a blood dragon on the hunt or not."

"Ah, surely you can come wit' us. If you turn, we can come back to this place, and you can take care of your business."

Rocco shook his head. "This time, my turning is different. The last time, I hunted only the people I had cursed. This time, my targets are less firm. If we cannot get back here immediately, I might harm one of the crew."

"What would you have us do?"

"Take Delgado on but keep careful watch. He is not loyal to any country, but I need to know he'll be loyal to us. Return here in five days. I shall be successful, either by killing Mercedes and ending my curse or by not turning because I have already ended it."

Chunk hung his head. "Yes, Cap'n, if those are yer orders."

Rocco grinned. "You've been a good first mate, Chunk, and a good friend. I know I will see you in five days."

The crew had been busily unloading gold, silver, and jewels from their last attacks, storing it in a small cave to the north of the beach, a cave they had to swim to access. In return, they brought back supplies that had been stored for safekeeping. Rocco supervised the process, giving a few orders on what to leave and what to take. He noticed that Luis helped carry and load, although he did not venture far enough to see where the cave was and did not even look in the direction.

He's a smart one, to not appear anxious to know our secrets.

"All set to hoist the anchor," Chunk told him.

Rocco nodded and approached the crew. "I am anxious to sail again, but I must take care of a task on this island. Chunk knows of my plans and when I am finished. *L'Implacable* will pick me up here before the new moon."

The sailors nodded and stood for a moment at their boats.

"Do not dawdle," Rocco said. "Harden up!"

They turned and pushed the dinghies out with backward glances as if reluctant to leave Rocco behind. Chunk sighed and walked to his boat, giving it a good push into the waves. He turned and held his hand up in goodbye. Rocco did the same.

Rocco watched them row back to the ship, unsure if he was making a mistake. He could go with them now and return at the crescent moon. There was a sourness in his gut, whether he remained or left with the crew.

But my men must not be endangered.

He turned away from the beach and climbed back up the path. At the top, he looked to the west and saw the dinghies pulling up to the ship. Soon *L'Implacable* would be sailing. Five days would go quickly, and he still needed to figure out how best to get to Mercedes.

Rustling flora and the sound of boots and swords made him whip around. Six men in uniform stormed him, weapons drawn. Rocco noticed immediately that these uniforms were not the same as those of the duke's castle. Before he could draw his own sword there was a blade at his throat held by a tall, hefty guard.

"Tristan de Rocco," the guard said. "You are to come with us." He gestured to another, shorter guard. "Disarm him—and tie his hands."

"Yes, Captain Simone." The short guard grabbed Rocco's hands and pulled them behind, tying them well with sturdy rope. He removed Rocco's sword from its scabbard and patted him down, taking the dagger as well.

"May I ask whose company I am being taken to?"

"You may ask." Alwan Simone pushed him forward so hard that he nearly fell but recovered himself.

Rocco paused to look behind him. "Very well. I often enjoy surprises." He proceeded down the path at a rapid march.

The six men quickly jogged forward to surround him,

preventing him from diving into the jungle. There was no way to escape, at least at the moment, so Rocco moved along with them. The time would come, he trusted. He only wished he'd trusted his gut as much in the moments before.

Lisette awoke from her nap with a start. Lamya sat at the fire, warming a leather bag.

"You are so quickly awake," Lamya said.

"I was dreaming." Lisette rubbed her eyes. "Rocco was on the ship, and I was on the shore. I waved to him, but he didn't wave back. Not a bad dream, yet I am unsettled by it."

"Because it is your fear that your dream of being with Rocco will not be true."

"It wasn't my fear until you mentioned it."

"I did not say it to make you afraid." Lamya took the bag away from the heat and shook it, massaging it as she did. "I said it to make you chase your dream with strength and focus. If it is your dream, do not let it be spoiled by circumstances you can prevent." She handed the bag to

Lisette. "Here. Drink."

Lisette put the bag to her lips and took a sip. "It tastes different than before."

"Yes, I added herbs. You need them for the baby."

"It's good." Lisette kept drinking. "I have grown so large with this child. Will it be time soon for me to give birth?"

"I do not always know the future," Lamya said, drawing circles in the sand with her finger. "But I believe that you must do one more thing before having Alara."

"One more thing?"

Lamya stretched and resettled herself. "I do not know what the thing is. I only know that your tasks—your pre-Alara tasks—are not finished. You must finish what you started. And then the baby will come."

"Finish what I started before the baby…" Lisette mumbled to herself. "I don't know what that would be. Before I knew I was with child, I planned to kill Mercedes to avenge my family and didn't."

"Why not?"

"I believed she was dead that night when I saw her body on fire." Lisette shrugged. "And now…she is so fragile and scarred and hated. Living with herself seems a worse punishment."

"But it does not fulfill the curse."

"No, but—wait." Lisette scowled. "I did not curse anyone, not like Rocco did. I didn't go looking for a way to become a blood dragon. A blood dragon feather got shoved into my ribs and dumped out its magic. Plus, I changed back to a human and haven't been a blood dragon since."

"You did not change back right away, not like Rocco did. You held your blood dragon shape until you had to call for my help." Lamya's tone was quiet. "Did you never wonder?"

"I wondered about all of it, Lamya. I had to stop wondering just to keep myself from going mad."

"Humans and their madness," Lamya scoffed. "Madness is not such a bad thing. Your lives are so rigid you do not accept your fears or your dreams or your needs. You have removed all of the life from living. Madness is needed sometimes to bring you balance."

Lisette finished her broth and sat back, leaning against an old log. "But even now, knowing Mercedes still lives and is perhaps more ruthless than before, I do not know that I can kill her. She was vain and mean-spirited, but now I can see the hurt in her wrath—the loss of Eric and her family and her beauty and her dreams—how does someone overcome such devastation?"

"I don't know, Lizzie." Lamya smiled. "How did you overcome so much?"

"I lost my family, yes, and my life of ease as a noblewoman in a castle. But being kidnapped set my feet on the path of love."

"And now you know who you are and what you want."

"Yes, but what do I need to do before Alara can be born? I have no desire to kill Mercedes."

"No, but someone else might. And that someone will need your help."

"Rocco?" Lisette sat forward again. "I wondered why he was a blood dragon again. That night at Mercedes' castle—he was hunting her, wasn't he?"

"There are but five nights before he hunts again. Mercedes is angry and hurt, but she is cunning. He will need your assistance." Lamya rose from her seated position by the fire. "Come. We practice the transformation again."

All afternoon, Lisette changed, dragon to human to dragon and back again. As the sun dipped behind a mountain, Lamya said, "One last time and we are done."

"You say 'we' as if you were transforming with me."

"In my own way I am." Lamya raised her hand, palm up. "Transform, please."

Lisette looked down at her arms. *I am a dragon.* The change had become so quick, she barely felt the flash of it. She hoped she did not dream of becoming a dragon—she might transform in her sleep.

"And once more, human."

I am a woman. Lisette saw arms where there were paws before. But something was wrong. She grabbed at her stomach and dropped to her knees.

"Alara, you have to change!" she screamed.

Lamya rushed to her side and put a hand upon her back. Lisette moaned.

"Tell her who she must be," Lamya said. "Quickly."

"Oww, Alara, you are a human baby," Lisette squealed through her tears. Alara as a dragon was too large for her, her tail poking at Lisette's spine and horns stabbing at her hip. "Daughter, please…you are a human…a girl…change your body…"

There was one extra-sharp stabbing pain, followed by relief. Lisette lay on her side, panting in exhaustion. Her arms cradled her body. A small hand slowly pushed out at her arm. Lisette moved her palm down to the source. A wee voice spoke in her mind.

I am sorry, Mama. I got confused.

"No, I am sorry, Alara. I have been practicing for too long. You must be tired."

Lamya stayed by Lisette's side, stroking her hair. "My apologies, too, Alara. I was driving your mother. It is important for her to be able to transform quickly and without doubt. But I did not take you into consideration."

Another hand pushed out toward the sound of Lamya's voice. The Ancient One touched Lisette's stomach at that point and spent a few moments silent and smiling.

"It has been much time since I got to know a human child. I had forgotten their simplicity."

"It's a shame we have to leave it behind as we grow older," Lisette said. After a few moments she sat up with Lamya's help. "Is there more broth?"

Lamya nodded. "I shall warm some for you."

As they sat by the fire, Lisette asked, "Have you any more insight into what kind of dragon Alara might be?"

"I do not know." She handed Lisette a warmed skin of nourishment. "When I put my hand on you, before she had turned, there was a strong presence of both peace and power. Her dragon will be capable, I believe, of both healing and destroying."

Lisette took a sip of broth. "How many kinds of dragons are there?"

"Oh, there are many dragons all over the world," Lamya told her. "Some are destroyers and bring pestilence, some are courageous and fight for their people and their lands. Some even bridged the gap between heaven and hell when the world was formed. They have become legends in most places, as if they never existed. But you and I know the truth."

Lisette drank her broth while Lamya tended the fire.

"I suppose," Lisette said at last, "Raising a child who can transform into a dragon will not be that difficult. I have come this far in such a short time and done all manner of things I never dreamed I could or would do."

Lamya continued to stir the ashes with a broad smile. "You have learned much."

"I still need your wisdom. You said before that I need to go help Rocco with Mercedes. Are you saying I should return to Île des Oiseaux and then come back here and have the baby?"

"It is always your choice, and make no mistake, there is danger there. I will not make you leave this place, and I will not stop you from leaving."

"That does not make my decision easier." Lisette frowned. "But if I have to help Rocco, I need to leave tonight. I do not know if I have the focus to fly such a distance before I turn human again."

"Ah, that will not be a problem. I have a ship that will drop you off at the pirate's harbor. All you need do is ask," Lamya said with a grin, "and show them your wrist."

Lamya led Lisette down the path to the sea, where a small rowboat awaited at the inlet. Lisette recognized the woman in the boat. Her heart leapt and she waded into the water up to her knees before she caught herself and faced Lamya.

"Thank you. I will return soon."

Lamya smiled and nodded. "Go now. I will wait for you."

With one more wave, Lisette turned back to the boat, now within her reach. She held her hand out to the woman at the oars for help getting in. "Pinar, how lovely to see you!"

Pinar was also smiling. "Lizzie, I am so happy that you are well."

Once Lisette was sitting as comfortably as possible

on the middle bench, Pinar picked up the oars and swept them back and down through the water. Although she was a slight woman, Pinar's arms pulled the oars efficiently.

"It will be so good to see the crew again," Lisette said. "How is Captain Derya?"

"She is well, although both you and Captain Rocco have occupied her mind."

"I hope we have not concerned her too much."

"It is hard to say." They had completely rounded the south point and were heading northwest along the lee side of the island. The *Dişi Aslan* was anchored ahead, awaiting their arrival. "The captain does not always share her private thoughts with the crew. She did not even disclose the unfortunate situation with Ruhee."

"I trust Ruhee is…well." Lisette wasn't certain what to say. She was unhappy with the girl's attempt to take Rocco from her, but she dreaded the harshness of pirate justice.

"A bit wiser for the experience," Pinar said, as they pulled alongside the ship.

Lines were dropped and the dinghy raised in short order. Many hands reached out to assist Lisette out of the boat and onto the deck. She recognized faces and there were greetings and hugs, until Oleta stepped forward.

"The captain would like to see you in her quarters."

Still smiling and warm from the happy reception, Lisette followed her below deck. The cabin was the way she remembered it, lush and comfortable with many silks and dark furniture.

"Welcome back, Lizzie." Captain Begum Derya was much herself, too. Still lean and fit, with large green-gold eyes. Her hair was a bit longer, hanging down her back in a thick braid.

"It is good to be back on the ship," Lisette told her, her legs acclimating to the roll of the floor. "It feels like home."

Begum gestured to the table, set with the copper coffee pot and fresh flat bread. "Sit. We will have coffee and talk."

Lisette did as requested and was soon sipping the dark, bitter brew from a small cup. "I am assuming that Lamya told you where I need to go."

"Yes, but not why." She pointed to Lisette's obvious belly. "Should you not be with her now, preparing for your child's birth?"

"It is where I would prefer to be, but Lamya has assured me Alara will not be born before the new moon. I must trust her on this. Rocco needs my help by the next waning crescent."

"Alara?" Begum grinned. "You know it is a girl?"

"Yes. That day I transformed to the blue dragon and flew from this ship, there was one thing I neglected to tell you. From early in my pregnancy—even before I knew I was with child—I was seeing a vision of a small girl who claimed to be my daughter Alara. She visited me that day and warned me that I was going to change." Lisette looked down at her coffee. "I do not tell many people in case they think me mad."

Begum laughed. "The old Begum might have thought that, but since my own experience with the blood dragon curse, and meeting Lamya de Sang, I now believe anything is possible."

"I admire you, Captain, in many ways. Have the ship and crew been well? I heard about Isla del Lagarto—is it true that all nobility have fled?"

"The island is thriving since the death of the Count de Medina, although you may not have been given the full story. Lawlessness is the rumor the island spreads to the nobility that still reign in the Caribbean. In truth, Isla del Lagarto has come under rule of the villagers and former servants. They live peacefully with a trio of governors who decide what is fair. Trina is one of the governors, as is Father Felix, and Nan."

Lisette grinned. "I am amazed—how wonderful! Trina is decisive and firm, Father Felix is compassionate, and Nan is practical."

"Yes, we visit them on occasion, buying and selling—imagine a pirate ship doing honest business." Begum laughed again. "But as Trina is our *Dişi* sister, we honor her new position."

"And now I go to help Rocco stamp out the last of the Medina family, the daughter Mercedes."

"Mercedes? I believed she was dead."

"I believed I had killed her at the wedding, but I burned her horribly instead. She still lives—disfigured, in pain, and very angry."

Begum nodded. "That is another part of the puzzle, then. When Chunk and I found that Ruhee had performed her little 'experiment' and that Rocco the blood dragon had flown away, we wondered who his victim would be."

"I'm surprised he could focus on a single victim, and that he picked Mercedes." Lisette reached for a round of bread, dragging a piece of it through the familiar and delicious, spiced bean paste. "I imagined his rage would have no target."

"Have you had much contact with him?"

Lisette's smile brightened her entire face. "I do not know if every memory has been restored, but he does remember me—and the baby."

"This is good news. I did not think the spell would last, but with no one prodding him, I wasn't certain he would ever regain what he lost." Begum frowned. "Is he still going to hunt for Mercedes?"

"No one knows, not even Lamya, whether he will turn into a blood dragon and seek Mercedes now that he remembers everything. But Lamya believes that I must be there to help him." Lisette sighed. "I have no stomach for killing. There is a part of me that feels great sympathy for that girl. I gave her worse than death. And there is a part of me that feels perhaps death would be both a kindness and a completion of vengeance."

"If Rocco requires you to kill her, can you do it?"

Lisette looked at her empty cup. "Only if he requires it."

Begum put her own cup on the table and rose. "You are tired, I am sure, and I must see to our course. Rest here. We will find you a more private place later."

Lisette placed her cup with the captain's and stood, stretching her back. "I confess, I will be happy to carry this little one in my arms and not in my stomach. She can be heavy as an anchor some days."

As if to protest, the baby kicked hard enough to fluff out Lisette's skirt.

Begum laughed. "She has an opinion about that."

"She has an opinion about most everything," Lisette said. "I do hope her opinion about resting is that it's a good idea."

The captain reached her hand to Lisette's face and cradled her cheek for a moment before leaving the cabin. Lisette eased herself onto the bed, wondering at the gesture but soon sighing from the comfort of silk covers. Not even her opulent childhood in the castle was this luxurious. She curled the corner of one around her hand and stroked it.

"Hush now, Alara. The silk covers are smooth and cool, and I would like a nap."

Mama? Do you remember the last time we slept here?

"Yes." Lisette closed her eyes and nodded. "Oleta and Ruhee were taking care of me, to save my life when I got stabbed." *When Rocco stabbed me.*

It hurt, Alara said.

"It did—did you feel it also?"

I didn't know the words, but I felt it. The sharp point hurt my home.

Lisette put her hand on her stomach, frowning. "Hurt your home?"

The place in your belly where I grow. The sharp point came into that place.

Now Lisette sat up. "I was stabbed in the womb?"

It's okay now, Mama, it healed, but there is a scar there. It sometimes feels hard, and I don't like it. But don't be mad at Daddy. He didn't know.

Sitting alone in the space, Lisette ran her hand over the place Rocco had put the dagger into. She thought it had only gone up, against her ribcage. It must have taken a downward slope first. Would it make childbirth harder?

Don't worry Mama. Go to sleep now.

Lisette laid back against the silks, but her eyes remained opened.

R occo kept easy pace with the soldiers. They seemed less like comrades and more like independent mercenaries. There was not much teamwork in the crew, more like each guard had been given a specific task, and they adhered to it without wavering. He did not recognize anyone.

Humorless, brainless, and you do not play well with others. I definitely would not take any of you on board L'Implacable.

When they passed the turnoff to the Duke de Martinmas castle he was not surprised. He was either being taken to the Mendoza castle, which did not seem likely, or to Mercedes. The Countess de Mendoza was righteously angry during Lisette's escape, but she was angrier at the priest. He could not imagine what she or the count would want with him.

But Mercedes de Medina might want an audience. As

they came to the fork to take them south to the Mendozas or east to Mercedes, Rocco's suspicion was confirmed. The guards pushed him down the eastward path. He was happy for the information. Mercedes was not a woman to wander outdoors in her condition. He would need more information about her movements in order to plan her execution.

The silence among the guards appeared strained.

"Going to the Medina castle, are we?" he asked.

A blow to the back of the head told him that the guards enjoyed the silence. He shut his mouth and walked the path, following the one they called Captain Simone. The captain's back was tall, broad, and burly, although not particularly muscular, and he had a head of dark curls.

Simone as in, Amoy Simone? Amoy's secretive behavior made sense to him now.

By the time they arrived at the castle the sun had set. One of the guards lit a torch to find their way. They marched Rocco directly to the dungeon and one of the cells. The clang of the door was the last sound he heard as they left, taking the torch with them.

"You could leave me some light," he growled as they exited. He sprawled on the stone bed, where a piece of sky could be seen from the small window. Sitting up, he attempted to locate the moon. It wasn't high enough yet, but the light it was throwing across the yard was bright.

He still had time to get out of this predicament. Relaxing back down, he watched the dance of treetops and the twinkle of stars. He had nearly closed his eyes when the dungeon door opened, and a torch entered, held by a slender figure dressed in black.

"Good evening, Mercedes," he said, "or should I call you Marquise de Medina?"

"You may call me Countess, as I inherited my title from my dead mother."

Rocco rose from his hard bed, stretching. "As I recall

the king's rules, I don't believe all children inherit their parents' titles—only the eldest heir and never a daughter."

Her head shot up and back snapped straight. "I am inheriting it all." She softened, whether from pain or something else Rocco could not guess. "But that is not worth the arguing. Tonight, I'm here to answer your questions. I assume you have some."

Rocco studied her, an apparition in black from head to toe. He briefly recalled his flight to this castle and seeing Mercedes disrobed, witnessing her disfigurement. What she could want from him, he had no idea, but he was not going to play whatever game she was inviting him to.

"Come along, Señor Rocco, do not be shy. You want to know how I found you, how I know you, why I want you in my dungeon. Yes?" Her voice had a happily proud lilt.

She wants to gloat, and to make me fear whatever she has planned for me.

"No." He sat back down. "No questions."

"So, you know why you are here?" Her face was not visible through the veil, but he assumed she was smiling.

"No. I do not know, and I am not curious." He watched her body shrink back a little, so he added, "I do have one question."

She leapt on his words like a striking snake. "Yes?"

"Can I get a meal? I haven't had much to eat today."

Mercedes whipped about on her heels, then stood for a moment to gather herself, obviously in pain. She took the torch and left him, locking the door behind her. She had been gone a few moments when Rocco heard an angry shriek.

He laughed and laid down again.

Darkness had grown heavy by the time he heard another key in the lock. This time, a small woman entered, carrying a tray with a candle lighting her way. She carefully put the tray on a table, picked up the candle, and lit the torches on either side of his cell.

"Good even," she said. "I am Ghreta."

"Tristan de Rocco at your service," he told her. "But you may already know my name."

"I do." She picked up a large bowl from the tray and slid it through the pass-door on the bars. As she handed him a mug of cider, she leaned in close. "But perhaps not in the way you think," she whispered and showed him her wrist.

"Ah, a sister of the lioness." He kept his voice low. "What can you tell me?"

"Mercedes knows that you are Lisette de Lille's lover. She will use you to lure Lisette back here, where she intends to destroy her."

Rocco nodded. He took a bite. It was surprisingly good, and the plate was full of meat and roasted potatoes. "Surely your mistress did not order that I be given such a feast. Will you not be in trouble for feeding me so well?"

Ghreta smiled. "The kitchen and I are close. I am friendly with most of the servants here, except for these new guards. Mercedes paid a large sum for ruthless men to do her bidding. They keep to themselves and abuse those who get in their way."

"Does Mercedes foresee exactly when Lisette would be here?"

"There is talk that Lisette will reappear by the new moon. A woman comes to our back gate, a stranger to me. I suspect she is from the duke's household and hears of Lisette through him."

"Is she tall, with island features, and her dark hair in a bun?"

Ghreta nodded.

"Amoy Simone, no doubt related to Captain Simone."

"Ah, a fine pair of mercenaries." She tapped her chin.

"I shall have to pay special attention to her visits."

Ghreta left, leaving the space lit by a torch. Rocco ate, wondering if Mercedes would be twice as angry in the morning when she saw the charred remnants of the torches. He chuckled—she would find something to be angry about no matter what. It would be perhaps easier for him to placate her, but the idea of goading her into rage pleased him.

But how to escape this gaol cell and also keep Lisette safe? Rocco looked out the window again. This time, he could see the moon in the trees. It was almost at the one-quarter mark. Four days until he could transform…if he could transform. Would his curse still work now that his memory had returned?

He patted his breeches, felt the feather. Taking it out of his pocket, he held it up to the light. Pale blue with dark tips, and a shaft as hard as any rapier. He knew the magic contained in dragon feathers. Lamya had told him years ago when he first embarked on his blood dragon journey. But what kind of dragon was Lizzie?

It didn't matter. He needed to protect Lizzie and his baby. Opening his shirt, he held the tip of the feather against his chest, took a breath, and shoved it deep into his flesh.

53

Something stinging entered Rocco's body, running both cold and hot across his chest and down his arms and legs. At the same time the feather shriveled in his hand until it was limp. He managed to stick the used feather back into his pocket before he lost consciousness.

When he woke, he was lying by a fire next to a crystal-blue lagoon. Lamya the warrior sat before him. It took him a moment to rub his eyes and remember what had happened.

"How did I get here from Île des Oiseaux?"

Lamya shook her head. "You are still there. I called you here to tell you that Lisette will be with you by the waning crescent."

"No, she mustn't. Mercedes is using me to lay a trap. That is why I did this—I need to be a dragon—I wasn't certain—"

"Yes, I understand why you do what you do. But do no worrying. You will awaken in two days. What will come will come."

Unconsciousness claimed him again and Rocco knew nothing but dreams of flying as a blood dragon. He was aware of his body being shaken and of a sharp poke in his side. Opening his eyes, he saw Captain Simone. His mind wanted him to leap up and disarm this toad who prodded him, but his body refused to obey orders. He felt a momentary panic before relaxing.

What will come will come.

"He's alive," the captain said, and jabbed him again with a long stick before he left the cell.

Mercedes stood outside, regal in her black outfit. "So, you join us again? I did not think a pirate would try suicide."

She pointed to his chest with her cane, and he looked down at the rusty brown stain of dried blood on his shirt. In his awakening fog he opened his mouth, nearly arguing with her before he shut it again.

"Now that you've returned from the dead, are you any more curious about your situation?"

He studied the veil, picturing what lay beneath. "No, but I'm still hungry."

Mercedes lifted her cane and pounded the bars. "You are going to hear it! I know about you and Lisette de Lille. I know that you are lovers. I know that she carries your child, and when she comes to rescue you, I shall kill them both!" She stopped to catch her breath. "I haven't decided whether to kill you, too, or let you live on in your grief. This would be dead wife number two for you, wouldn't it? Not having very good luck with them, are you?"

"Better luck than you," he said. "And that's not a very nice way to speak of your own mother."

Mercedes' entire body shook, and she raised her cane, taking a step forward into the cell. Rocco assumed he was about to be pummeled. As quickly as her anger ignited, she lowered her cane and grew still.

"When I am finished, you will never know love again." She withdrew and left the dungeon.

Captain Simone was still in the cell with him, watching Mercedes leave. He turned back to Rocco. "You don't seem like a man who would end his life."

"It was all quite accidental."

The guard frowned. "You don't seem like the clumsy type either."

Rocco smiled. "People are not always what they seem. What is your name again—Captain Simone?"

"What does it matter?"

There was a tingle in Rocco's toes and fingers, radiating up his limbs. "I like to know my gaolers. It's sometimes the difference between letting them die and letting them go."

"Awfully bold for a man on his back." The guard walked from the cell and clanged the door shut.

"Alwan!" Mercedes' screech pierced the air from outside.

"Alwan, eh?" Rocco gave him a head-to-toe inspection. "We'll see which side you end up on."

The captain pivoted on a heel and strode from the dungeon, slamming the door and jamming the key into the lock. Rocco chuckled. For being in charge of Mercedes' elite guard, Alwan was quick to anger and easy to goad. That could prove useful.

In the meantime, he needed to be able to move again. Beginning with his hands, he closed his fingers and opened them. They were shaky at first, so he repeated the motion until his hands responded when asked. Arms were next. He worked his way up to his shoulders, focusing on each motion, until they behaved like normal.

The legs were more difficult, and it took many tries

to roll his ankles and bend his knees. He spent the whole morning trying to sit upright. The sun was almost at midday when the dungeon door opened. Rocco looked up to see Ghreta and a tray of food.

"Sorry I am late, but the guards were milling about the kitchen, and I could not get away."

"I suppose m'lady aims to starve me before she tortures me."

Ghreta set the tray on the table and held the bowl of food out through the pass-door. Rocco stood gingerly, testing his leg strength. His legs held until he took a step forward. The left leg collapsed and so did he, to the floor.

"Captain Rocco," Ghreta returned the bowl to the tray and turned back to the cell. "Are you alright?"

He smiled and scooted over to the bars. "I am recovering from a brief illness. But do not trouble yourself, I will be back to my strength soon." Holding his hands up, he said, "I'm sure I just need nourishment."

She retrieved the bowl and passed it in and down to him, along with the mug of ale. "I'm sorry to see you taken ill. Is there anything I can do?"

"Perhaps," he said between bites. "What do you know about Mercedes' elite guards?"

Ghreta made a face and spat on the floor. "Dogs, all of 'em. They's mercenaries, not even fit for pirating because they cannot be on a crew. Don't make good captains because they sow unrest on every ship."

Rocco nodded. "They did not seem to be working together when they brought me in. I suppose they were only successful because they never spoke to one another. How many of these elite guards are there?"

Ghreta looked at the ceiling and fussed with her fingers. "Fifteen, and ten of the regular guards, the ones that came from the d'Auguste castle, although it would not surprise me if the regular guards found their way back, now that the castle is occupied by the Count de Mendoza and his family."

"And Alwan?"

"Was not from either castle. I believe he came from Isla del Lagarto with Mercedes. He might be the meanest of the team. Angry all the time, threatens to kill the cook for too much salt in the broth, wants to kill the stableboy because his horse isn't tacked before he asked for it, you know the type."

"Yes." Rocco handed his empty bowl to Ghreta and drained his mug. "Thank you, I was most hungry. And now let us see if food performed the miracle I am hoping for."

Grabbing the bars, he pulled himself to his feet slowly, checking the strength of his leg muscles. He managed to hold himself up in a standing position, so he let go of the bars to test his balance. Smiling with his success he put his hands back on the bars again, lightly, and lifted one leg, stepping it forward, bearing weight on it again. It held.

"I believe I am almost back to normal," he told Ghreta and proceeded to walk in small, careful steps from one end of the cell to the next, keeping his hands close to the bars in case he stumbled.

"I am happy to be part of your miracle." Ghreta picked up her tray. "I'll return tonight with more food, God willing that the guards are not in my way again."

She left and Rocco returned to his labors, walking his cell until his legs felt like they belonged to him again. He practiced getting up, swinging his arms, and bending his torso, all while considering how to escape and protect Lisette.

Not that she needs protecting. She's killed men who threatened her, whether in human or dragon form. But twenty-five guards may be a lot for both of us to handle, even as dragons—if I can transform.

54

Lisette lay on the captain's bed attempting sleep but could not stop thinking of the scar on her womb and what that would mean for childbirth. What if the labor of pushing Alara out broke through? She would bleed uncontrollably and die without raising her daughter.

She rose. Wrapping her robe around her, she opened the cabin door. "Some sea air will clear these thoughts, and perhaps I shall seek the counsel of the captain."

The ship at full sail cut through the water like a dagger. Lisette walked to the bow, reveling in the wind and spray on her face. It was like coming home. She looked down at her swollen belly.

"If you weren't so large, I should like to be up in the crow's nest."

"You will be again." Captain Derya had walked up beside her. "You didn't sleep very long."

Lisette huffed. "I didn't sleep at all."

"There is much on your mind, I know, but we will not be in the harbor for another day. You cannot change anything from here."

"There seems to be a new problem." She described Alara's unsettling news.

The captain's face crinkled with worry. "We would not have known that when you were injured. This is unfortunate. There will be no room to delay—you must complete your task quickly and return to Lamya. Your *Dişi* sisters will do everything they can to help you."

"Thank you, captain. I am less worried already." She turned back to the horizon. "I just hope I know what to do to help Rocco."

The captain's hand rested on her shoulder. "It will come. It always does."

Captain Derya returned to the helm, leaving Lisette to enjoy the ship's movement and the view of open water. She tried to conjure the same happiness and feeling of freedom this usually brought, but her mind kept leaping into the future.

"I should have a plan," she told the wind. "Perhaps several."

She spent the afternoon walking around the deck, having brief conversations with the crew, and considering her options, and the worst that could happen in each. By the time four bells rang, she was again hungry and now exhausted.

Half the crew filed below deck to the mess, leaving the other half to man the ship. Lisette watched Oleta and Pinar heading down the steps. Behind them slipped a small girl she recognized, Ruhee, who was obviously trying to stay out of Lisette's view.

Lisette smiled. Ruhee was so young and still naïve. It was difficult to be angry with her for falling in love with Rocco and attempting to make him feel the same. Lisette was surprised to think that she wouldn't have been angry if Rocco had taken Ruhee to his bed. *There is pleasure and there is love, they do not have to be in the same place at the same time.*

She followed the crew, only to be stopped by Captain Derya. "Do you not wish to take your meal in my cabin?"

"If it is permitted, captain, I'd like one meal with the crew. I have missed them, especially Pinar, who was my confidant at my—the duke's—castle. This evening, I could join you for coffee before I am shown to my quarters."

Captain Derya smiled. "Yes, of course. Coffee tonight is excellent. We can discuss your plan for battle."

Lisette's eyes widened and she shook her head. "Apologies, it becomes a different thing when you describe it as a plan for battle. But that is what I shall need."

Excusing herself, Lisette carefully descended below deck, trying to maintain her balance while carrying extra weight. She walked down the narrow path to the mess and entered the space feeling quite too large to maneuver. Turning to leave, she caught the cook's eye and grinned.

"I had an idea to eat with the crew," she said. "But it appears I don't fit anymore."

"Nonsense," Cook said and shouted to the women at the table. "Move down! We got a visitor."

The chattering arose until it was almost too much for the room, everyone scooting to give Lisette room while asking her a thousand and one questions.

"Where have you been?"

"When is the baby due?"

"Who's the father?"

"Are you coming back to crew with us after it's born?"

Pinar had switched places to sit next to Lisette. She

patted the bench beside her.

"Ignore them wenches," she said with a laugh. "Come tell me everything."

"You know most of it," Lisette told her as she spooned a helping of stew on her plate. "I am on my way to Île des Oiseaux to help Captain Rocco. After, I shall return to…the other island to have the baby."

"If you will permit my saying, are you certain you will have time?" Pinar looked at Lisette's belly. "You look like you are ready now."

Lisette shrugged. "I was assured that there is time for all, as long as I did not dawdle."

Pinar stifled a laugh. "When the baby decides it's time, there will be no dawdling."

"I must trust my mentor," Lisette said. "I am grateful that you are taking me to Île des Oiseaux. Does the *Dişi Aslan* have other reasons to be at the island?"

"We will get our reports from our sisters and restock our food and drink." Pinar leaned in. "If you require our help, we will be in harbor for three days."

"Wow, that's quite long for you. Is it safe?"

"If it is not, we make an early departure. We have done it before."

Oleta patted Lisette on the shoulder. "We should like to stay with you, but our meal is over, and the next shift is hungry."

"Yes, I'm certain." Lisette rose with the rest and moved out into the alleyway, away from the ladder to the deck. "Please, you go first. I do not scamper up these as quick as I used to."

As each woman passed, they said a blessing for the baby. Some gave signs of their religious beliefs, and a few touched her stomach while saying a specific prayer. The last woman had gone up and Lisette stepped forward to grab the side rail when Ruhee appeared from the shadows.

"Oh, Ruhee, I thought everyone had gone up."

The girl gaped at the floor, shaking her head, hands clasped to her chest. She unfolded her arms and extended a hand to Lisette, palm up. When she opened her fingers, they revealed a gold chain with a charm on it. The charm looked like a cross, except the top of it was shaped like an upside-down teardrop.

"This is for the baby," she whispered.

Lisette took her hand and folded the chain in it. "Ruhee, you owe me nothing. I am not angry. We all make mistakes, and hopefully we all learn to do better."

Ruhee looked up at her, tears streaming down her face. "You should be angry! You should not forgive me! I did a bad thing, and it went wrong—and I do a worse thing now because I am not sorry, and I still wish he loved me."

Lisette sighed and smiled. "I cannot be angry with you because you are so angry with yourself. Yes, it is easy for me to be kind now. The spell did not work as you planned, and Rocco still loves me. But I am sorry that you are in pain, and there is nothing I can do to make you feel better."

Ruhee thrust the necklace at her once more. "Yes, you can. Take this from me. It was my grandmother's, and her mother's before. My father is Bhārat, but my mother was Egyptian. This is the ankh, the symbol of eternal life. I wish your baby to have it, and to have eternal life."

"Oh, no, Ruhee, I cannot take your family heirloom." Lisette recalled her emerald that she had given to Begum for safekeeping. "You must give it to your child someday."

"Yes, you will take it. It is my punishment for trying to outsmart the gods. Being punished is the only way I can leave this memory behind and heal."

"Very well. But it is borrowed between friends, not given to a victor. Someday you will have need of it. Come to me and it is yours again. In the meantime, I shall cherish it and honor your family."

Ruhee burst into wracking sobs and Lisette drew the girl into her arms, patting her back to soothe her. She was no shorter than Lisette, and yet she seemed so small. Lisette reasoned that it had something to do with the large belly in between them. When Ruhee had run out of tears, Lisette took the necklace and put it around her own neck. Ruhee nodded, her eyes swollen and raw.

"There it will stay," she said.

"Until you return for it," Lisette told her.

Ruhee teared up again and ran over to the ladder. Lisette followed her. Climbing up the narrow, steep ladder was harder than climbing down. With each step, she had to push with her legs to shove her body upward, as she curved her back to keep her stomach from getting caught on the rungs and pulled with her arms at the same time. By the time she was on deck, she was exhausted.

Now I'd like that nap.

Begum was still at the helm, staring forward and looking cross. Lisette followed her gaze and saw a ship on the horizon. It was too far to see their flag, but the vessel was moving in the same direction as the *Dişi Aslan*.

Lisette stepped up to the helm. "Looks like we are following, but not for long. Any idea who it is?"

"Hmm, perhaps," Begum said, her eyes still focused on the sea ahead. "You are right, we shall catch up soon, and I shall know for certain."

Lisette kept watch, excited to find out what flag the ship sailed under and mesmerized by the swooshing water and steady creaking of the deck. The *Dişi Aslan* whipped across the waves, growing ever closer to the strange ship. Looking ahead, Lisette could see the tip of an island mountain—it was the tallest point on Île des Oiseaux.

She felt a small hand in hers and heard her daughter's voice. *Mama don't be worried. Pinar is right. I shall be ready soon. You will not return to Lamya before I am born.* Alara's hand was gone, and Lisette looked up with a start.

The captain was putting a spyglass up to her eye, moving it back and forth. She lowered it and exclaimed, "Good news, we are about to meet up with *L'Implacable.*"

As excited as Lisette was to see *L'Implacable*, she was still reeling from Alara's words. She could not have this baby without Lamya. And yet she had been given direction by the Ancient One to help Rocco, along with a promise that she could return to give birth safely.

Perhaps Begum would have counsel for her. She took a breath, slowly let it out, and her body relaxed. Worrying about the future was useless. At the moment, there was a ship to hail and friends to greet. Later, hopefully with Begum's help, she would make a plan.

The *Dişi Aslan* rolled up beside *L'Implacable* and flags were run out as greetings. Lisette moved to the port side and looked up at Rocco's ship, looming so much larger than the sleek vessel she sailed on. A large, ruddy man stood at the starboard rail, waving his arm.

"Ahoy, Captain Derya! Permission to board?"

The captain waved from the helm. "Ahoy, Chunk! Permission granted."

Within the hour, Chunk sat in Captain Derya's quarters, shifting in his seat, and looking uncomfortably at the selection of bean dip, flat bread, and skewers of meat. Lisette filled her plate as Begum filled the copper pot with black coffee and set out the small cups.

"Do have a bite, Chunk," Lisette encouraged, demonstrating how to pack the meat into the pocket of the bread and drag it through the dip. "It is warm and filling."

Chunk nodded, smiling nervously. "Sure, Lizzie. It's so good to see you again." He mimicked her, building a bite, and tentatively sinking his teeth into it. "Hey, this here is good! Thanks indeed, Cap'n Derya."

The captain smiled and poured the coffee before taking a seat. "What news?"

"We last saw Cap'n Rocco three nights ago." Chunk relayed the meeting, the taking on of Luis Delgado, and Luis' tale of being arrested for allowing Lisette to escape. "Pardon my saying, Lizzie, but Delgado told us quite a yarn about your exit from the castle."

"If it involved feathers and flight, it was all true," Lisette said.

Chunk took a tiny sip of coffee and his face puckered. "Sorry, Cap'n, this might take a bit to git used to."

Begum laughed and brought out a bottle and a mug. "You are excused. Rum is probably more to your liking." She filled the mug with a generous pour and handed it to him.

"Aye, yes." He took a swig and smiled. "Any news from the *Dişi Aslan*?"

"We are just back from Isla del Lagarto," Begum told him. "I am very pleased, they are thriving. We exchanged goods and checked in on Trina. She is enjoying her new role, dispensing rule and justice away from the stifling European overlords."

"Where are you on your way to now?" he asked.

"We sail to Île des Oiseaux." Begum sipped her coffee. "Lisette has a job to do there, and we have business to attend to."

"Seems we'll be sailin' companions for a stretch, then," Chunk said. "We also aim for the island, to pick up Cap'n Rocco."

Lisette looked at him. "After Rocco has finished what he came for, he'll rejoin the ship?"

"Aye, Lizzie. Ya know, it'd be nice if you could come wit' us."

She smiled and patted her stomach. "I think I might be busy."

Chunk blushed a light rose. "Sure, I forgot."

"I see that Ruhee has apologized." Begum changed the subject, gesturing to the necklace on Lisette.

"Her spell made things most difficult," Lisette said, fingering the gold charm. "But I do not have it in me to be angry. She insisted I take this."

"Ruhee is a simple girl without much in this world. The ankh is a symbol of her family, a link to her home."

"I protested for that very reason. Why did she insist that I take it?"

"She took something important from you. Giving you something important to her is her penance."

"Hmpf," Chunk puffed. "She took somethin' important from us, too. We need Cap'n Rocco back. Instead, he's chasin' off to kill a wench he got no grudge agin."

"And I must help him, according to my mentor," Lisette said. "I pray it goes well."

"We will help you in any way we can," Begum said.

Chunk nodded. "We'll be standin' by to jump in, too."

"I am uneasy about this task, especially now that

Rocco has his memories again," Lisette said. "He knows that his curse was lifted, but I think he has committed to slaying Mercedes—the question is, will it be as dragon or as man?"

Begum shrugged. "He will only know when he knows."

"True enough." Chunk rose from the table, nodding. "But we'll be there if he needs us. Now if you will excuse me, I need to git back to the ship."

"Yes, of course," Begum stood and led him to the door. "Good luck, Chunk. We will meet again on Île des Oiseaux."

Lisette rose and stretched, wondering how she would help Rocco and how in the world she would have a baby without Lamya. Having the crews on two ships available to fight was comforting, but no amount of fighting skill could deliver a dragon child.

Begum went to a chest in the corner of the room, extracting something from a drawer. "I've been keeping this safe for you." She proffered a closed fist.

Lisette held her hand out and Begum dropped something into her palm. "My emerald!" She held it up to the light and then placed it around her neck. It hung lower than the ankh, cool against her skin. Wrapping her fingers around the jewel, she recalled her father's embrace and the last time she saw her family. The tears worked themselves up from her heart.

Begum put her arm around her shoulder. "It will be well, Lizzie."

"My apologies. This brought back memories of my father. I wish he could be here to help us—and my mother to help with the baby."

"Yes, your mother," Begum said with a wan smile. "But you will have Lamya to help you."

"Maybe not." Lisette told Begum of Alara's latest visit. "I confess, I am afraid."

"Would you really trust the word of an unborn child over that of an Ancient One?"

"It does sound ludicrous, but after the last couple of years, I've found that I can't discount anything, especially my own intuition."

"And what is your intuition telling you?"

She sighed. "That I shall soon be in danger, without and within."

Begum paced across the cabin. "I cannot help with childbirth, although there are many on my ship who have healing knowledge."

"Like Ruhee?" Lisette waved her hand. "My apologies, that was uncalled for."

"No, it is understandable. Yes, like Ruhee. Oleta for one." She stopped and looked at her wall of maps. "What I can help you with is Rocco. What is your plan?"

Lisette sat again, tired by the baby's weight. "If Rocco escaped the duke, he will not return to the castle de Lille. His goal is to kill Mercedes, so he shall go to her, learn what he can about her strengths and weaknesses in preparation for the waning crescent."

"Yes, that is reasonable."

"That said, I do not know exactly where to find him. My choices at the moment are to travel to Mercedes' castle to be prepared to help, or to go to my old home to see what news Marisha can tell me."

"Ah, I would recommend Marisha first, then Mercedes," Begum said. "My *Dişi* sister is very good at keeping her eyes open and mouth closed. She can relate the latest intrigue."

Lisette nodded. "And as far as a strategy for helping Rocco, I can now transform into a moon dragon without hesitation. I can also transform back and have a dagger at the ready."

Begum pointed to her midsection. "If you can reach beyond your current situation."

"Ugh." Lisette looked down. "If the gods are willing that this baby can wait until after I come to her father's aid."

"We will help where we can."

"Begum? I—I hardly know how to ask but I must…" Lisette hesitated, drew a breath, and continued. "If Alara should come into this world and I should not—survive her birth…she will need to be taken care of by someone who knows what she is."

The captain took a few steps around the cabin before facing her, the candlelight giving her eyes a glassy shine. "Of course, I will do this thing. Never worry about your daughter, she will always be cared for. And you will survive this.

Begum cleared her throat. "In the meantime, I will have a contingent of my crew at the ready. They will be under orders to watch carefully and step in if you need them. I will join you as soon as I can."

"Thank you." Lisette smiled. "Having so much support makes me a little braver."

"Now, the hour is late, and you need sleep." Begum gestured toward her bed. "You will sleep here tonight. I will take the smaller space."

"Oh, Captain, I couldn't—"

"You will. Consider it captain's orders, although I would prefer it if you accepted it as a gift from a friend."

"Thank you," Lisette repeated, and rose to hug her. "I hope to repay your kindness someday."

"Someday? Do you forget your gift to us of Sandoval's gold?" Begum laughed. "Go to sleep."

Lisette watched her leave before reaching down to remove the dagger's sheath from her thigh. She slid the blade out and tested its edge. Still sharp, but with a few burrs. She was rooting around Begum's cabin looking for a whetstone when there was a knock at the door.

A young woman stood on the threshold. "I come to

take the dishes."

"Yes, of course." Lisette moved out of the way and helped her set the plates on a tray.

"M'lady, there is no need for you to work," the girl said, frowning.

"First, I am not m'lady on this ship. I am Lizzie and wear the mark of the *Dişi Aslan*. Second, I am neither afraid of nor too proud to work. Four hands make the job go faster."

The girl grinned. "Thank you, Lizzie."

"Do you know if the captain has a whetstone in her cabin?"

"Yes." She nodded toward a cabinet in the far corner. "Third drawer, port side."

Gathering up the last plate, the girl excused herself and left. Lisette walked to the cabinet and opened the drawer. The whetstone was where the girl said. On the right side was a carefully folded pile of small clothes. Lisette held them up, surprised.

It was a baby's gown and biggins, both in a fine-textured tan felt. A slip of paper fell from the cap. Lisette picked it up and read.

My dearest Amarissa,

I long to keep you with me always, but it is not to be. I shall cherish and treasure you and you will never be far from my heart.

Mama

The shock knocked Lisette down into a chair. Begum had a child? It was almost too much to take in. She read the note a few times. Underneath the word Mama, there was a squiggle of strange yet familiar characters. A backward J with two dots under it, followed by a sideways W.

She unclasped her emerald and held it to the light. Engraved in the gold setting were the same characters—a backward J with two dots and a sideways W. She had assumed these were the jeweler's marks. Why would Begum have signed a letter with the exact symbols?

And where was the baby? Perhaps something bad happened, or perhaps she had to give little Amarissa to someone for safekeeping. Begum had never shared this story.

"Of course, she wouldn't share this experience with me," Lisette told the empty room. "Who would tell a pregnant woman a story about a baby without a happy ending?"

She put the note back and carefully folded everything, putting it away just as she found it, and closing the drawer. Her dagger would have to keep its burrs. She would not have the captain finding out she opened that drawer and learned its secret.

Taking off her robe, she snuggled deep into the fine silks of the captain's bed and closed her eyes.

Light had barely peeked into the room when she heard the cry of "Land!" from the crow's nest. She rolled to the edge of the bed, awkwardly rocking her body until her feet were on the floor. Fastening her robe about her, she left the cabin and climbed the stairs, anxious to see Île des Oiseaux.

The captain was at the helm. Lisette stepped up, wishing she could be in the crow's nest with the best view. From the helm, she could see the tall cliffs of the island, just west of the port. They had carefully swung out and past the village during the night, to escape detection. The land before them appeared rugged and impenetrable.

What lay beyond was the small harbor that any sailor with half a brain could find, but only the best sailor could steer through.

"I trust you slept well," Captain Derya said. "I will have Emil bring you food in my cabin. You have a long journey ahead of you. It will require strength for you and the baby."

"Yes, thank you," Lisette said. She descended to the deck and down the stairs to the cabin, speaking to herself. "I have a long journey, even if I fly there."

Rocco watched the moon through his cell window. The third quarter grew slimmer each day. In two nights, perhaps only one, he would become a blood dragon—or some kind of dragon, he hoped. Would this cell hold him? He'd never had to break out of a confined space.

Morning came with its usual boredom. He hoped Lisette would not risk herself or their baby to come here and rescue him. *Of course, that sort of restraint is impossible.*

The dungeon door opened, and he expected to see Ghreta with another meal and perhaps more information. A bent, black figure entered, Mercedes and her favorite guard Alwan.

"Good morn, Mercedes," Rocco said. "Or should I call you Marquise de Medina?"

"Countess will do. We have had this conversation."

"And yet I remain unconvinced. Did El Rey confer the title to you?"

Her voice betrayed her irritation with him. "When I said I was keeping you to lure Lisette de Lille out of hiding, I did not say you had to be healthy and unbroken."

"If I am harmed it will make her quite angry." He leaned upon the bars. "How many dragons does she have at her command?"

"I hope she brings them all." Mercedes stood firm, but Rocco saw her knuckles tighten on her staff. "The guards will make quick work of them, I'm certain."

"Surely you have seen the dragons fight. Swords do not pierce them, nor arrows." He grinned. "Have your guards a secret weapon to bring them down?"

She neared his cell. "How do you know so much about the dragons?"

"There is a network of gossip on the islands, and many tales to tell."

She pounded the bar with her cane where his hand rested, but he was quicker and pulled back. "You were there! I remember!"

"Where, Marquise?"

"Lisette and I were fighting. She must have thought she had me bested, but I was just waiting for the right moment to kill her. You pulled her from me. I remember."

He stared at her, silent.

"Answer me!" His silence seemed to infuriate her. "You were there, weren't you?"

Rocco turned his back to her, went to his bed, and laid down.

"Come back here and answer me!"

He was surprised she didn't burst into flames. She stepped aside and gestured for Alwan, who strode forward and put the key in the cell door.

"I've been looking for a chance to give you a good

beating," he said.

Rocco stood and glared at him. "Do your best."

The dungeon door flew open and Ghreta burst in. "M'lady, the Count de Mendoza is here. He says it is important and that he must speak to you."

Mercedes cocked her head. "Very well. Alwan, leave him and come along."

"But m'lady, I can still give him a good thrashing."

"Not unless I can watch." She turned toward the exit. "Come. We have plans to make."

The trio left, and Rocco reclined on his bed, his heart still pumping with the desire to fight. This cell was more than confinement to him. He was accustomed to the ship and being active. His legs and arms ached for action. For the next hour, he paced back and forth, swung his arms about, and practiced his sword and dagger skills, although he had neither weapon.

He was in mid-thrust when the dungeon door opened. Throwing himself onto his bed, he feigned sleep.

"Can you really relax at a time like this?" Ghreta asked, carrying a tray of food.

Opening his eyes, he sat up. "I thought you might be Alwan, come to try to beat me."

She sat the tray down. "Stay on your guard against Alwan. He is not only strong and a bully, he also cheats and will pull a blade on you. Anything if it means he wins."

Rocco took the bowl of food and the mug she passed to him. "I am glad for this sustenance at least. Any news?"

"Much." She nodded. "It seems the Count de Mendoza was alarmed by the recent evening at the Duke de Martinmas' castle. He is meeting with Mercedes to enlist her protection against a dragon, of all things."

"Hmm," He took a long drink. "Does Mercedes seem keen about this proposition?"

"I saw her speaking with him energetically. He was happy to accept protection and hinted that they could work together to get more wealth from this island. Mercedes sounded quite agreeable. However, after he left, she spent some time in huddled discussion with Alwan." Ghreta lit the torches beside the cell. "If I know nobility, I'd guess she is planning to play the duke against the count and take both castles for her own if she can."

Rocco huffed. "And they say pirates pillage. We have a long way to go to catch up with the nobility."

"I have heard Mercedes speak of her desires before. Total rule of this island, taxation of every ship that harbors, and percentage of every crop."

"It may not be enough then," Rocco said, "for me to kill Mercedes. I shall have to do something about the Mendozas."

"That is a lot of killing," Ghreta said.

"I don't have to kill them. I can encourage them to return to Spain." He smiled at her. "I believe that can easily be done."

Ghreta sighed. "Thank the gods. If you don't mind me saying, I consider killing Mercedes to be a kindness, seeing as the pain she is in. But people like the Mendozas—"

"People who want to rape this island, strip it of everything good and plentiful, so that those who can leave and those who can't are miserable? People like that?"

"When you say it out loud, I suppose I can't object if they're laid into the ground."

"In the meantime, I need to get out of this cell." Rocco looked around. "Any chance of slipping me a key, or a piece of metal to pick the lock?"

She shook her head. "Even if I did, there is a guard stationed outside the dungeon. He is only away from his post when I deliver food."

"I shall manage." Rocco reached through the bars and

touched her arm. "Thank you for what you have been able to do. I hope you don't get into trouble."

Ghreta patted his hand. "I'm a *Dişi* sister. Trouble is my natural state."

She took the emptied bowl and mug and walked toward the exit. At the dungeon door, she turned to him. "I will see what I can bring you."

Rocco returned to his exercise, jumping and running in place. It was ludicrous, but he was on his way to madness if he didn't keep busy. His dragon flights ran across his mind.

Lisette is lucky. What a gift, to wish for transformation and receive it. I wonder if she'll retain the ability after the child is born.

The dungeon door swung open again and a man in a long robe stumbled inside. It was Tumas, followed by one of the regular guards. The guard grabbed Tumas' arm and dragged him to the cell next to Rocco, shoving him in.

"Priests who take sides deserve hangin'," the guard spat as he slammed the door shut.

Rocco watched in silence until the guard left the dungeon.

"Priest, how did you get here?"

"I confess I do not know." His face wore bruises, and his robe had a few tears amid patches of dirt. "I was counseling the duke about his son and about Lisette. I had encouraged him to keep an open mind about the young woman. This morning when I went out to gather mangos, I was surrounded by guards and dragged here."

"I guess Mercedes was unhappy when you left her for the duke's castle."

Tumas shrugged. "She should have treated me better. I know that Jesus suffered many indignities and wounds, but I was trying to give counsel and aid to a woman in pain, and she rebuffed me at every opportunity."

"Why were you picking mangos? Usually, one of the

kitchen servants collect those."

"Yes, usually." Tumas smoothed at his robe, studying each rip. "But Amoy asked me to do it today. She said the kitchen help was too busy."

"That wench is dangerous." Rocco frowned. "She is passing information about the duke's place to Alwan, who shares it with Mercedes."

"We need to get a message to the duke."

"Forget the duke. We need to get a message to someone who knows what to do with it."

"What do we do?"

Rocco sat back down on his bed. "We wait for the next meal."

Lisette came ashore in the dinghy with the captain. *L'Implacable*, being slower, had not joined them yet, but they knew she was no more than a half day behind. Lisette was quiet during the trip from the ship to the surf. She was glad that Begum did not prod her for conversation.

Helping Rocco would mean a battle, she knew, and she would have to put aside her moon dragon instincts of nurturing in order to slay Mercedes. She wished for a message from someone granting her permission. It could be Alara, or Lamya, or even God Almighty. She looked up at the sky, as blue as Rocco's eyes, and prayed for wisdom and courage.

"Can you get out when we get to the surf?" Begum asked. "Or do you need help?"

"I'll try to do it," Lisette said, looking down at her stomach. "I should be able to float."

She waited until they were almost at the beach and the waves were small before rolling her legs over the port side and attempting to stand. The sand under her feet shifted back as the boat shifted forward, depositing her on her backside in the surf. Maintaining her grip on the dinghy, Lisette pulled her feet underneath her and stood, rocking to and fro to keep her balance.

"Are you alright?" Begum shuffled through the surf toward her.

"Yes," Lisette chuckled. "It was not graceful, but it was done."

The rest of the crew rowed in, stashing their boats in nearby caves and rock formations. Begum gestured to them. "I need four of these women to come with me, and the rest will be on lookout for you. Good luck."

Lisette gazed around. Flying to the castle would be so much faster. It would also attract the most attention. She'd have to fly high and use her cloud skills to hide herself.

"You are trying to make a decision?" Begum asked.

"Yes, it would be faster, but if I'm seen…"

"It would give away any advantage for surprise."

"For now, I shall walk." Lisette took two wide steps forward. "Actually, I shall waddle."

Begum smiled.

Lisette started up the winding trail that would take her to the top of the cliff. Her castle was a half-day journey on foot. She could get there by the noon sun and find a way to contact Marisha.

Walking up the traversing path, she had to stop at the first bend to catch her breath, and again at the second. Getting to the castle by noon might have been optimistic.

She patted her stomach. "Alara, you get heavier and harder to carry each day."

"What did you say?" Begum had walked up behind

her, leading her crew.

"I'm telling my little girl that she is not so little to carry uphill." Lisette lowered her voice. "It would be so much easier to fly."

"True," Begum said, "but it would startle my crew. Besides, I am sending someone to help you—and she cannot travel on the clouds."

Begun turned and whistled, gesturing toward Lisette. Pinar ran up the path to join them.

Lisette grinned. "Pinar, I would love your assistance, but I do not want to put you in danger."

"The captain has a good idea," Pinar said. "I know the castle and can slip in unnoticed—just one more servant. You might get caught up in the duke's web again."

They continued to climb the cliff. Lisette's breathing was ragged and heavy, but she refused to take another break. By the time they reached the summit, she had to stop to calm her pounding heart. "My apologies. I am not as agile these days."

"All the more reason to let us help you," Pinar said.

Lisette sighed and nodded. "All right. You win."

The crew joined them at the top.

"Go with God's strength and mercy, Lizzie," Begum said.

"Thank you, Captain."

They hugged one another and split up, Begum and three women heading toward the village, Oleta leading the rest toward the jungle outside Mercedes' castle, and Lisette and Pinar walking toward the castle de Lille.

"When is the baby due?" Pinar asked.

"Soon. I do not mean to be terse, but Lamya told me I could return to her and have the baby after I help Rocco, but I had a vision, a premonition that I shall have the child sooner. I admit, Pinar, I am uneasy."

"My grandmother used to say, 'hayat bir yol bulur.' It means, basically, that life finds a way to live. You are strong, m'lady—" she held up her hand to stop Lisette's protest, "and I mean m'lady. You are regal and confident, and capable of doing whatever you attempt."

"But what about nature?"

"If the baby is strong and you are strong, life will find a way to keep living."

"Thank you, Pinar, and thank your grandmother. They are good words to keep in mind."

Pinar pointed to the charm Ruhee had given her. "You wear the ankh. It is a symbol of eternal life. Trust me, all will be well."

The castle was a short distance away when Lisette stopped, holding her stomach, and blowing her breath out in an attempt to stop the pain in her belly. "I need to sit down."

Pinar guided her to a small grove, well off the path and partially hidden and eased her to the ground. Lisette rolled onto her side and curled up, panting. She had, early in life, experienced the rolling pain of her menstrual cycles, but this was heightened.

Oh, Alara, tell me you are not ready yet. This is not a good time.

One more tightening of her muscles, one more pinching roll, and her body relaxed. She stayed on her side, catching her breath. Raising her hand, she asked, "Help me up?"

Pinar pulled her to a sitting position and stopped. "Sit for a few moments. Make certain the contraction has passed."

"Contraction. So that's what it was." Lisette curled her feet underneath her. "Please, I must get up, we must keep going."

"No." Pinar stood over her, hands on her hips. "You will stay here, rest your body. I will go to the castle and return with news."

"But I need to—"

"You need to help Rocco and have a baby. That is all. I can move faster if you are not with me. If you will forgive me, you do not move very quickly."

Lisette laughed. "Go. Find Marisha and come back."

Pinar trotted down the path toward the back of the castle. Lisette could see her approach the gate, knock, and be allowed inside. She said a prayer for her *Dişi* sister, appealing to any god listening to keep Pinar safe. Now it was time to wait.

Lisette leaned her back against a tree and stretched out her arms and legs. The baby stretched her limbs in response, pushing a tiny hand up Lisette's ribcage and a tiny foot into Lisette's hip.

"There must be very little space left in there," Lisette told her, "but please try to stay where you are, at least until this is over."

I'll try, Mama, but I cannot promise you. Hayat bir yol bulur.

"You are a parrot."

No. I am your daughter. And a dragon.

Rocco's face popped into her mind. She would see him again soon and allowed herself to dream that he was with her and their baby and living in a little house where they could be together without troubles.

She laughed out loud. Who in this life did not have troubles? "All right," she said. "We can live together in relative happiness. Rocco can sail his ship, and I can miss him until he returns." *And when Alara is old enough, I can sail with him and sit in the crow's nest again.*

Looking at the castle, it surprised her to not want to live there. Life had seemed so lovely as a child within its walls. Surely, she and Alara could wait for Rocco's return here, in luxury.

But it wasn't the same. The happy memories had a dark stain across them now that her family was gone. The duke was a pleasant enough fellow, if stubborn and arrogant, but having someone take possession of what was once hers made the castle less important to her.

"A little place, for the three of us," Lisette told her baby. "Unless you have brothers or sisters. Then we will need more room."

She saw a shadow move on the castle wall. The back gate was opening. Hoping that it was Pinar, she leaned forward. A tall, big-boned woman exited. Lisette recognized Amoy.

The housekeeper walked to the edge of the jungle and reached down to examine a plant. The castle gate shut, and Amoy stood, looking back. After a moment, she turned and strode away from Lisette, taking the path toward the other castles. At the top of the ridge, a tall figure stood, waiting.

His features were unclear at this distance, but Lisette recognized his form. This was Alwan. Amoy met him and the two stood together, obviously in conversation, although Lisette could not hear the words. They appeared to be engrossed in whatever they were discussing.

As Lisette strained to hear a snippet of anything, she heard the gate open and looked over to see Pinar peeking out. Seeing the figures on the hill, the girl pulled the door back a little, continuing to watch the pair. Lisette regarded the scene, trying to think of a way to shoo Amoy toward Mercedes and allow Pinar to come to her.

Like the Medina castle, the wall around the de Lille home was wide enough for soldiers to mount a defense. The land had been cleared around the wall to keep the enemy from hiding in the jungle. Unfortunately, the verdant island rejected its baldness and grew back with ferocity.

The gate had closed and two figures were crawling

along the wall toward the corner furthest from Amoy and Alwan. They disappeared behind a tree that obscured the view.

Losing sight of the figures on the wall, Lisette turned to see that Alwan was gone, and Amoy was trotting back toward the castle. Lisette pushed herself back into the shadows until the woman had opened the back gate, taken one last look over her shoulder, and disappeared.

A rustle in the tree by the wall caught Lisette's attention and she saw two figures drop to the ground and run toward her. Pinar was in the lead, carrying a leather pouch. Huffing behind her was Marisha. They arrived at the top, breathless and excited.

"Lizzie, we have much to tell." Pinar shoved the pouch at her. "Here, I brought you a meat pie and some cider. You will need sustenance for the baby."

Lisette took the food. "Thank you. Now sit beside me and give me the news."

"Rocco indeed escaped from the duke," Marisha said, "but he was captured by Mercedes. She has increased her guards by at least double. These new guards are different, hardened men who are ruthless killers, no doubt kicked out of some military. She is holding the captain prisoner in an attempt to lure you to her."

Pinar shook her head. "This is dangerous. You are not as fast or agile in your present condition. What are you doing? Eat. You have taken one small bite."

Lisette held the pie up. "I am eating. I wanted to be careful with the first few bites in case Alara has an opinion about the filling."

"There is a rumor," Marisha said. "Count de Mendoza has been sent here by the king to determine which noble should ultimately rule this island. Mercedes has seized on this as an opportunity to play the count against the duke and take control for herself."

"How is this to happen?"

"The count approached her for protection from the dragon, promising to help her amass more wealth by removing the duke and increasing taxes on the people. She agreed, but in her own turn, sent an emissary to the duke to tell him of the count's plans and recruit him to help remove the count." Marisha stopped for a moment to catch her breath. "The duke was not as enthusiastic as Mendoza. It seems that as a duke, he does not make contracts with emissaries, nor with counts, and certainly not with a marquise who has labeled herself a countess."

"I'm guessing Mercedes is not pleased with his arrogance," Lisette said.

"She is furious. I believe the plan is to take care of you and Rocco, and then use the count's forces to dispatch the duke. She still has spies within the duke's household and can use them easily to gain access. Mercedes is mad with power and wants even more than she has now."

"I know of one spy." Lisette told them both of Amoy's visit with Alwan. "Have we any idea how many men the count will bring to the battle?"

"He employs ten men of varying degrees of skill," Marisha said. "Still, with Mercedes' twenty-five, that is a large contingent of fighters, and even the most timid may find strength and courage when surrounded by braver souls."

Lisette rubbed her temples and took a swig of cider. "We need to free Rocco, although at sunset, he might free himself."

"You need to rest." Pinar pointed to the half-eaten pie. "And nourish yourself. Of truth, Lizzie, I do not know how you can go into battle while a baby is begging to be born."

"Is this true?" Marisha asked. "I did not realize it was so close."

"She is having contractions," Pinar said.

"One. I had one contraction." Lisette scowled at them

and took another nibble. As she swallowed, a cramping pain rolled through her again, under her ribs, slowly and torturously, working its way down to her thighs. She resisted, taking another gulp of cider and attempting to breathe naturally. When the sweat rolled down her temples and her breath turned into panting, she curled sideways at last.

"You see?" Pinar knelt beside her, rubbing her back. "We need a midwife."

Lisette waved at her and shook her head. She took a deep breath and let it out, feeling the pain subside. Lying still for a moment, she massaged her belly and felt the baby adjust.

Not yet, Alara, please. We need to rescue your father. She sat up carefully. "Do not worry. The baby will not come yet."

"How do you know?" Marisha frowned. "Have you ever had a baby?"

"No, but I must trust my mamha. She told me I could help Rocco and come back to her before Alara comes." Lisette put the food away and tucked her feet under her. "Now, could someone help me stand? The sooner this is done, the sooner I have this baby."

Pinar took Lisette's forearm and guided her to standing. "I hope you are right. Marisha and I will go with you and help lead the charge against Mercedes' forces."

"No, one of you must return to the harbor. *L'Implacable* should be here by now," Lisette told her. "Those men are fearless in battle and I'm certain would fight for their captain's freedom." Lisette pressed Pinar's shoulder, gesturing toward the pirate's harbor. "Go, get Chunk and his men. And Marisha, you should probably catch up to Oleta and lend your sword."

It took a little more pushing and a lot of cajoling, but Pinar finally turned back toward the cove and Marisha toward Mercedes' castle. Lisette watched them both walk on, getting further apart and turning to look at her every few steps.

"You will turn into pillars of salt if you are not careful," Lisette called after them.

She regarded the sky. In the very few moments of their conversation, the sun had disappeared, its orange light giving way to twinkling stars and a crescent moon. Kneeling in the soft undergrowth, she closed her eyes.

One river, many streams. I am Lisette de Lille, and I am a dragon.

58

The next time the dungeon door opened, Rocco was glad to see it was Ghreta and not Alwan returning to beat him. He'd be happy to take Alwan on, but Rocco assumed he'd have backup men to help him if he needed it. And he'd need it.

"Good afternoon, Ghreta. We have a new occupant." Rocco gestured to the next cell. "Do you know Father Tumas?"

She smiled and put the tray down. Handing a bowl and a mug to each, she said, "Hello, Father. Sorry to see you in here."

"Any news?" Rocco asked.

"Mercedes believes that Lisette will soon be on the island, so she is preparing her guards. She has also enlisted the guards of the Count de Mendoza, so there will be as many as thirty men here at the ready tonight."

"She thinks Lisette will come tonight?"

Ghreta shrugged. "That I do not know, only that they will be ready tonight and will continue to be ready until Lisette comes."

"I cannot let her walk into this."

"I have been in touch with my *Dişi* sister at the duke's castle. Hopefully, she can get word to Lisette. I will be on watch."

"If you need an ally, I stand at the ready," Tumas said. "I may be a man of peace, but as a lad, I fought for my country. I have not forgotten how to wield a sword."

"Thank you, Priest," Rocco said. "First we need to escape this place."

"Ah, yes." Ghreta reached into her pocket and withdrew two slender metal rods, sharpened at the end. "I could not sneak away the key, but a wise pirate like yourself might put these to use."

Rocco took them and felt their edges. "Yes, I believe these will work their magic."

"Know that the weapons are kept in the stables not the barracks. There is usually a guard on duty."

"Thank you. Anything else?" Rocco asked.

Ghreta picked up her tray and walked toward the door, then turned. "Yes. Although there are many men here, they are not stationed strategically. Most of them are outside the wall, waiting no doubt for Lisette to show up. Be cautious, but it is likely you will not encounter any resistance to stealing a blade and escaping. Mercedes is not expecting you to get out, she is expecting Lisette to get in."

She left and Rocco went to the window. If he was going to leave this place, he needed to unlock his cell now. The moon would be in its full waning crescent tonight. If he was going to transform, it would be at sunset.

Embracing the padlock on the door, he put the tools in the keyhole, pushing and lifting with one and searching for the mechanism with the other. This was a fairly quick task when he was facing the lock but finding everything from behind gave him a distinct feeling of being in a mirror. He slowed his movements, closing his eyes and realigning himself to think backward.

The lock rewarded him with a loud click before falling open. Rushing to Tumas' cell, he opened that one more easily.

"You may come with me, Priest, or wait until nightfall to escape."

"Why do you not wait for darkness?"

"I may not be able to by the time the sun sets."

Tumas looked at him, head cocked in confusion.

"Remember what you saw Lisette do?" Rocco asked. "It may become a little crowded in here."

The priest's eyes widened, and he nodded. "Let us be gone then. I shall travel with you."

Opening the dungeon door, they crept up the few stairs into the long-shadowed afternoon. An extra outline revealed a guard to their right. Rocco nodded to Tumas and gestured to a clump of bushes at the side of the path. As Rocco continued to climb the steps, Tumas reached down for a rock, took aim, and threw it.

The two men easily overpowered the distracted guard, choking him to unconsciousness. Rocco searched him for weapons but found only a sword.

"I was hoping for a dagger so we would each be armed." Rocco handed the sword to Tumas.

"Oh, no," Tumas protested. "You should have the blade."

Rocco grinned. "Don't worry, Priest, I shall find a better one."

No one else seemed to be in the vicinity, so they continued to inch forward. By the time they stood, flattened against the dungeon wall, they heard nothing but birdsong.

"Which way to the stables?" Rocco whispered.

Tumas pointed to the west side of the gardens. "That long building."

Rocco checked the area in all directions and saw no one. The path to the stables was lined with trees that provided a canopy of shade, all useful for men trying to evade capture. Still, there was an unease in his gut. It wasn't normal for the grounds to be this quiet.

"Be ready to use your metal," he said, pointing to Tumas' sword.

They were halfway across the garden when Rocco heard a distinctive hiss, followed by a thudding noise. He turned to see an arrow buried in the dirt at his feet. Tumas looked up at the sky, gasped and fell backward, an arrow through his chest.

Rocco ran to him, dragging him behind a thick tree trunk before hefting the priest into his arms and sprinting for the stable door. More arrows drove into the ground as he flew, zigzagging to make himself a harder target. The last arrow impaled the door frame as he leapt into the stable.

Once inside the door, Rocco set Tumas down, taking care not to touch the arrow still embedded. Tumas opened his eyes and let them drift upward.

"Thank you, friend," he said in a soft labored voice. "I should wish to help you…I have to meet…someone…I'm afraid He won't wait."

The priest's head fell forward as his body relaxed. Rocco made the sign of the cross, kissing his thumb and laying his open palm on Tumas' chest.

"Go with God, Priest. And thank you for your service."

Rocco looked around at the space, a large entryway with hooks along the wall, hung with a few bridles. There was an open door to his right, and a double door at the back. He had been too busy running to pick up Tumas' sword, so he grabbed a stiff riding crop from one of the hooks and slapped it against his palm. It would do as a weapon until he found a blade.

Flattening himself outside the door on the right, he listened for a few moments. He heard an intake of breath, small but definitely there. Rocco stomped into the doorway and jumped immediately backward. He was rewarded with a guard charging him with a broadsword.

The guard overshot his exit from the room, allowing Rocco to sidestep and bring the crop down on the guard's wrist. The broadsword hit the floor with a muffled clang, the guardsman reaching to retrieve it. Rocco rushed into the room and grabbed the first sword he saw. The guard had picked his blade up from the ground and turned to face the pirate.

"Hmpf," the guard huffed. "That one's much too dull."

"Pity," Rocco said. "It will hurt a lot more when I kill you with it."

He thrust forward, causing the guard to lean back, his sword held sideways to block the attack. As the guard did so, Rocco swung slanted and down, catching him across the waist, driving the blade into his midsection. The guard screamed and crumpled to the floor, where his screams fell to moans.

Rocco went back into the room and examined the weaponry. He chose a fine rapier, a razor-sharp dagger, and a well-weighted bow and quiver. By the time he had finished his shopping, the guard was silent.

"Yes," Rocco said, stepping over the body. "That did hurt."

There was still no sound outside the stables, but Rocco did not dare exit. He glanced at Tumas. Poor priest. He had a good heart. God would be welcoming him home.

The little bit of sky he could see was deeply crimson,

blurring into purple and chasing a sliver of blue. Soon he wouldn't need these weapons, nor would he need to hide.

He took a spot against the wall, at a perfect angle from the door to catch anyone trying to come in. The weapons by his side, he waited.

The shadows continued to grow in the entryway, darkening the room. He could see the crimson sky replaced by a velvet twinkling. Frowning, he carefully crossed the space to look at the sky from the other direction. Sunset had come and gone. It was night—and he hadn't transformed.

A splatting sound, followed quickly by more of the same made him look at the ground outside. Patches of dark soil, like large dots, were connected with each splat. In moments, a storm arrived, harsh and driving. It would be a miserable time for a battle but an easy escape from his confinement if he could be quick about it.

Going back into the stalls, he saw a large barn door that led into the paddock which had been left unlocked and open. He went down the stalls, opening each one wide, shushing the horses out. They obliged by trotting to the door where they stopped and peered out at the storm.

Even they were not anxious to trade freedom for a soaking.

Rocco grabbed a whip and snapped it, shushing them forward. They sprang like a single body with a single thought, running out to the nearest tree to find cover.

Grabbing the mane of one from the middle, he swung up and laid his body flat on its back. The herd rewarded him by galloping across the gardens in a clump. He could hear the guards on the wall and the balconies, yelling that the horses were out, that he might be among them, and that no one could see anything.

The herd got to the far corner, pivoted, and ran for the next one. As they turned, Rocco dropped off and rolled to a rough-barked tree, where he crouched and waited.

The yelling was still going on, but a high-pitched screeching had joined them. This had to be Mercedes, and she sounded livid. Rocco heard "find him," and "imbeciles."

The rain was lessening, allowing him to see and hear with more clarity. Escaping this place would not be difficult now. The guards on the walls would soon be called to come down and hunt for him. When they climbed down, he'd climb out.

Running to the wall ahead of him, he put a foot on the uneven rock and stopped. Escape was not what he needed, not as much as reckoning. Alwan was a mad dog. And for Lisette's safety, Mercedes had to die.

He turned back toward the castle in time to see a guard charging him, sword drawn. Rocco grabbed at his rapier, cursing that he'd left it in its scabbard. The guard's face assumed a curious wonderment as he pitched forward into the dirt, an arrow buried in his back to the feathers, its point protruding from his chest.

Rocco looked behind the fallen man, to see a familiar, smiling face.

"Delgado! I was going to run him through."

"My apologies, Captain Rocco. I let my bloodlust rule my bow. We have come to rescue you, but I see there is no need."

"True, I am free for the moment, but Mercedes will not rest until I am dead."

Luis looked through the trees, aimed his arrow and released it. The sound of a scream and the thud of a body made him turn back to Rocco. "Then we should make your freedom permanent, at least from Mercedes de Medina."

Rocco smiled and nodded. "I leave you to your task. I am off to settle a score with Alwan Simone before I dispatch that witch."

59

The change was a soft pinching, and Lisette pushed away from the grove. Unfolding her wings, she wasted no time soaring toward Mercedes' castle and Rocco.

As she lifted away into the darkness, she placed a paw on her expanded dragon belly. She could feel limbs pressing back, but not hands and feet. A pointed tail prodded her paw, and tiny wings attempted to expand in the small space.

Wait, Alara. Soon we will be with your father, and you can greet us both.

Very well, Mama, but I cannot wait long.

The night air was heavy, and clouds obscured the sliver of moon. Monsoon season would soon replace the occasional cloudbursts, bringing unending days of rain. Lisette flew high to avoid being seen, although her wings felt heavy in the thickness of the charcoal sky.

I hope the rains hold off until this fight is settled and Alara is in my arms.

As if to mock her, a fat drop of water landed on her nose, exploding spray in her eyes. The drop had friends, who splatted themselves about Lisette's head and body until the drops united into an expanse of pouring water. Like her daughter, the monsoon was in no mood to wait.

Lisette pressed on through the rain, following the curve of the jungle to the Medina castle. Even her dragon's enhanced eyesight strained to see the thick battle wall surrounding the fortress and the dark spires that rose from the middle. At last, she could perceive lights—torches running across a courtyard, being snuffed by the downpour to leave trails of thick smoke.

Looking up, a single window in the castle held light. Lisette banked right, lowering herself through the pouring rain, settling quietly on the balcony outside the room, and breathing a slow, steady fog that blended in with the storm. Cocooned within her own cloud she looked into the lit chamber and listened.

"Rain!" The guttural rasp of Mercedes' voice was easy to recognize. "How am I going to coax Lisette to her death if I can't tie Rocco out to be dragon food?"

A deep male voice responded. "Countess, this storm shall pass. I say we keep to our—your—plan. The guard contingent from the Mendoza castle is already here, and spies tell us the Martinmas guards will arrive shortly."

"The duke acquiesced?" Her voice held both anger and distrust. "Since when?"

"Since today." The man's voice was steady. "My sources say the duke and his son had an argument. The son swore he would send the guard with or without his father's agreement. The duke surrendered."

Lisette did not believe Connie or the duke would throw in their lot with this woman.

"Very well," Mercedes said at last. "We will use

them to take the other castles—after we dispatch that demon and her lover.”

Wet, flapping footsteps caught Lisette’s attention, stopping with one last watery stomp.

“Captain!” A higher male voice barked. “We have a problem!”

Rain continued to pound, making Lisette struggle to hear the high-voiced guard in Mercedes’ chamber. She caught a few words, one of them being “Rocco.” As quickly as the rain began, it stopped in time for the man to squeal, “It was not my fault that he escaped!”

She heard the metallic whoosh of a sword being withdrawn, and a body hitting the floor.

“Don’t leave that in my room, Alwan,” Mercedes said. “Toss it into the yard.”

Lisette lifted straight up and over to the roof as the guard strode to the balcony’s edge, a lump that used to be a man over his shoulder. He launched the lump into the courtyard. To Lisette it appeared that he was trying for distance.

“Rocco’s escaped.” Mercedes was almost growling. “What do we do now?”

“We find him. He could not have gotten far in this downpour.”

“Now the rain has *stopped*. Get to work.”

Lisette searched for Rocco in the courtyard, but Mercedes reclaimed her attention.

“Wait—don’t leave! What if Rocco comes looking for me?”

“Of course, Countess. Let me help you.”

Lisette hovered, watching both the balcony and the courtyard. Soon, she heard a scraping noise and saw Alwan dragging a figure in black across the balcony. He propped the dummy upright and fluffed the clothes out.

“Excellent,” Mercedes said as she hobbled out to

him. She was dressed in a bright blue gown, jewel-encrusted and off the shoulder. Her shoulders were blackened and scarred, all the way down her arms. One side of her face was drooping and raw. Patches of her hair were missing, with pearl combs barely holding the fine wisps.

Her appearance made Lisette draw back in momentary pity until Mercedes spoke again.

"Go. I shall stay here in the shadows. When he attacks the dummy, I shall catch him by surprise."

Lisette opened her wings to fly down and pluck Mercedes from the balcony, but the woman limped inside and out of her grasp. A sudden noise made Lisette look up. Guards were falling off the wall of the courtyard, and she could see figures leaping over the stone, swords drawn. She could tell by the lightness of their movements that these invaders were from the *Dişi Aslan*.

Lifting higher, Lisette flew over the courtyard, watching the skirmish and wondering where she might help. A layer of fog would not aid the situation, as it would blind the pirates as much as the guards. She could see Oleta, Pinar, and Marisha wielding swords against Mercedes' men with success. The ones who were not cut down turned and ran.

A movement to her right caught her attention. Luis Delgado was crossing swords with a short, slender man. The guard quickly lost his blade to Delgado and fell to Luis' sword. A group of men ran toward Luis, and he spun to meet them, weapon ready.

"Captain!" one of the men shouted. "The duke has sent us to aid in defeating Mercedes!"

"I guess the duke has forgiven me," Delgado said with a smile. He pointed to the enemy still fighting and they dispersed, running to add their swords to the fight.

Thank you, Uncle Oscar. The duke had his faults, but his moral compass was clear.

A pain stabbed at her ribcage. Alara, in her dragon state, poked Lisette's insides with her tail. Lisette lost a bit of altitude as the sharpness gouged her. She cradled her stomach with both front paws and forced her wings to carry her higher.

Alara you must wait. She searched for a place to land unseen. *At least let me find your father and do something about Mercedes.*

I am trying, Mama, but this space is so small, and my body feels so big.

Soon, my girl. Soon you can stretch out as far as you can reach. She found a patch of roof over Mercedes' chamber and lit softly. *It might be better to transform in case the baby cannot be delayed, but this is not the place or time. I must be here, where I can be of immediate use against that woman.*

The first guard Rocco encountered was a young, wide-eyed lad with fear pouring from his skin. He swung his sword at Rocco in a reckless arc, an easy opening for the pirate to end him quickly with a slice across the throat, but pity stayed Rocco's hand. Catching the youth's wrist in mid-swing, he pushed his rapier at his chest without drawing blood.

"Are you determined to fight and die for Mercedes de Medina?" Rocco asked.

The guard's eyes filled with tears as the front of his breeches showed the stain of his terror. "I don't want to die."

"Then throw your weapon down and run for it." Rocco nodded toward the wall. "Don't stop until you get to the village."

Dropping his broadsword, the guard wiped at his face

and dashed to the stone wall, which he clambered up and over like a frightened squirrel. Rocco picked up the broadsword and moved on, hoping to find Alwan.

The castle's yard was large, criss-crossed by strolling paths and scattered with outbuildings. Rocco slunk past a bench surrounded by fragrant bushes. A figure leapt out and grabbed him by the throat, dagger in hand. Rocco dropped the broadsword and grabbed the wrist with the dagger, bringing his own blade back to strike.

"Captain Rocco!"

He lowered his weapon. "Oleta! Is Captain Derya here? How many are you?"

"We are but ten—Captain should be here soon, as well as crew from your ship."

"I've seen one of my crew, but I'll be glad to find the rest." He picked up the young guard's broadsword and handed it to her. "Might do better with this. Longer reach."

She took it, smiling. "Thanks."

"Have you seen a big, beefy guard? Wears a different uniform."

"Alwan? I know him. No, I have not seen him."

"I'd like to kill him myself," Rocco told her. "But I'll give anyone who kills him a handsome reward."

"No reward will be necessary." Oleta spotted a nearby skirmish and ran toward it, yelling over her shoulder, "We all want to kill him."

Rocco ran across the grounds toward the castle. He could still see the shrouded figure of Mercedes watching the action. A red blur caught his attention, so he turned and found another of the regular guard, with four more scurrying toward him.

"Think to gang up on me?" he asked as the guard slashed at him.

Rocco blocked the man's blade with his sword and crossed under to have at his belly. The guard parried quickly and brought his sword toward Rocco's chest. Raising his steel to check the guard's, Rocco smiled.

"What are you smiling at, pirate?" the guard sneered.

"You're better than the last man." He lifted his sword, feinted, and drove it into the man's midsection. "But not better than me."

The four guards coming towards him attempted to surround and overpower him. Rocco leapt to a bench and, grabbing the branch of a tree, hoisted himself out of their range. He took the bow from his shoulder and lined up an arrow. The first man went down and the rest scattered. He managed to hit one more before they were out of range.

"That's for the priest," Rocco shouted after them.

Leaping down from the tree, he dashed to the castle and leapt up the climbing vines, finding footholds in the stone edifice, and pulling himself along. He kept watch on both Mercedes and the action below.

An arrow hissed by his head. He looked back, preparing to unleash his own in response, but Begum Derya had grabbed the man from behind, holding his head back to slice his throat. She glanced up at Rocco, nodded, and kept fighting.

The night was well dark, and the rainstorm had doused all the torches and left them too wet to relight. Clouds still blocked both moon and stars. Rocco desperately wished he had transformed. *Why didn't I? Did Lisette's feather take my magic away?*

He grew closer to the balcony, but the figure in black had not moved, still looking out at the fray. Rocco hesitated. It was not like Mercedes to be so quiet. She would be screaming commands at her troops, especially now that she could see others had come to Rocco's aid.

He jumped to the balcony, landing softly but still with enough sound that she should have turned. Striding forward, he kicked at the figure. It wobbled a bit, and fell to the floor, knocking its hat off and revealing it to be made of straw.

Rocco quickly turned to the chambers inside. Mercedes lurked in the doorway, and he recoiled at the sight of her. Somehow seeing her in a beautiful gown was more disturbing than seeing her with no clothes at all.

"Don't you like my outfit?" she asked. "I was going to wear it at our first dinner party, Eric's and mine." She gazed down at the floor. "We never had it, did we?"

"It's a lovely dress." Rocco felt a pinch of sorrow for her.

"And now it's ruined. Ruined by that wench Lisette de Lille." She smiled and inched toward him, bristling with rage. "She needs to pay. For what she did to me, she needs to pay."

"I know you think that you are owed something," Rocco said, backing away. "But you did have her kidnapped, steal her fiancé, and kill her parents."

"For the crown!" She stomped her foot and gasped from the pain. "I am loyal to El Rey! Everything I do is for His grand design."

Rocco glared at her. "No. Your family has no regard for anyone else. Your father stole my wife, impregnated her, and killed her. Was that for El Rey?"

"I'm certain it was." She lifted her chin.

"It is a pity. You are the child of my wife and the count. You should have been my child. Knowing you were Tempest's stayed my hand. Wanting you to live made me turn on Lisette." He shook his head. "But you are your father's daughter—bitter and evil and ugly, even when you were beautiful."

A shadow crossed behind him and grabbed his arms. As he struggled to free himself, he heard the voice he'd been looking for.

"Shall I kill him, m'lady?" Alwan said. "Or would you like the honor?"

"I should like to do it," Mercedes replied. "I've never

used this dagger before."

She straightened her spine, wincing as she did, and picked up an ornately carved dagger from the table. Holding it up, she asked, "Isn't it beautiful? I had it made especially for you and Lisette. You can die by the same blade—isn't it romantic?"

Rocco continued to struggle against Alwan, whose arms were as solid as any rock. "You'll not have Lisette."

Mercedes advanced toward him, holding out her dagger with a crooked smile. As she neared him, he pushed back against Alwan and lifted both his feet.

"I'm not ready to go either!" he spat, kicking her in the stomach.

Mercedes crumpled against the balcony railing, curling her body inward, moaning. Alwan pushed Rocco away and kneed him viciously in the back. Rocco winced and his legs collapsed. Alwan dragged him back up by his arms, nearly pulling them from their sockets.

"Shall I punish him?" Alwan asked.

"No," Mercedes said between heavy breaths. "I'll do it." She staggered toward Rocco, the blade held over her head. "I was going to kill you right away, but I think I'll carve you up a bit first."

Rocco bucked his body, kicking back at Alwan, attempting to escape. Mercedes shuffled closer, her eyes scanning his body as if picking the right place for plunging the dagger.

Alwan's grip on Rocco weakened. "Countess?" he whispered.

"You should have just stabbed me." Rocco pulled away from Alwan and pointed.

Mercedes turned to see a blue dragon, wings fully spread, jaws open wide to display pearlescent fangs. She fell back, nearly going to her knees before lifting her dagger and staggering toward Lisette.

"Tell your mistress it's her I want!" Mercedes

screamed, shuffling forward, and plunging her weapon into the feathers, which instantly puffed and hardened, shattering the blade.

"It's her you've got, Mercedes," Rocco said. "Lisette is the dragon before you."

He glanced around for his weaponry, still keeping an eye on Mercedes and Lisette. Alwan stood at the chamber door, watching Mercedes, sword upturned in preparation and his face ashen.

Mercedes whipped about to face Rocco. "Then I shall have to kill you instead!" She raised her broken dagger. "This is still sharp enough to bleed you with."

She took but a single step before a large paw grabbed the top of her head, razor-sharp talons gripping her scalp. Mercedes yelped as another paw wrapped around her waist and lifted her off the balcony. Lisette sat back on her haunches, holding Mercedes aloft briefly, before wrenching the woman's head sideways and snapping her neck.

Tossing Mercedes to the balcony, she stepped forward to Alwan, creeping at him like a hunting lion, eyes narrowing and jaws clenching. Alwan ran at her, trembling and swinging his sword at her chest. She growled and reached her talons out to him.

His weapon sank between the toes of her paw, causing her to pull back and roar in pain. She grabbed the sword with the other paw and crushed it.

Anger swept through Rocco like a squall. He stepped forward to put his sword through the guard when he felt a familiar burning sensation and sank to his knees. When his brief transformation ended, the red feathers that he'd worn as a blood dragon were now white with red tips. He raised his paw and extended the long deadly talons…then he looked at Alwan.

The guard uttered a guttural scream and ran inside the castle.

Rocco and Lisette exchanged glances. Lisette nodded her head toward the castle and entered Mercedes chambers. Rocco opened his wings and spanned the courtyard, waiting for Lisette to chase Alwan into the open.

As he circled, Rocco saw the crew of *L'Implacable* had joined with the soldiers from the Duke de Martinmas to fight the elite guards. Captain Derya and her group had dispatched almost all the regular guards. Thirty guards were no match for a dozen pirates, especially when their loyalties were not bound to the Medina family.

A guard had Chunk against the stable wall, hacking at him furiously with a broadsword. Chunk answered blow for blow, deflecting everything the man threw at him.

At last Chunk pushed away from the wall, nabbing him with a hefty slice to the shoulder. The guard grabbed his arm in pain and bent down. Chunk moved forward to finish the job.

Rocco saw it before Chunk did—a dagger in the shaft of the man's boot. The ruthless guard reached across with his good hand and flicked it at Chunk, catching him in the thigh, embedding the dagger to the hilt. Chunk fell to his knees, yanking at the dagger to get it out.

The guard picked up his broadsword to deliver the death blow but was grabbed himself by Rocco's talons. Rocco speared through the guard's middle with one paw and twisted the man's body with the other. The guard yelped once and was silent.

From the corner of his eye, Rocco spied movement across the yard. Alwan had appeared, running toward the stables with Lisette on his heels. Rocco threw the dead guard's body aside and flew to cut off Alwan's escape.

Lisette joined Rocco in the hunt for Mercedes' henchman. Alwan pivoted and ran toward the courtyard wall, zigzagging as he scrambled. The dragons pursued at his flanks, driving him toward the corner. Rocco swooped forward, reaching out with his claws to grab the guard.

Fat, hard raindrops splashed in front of him, followed quickly by a thunderous shower. Alwan sank with the sudden onslaught of water, causing Rocco to miss his midsection. The man continued toward the wall, where he grabbed at the slick rocks and tried to climb to freedom.

Lisette got to the guard first and fastened her paw around his leg, sinking her smaller claws into his flesh. He screamed as she pulled him away and held him upside-down to Rocco.

Roaring in anger, Rocco grabbed Alwan and thrust his talons through the guard's stomach. He'd never heard the kind of scream that Alwan produced, a high yet throaty cry of sheer terror. He smiled, showing rows of white, razor-sharp teeth, and squeezed until the guard wept. Rocco opened his mouth to spew fire at the guard, but the steady downpour dowsed his flames each time he breathed out.

As he tried one more time, Lisette flew to his side and opened her mouth. A steady white cloud mixed with his fire, making a steam as hot as that from a blacksmith's bucket. The body quickly went from beet red to white blisters before the skin turned completely black.

Rocco dropped the body and turned to Lisette, wishing they had some kind of language. *Thank you.*

She opened her mouth in a near-smile. *We make a good team.*

He pulled back in shock. *You can hear me?*

I am also surprised. Lisette looked back at the courtyard. The rain had ceased as instantly as it had arrived, allowing the sound of battle to be heard. *There is still fighting. You should help.*

Rocco turned and nodded. *Yes. And you?*

She bowed her head. *I'm afraid I cannot join you. Alara is coming soon. And I have one last thing to do before she arrives.*

He gazed at her, torn between helping his crew and being with Lisette for their daughter's birth. Lisette nudged his shoulder with her paw, toward the sound of swords, before extending her wings and flying off.

This is the path she wants. He flew toward the fray.

61

Lisette launched herself toward the sky, glancing briefly at Rocco as he headed toward the battle. She was glad he did not try to follow. He would regret not helping his crew defeat the guards, and she needed time to get back to the castle to have their baby.

Alara was right. I will never get back to Lamya in time.

The rains ended as she landed lightly on the balcony where Mercedes lay. A deep sigh and a confident command transformed her back into human form. Transforming was a risk, but she needed to make peace with what she'd done. In the moment, she had been so afraid for Rocco, she had acted without thought, killing Mercedes with an easy twist.

Saying a prayer over the dead was not something a dragon could do.

"I am sorry, Mercedes," Lisette said, making the sign of the cross. "If it's any consolation, I truly wish I had killed you the first time."

She moved away from the body, preparing for one last transformation to dragon so that she could fly quickly back to her castle. Before she reached the archway, a contraction tore through her stomach, small, short-lived, but powerful, driving her to her knees.

Mama, Alara said. *There is no more time. I am coming now.*

"Oh, no, this is not a good time," Lisette cried, pushing herself up to her feet. "I am not at home yet."

I cannot wait.

Warm liquid trickled down Lisette's legs. She looked down to see something clear pooling between her feet. Alara was not kidding—her water had broken.

Lisette looked over the balcony. The fighting continued although Rocco was ending most skirmishes with talons and fire. She did not want to have her child on Mercedes' balcony, with Mercedes lying dead next to her. Shuffling forward, she went into the chambers and found the stairs. Halfway down, another contraction hit her, not as painful but longer. She clung to the banister and continued to inch downward.

She was almost at the bottom when she saw Amoy waiting. The housekeeper had a cleaver in her hand and was crying.

"My brother was everything to me!" she wailed. "It's your fault, all your fault!"

"If you want to blame someone," Lisette managed between heavy breaths, "blame Mercedes. She could have just left me alone."

"Amoy!" Marisha strode into the room, sword at the ready. "Put down that cleaver or join your brother."

"I'd be better off joining him." Amoy turned and rushed at Marisha, staggering in her teary rage.

Marisha stepped to the side and stuck her foot out, tripping the woman. Amoy sprawled across the stone, her weapon flying away, clattering. Marisha walked over and picked up the cleaver.

"Go back to your village, Amoy."

"Alwan was my family," Amoy said as she wrestled her body up from the floor. "My only family. I have nothing to return to."

"Then make a new life," Lisette said as she panted through another contraction.

"Wise words." Marisha took Amoy by the arm and hoisted her to her feet. "Find a man. Settle down. But get out." She shoved the woman out the door with a kick and scurried to Lisette.

"Lizzie, let us get you somewhere comfortable." Marisha put her arm around Lisette's back and eased her to the bottom of the stairs. Pointing to her hand, she added, "You're bleeding."

"It is nothing," Lisette wiped her hand on her robe and shook her head. "I cannot have my baby in this house. Not Mercedes' house."

"Very well, but it's not convenient." Marisha half-walked, half-carried Lisette from the castle. "Where's best, your highness?"

Lisette looked around. "The back gate." She gestured. "There's a soft clearing just beyond."

Marisha scowled but led on. Three contractions later, Lisette was lying in a mossy bed, looking up at the sky. The pains were coming faster now, and she knew the baby would arrive soon. She put her hand up to where the scar was on her womb.

"Something doesn't feel right," she told Marisha.

"Of course, it doesn't feel right. Have you ever had a baby?"

Lisette took a big breath. "I need a healer. Get Oleta."

"I don't want to leave you alone."

"You won't be gone long. Please, Marisha. I have a bad feeling about this."

Marisha frowned. "I will do it because you are begging, but I do not wish to." She leaned down and gave Lisette a hug. "I will run."

Lisette heard quick steps as Marisha hurried off. She continued to watch the dark sky as clouds drifted across it. Her backbone arched with each contraction, and she bit down on her sleeve to keep from shrieking. Marisha would find Oleta. She had to.

After one hideous cramping contraction, Lisette wanted to push—was it time?

Alara, can you not wait until Marisha returns?

No, Mama. Alara's voice was insistent. *I'm coming now.*

She could not stop it. Her body pushed as if it needed to expel everything inside her. Lisette abandoned any pretense of being quiet and roared her pain. She continued to push and continued to scream until she felt a large object push past and give some relief.

Leaning forward, Lisette saw a head between her legs. She quickly grabbed the hem of her robe to place it under the baby, who promptly slid out. Gathering up the tiny squirming body, she held it on her chest and hoped Marisha would return. She could feel more liquid leaking between her legs. Looking down, it was as she feared— blood, a lot of it.

Please, help me, she prayed to any god that might hear and closed her eyes.

Someone shook her arm and she awakened. Marisha's face appeared, looking worried. "I'm back. I found someone who can help."

"Good," Lisette whispered. "I'm so tired and cold."

"It is me, m'lady," a little voice said. "Ruhee."

"Ruhee," Lisette repeated.

"I am skilled, m'lady. I can do this. Where is the ankh?"

Lisette raised her hand to her neck.

"Marisha," Ruhee said. "Go up that hill and look for a small plant with white flowers. Bring at least two handfuls. Hurry!"

Lisette heard the rustle of feet in brush. Alara was being lifted from her arms, and she held on.

"No, don't take her."

"You will have her back soon," Ruhee said. "I need to heal you, and I do not want the baby to be hurt."

"I am holding her for you." Pinar's voice was at her side.

"Pinar, I am so glad…" Lisette tried to say more, but Ruhee shushed her.

"Save your strength."

Lisette closed her eyes, wanting sleep but fighting to stay awake. She was so tired. A voice startled her into consciousness.

"Lizzie, chew on these flowers."

Marisha had returned. Something was being held to her lips.

"They will help with the pain," Ruhee said.

Lisette whispered, "Please. I don't want to bleed to death."

"You must trust me," Ruhee told her. "No matter what, let me complete what I must do."

Lisette was aware of something warm on the left side of her stomach, right where the old knife wound was. Ruhee held it there with both hands, pressing. She was saying words in a language Lisette had never heard.

The object grew in warmth, getting warmer and warmer until it was hot and surpassing hot into burning and from burning into feeling like her entire body was on fire. Lisette tried to pull away, but Ruhee was relentless, her words now sounding like a chant that never ended. The fire in her side burned bright and fierce, reaching out in waves to the rest of her.

There was nothing to do except scream, which she did before passing out.

Lisette opened her eyes. She let her vision drift around the space while she tried to identify where she was—this was her mother's room. The sun was high, and she wondered how long she had been asleep.

A mewling cry got her attention. She propped herself carefully on her elbows. It felt like she had been beaten severely about the stomach. Looking to the end of the bed, she caught the glimpse of a cradle.

Alara was here. Lisette peeked down inside her gown at her body and saw bruises on her thighs and hips—and a burn mark on the left side of her now-flaccid stomach. It was raw and blistered, and in the shape of Ruhee's ankh.

Her mind slowly filled in all the blanks. A glimmer on her chest made her reach up to her neck. Two necklaces hung there, an emerald with an Arabic message, and a small golden ankh.

She sat up, scooting to the edge of the bed, to get to her baby. It was a slow and painful process. As she pushed herself against the covers, she noticed the bandage wrapped around her hand.

"I guess I am not as invincible as I thought," she said as she remembered Alwan's sword.

She'd just swung her feet over when the door opened and Pinar came in, carrying a tray.

"What are you doing?" Pinar asked.

"I want to see my baby."

The girl set the tray down and rushed to her. "Get in bed. I will bring Alara to you."

She helped Lisette return and adjusted her pillows for greater comfort. Going to the end of the bed, she leaned down to pick up the baby, and stood up, shaking a finger.

"You understand, you can hold the baby for a moment, but you have a meal to eat. After breakfast, you may hold her all you like."

"Must I get used to being ordered about?" she said with a smile.

Pinar chuckled. "My apologies but I was instructed to make you healthy."

Scooping up lace and blankets, Pinar walked over to Lisette and laid the baby in her arms. A tiny girl with dark curls and green eyes looked at her. She appeared to be smiling.

"Instructed by who?"

"Everyone with the authority." Pinar counted on her fingertips. "The duke. His son. Captain Derya. Captain Rocco."

"Captain Rocco is the only one I care about right now. Is he here?"

Pinar shook her head. "He is down at his ship, but he should return before nightfall."

Lisette's disappointment was quickly erased by her

captivation with Alara. "She is beautiful. And my green eyes—I thought babies were born with blue eyes."

"They usually are. They are also usually squirming, fussy creatures who demand attention." Pinar pointed to the baby. "She is different."

"Yes, I knew that."

Pinar stood beside the bed, arms crossed, foot tapping. Lisette smiled and handed Alara to her.

"Only because if I eat quickly, I can have her back."

Her tray was a cornucopia of food. Three kinds of meats, two roast vegetables, breads, sauces, all overwhelmed her.

"Let me guess…the duke ordered this meal," Lisette said.

"Even down to the rum."

Lisette sighed. "I appreciate his attention to me, but I cannot eat all this, and especially not those sauces. I know they are very rich."

"I agree," Pinar said. "Eat what you can."

"Why don't you share this with me? The duke doesn't need to know. All he will see is a cleaned plate."

"Making him give you more," Connie said as he appeared at the door. "I wanted to see how you are doing." He walked over and gave Lisette a kiss on the cheek.

"I am well. Where is the duke today?"

"He is at the castle de Medina, assisting in the disposition of the dearly departed."

Lisette put her fork down. "How many dead?"

"All of the elite guard, most of Mercedes' regulars. The men provided by the Mendozas surrendered as soon as they saw they were outnumbered—I guess they signed on to guard the castle, not fight for the castle. And of course, Mercedes."

"Did we lose anyone from the duke's guard or…the ships?"

"Trying to be delicate?" Connie grinned. "My father's men all returned, and no pirate lives were lost. Man and woman, they know how to fight to the death—but not *their* death."

"Such a waste of life for such a useless cause. One woman's pride." Lisette raised her goblet of rum. "God have mercy on their souls."

"Amen." Connie moved to the cradle and looked inside. "A child is born. Good work, Lizzie, she's very pretty."

"I think so."

He walked back to the door. "Take care and see you tomorrow."

Lisette ate a bit of meat and a vegetable, then pushed the tray away. "I don't dare eat more, Pinar. My body is not ready for a feast."

Pinar set the tray to the side and brought her Alara again. "Take your time getting to know her. I will be back later to help you."

Lisette snuggled back into the pillows and held her daughter close. "We're going backward, in a way. You've been talking to me this whole time, and now you're a baby and cannot talk. At least, I do not think you can. But I'm so glad you're here."

She had lost track of the hour and the sun's movement across the room when Pinar reappeared and scooped the baby from her arms, placing her back in the cradle. Lisette opened her mouth to protest but Pinar held up her hand.

"You are going to have years with this baby. Right now, you need sleep." She frowned. "You lost much blood last night. The duke is correct to want you to eat. We almost lost you."

"Yes, my body remembers." Lisette smiled. "All right. Hand me a roll."

Pinar placed plates on the bedside table, within reach,

and gave Lisette a warm crusty roll. "Eat a little, sleep a lot. Do not worry about your baby—Alara will be taken good care of."

"Yes, ma'am," Lisette said as Pinar walked to the door. She picked at the roll, putting a bite in her mouth and watching the door close.

Alone, she looked at the shadows on the floor and imagined her mother lying in this bed after bearing a child. Her face grew flushed, and the hot tears built but she forced them away along with her memories. She needed to focus on the future. A daughter must be raised…a most unusual daughter. And was she going to take possession of this castle, live here with Rocco?

I might not get the choice. Politics might make this decision for me.

The roll was filling, but dry, so she reached to the table for her rum. As she did, she saw a piece of leather sticking out of the table's drawer. Opening it, she discovered that the leather was the binding for a journal. Lisette picked it up. Embossed on the front was "JdL." Juliette de Lille. This was her mother's journal.

Thrilled and frightened, Lisette opened it. She recognized her mother's neat, perfect script. Nothing the duchess did was ever sloppy, not even a journal where she might pour her heart onto the page.

Most of the entries listed the drudgeries of life in the castle—problems with the servants, getting good meat for the table, finding a seamstress, etc. Lisette skimmed through these, disappointed that her mother's hard shell could not be cracked, even in her most private moments. She took another swig of rum and turned the page, expecting the same drivel.

May 12th

Is there no end to the indignities I must endure married to this man? I realize that we were not joined by love or even choice, but his behavior is beyond the pale.

We had but three short weeks after our wedding to consummate our marriage, and yet he was never able to even be in the room with me after sunset. When he was ordered to lead an expedition to the Ottoman Empire, he left with barely a peck of a kiss good-bye.

Four years and no letters. I knew not whether he lived or died, so I ran the household as I saw fit. Yesterday he arrived home unannounced with a gift for me—a baby!

According to him, he found this child on the road, abandoned, but the babe looks too much like him. I knew confrontation would not work so I fed him rum until his tongue loosened. He met a woman, different from the putains who usually serviced him. She was independent and took him to her bed whenever it suited her needs.

He lost track of her for almost a year and did not find her again until his tour was over. His plan was to convince her to move to our island—our island—to continue their dalliance. She refused and handed him a package instead. A baby.

"I cannot go with you," she said. "But you can raise Amarissa as the daughter of a duke. It will be a better life than the one she would have with me."

I'm certain there were loving words of promises made—he can be charming. But yesterday he dropped this woman's child in my lap, told me to raise it as our own, and left to walk the grounds.

How am I to do this?

Lisette sat back, the journal falling against her lap. *My mother is not my mother.* The words were alien to her.

"My mother is not my mother," she said to the room, trying to make sense of what she read. "My father is my father, but my mother is not my mother. My mother is someone far away who named me—"

The name jogged her memory. In the letter she read in Captain Derya's cabin, the captain referred to a baby named Amarissa.

"Can I be Begum Derya's daughter?" Lisette's limbs grew shaky, and her heart pounded. She flashed through her memories of talks in Begum's cabin. Did Begum know who she was?

The answer had to be yes.

She put the journal back, afraid to read more. The chamber door opened slowly, and a small face peered in. Ruhee crept into the room.

"M'lady?" She stood at the doorway, hands clasped and head low.

"Yes, Ruhee, come in." Lisette watched her walk to the bed, her footsteps halting. "I was hoping to have a chance to thank you. You saved my life."

"I'm glad you are all right." Ruhee stood at the end of the bed, looking down at Alara. "And the baby."

Lisette reached up to her neck and unclasped the ankh, holding it to Ruhee. "I believe this has completed its task with me. It belongs with you again."

Ruhee's eyes widened as if in fear. "Oh, no, m'lady, it is not—"

"Do not argue." She straightened her arm further toward the girl, shaking her hand. "I appreciate your gesture of atonement, and I greatly appreciate your efforts to save me. I insist—this is yours."

The girl walked forward, her hand stretched out and trembling. She was nearly in tears when she whispered, "Thank you." Quickly dropping the necklace into a pocket, Ruhee ran from the room.

That was odd. She noticed the quaking of her own hand. Her entire body shuddered and shuddered again, head to toe, without stopping. Why would such an exchange make her react so?

It wasn't Ruhee, it was finding out about my mother, who is not my mother.

Wanting to weep, she could think of only one option—she downed the rest of the rum. After a few minutes, the alcohol quieted her body and she closed her eyes, not to sleep but merely to relax her mind. When Rocco came, they could talk, and he would calm her.

A knock at the door awakened her. Rocco strode to the bed and scooped her in his arms, kissing her as he did. Lisette wrapped her arms around him, grateful and exquisitely in love. Whatever it meant to be the daughter of a pirate and a duke, she could face it with him.

"I have missed you," she said. "There is so much to tell."

"We will lose our voices with all our stories." He kissed her again. "But first, let me see what we have made."

Rocco walked to the end of the bed and looked into the cradle. He looked back at Lisette. "Where's the baby?"

Lisette pushed up against the pillows. "Isn't she in the cradle?"

"No." He reached down and pulled out a small feather, deep violet with a familiarly rigid shaft. "Tell me she's too young to have transformed."

"It doesn't seem possible." Lisette trembled. "Are her swaddling clothes in the cradle?"

Rocco shook his head. "Everything has been taken from her bed, blankets included." He looked up at her. "She…"

Lisette nodded, knowing what he did not want to say. "She's been taken. Ring for Pinar!"

63

"Are you certain this ship will have room for us?" Ruhee asked from the bed of a buckboard. She steadied a basket of silks next to her, hiding its contents from the driver.

"Oh yes, they sail at noon." Amoy turned to the large dark man holding the reins. "We will get to the port in time, won't we, driver? My daughter and I are carrying a gift back to my husband on Isla del Lagarto, and we can't miss this ship."

"Yes'm." He nodded, smiling to show his gold tooth. "You can count on Horace to get you there."

Ruhee sat back, hoping the basket did not start crying. Lisette could never be a good mother to this child. She'd make Rocco see that. This was her baby now.

She peeked under the silken covers to see two large green eyes looking up at her. The baby did not make a sound but seemed to study her with a somberness that made Ruhee flinch. She reached to cover the basket again when the baby held her hand out to her, fist closed. Ruhee extended her fingers down to the tiny fist which opened, revealing a feather.

She took it from the baby. It was unlike any feather she'd ever seen—small and violet with a hard shaft and a sharp end. She frowned, turning the feather about to examine it. Looking back at the baby, Ruhee's spine felt an immediate chill.

The baby continued to stare at her, as if in judgment.

THE END...almost

But what happens next?

Lisette's story concludes in Book 3 of Dragon Shadows, NEW DRAGON SOARING.

Here is a brief excerpt:

The boy stuck one valise under his arm and grabbed the other before reaching for Ruhee's basket. She yanked it away from his hand and heard a small mewling in protest from underneath the silks. The young man stopped and looked at the basket quizzically.

"My kitten," Ruhee told him. "I'll carry it."

He led the two women up the plank and across the deck, to stairs that deposited them on the lowest passenger tier before the mast. Their cabin was at the end of the step, a tight affair with bunk beds, a wash basin, and a porthole. Dropping their bags, he bowed and left.

"Ugh!" Amoy looked around the space. "It's so small in here! A cockroach would have trouble turning around."

Ruhee shrugged and set the basket on the floor, kneeling beside it. "No smaller than any other cabins, except maybe the captain's." She opened the silk bedding and looked at the baby inside. "She looks hungry. Where's the wet nurse?"

"The what?" Amoy was digging through her bag and throwing things on the lower bunk.

"The wet nurse," Ruhee repeated. "For the baby."

"It won't need a wet nurse." The large woman continued to root about. "Soon as we get out far enough, we're throwing it overboard."

Ruhee opened and closed her mouth, like a fish flopping on deck. Amoy glanced at her, a warning in her scowl. Ruhee held her breath to keep from arguing, especially when she saw the large knife Amoy placed on the bed.

What am I to do? She looked down at Alara, who still

stared at her as if she might also pull out a blade. "It will be some time before we are far enough to dispose of a—anything without being detected. Should we not have milk for the child until then?"

"Why?"

As if on cue, Alara opened her mouth and wailed an infant's cry so loud it pierced ears and brought an immediate knock on the door.

"Is anything wrong?" A female voice asked through the wood.

Amoy shushed at the baby, but it only screeched louder. Ruhee picked Alara up, which made the baby's face redden and stop long enough to take in a breath and wail with even more volume. Ruhee ran to the door, Alara in her hands, over Amoy's protests.

Standing at the doorway was a small woman, dark-skinned and bent with the years. Her gray hair was knotted atop her head and her hazel eyes sparkled.

"Oh, I knew it was a baby," she said, lighting her face with a smile. "Is she okay?"

"Yes, she's—" Amoy snapped.

Ruhee cut her off, still trying to bounce and cuddle this siren of a child. "Actually, we are in trouble. This child's mother died giving her life. I am—we are—to take her to her mother's sister on Isla de la Soledad, but our wet nurse abandoned us, along with all of the supplies for the child."

The old woman nodded at the story, expressing astonishment. "I am so sorry. Perhaps I can be of some help. I have raised many babies and know their needs well." She held out her arms. "May I?"

Ruhee did not want to relinquish Alara, but her unhappy screams were relentless. She handed the baby to the woman, who cradled her in both arms, nestling her against her shoulder and rocking back and forth. As soon as Alara left Ruhee's arms, the screaming stopped. The baby snuggled the woman, cooing her pleasure.

Amoy scowled at the woman, but Ruhee saw her shoulders relax. "Thank you," Amoy said, biting her words tersely, "but we shall manage, I'm sure."

The old woman smiled at Ruhee, a strange smile. Her eyes penetrated Ruhee's to the point that Ruhee flinched and looked at the ground. She handed Alara back to Ruhee.

"If you need me, I'm down the hall, second door left. My name is Kurta."

Ruhee took Alara into her arms and closed the door. Alara stared up at her, green eyes wide as if sizing her up and finding her lacking. Wrinkling her face, the infant wailed again.

"Shut that baby up!" Amoy snapped.

"She's hungry," Ruhee said. "It will be days before we are far enough away to do what you want. She will not stop crying until then."

Amoy stepped toward Ruhee. "Then maybe we don't throw her overboard *alive*."

The girl stepped back, holding Alara away. "And how do you explain it? The old woman has seen her."

"Whose fault is that? I told you not to open the door. So much for your kitten!"

"I doubt if anyone in the whole ship believes this is a kitten!" Their voices kept rising over the wails of the baby, who seemed to be competing with them for volume.

"Fine!" Amoy screamed at last. "Get the old woman to feed the brat!"

Ruhee opened the door and trotted down the hall, carrying the screaming Alara. Kurta was standing outside her room, smiling.

"I heard you coming," she said, opening her arms. "Let me have her and come inside."

Kurta's room was no larger than Ruhee's, yet it

appeared spacious. The two bunk beds had been draped in richly colored silks, the basin was surrounded by a wooden shelf, and a small table and chairs sat in the middle. Kurta also had a porthole but hers brightened the space with light.

"I have milk prepared for the child," Kurta said, gesturing to the shelf as she sat down. "Could you bring it to me?"

Ruhee turned to the shelf and picked up a bubby-pot to hand to Kurta. She stood for a moment, watching the old woman cradle Alara, bouncing her gently and offering her a gnarled finger to mouth. Anger flashed through her that this old woman was bonding with her child. Handing Kurta the pot, Ruhee took a seat at the table.

The child is just hungry. Once she is full, once I know how to fix her food, we will bond.

Kurta offered the cloth-tipped pot to Alara, who sucked at the milk, her eyes soft, holding the old woman's finger in her tiny hand.

A small jolt rattled the room, followed by a familiar sound. The anchor was being hoisted, the chain's metal clanking against itself as it was wound. *El Buscador* was heading out, on its way ultimately to Isla del Lagarto. Soon they would be asea.

Ruhee wondered how far out the ship would be before Amoy decided they could toss the baby. She looked at Kurta and frowned—this old hag comforted Rocco's daughter when she could not. These women were both interferences in their own way.

But she would have Rocco in the end—no matter what it took.

Yes, you can have it all—on February 10, 2023 when Book 3 is released in print and ebook!

Acknowledgments

Even though this is part two of a single story, I suppose it needs its own acknowledgment page. After all, I am thankful that I wrote it.

When I was a youngster, one of my favorite pastimes was to sit with a large sheet of paper and my crayons. I always started in the lower right corner with a house, a tree, a horse, and a dog. And I would tell a story of where my horse and dog and I would go and what adventures we would have, and I would draw the story as I thought of it. There would be forests and lakes and mountains, and cities by oceans with ships in the harbor. When the bomber planes showed up, that's where the dragon would come in.

My family took one look, pronounced me an artist, and spent the rest of my childhood providing canvas and paint. After a year as an art major in college, I realized that I would never be happy trying to get the picture on the canvas to look like the picture inside my head and left it behind. I look back on those times and see clearly that I was a storyteller.

I tell you this story to say how thankful I am that I figured that out.

I'm always grateful to my editor and friend Jennifer Silva Redmond, and to my family for their support and patience, especially when I'm trying to explain a plot hole I'm trying to solve, and they just want to watch the game.

Finally, I want to thank Star Wars. I began writing this second book with an outline and some rigid ideas. After three or four chapters of joyless key-pounding, I decided listen to Obi-Wan Kenobi and "trust the Force." I let my inner child have her crayons again and stopped trying to control the narrative.

I hope you enjoy reading it as much as I enjoyed writing it.

ABOUT THE AUTHOR

G.S. Carline did not plan on writing a fantasy, but one morning in the shower it occurred to her that there weren't enough girl pirates in literature. She thought she would write a single story, perhaps a novella, about a young woman who has Important Life Goals and instead becomes the terror of the seas…and then the dragons came. The whole thing ended up as a trilogy and here we are.

At the time of this bio, G.S. is living happily with her husband and a Corgi. She also has a son and two horses, all of whom she thoroughly enjoys even if they don't live with her. You can find out more about her by visiting https://gaylecarline.com/

Did you enjoy the story?

I'm certain that you are such a wonderful reader, you ran out and posted a review of Blood Dragon Rising with many stars and lovely words. And now you've read and (hopefully) enjoyed the second book and think, "Ah, I've reviewed the first book, do the rest really need my praise?"

Yes, I'm sorry to say, the rest really do. Even though each book is a part of the whole and you really must read them all and in order, they stand alone on internet shelves.

Again, you don't have to write a thesis. It doesn't even have to be a term paper. A title. Stars because all these sites require stars, even though I think they're almost useless. Then a sentence. Here, let me help you:

> ★★★★★ **What happens next?**
> The second book is just as exciting as the first. I can't wait to read more—I love Lisette!

You may leave it on Amazon, or Goodreads, or wherever my books are sold.

Thank you so much. Really, I do appreciate you.

9 781943 654239